Chapter One

Maynard Charles, erstwhile director of the Buckingham Hotel, often wondered if life would have been easier if he had been able to remain in post, tending to the whims of that establishment's esteemed guests and wondering only about the quantities of foie gras in the hotel restaurant, or the vintage of the cocktail lounge's finest Champagne. Yet that was a lifetime ago. Tonight he stood in the swirling snow of a Piccadilly backstreet, lighting up one of the White Owl cigars on which his constitution depended, as he waited for his driver to appear. Behind him, the doors to the Deacon Club opened and closed, either admitting some shadowy figure into the warm interior or ejecting another into the bitter night. His face was set in a scowl beneath his black Homburg hat. His fingers fidgeted constantly, in time with his hammering heart.

The car approached with scarcely a sound, gliding over the hard-packed snow. No headlights illuminated the blackout, so Maynard could not be certain the vehicle was for him. All the same, he hurried over – and, in an act of faith, slipped directly into the back seat. Maynard was a middle-aged man of porcine proportions, but the driver was his exact opposite: tall and angular, he had to hunch to keep inside the confines of the vehicle.

'I came as fast as I could, sir. The second I got the call, I—'

'Cartwright, I've no doubt about it. But drive, will you?' Mindful of the brutish tone of his voice, Maynard pitched forward and touched the man's shoulder. 'This one sounds serious, old man. I'm grateful for your company.'

Travelling in the blackout was no easy feat, but Cartwright was used to it by now. No night was the same, of course, but the Luftwaffe's raids had grown fewer, and it had been many weeks since Maynard last heard the roar of the ack-ack guns in the east. Unlike so many of his fellows at the Office, Maynard was not driven by faith – but he found he was kneading his hands, as if in prayer, and the dark mutterings he was making beneath his breath would have sounded, to anyone else, like a petition to God above. Sometimes, in this line of work, you got a sense of foreboding that it was difficult to either acknowledge or ignore. Maynard Charles could not help feeling that something significant was coming tonight.

It was the voice that had trembled down the telephone line, only hours ago.

The way the young man had whispered, 'I can't tell you – not like this, not on the line. Mr Charles – I need to come in.'

The streets around St Paul's were either blockaded or impassably ruptured – but Cartwright slid the car between hoardings and into the tangle of streets beneath the ruined cathedral.

They stopped at an intersection, somewhere near Cheapside.

'Wait for me here,' said Maynard as he stepped out into the snow.

'Will you be long, sir?'

Maynard took a breath. It was good to be out in the bracing air; it focused a gentleman's mind.

Readers love Anton Du Beke's sparkling fiction . . .

'Beautifully written'

'What a triumph'

'A story full of true emotion, heart, poise
and survival'

'I was enthralled from start to finish'

'Anton Du Beke has done it again'

'A truly fabulous read'

'The story of The Buckingham just gets better
and better. Couldn't put it down'

Anton Du Beke – the King of Ballroom, *Strictly Come Dancing* royalty and household name – is one of this generation's all-round entertainers. In 2018, he realised his boyhood ambition and published the first in a series of bestselling novels set in the 1930s world of the exclusive Mayfair hotel, The Buckingham.

Also by Anton du Beke

ANTON DU BEKE

The WINTER BALL

A Buckingham Hotel novel

ORION

First published in Great Britain in 2025 by Orion Fiction,
an imprint of The Orion Publishing Group Ltd.
Carmelite House, 50 Victoria Embankment
London EC4Y 0DZ

An Hachette UK Company

The authorised representative in the EEA is Hachette Ireland,
8 Castlecourt Centre, Dublin 15, D15 XTP3, Ireland (email: info@hbgi.ie)

1 3 5 7 9 10 8 6 4 2

A CIP catalogue record for this book is
available from the British Library.

ISBN (Hardback) 9781 3987 2229 3
ISBN (eBook) 9781 3987 2231 6
ISBN (Audio) 9781 3987 2232 3

Typeset at The Spartan Press Ltd,
Lymington, Hants

Printed and bound in Great Britain by Clays Ltd,
Elcograf S.p.A.

www.orionbooks.co.uk

With all my love to Hannah, Henrietta and George.

ORION

'I'd pull up a blanket, if I was you,' said Maynard – and trudged along the ill-lit row.

The house was almost unnoticeable, sandwiched between two grander townhouses. Like every house in this row, from without it looked abandoned – but half of London looked abandoned in the blackout, and that was as it should be. Behind the wrought iron railings, frosted steps led up to a front door painted forest green. Maynard was irritated to see the boy's footprints in the ice – but at least there was only one set; that meant he'd listened to instructions, and come alone.

Maynard's key stuck in the lock, the mechanism contracted in the deep December chill, but he forced it to turn and slipped into the safehouse.

Relief came over him, the moment he stepped inside. His trembling fingers produced another White Owl from the case in his pocket, and he lit it as he tramped through the darkened house.

'Show yourself, boy. It's only me.'

The safehouse might not have had the trappings of the other townhouses along this street, but it was by no means a barren shell. Its kitchen was stocked better than many family homes, and the whole place had a familial air, with thick shag rugs in the hallway, a newspaper rack and hatstand bedecked in old coats.

Maynard drifted along the hall and through the door at the foot of the stairs.

'Bogart,' Maynard said as he ventured through.

The boy was waiting in a well-appointed drawing room, where portraits hung on the walls and a tinny gramophone in the corner was playing a record from the collection by the chimney-breast. Elgar's Second Symphony, if Maynard was correct. An odd choice for the young man who stood in front of him. He looked as out of place here as he would have done in the palaces of Westminster – a raggedy young man, his face etched in deep lines that belied his youth. He was scarcely eighteen years of age, tall and lean, with sad almond eyes feathered in grey. He stood in his shirtsleeves and trousers rolled up to the knee – and, by the look on his face, he was terrified.

Maynard lit him a cigarillo. The young man's fingers trembled as he fumbled it to his lips.

'I'm not crazy,' he began, with voice as jittery as his hands. 'You'll say I am, but I'm not. I saw his face, Mr Charles. I looked into his eyes as he said it. At the very least, *he* believes it – and he said it'll get us all killed.'

There was a decanter on the counter by the fireplace. By the look of it, the boy had already taken a brandy to steady his nerves. Maynard decided he needed another, so filled the glass to the brim.

As he was pouring one for himself, he said, 'Bogart, I understand you're frightened – but if you don't tell me what happened, how am I to help?'

The young man glugged half of the drink at once.

'It just sounds so inconceivable, sir.'

'There are a lot of things happening in the world that sound inconceivable.'

'You might think me a fool.'

Maynard invited him to sit – but the boy would not sit. 'How long have we worked together, boy? Twelve, eighteen months? You ought to trust me by now. We look after our own. Whatever it is, we'll investigate.' Maynard sighed. 'This is war, boy. I daresay you can risk being labelled a fool, if it's for King and Country.'

Bogart drained the last of the brandy. He looked like a caged animal, thought Maynard, constantly prowling up and down some imaginary bars.

4

'It was just another night in the Pink Sink, sir. I didn't think anything of it, not at first.'

The Pink Sink. Sometimes the words still gave Maynard a shudder of guilt. 'The Pink Sink' wasn't the club's formal name, but sometimes institutions assumed names of their own – and no amount of intervention could change a thing. As far as respectable members of society were concerned, it was the Lower Bar at the Ritz Hotel. But those men who needed to keep their romantic lives private – those men, in short, who enjoyed the company of other men – knew the Pink Sink for what it was: a place where they could be themselves, could meet lovers, make connections and barely have to *pretend* at all. Maynard shared the sympathies of those men, but he also knew that the Pink Sink was a breeding ground for secrets and lies. Men with certain inclinations could be manipulated, used, blackmailed and bartered with. It wasn't kind. It wasn't gentlemanly. But it wasn't just courageous soldiers and talented generals that won wars; they were won in the shadows as well. And that was why Maynard ran agents in the Pink Sink, sniffing out stories, feeding back on compromised individuals, chasing gossip.

Bogart had been useful before.

Perhaps he'd be useful tonight.

'What was so special about this night?'

'It was about a week ago, sir. I wasn't expecting it. But there are Americans in the Sink now. We see more of them every month, as word gets round. I don't know what it was about this particular guest. Just another middle-aged man, looking lonely and in want.' Bogart stopped suddenly, for he'd seen the way Maynard's eyes were creasing. 'That is to say, sir, there's nothing wrong with being a middle-aged man, lonely and in want.'

Maynard's scowl deepened. His job was to probe people's private lives and exploit whatever he could find, but whenever anyone ventured close to suggesting that he himself might have a private life, his hackles rose.

'Spit out your story, Bogart. This is a Department safehouse. It isn't a rest stop for beleaguered agents.'

Bogart hadn't stopped pacing. His hands fidgeted and writhed.

'I took a drink with him, sir. Then I took him to my rooms.'

Not rooms at the Ritz. There were plenty of lower-level establishments where the Department kept rooms, entirely for this purpose. Maynard was not immune to feeling terrible about it. He had to remind himself that they did it for King and Country – and that, if they won, there were surely kinder days ahead.

'And?'

'It was afterwards, sir. He started sobbing, as some of them do. Except, when I tried to console him, it wasn't who he was, what we'd done, he was crying about. He was scared, sir. No – *terrified*. I've never seen a man as frightened. And he said...'

Maynard watched as the blood drained from his cheeks.

'He said *what*, boy?'

'He said the world was going to end, sir – and that it was his countrymen who were going to end it.'

Now Maynard was interested. He sat up straight, made a steeple of his fingers.

His interest only unnerved Bogart more.

'I was hoping you'd tell me I was a fool to listen to it, sir. I was hoping you'd tell me it was fantasy.'

'What else did he say, son?'

Son. Maynard used the word deliberately for the emotional reaction it provoked – and there it was, softening the boy's features.

'He said there was a programme. An American military team, comprised of scientists and engineers. They were building a bomb to end the war – except, if they got it wrong, its effects could ripple outwards and end everything it touched. Kill everyone who ever lived. Sir, I thought he'd gone mad. He was just a supplies man, that's what he said. But then he said – he had a friend in the US Embassy, right here in London. That's where he got his information from.'

Maynard closed his eyes, trying to think it through.

'Sir, he said his friend was spooked. He wasn't meant to know what he knew. But this man had seen the evidence and he thought: Well, what's the point of winning a war, if it ends civilisation as well? What's the point of a victory, if everyone loses? What's better – a world run by Nazis, or no world at all? And he decided…'

Bogart hung his head.

'Decided *what*, son?'

'He decided it wasn't right. That nobody should have a weapon that powerful. And if he couldn't stop it from happening – well, he'd do the next best thing. He'd sell the secret, sir. He'd sell the secret to the enemy, to save the world.'

'Are you telling me, son, that there's a man in the US Embassy ready to betray us?'

Bogart's eyes were brimming. He wiped his tears away. 'I'm only saying what I heard.'

'This man you were enamoured with – did he say who it was?'

'No, sir. I only know he's one of the new appointees. Ones who came to London since what happened at Pearl Harbour.'

Now Maynard rose to his feet. The truth was, he knew nothing of what the boy had been splurging. There was every chance he had been fed the fantasy of some deranged mind. Yet he was privy to other secrets, and he was well aware that secret programmes existed, as Allied scientists and engineers battled with their Axis counterparts to develop ever more dangerous, fantastical weapons to turn the tide of war. 'Where is he? This man you took to bed – where can I find him?'

Bogart's brimming eyes let loose their tears. 'That's the problem, sir. That's why I had to come in. He's gone, sir.'

'Gone?'

'Vanished. He was to come back to the Pink Sink two nights ago – but, sir, he's gone.'

Maynard started pacing. 'Is that so unusual? A married man has an illicit liaison, then vanishes from sight?'

'It's not just that, sir. Sir, I'm being *watched*.'

'Watched?'

'I can't put my finger on it. But there are eyes on me. Somebody came to the Pink Sink when I wasn't there, and asked for me by name. I've no idea who. And then … when I'm walking, when I leave my digs, there are *eyes* on me, sir.' Bogart clenched his fists, as if about to brawl with some imaginary enemy. 'What if the Americans are trying to cover up their secret? What if it's true, and they need to plug the leak? They went after the man I befriended in the Pink Sink and cleaned that up – but now they know that *I* know too.'

The emotion got too much for Bogart. He rushed to Maynard, as if trying to take comfort in the older man's arms – but Maynard put up a single stolid hand and thrust him back.

'I'm sorry, sir,' Bogart wept.

'A better-trained handler would have killed you for less,' Maynard snapped.

'I'm just …'

'I know what you are. We're all frightened, boy.'

'But could it be true, sir? Could there really be a weapon capable of killing us all?'

Maynard said, 'I expect there are thousands.'

Bogart just wept.

After a moment's thought, Maynard gathered his composure. It was true that he'd been trained to keep his agents at arm's length – one never knew when one was being double-crossed – but it was also true that he had some sympathy for the boy.

'Dry your eyes, boy. You're safe here. You're to stay here, under this roof, until you receive further instructions, do you hear? One of the staffers from the Department will come and take a statement from you. We'll deliver supplies. Do nothing, and *say* nothing to another soul, until you hear from me. Do you understand?'

Bogart discovered stoicism at last. He dried his eyes and nodded. 'I do, sir.'

Maynard crossed the room. In the corner by the hearth sat a jet-black telephone. He lifted the receiver, dialling a number he knew by heart. When one of the secretaries' voices buzzed at the other end, he announced himself as Maynard Charles, delivered his number and whispered three codewords in sequence. Some moments later, just as his impatience threatened to spill over, the voice of one of the Department officers sounded on the line. 'We'll need to move fast,' Maynard said, after making his introduction. 'This thing may play out in days, not weeks. But I have a man in mind – the perfect man for the job. This Home Away From Home programme – we can turn it to our advantage. American soldiers going into British homes for Christmas – well, it can't all be roast goose and trimmings, can it? There has to be something of advantage beyond a bit of extra bacon. So here's how we'll play it. We'll identify the new appointees at the embassy and send them to his house, tell him to sniff out the rat. Yes, sir. I have absolute faith in the man. Send word for him at once. I'll meet him at the Deacon Club. His name? Raymond de Guise.' There followed much whispering and hushed instructions, Maynard's voice dropping low so that Bogart could not hear the particulars of his plan. Then he checked his watch. 'If I'm right, you'll find him at the Buckingham Hotel.'

Then Maynard slammed down the phone and turned to look at Bogart one final time.

'Keep your chin up and your shoulders straight, soldier. The world hasn't ended yet. Indeed – if what you're saying proves right, there's every chance you just saved it.'

At least this seemed to lift the boy's spirits a little. Whatever inner turmoil the boy was enduring tonight, he would have to suffer alone. Maynard was not without sympathy – but his duties would not wait.

Cartwright was waiting for him on the snowbound street.

'Where to, sir?'

'The Deacon Club,' Maynard returned, 'and twice as fast as we came. I'm afraid the wheels of this war keep turning, my friend. I'll get no sleep tonight.'

In the back of the car, Maynard tried to think the situation through.

A man in the American embassy, in possession of the most terrible secret.

A man whose conscience had already led him to spilling that secret to a friend.

A man whose conscience was, even now, directing him to trade in that secret.

And sell it to the enemy...

What twisted logic was this?

'Cartwright,' he began, 'humour me for a moment. I'd like to ask your opinion on—'

Suddenly, the car skidded. One minute, they were roaring down the empty thoroughfare of Ludgate Hill. The next, the car was colliding with a lamppost, riding up onto the ruptured kerb with its wheels still spinning.

Behind the wheel, Cartwright caught his breath. 'Are you all right, sir?'

Maynard checked himself. 'Nothing a brandy won't fix. And you?'

'We'd better check the damage, sir.'

At least there was starlight enough to step outside and see the damage firsthand. Out on the frigid street, Cartwright bowed to check the buckled bonnet, lifting it to see smoke and steam billowing out. 'I'm sorry, sir. We're a long way from home, and this old girl needs patching.'

Maynard looked to the skies, as if he could see the passage of time in the wheeling stars.

'It's been a long time since I marched in the snow,' he said, drawing his collar tight against the cold and dark.

'Must you, sir?'

Maynard felt flakes of snow settling across his shoulders. 'I can't tarry, Cartwright. This one's too important.'

'Then I'll march with you, sir. It's been some years since I put many miles into these legs, but I'll do my best.'

Maynard clasped his shoulder. He hadn't known Cartwright during the Great War, but you always recognised a man who'd come home from that conflict. You were brothers, even if you'd never met.

'Stay with the car, old man. That's Departmental property. Don't let the scavengers come for it.' His eyes flashed about the midnight street. 'This city is full of the courageous, but it's full of the criminal too. I'll send help as soon as I reach the Club.'

Cartwright would have put up more protest, but he knew Maynard Charles well enough to know that he would tolerate no argument. Instead, he bowed again to the crumpled bonnet and started ferreting around inside.

*

Two miles separated Maynard Charles from the Deacon Club – in the snow and ice, that might take him an hour yet. He only hoped the bracing air would help him unpick this particularly thorny little problem.

If any man could help him, it would be de Guise.

The problem was: he'd have to involve de Guise's family.

Raymond would put up some protest at that.

He was too honourable not to.

And yet... honour worked in different ways as well. Their loyalty, first and foremost, was to King and Country. Yes, de Guise was the man. Maynard would just have to convince him that the dangers were worth it.

A shot rang out in the night.

Maynard hadn't grown used to the sound of gunshots, not even after his years in Flanders and France. He wheeled round, searching out the source – and must have slipped on the ice, because the next thing he knew, he was crashing to the ground.

Only as he hit it, and felt the pain ricochet through his body, did he realise he wasn't really wheeling round in shock at all.

He was wheeling round because of the force of a bullet.

It had struck him full in the breast.

The world fell out of focus.

He lifted his hand to his chest and found it hot and sticky with blood.

All the buildings, the lampposts, the stationary vehicles of Ludgate Hill faded into darkness.

A lifetime of memories crashed across him, like waves breaking on the shore.

He thought he could hear his name being called. He thought it was his father. Funny, for Maynard hadn't thought about the domineering old man in decades.

'Mr Charles,' came a voice. 'Mr Charles!'

Strange: his father had only ever called him 'boy'.

A silhouetted figure hung above him.

Death, kneeling down to carry him away.

But that voice, it didn't belong to Death. Nor did it belong to his father. It belonged to Cartwright, loyal Cartwright, who was kneeling down and taking Maynard's head in his lap, urging him to look directly into his eyes. 'Sir,' came Cartwright's voice, from the other side of the veil, 'stay with me, sir. Stay with me.'

Maynard rasped, 'You've got to get out of here, good man. The enemy…'

Cartwright gripped him more forcefully. 'The enemy hasn't got you yet, Mr Charles. We're back in the trenches now, you and I. I carried my fellows out of the deeps before. It may be years since those days, but I'll – I'll do my best.'

Two men on a frozen roadside, one of them leaking his life's blood into the other's arms.

London at war.

And out there: a secret in the hands of a traitor.

The clock was ticking.

Day One:

Wednesday, 16 December 1942

Chapter Two

THE BUCKINGHAM HOTEL PRESENTS

THE WINTER BALL

SATURDAY 19TH DECEMBER

**FEATURING THE MAX ALLGOOD ORCHESTRA
AND THE BUCKINGHAM DANCERS**

led by

THE KING OF THE BALLROOM, RAYMOND DE GUISE

*With guest stars Francesca West and Dorothy Potter,
and the return of Hélène Marchmont*

~

The snow on Berkeley Square had a different quality to the snow that had fallen across the rest of London, but the three American infantrymen who tramped into its perfect peppermint surrounds were too blown away by the hotel in front of them to marvel at the square's pristine white pastures. One year ago, the idea of being drafted to war and posted to London had been unthinkable – but the idea that they might spend Christmas in an institution as garlanded as this was more unthinkable still. Yet here they stood: three young men from Madison, Wisconsin, about as far away from home as the civilised world would allow. Each had a pack slung over his shoulder. Each stood proudly in his infantry fatigues.

And each, though they wouldn't admit it, trembled with anticipation at what was to come.

'It's gotta be better than barracks,' said the tallest. His name was Buxton May – and when the second lieutenant had read out his assignment, he had hardly been able to believe his luck. The Home Away From Home programme was designed as a greeting from gracious British hosts to the American soldiers sent to help them win this war. All across this great sceptred isle, American GIs were being sent into the homes of local host families for good old-fashioned family Christmases – but to be sent to the Buckingham Hotel was something else altogether. 'God bless British hospitality!' he beamed, striding out across the snow.

'It's at the personal invitation of the King, don't you know?' grinned the second soldier, a thick-set redhead named Eugene Tuck.

'I heard it was the Hotel Director,' replied Buxton May. 'He wants to do his bit as well.'

'The only thing better,' added Eugene, 'would have been Buckingham Palace.'

The third soldier smiled, inwardly. As far as he was concerned, there was no better assignment in the whole of the world. His name was Joel Kaplan – and, since the heady days of summer, he had named one Rosa Bright, a senior chambermaid in the hotel that hung above him, as the love of his life. It was Rosa who made this war worthwhile. It was Rosa whose laughter had cured every ounce of homesickness in his heart; Rosa, whose touch had made the prospect of some day being sent to liberate France bearable. It could only have been the hand of Fate that brought Joel to Berkeley Square this morning. He liked that idea.

He liked the idea that, for the next few days, he would be under the same roof as Rosa even more.

The Buckingham Hotel sat at the head of Berkeley Square, its striking white façade topped with turrets of snow. In front of the hotel, a grand marble colonnade gave it the impression of a palace from a much earlier age, and the doorman at its famous revolving bronze door had the look of a royal sentry. A stream of gleaming Rolls-Royces lined up at the colonnade, ready to escort the hotel's esteemed guests to whatever exclusive occasions they had come to London to enjoy. And there, behind the glass pane of a noticeboard at the foot of the sweeping marble stairs, lay the announcement of the Buckingham's Grand Winter Ball, taking place in but three days time.

'I rather think we're not invited,' said Eugene. Ahead of them, the grand doors had opened – and out walked a gentleman in finery, the lady on his arm draped in a fox-fur stole. Three infantrymen dressed in fatigues probably wouldn't be dancing with royalty on Saturday night – but perhaps they'd get a taste of the high life in the cocktail lounge.

Joel didn't mind. Rosa had told him about the way the hotel underlings – the chambermaids, the porters, the concierges and pages – turned the Housekeeping Lounge into a party every bit as worthy as the balls in the hotel ballroom. He was looking forward to nothing more than drinking and dancing with her in her own world.

'Hey,' said Buxton as they tramped up the stairs, 'you don't *really* think King George's gonna be at this ball, do you?'

The others just shrugged.

'My grandaddy fought against the old King George,' said Eugene.

Joel shook his head wearily. 'I think you got your mathematics wrong.'

But Eugene was adamant. 'We have babies old in my family. My pa was sixty-three when I come along.'

'Winter romance,' laughed Buxton.

'And *his* pa was seventy-one.'

'Something still don't add up,' said Buxton. 'He must have been a damn young soldier, to join the Revolution. Hardly out of diapers, I should think.'

'What can I say? We make 'em tough in my family.'

By now, they had reached the top of the steps. The doorman, his royal blue coat glittering with golden buckles, looked on them suspiciously, as if to say they must be approaching altogether the wrong establishment.

'Look,' said Joel, 'whatever your grandaddy or your great-grandaddy did, leave it at the door. We don't want any old family rivalries bubbling up. Leave *this* King George alone. We're here at his invitation, remember? Come Christmas Day, we'll be eating his goose.'

They were heading for the revolving bronze door when the doorman took three defiant strides and placed himself in their way. 'Excuse me, gentlemen,' he began, in a rich baritone. 'I think, perhaps, you might be—'

A second voice came from the revolving door. 'I'll take this from here, James.'

A short bespectacled man dressed in a brown suit emerged. He was unremarkable in appearance, with rounded cheeks and short-cropped hair, but he held himself with the supreme confidence of a leader. Joel had known commanders like this: some needed to stamp their authority with a brusque manner and insistent demands, while others just exuded the quiet authority of intellect, knowledge and experience. This man was certainly one of the latter.

What was more, he spoke with the accent of New York City.

'Am I looking at general infantrymen Kaplan, Tuck and May?' the bespectacled gentleman enquired.

The infantrymen answered as they would a commanding officer: 'Yes, sir.'

'Well then, allow me to introduce myself,' said the stranger. 'My name is John Hastings. I'm the director of the Buckingham Hotel – and, for the next week, gentlemen, you are my hallowed guests.'

Hastings clicked his fingers, and at once two porters appeared from the doors. Neither Joel, nor the other infantrymen, seemed to understand what they were here for – Buxton even resisted when the first porter tried to take hold of his packs. 'You're guests here, boys,' Hastings explained. 'Let us *serve* you.'

'A guy could get used to this,' said Eugene, as the porters took their packs.

'There'll be a lot to get used to,' Hastings announced. 'Come this way!'

The moment Joel stepped through the doors, to be hit by the wave of unseasonable heat in the hotel lobby, he was amazed. Rosa had told him about the opulence of the Buckingham Hotel, but none of her vivid descriptions had prepared him for this. The grand reception hall of black-and-white chequered squares felt more like the inner sanctum of a temple than a hotel. Around its edges, gleaming mahogany check-in desks were crowded with guests – while, in its centre, a fir tree bedecked in gold and silver baubles, and twinkling with electric lights like clusters of stars, reached to the domed roof above.

On one side of the reception hall, golden elevators ascended to the storeys above. On the other, doors led into the fêted Queen Mary restaurant. 'You'll be taking luncheon there, of course – and dinner, should you wish. All of it courtesy of us. And on Christmas Day I'll be hosting you myself, through those doors, for Christmas dinner. Make sure you make your requirements known to the desk beforehand. There's goose, of course, but we'll serve partridge and venison too. I took the venison last night. It simply melted on my tongue.'

Joel had always known places like this existed – but to be standing here, right in the centre of one, the beating heart of the Old World itself, filled him with the strangest feeling of all.

'What's down there?' he asked.

On the far side of the reception hall, masked from view by the Christmas tree's sparkling boughs, stood an ornate marble arch. Through the archway a passageway sloped downwards, until it reached heavyset double doors at its end. For a moment the doors came apart, revealing a whisper of what lay on the other side.

'The Grand Ballroom,' Mr Hastings announced, 'the crown that sits upon the Buckingham's head.'

Joel had heard of it, of course. He took two faltering steps in that direction. He was quite certain that, underneath the hubbub of the reception hall, he could hear music floating up from the ballroom. Rosa loved to dance. It was how they'd met, out in the clubs of Soho. It was how they'd fallen in love. How many times had she spoken of the Grand Ballroom? How many times had she whispered her dream, that they might get the chance to waltz there together? Joel preferred a wilder dance – and Rosa was *so* wild, jitterbugging in the Midnight Rooms or the

Ambergris on a Saturday night – but, right now, Rosa's dream surged up inside him.

'Sir, is it really true you've got King George and his family attending your Winter Ball?'

It was Eugene who had spoken, quite breaking the bewitchment cast over Joel.

'We talked about this,' Joel said, through gritted teeth.

'Hey, I'm intrigued!' Eugene laughed.

'As a matter of fact, I can't rightly say,' Hastings replied.

Eugene tapped his nose. 'A matter of national security, I expect.'

'I wish it was only that!' Hastings laughed, and started shepherding the soldiers away from the doors of the Grand. 'The royal party has yet to declare. I'm hopeful we may host them this Christmas – but the Imperial Hotel in Knightsbridge has also laid a claim.'

'Laid a claim!' laughed Buxton. 'It's positively medieval in old England.'

Hastings smiled, 'You rather get used to it. An American man can find much to enjoy if he gives in to Old World temptations.' By now they had reached the check-in desks. Hastings waved for one of the attendants. 'I'm afraid, boys, that – whether the good King George brings his family to our celebrations or not – the Winter Ball isn't part of the Home Away From Home programme. I'm sure you'll understand.'

Joel felt a little stab of disappointment: some tiny part of him must have entertained the idea of walking in there with Rosa on his arm.

'Look lively though!' Hastings declared. 'The opulence of the Buckingham Hotel is yours. The Queen Mary for dinner tonight. Cocktails to follow, in the Candlelight Club above. And if it really is dancing and music you're after, well, you can visit the demonstration dances tomorrow afternoon. Our whole troupe will be performing demonstrations for the crowd. The Max Allgood Orchestra – he's another gentleman from our side of the Atlantic – will be at full strength. You'll see some wonders in there. But, for now, let's get you into your quarters.'

In the same moment that the doors of the Grand Ballroom had fluttered open, revealing a glimpse of the baroque interior and its swooping music to Joel Kaplan, the dance troupe had been assembled on the beautiful sprung dance floor. Among them stood Frank Nettleton, sometime page, and rising star of the ballroom.

At twenty-three years old, Frank had grown out of the gangliness of his youth. Dancing had made him strong and supple, wiry and taut. On the night of the ball he would scythe across this dance floor in a suit of forest green, golden cufflinks at his wrists – but, right now, he stood in the same slacks and shirtsleeves in which he'd this morning been running errands for hotel guests. At his side, his dance partner Mathilde – elfin and slight, with dark hair cut short and bright cerulean eyes – kept trying to return his attention to the leader of the troupe, who was in the heart of the dance floor, illustrating a piece of choreography with one of the other dancers. But Frank could not help his eyes returning to the doors, for he'd just caught a fleeting glimpse of the soldiers.

'The Buckingham's a big place, Frank,' Mathilde whispered. 'Chances are you'll never see him.'

'I know it,' said Frank.

'And if you did, would it hurt that much?'

Frank shook his head wearily.

'It's been six months.'

'But before that,' said Frank, 'it was going to be my whole life.'

Rosa: Frank had been trying not to think about her since she'd called things off this summer. Most of the time he managed it. And yet, when he'd heard that the very same soldier she left him for was to be hosted here, right here at the Buckingham Hotel, a multitude of old feelings had rushed back to the surface. Late at night, manning the observation post on the Buckingham rooftop, Frank was plagued by the feeling that he wasn't good enough. That, if only he'd been permitted by the Medical Board to go off to war, Rosa might have looked on him differently.

That he too might have been a hero of the war.

'It's the Winter Ball, Frank. You deserve to shine. But you're not going to if you don't—'

In the heart of the dance floor, the troupe leader pivoted on his heel and said, 'Miss Bourchier, are we listening?'

Mathilde blanched, and dug her elbow into Frank's ribs. 'I'm sorry... Mr de Guise.'

Raymond de Guise – looking debonair as ever, despite the fact that he wasn't in his suit of midnight blue – ran a hand through his tangled black hair and surveyed his troupe.

'Ladies and gentlemen,' he began. 'Three days separate us from the Winter Ball, but there is no denying the facts: we have already been dealt a devastating blow. Marcus will not be dancing with us on Saturday night. It is unavoidable.'

Marcus Arbuthnot, the leader of the troupe, had been preparing the dancers for months to dazzle the crowds in the Grand – yet, three days ago, the most devastating news had swept him from London and beached the troupe. Lady Margot Arbuthnot, Marcus's dowager aunt and the woman who raised him, was to slip out of this world before Christmas night. With the Hotel Board's blessing, Marcus had gone to sit by her bedside as death hoved into view, leaving the troupe in Raymond's good hands.

It had been some time since Raymond de Guise had led the troupe at the Buckingham Hotel. Sometimes it seemed that a lifetime separated him from those days. Three years of warfare, and a year in the deserts of North Africa, certainly did. Yet there was nothing he wouldn't do for this hotel, and he had seized the opportunity to rally the troupe with aplomb.

'As you all know, changes have to be made. We have assembled a most magnificent company.' He looked across his dancers, their ranks swollen by a number of new hires, and then to the stage behind him – where Max Allgood, leader of the Orchestra, was holding his trombone Lucille aloft in front of his players. 'But in losing Marcus, we have lost the gravity at the heart of our routines. We are all lost planets, without a sun to spin our orbits around.

'Yet fear not! We have been in tricky situations before – and we have always come through. King George and his daughters may yet be waltzing with us on Saturday night. I expect us to prepare as if we are certain of it. Our guests deserve nothing less.'

Up on stage, Max Allgood shambled to the parapet and said, 'Sorry Mr de Guise, but when you talk about *changes*, I hope you're not thinking of changes to the set? We've got our new pianist landing tomorrow – Alix Monet, all the way from Paris, France. I reckon we'll need all the time we can get to work Alix into the band.'

'Max, I wouldn't have it any other way,' Raymond announced. 'We need the set to stay exactly as it is, while we work our choreography around it.'

'I'm grateful, sir. We've had a hell of a time finding Alix. A whole year without a permanent piano player, while ...' Max was going to say more, but nobody needed to hear a word to understand: Max had been banking on his nephew Nelson taking a place in the Orchestra, but the boy was wilful, wild and wholly unpredictable. After an unexpected performance at the Albert Hall this summer, he'd been approached to play at the Imperial Hotel – and since then the Society Pages had been quite full of stories about the drama, passion and glamour at the Imperial Ballroom. Max had been brooding over the betrayal ever since.

'To dance then,' Raymond declared. 'Tomorrow night we'll run a full rehearsal of the opening numbers. We'll reallocate Marcus's dances with the guests among us. By midnight on Saturday, we'll be dead on our feet. But just imagine the *wonder* you'll feel. Just imagine the splendour, the magic.' He turned to Max. '"Cubana Moonlight", Mr Allgood? Let's give this a try.'

The dancers started limbering up. On stage, the Orchestra settled into their seats and brought their instruments to bear.

But in the same moment that Max started counting the musicians in, a concierge appeared through the doors of the Grand, sashayed over to where Raymond was about to take the Austrian dancer Karina Kainz in hold, and handed him a folded slip of ivory card.

Raymond inspected it:

DINNER MOVED. UNAVOIDABLE. ATTEND AT ONCE.

The moment Raymond saw those words, something in him changed. Frank, Mathilde and the other dancers all noticed it. Raymond had not been quite as light on his feet since returning from war, but suddenly he looked even tauter, more rigid, more ill-at-ease.

He was trying to hide something – Frank was certain of it.

The concierge had barely slipped away when Raymond turned with a wan smile to the troupe. 'My friends, after everything I've just said, I must beg some patience. Max, I suggest you carry on with preparations. Dance, my friends. I'll return as quickly as I can.'

As he strode away, mounting urgency in his steps, Mathilde called out, 'But Mr de Guise – you've just said … three days. It's three days, and we're not ready. The King himself might be here.'

Raymond had almost reached the marble arch that led to the hotel reception.

He pivoted on his heel. 'I wouldn't go if it wasn't urgent. Rehearse!' he exclaimed – though everyone in the Grand could tell there was something forced about his expression. 'I shall look forward to seeing what you've accomplished on my return.'

Raymond couldn't bear more doubting eyes, so he made haste from the Grand Ballroom, stuffing the ivory card into his pocket as he marched.

It had been some months since he last received a missive like this.

He'd almost forgotten he wasn't actually invalided home from the war.

Autumn had been quiet – quiet enough that he *almost* believed he was back in his old life, caring about nothing but dance.

But nothing could have been further from the truth.

The truth was – this wasn't an idle message from his wife. It was how the Office contacted him: a summons to the Deacon Club, and whatever awaited.

The reception hall was busy with guests coming and going. Raymond picked his way through, heading for the Housekeeping corridor and the tradesman's entrance beyond – but he didn't get far. The Hotel Director, John Hastings, was standing by the golden elevators with three infantrymen in their khaki fatigues – and he was calling Raymond's name.

'Mr de Guise,' Hastings exclaimed, 'I should like you to meet our honoured guests for this Christmas.' He spread his arms out to the infantrymen, who each extended their hands for Raymond to shake. 'Buxton May,' Hastings began. 'Eugene Tuck. And this is...'

'Joel Kaplan, sir,' said the swarthy serviceman, with the firmest handshake of the three. 'I've heard so much about you. Mr Hastings here was saying we might catch a glimpse of you in the demonstrations tomorrow.'

'Not to mention that Mr de Guise will be joining us for dinner on Friday night in the Queen Mary,' said Mr Hastings.

Joel's hand was still in Raymond's own. Raymond fixed him with a glare. He knew it wasn't right to feel any enmity for the soldier – but Frank was his brother-in-law, dancer and friend, and the sight of the man who had broken his heart tightened Raymond even further.

But he was a practised liar.

He swallowed it down.

'I shall look forward to it,' he said. 'I'm glad you boys are here. It's been a trying few years. But here come the cavalry...'

The infantrymen laughed at that. 'Pleased to do our part, sir,' said Joel.

'And even more pleased to spend Christmas like *this*,' chimed in Eugene.

A tiny bell rang and, in front of them, the golden grille of the elevator rolled back. Inside stood the elevator attendant in his burgundy jacket and peaked cap.

'Mr de Guise, we'll catch you soon,' said Joel as he stepped into the elevator.

Then a strange, faraway look came over his eyes.

Raymond followed his gaze.

At the end of the Housekeeping hall, a darkened corridor vanishing behind the elevator shafts, the chambermaid Rosa had appeared.

Raymond fancied he could almost feel the electricity and expectation passing between them.

But then Mr Hastings stepped into the elevator with the soldiers, the grille was drawn shut and they vanished from view.

Rosa was gone when Raymond looked again – and thank goodness, because he was quite certain now wasn't the moment to become embroiled in some romantic tragedy.

The ivory card felt like it was burning a hole in his pocket.

They wouldn't have summoned him to the Deacon Club if it wasn't serious.

He'd started the week with the warmest of feelings: Christmas on the horizon, his first since returning from the war; the first he'd get to share in the company of his son. Now, not only was Marcus gone, and Raymond responsible for the spectacular of Saturday night – something else was to be asked of him as well.

Raymond de Guise caught sight of his reflection in the elevator's golden doors.

How many different faces could a man wear?

How many different lives could he lead?

Moments later, he was striding out across the snowbound Berkeley Square.

He didn't know it right then, but time was already running out.

Chapter Three

In the sitting room at Number 18 Blomfield Road, Maida Vale, Nancy de Guise lifted her infant son Arthur to the top of the Christmas tree and tried to guide the cloth angel in his chubby fist onto the top of the tree.

It did not go well.

Moments later, with the angel lost somewhere in the branches – already liberally festooned with baubles by her nephew Stan – she was staggering backwards to land in one of the armchairs, while Arthur's laughter filled the air.

She looked up at the tree. Lopsided, imperfect – but beautiful.

Just like her family, in fact.

The de Guise family had been living at Blomfield Road since the days when war was still only a dark storm cloud on the horizon – but the dream of a simple family home had been vanquished in that first year of war. Now Blomfield Road belonged not only to Nancy and Raymond, but to Vivienne, widowed when Raymond's brother perished at Dunkirk, and her son. Stan was rampaging around somewhere now, a wooden spoon in his hand and cake mixture spread across his face (at nearly four years old, he could be forgiven). Nancy's brother Frank, too, had been making Blomfield Road his home, ever more so since summer. There'd been a time when he spent almost every evening in the chambermaids' kitchenette, listening to music and playing at making home with Rosa. Now, when he wasn't at the hotel he could often be found right here, where he belonged.

A hotchpotch family, Nancy often called it – and if the truth was that home life often felt just as chaotic as her role as Head of Housekeeping at the Buckingham Hotel, well, she wouldn't change a thing.

Except, perhaps, that angel, buried upside-down in the branches.

Nancy was suddenly aware of a presence behind her.

There stood Vivienne, Stan running rings around her legs. She looked, thought Nancy, more *enlivened* than she had of late. Life had been cruel to Vivienne. It had bullied and harried her, cut her adrift, offered her a new start, then widowed her and told her to keep marching. But there was something about this Christmas that seemed to have brought a bit of colour back to her eyes. She was still only twenty-five years old, with fiery auburn hair cut short, and fiercely striking eyes. The apron she'd been wearing was crumpled in one fist, and her house dress was sky-blue and white – a dress for a summer's day, not a winter's night.

'They must be here any minute,' Vivienne began, her accent dripping with the timbre of her native New York. 'The soup's on the stove. The wine is cold.'

'The bread still warm,' Nancy grinned. 'Vivienne, you've done *more* than enough. These boys have been living on meals from the mess hall. They'll be aching for some home-cooked comforts.'

'I only wish we could have got hold of a turkey. Some pecans for a pie.'

'You found a pumpkin. Isn't that enough?'

Nancy carried Arthur past Vivienne, out into the hall to the foot of the stairs. 'I only wish we could offer them rooms of their own,' she said, looking up. 'Three to a bedroom seems awfully improper. Not very … hospitable.'

'It's like you said: they've been sleeping in barracks. They'll think this is luxury.'

'Not quite as luxurious as the ones going to the Buckingham Hotel,' remarked Nancy.

The Home Away From Home programme – the moment Nancy had heard of it, she knew she wanted to volunteer. London was flooded with American soldiers, anticipation rising for the moment the European offensive might begin in earnest – and it was a shame to think of them stranded in barracks on Christmas night. Nancy had grown up motherless; at eight years old, she'd been looking after her baby brother, cooking meals for her father, determined to do some good in this world. Then she'd come to London to begin her life anew. She knew what it was like to be far away from home – so throwing open the doors of her house to three American soldiers, making them part of her hotchpotch family for Christmas, had felt like the most natural thing in the world.

'It's poor Frank who's going to have to sleep in the Anderson shelter,' grinned Nancy.

'I rather think he likes it,' said Vivienne. 'His own private space.'

'I want to sleep there too!' chirruped Stan.

As Nancy drifted upstairs, eager to give Arthur one last nap before their visitors arrived, it struck her suddenly that perhaps this was the reason Vivienne seemed more lively of late. It had been seven long years since Vivienne last set foot in the country of her birth – but now, for the first Christmas in her adult life, America was coming to *her*.

Nancy was glad.

She deserved new beginnings.

Downstairs, Vivienne looked at herself in the hallway mirror. She wasn't sure why she had decided to fix her hair this afternoon. Perhaps it was just good old British first impressions – or perhaps it was something more. A prickle of guilt coursed through her when she thought about the future. That was the curse of the widowed woman, forever chained to the past. For two years she had dreamt of Artie every single night – but of late those dreams had started changing.

There was still tidying to do in the sitting room. Raymond had been playing his records last night, and left them strewn across the sideboard as he so often did. As Vivienne started tidying them away, she realised he had almost exclusively been listening to the recordings he'd collected on his trip to New York: Cab Calloway, Glenn Miller, the Count Basie Orchestra and the Mills Blue Rhythm Band. It had seemed, in the last year, that the whole of London had fallen in love with America, but, as she tidied the records away, Vivienne couldn't help thinking that there was something slightly *amiss* about Raymond and his records.

He'd been invalided back home after an ambush in the deserts outside Cairo, where he was stationed. Sent home from the Western Desert, deaf in one ear and half-deaf in the other after their convoy was attacked, Raymond had cut a forlorn figure when he returned to London. The fact he'd found his way back to the Buckingham, back to music and dance, at all, seemed a victory. And yet...

'All set, Viv?' came Nancy's voice from the door.

Apparently, Arthur had gone down easily, as always. Vivienne wished Stan would be a little more co-operative with his sleep – but then, he had the wolfish wildness of his father running through his veins.

'Raymond hardly ever mentions his injury anymore, does he?' Vivienne ventured. Then she caught herself and added, 'Unless, perhaps, in private?'

'He won't talk about it. He hardly wants to talk about Cairo at all.'

Vivienne could understand this. Why would any man who'd seen what Raymond had seen want to bring it into the house where his family lived? 'He just seems to be enjoying his music more than ever,' she went on. 'Maybe he's getting his hearing back?'

Nancy lowered her voice to a whisper. 'Part of me's afraid of it. What if they sent him back to the front?'

'They wouldn't do that … surely?'

Nancy shook her head as she swept up Stan.

'*They* might not,' she said as she hustled him towards the kitchen, 'but if Raymond thinks, for even a second, that he can go out there and do his bit again, what do you think he's going to do?'

Vivienne brooded on that as she straightened the sitting room.

Nancy was right, she decided: if Raymond was healing, his sense of duty would surely kick in. The obligation he felt to King and Country would eclipse everything he was doing in the Grand Ballroom – just as it had done in 1939, when Mr Churchill first made the declaration of war.

The only reason she could possibly fathom that he'd be keeping his healing a secret was to avoid that responsibility.

Yet that wasn't the Raymond she knew.

That wasn't the Raymond Nancy had married, the Raymond who had already given so much to the battle.

The problem was: she was quite certain things had changed in him.

She was brooding on it still when a sharp knock came at the door, and Nancy strode back to the sitting room to collect her. 'Here we go then, Vivienne. It's time.'

With one last look in the mirror – really, *why* did she care so much? – Vivienne rushed to join Nancy at the front door.

The shapes of three figures stood on the doorstep, their features obscured by the frosted glass in the pane.

'Let's treat them as lavishly as they're getting treated at the Buckingham Hotel,' beamed Nancy.

Then she opened the door.

Raymond broke into a run the moment he was certain he couldn't be seen from the windows of the Buckingham Hotel, sliding in the snow until he reached Piccadilly and the black face of the Deacon Club beyond.

It had often occurred to Raymond that the most important places in London often looked the shabbiest. So it was with the Deacon Club. Raymond had spent many long nights in private clubs – the Academy des Artistes in Covent Garden had once been a home away from home – but the Deacon Club was unlike any other. Behind its nondescript door there was a restaurant, a bar, lounges and countless private nooks and crannies for surreptitious meetings – but the Department spent as little on its upkeep as possible. Consequently, the club had a persistent smell of rising damp – and, as Raymond greeted the doorman and rushed to the stairs, the floorboards creaked.

Up the stairs, across the restaurant, round the bar and into the shadowy back hall to the office where he took his instructions. He rapped on the door, but didn't wait to be admitted. The man on the other side would be pacing up and down, White Owl cigar hanging out of his lips, waiting for Raymond alone.

'Mr Charles,' he began, 'I came as fast as I…'

But the man sitting behind the great oaken desk was not Maynard Charles.

No reef of smoke from a White Owl cigar filled the air.

'Mr de Guise, I suggest you remove the inscrutable expression from your face. It is not a good look for an espionage artiste.'

The man had a peculiarly effete air, with matinee-idol good looks and close-cut black hair that matched perfectly the fuzz around his jawline. Pointedly, he did not stand. Instead, he kicked out a leg underneath the table sending the opposite chair skittering outwards, as if inviting Raymond to sit.

Raymond did not sit.

'I'm sorry, sir,' he said, with deference – for, whoever this was, he was certainly Raymond's superior. 'I imagined the summons came from Mr Charles. I've never dealt directly with another.'

'I'm afraid, sir, that this situation is rapidly evolving. You may want to sit for this.'

Still, Raymond stood.

'Very well,' the stranger went on. 'Mr de Guise, it is my regrettable duty to tell you that, two nights ago, Maynard Charles was shot on Ludgate Hill.'

The silence in the study was deafening.

Still Raymond did not sit.

'Shot, sir?' he said, at last. 'Does he live?'

'For now,' said the stranger.

'But I don't understand, sir. Shot by whom?'

'Why,' said the man, as if it was the most natural thing in the world, 'by an agent of the enemy, of course.' Then his blue eyes narrowed and he said, 'Sit, Mr de Guise. We have much work to do.'

This time, Raymond relented. His mind was still whirling, his thoughts in freefall, as he sank into the seat.

'My name is Vernon Fox,' the stranger went on. 'I'll be your associate now. You report to me and me alone, de Guise. Is that clear?'

'Of course, sir,' said Raymond at once. 'We must catch his attacker at once.'

'We'll do no such thing,' Vernon Fox replied. 'They're long gone now, and it was probably some local criminal in any case.

Some men will do anything for a pay packet. I'm afraid London is rife with agents of the enemy now.'

'Then why am I here, sir?'

Vernon Fox fixed him with a look. 'You're here because it was his last request. Let me be plain with you, de Guise: I neither know nor approve of you. You've been instrumental to this Department in the past, but Maynard Charles put trust in you that many of us don't share. It seems to me that, for the last six months, all you've been doing is dancing. Not one piece of gossip you've fed back has proven to have any Intelligence value since the height of last summer.'

Raymond bristled. He was quite sure he'd done his duty to the very best of his ability. His purpose in the Buckingham Hotel was to *listen*, and that was precisely what he'd been doing.

'But Maynard Charles trusted you, so here we are.' Vernon paused. 'On the evening he was attacked, Mr Charles was visiting an Office safehouse in St Paul's. He'd been summoned there by one of the Departmental assets. No,' Fox went on, seeing Raymond's expression change, 'you don't need to know who. As it happens, this particular asset has gone to ground, but we're working under the reasonable assumption that he wasn't part of the attack.'

'He may have been bait for a trap, sir.'

'Maynard trusted him, in quite the same way he trusts you. We think he *needed* Mr Charles. But he was a frightened man. A haunted man. Mr Charles had offered him protection, and in return he gave up certain information that has sent ripples of concern around my community. To wit, Mr de Guise: this man identified a traitor. The problem is: he doesn't know who it is.'

'Sir, I'm not sure I understand.'

'Maynard Charles did. So, while he lies in a bed in St Thomas's hospital, fighting for his life, let's honour him and do as he asked, shall we?' Fox hesitated before he went on, 'I understand that your family is signed up to the Home Away From Home programme. Am I right?'

Raymond nodded, though some instinct deep in his belly told him that this conversation had just taken a sinister turn. What could his family possibly have to do with his undercover work for King and Country?

'This programme sounds very optimistic and neighbourly, but it's been a logistical nightmare for the Department. American soldiers going into British homes – what could go wrong?' Fox snorted and consulted his papers. 'You were, it seems, allocated three airmen from Camp Griffis as your guests, but at Maynard's instruction plans have been changed. Instead of accepting those airmen as your house guests, you will be playing host to three staffers from the US Embassy on Grosvenor Square.'

'Why, sir?'

Vernon Fox darkened yet further. 'Because, according to the gossip picked up by our missing asset, one of these three men is in possession of secrets, the magnitude of which you could barely begin to comprehend. Because, according to that same asset, this man's plan is to sell them to the enemy.'

Raymond's face paled. 'Sir, do you mean to say you expect me to host a dangerous traitor to Christmas dinner? That I should sit him at the same table as my son?'

Raymond's voice had risen in fury, but Fox met his rising ire with an implacable, icy glare.

'Not my plan, de Guise. This plan belonged to your bene-factor, Maynard Charles.' Vernon Fox paused. 'I'm not without sympathy for you. But this is what you were brought home for. If it helps, it is not the belief of this Department that he's selling secrets for selfish reasons. We believe this man's principles have been tested – tested to the point that they've shattered. This secret he's acquired pertains to a new weapon being developed in the United States. Perhaps he sees his own side gaining an unfair advantage in war, and thinks to even the balance.'

To Raymond, it seemed madness. Surely this war had to end, one way or another? Was any advantage unfair, when facing this enemy? Could a man really have lost sight of good and evil, right and wrong, so much that he might seek to trade with the enemy out of *honour*?

'But the fact remains,' Raymond seethed, 'you want to dispatch an enemy of the people into my home, at Christmas. You want him to sit at the table where my wife, my son, my nephew all live? You want him toasting, playing charades, eating mince pies, with my family? And you want me to *agree* to this?'

Vernon Fox stood. 'I don't need you to agree to any of it, de Guise. It's already agreed upon. In fact,' and he checked the watch at his wrist, 'it's happening right now.'

Raymond's eyes flared.

'I'm sorry, de Guise. The clock is ticking, and we may not have much time. One of these three men means to make a deal with the enemy. Your job, whether you accept it or not, is to find out which one.'

Raymond wheeled round, reaching for the door handle.

The heat inside him was indescribable.

'You shouldn't have brought my family into it.'

But Vernon Fox simply said, 'This Department is at your beck and call. I'll be waiting for your call.'

The fire was still burning in Raymond as he reached the club's crooked stairs and started loping down. Outside, a taxicab was trundling past in the last of the ailing light. He whistled for it, watched as it ground to a halt some way along the row, then leant back into the club.

The doorman was waiting.

'I need you to put in a call for me. Get a message to the Buckingham Hotel. I'm meant to be back in the Grand.'

'Yes sir.'

'Tell them they're to dance on. I'm sucked into a family emergency. Do you hear?'

Raymond hardly waited for a reply. He was already hurtling towards the taxicab.

The journey to Maida Vale had never felt as tortuous and long. More than once, he snarled at the driver, telling him to take another route; more than once, he entertained the idea of leaping out and running the rest of the way on foot.

When he finally reached Blomfield Road, he had just about stopped the stampede in his heart.

He'd been lying to Nancy all year. They'd told him he had to – that he was the King's agent now, that secrecy was paramount; that to tell her the real reason he'd been brought back from war, to insert himself back in the Buckingham Hotel and feed back on the gossip of all the industrialists and aristocrats who walked its halls, would put her in harm's way.

But she was already in harm's way.

What use was his secret, if they put her in harm's way themselves?

He had to control his breathing as he approached the door. Through those doors, Nancy and Vivienne were already playing host to the enemy. Now he'd have to do the job he was paid to do, right in front of their eyes.

Under his breath, he made himself a promise:

If a hair on her head was ever in threat, he would tell her the truth.

Raymond would finally tell his wife who and what he was.

He opened the door.

A wave of warmth rushed out to meet him, drawing him inwards. Nor was it the only thing – for here came Stan, rampaging forward to throw his arms around Raymond's legs and scream 'RAYMOND!' at the top of his voice. It was his usual way. So ordinary was it that Raymond felt his heart start to beat a less strident rhythm. He picked up Stan, cuddled him tight – 'Stick with me, little man' – and closed the door behind him.

Voices.

Voices sailed up to him from the kitchen at the end of the hall.

He could hear Vivienne laughing – she sounded strangely light – and, beneath that, the rumble of voices he had never heard before.

Raymond walked into his own kitchen – and found a traitor sitting at his dining table, drinking wine from one of his glasses.

He was silent as he surveyed them. Three men were ranged around the table – and, by God, one of them was bouncing Arthur, Raymond's own son, on his lap. Not one of them looked capable of treachery. At first glance they were just ordinary fellows, younger than Raymond, faces open and clear, their laughter ringing.

At Raymond's appearance, they stood.

Well, at least they had manners.

Nancy rushed to greet him. As she rose on tiptoes to kiss him on the cheek he heard her whisper, 'There's been some mix-up in communications. We were expecting airmen, but they're from the Embassy.'

Raymond controlled himself. 'The more the merrier, Nance,' he lied.

Then Nancy turned to the strangers. 'Allow me to introduce my husband, Raymond,' she declared. 'Raymond, these are our guests for Christmas. This is Ellsworth...'

'Ellsworth March,' announced the first American. Perhaps thirty years old, he was a beanpole of a man, tall and lean, with a fuzz of red hair and a dusting of freckles. His handshake, when it came, was tight and firm.

'Hello sir,' said the second, a dusty blond man who carried more weight around his belly. He seemed a little more nervous as he took Raymond's hand, and his handshake was gentler, as if he wasn't altogether certain of his own place. 'The name's Linden, sir. Jonah Linden. I'm real happy to be spending Christmas with you. Honestly, sir, we couldn't be more grateful.'

'You're most welcome,' Raymond said, his smile painted on.

'And this,' Nancy weighed in, 'is Mr Henry McCord.'

It was Henry McCord who had been bouncing Arthur on his lap. Although he was the youngest of the three, he was also the biggest. As he stood to greet Raymond, he *loomed* – tall, statuesque and with a rugged air that put Raymond in mind of the America he knew from the silver screen. More of an infantry type, thought Raymond – or a cowpoke from the Old West – than an embassy office worker. His dark hair was cropped short – and, though he'd evidently shaven that morning, his jaw was already darkened by stubble. 'You've got a sweet kid here, Mr de Guise. It's an honour to share his Christmas.'

Raymond had to stop himself bristling. He set Stan down, took Arthur in his arms and only then did he greet Henry McCord with a twinkling smile. 'You're most, most welcome,' he replied.

Then his eyes flashed around, taking them all in:

Red-headed Ellsworth, tall and lean.

Dusty blond Jonah Linden, with his nervous, darting eyes.

Henry McCord, and his bright white smile.

One of them was carrying treachery in his heart – while Christmas baubles glittered all around.

Chapter Four

At the Buckingham Hotel, postmaster Billy Brogan was poring over his private ledgers when his office door burst open, and in marched Frank Nettleton, looking about as harassed as Billy had ever seen him.

Startled, Billy started scrabbling his papers into drawers. As a long-time employee of the Buckingham Hotel, he took his duties seriously – but this particular ledger was not for prying eyes. It detailed the minutiae of Billy's business enterprise. That some of these activities were not altogether savoury – much less legal – was not a secret that Billy cared to share very widely. Nevertheless, in private moments, he often liked to pore over the pages. It was proof to him, if to nobody else, that a man did not need the boon of lands and titles to make something of himself; that he did not have to be born to wealth and privilege in order to succeed. Highborn men were born into greatness, but lowborn men had to acquire it through courage, cunning and guile.

'Frank, what the devil's going on?'

Frank had started pacing up and down. Billy had to admit that he was an elegant pacer – all that dance training certainly paid off – but seeing him so pent-up was outside the natural order.

'It's meant to be the season of cheer, isn't it? Good will to all men. But it's all going to hell, Billy. We've lost Mr Arbuthnot,

Raymond just *vanished* from the Grand this afternoon – and, and... *he's* here.'

Billy had stashed half a bottle of brandy in the bottom drawer of his desk for occasions just like this. He took it out and filled two crystal glasses to the brim. Crystal glasses were easy enough to swipe from the Candlelight Club, or from the room service trolleys. Billy was careful not to take too many, but a good number could be written off as breakages.

Frank did not really like brandy. He hardly liked a drink at all, unless it was a pot of nicely brewed tea with brown sugar. Nevertheless, he glugged it straight back.

'There are a thousand families taking part in the Home Away From Home programme,' said Frank. 'Ten thousand, maybe. All those families taking in American soldiers for Christmas... and *he* has to come here.'

Billy said, 'Fate, Frank. *Fate.*'

'That's what Rosa will think. She'll be up in the kitchenette, talking about star-crossed lovers. That's just her thing. She'll think destiny had something to do with it. But it's just rotten luck.'

'The thing about ladies, Frank, is they like a bit of romance. And if it wasn't him, Frank, it would have been somebody else.'

'Exactly. Just about *anyone* else would have done. I know Mr Hastings wants to do his bit. I know he thought the programme was a good opportunity for the Buckingham. I know he's keen on American custom and grabbing the American dollar. By goodness, we've got Max Allgood with an all-American orchestra! He's just about got them jitterbugging in the Grand.'

'Now, steady on, Frank...'

'But why did Joel Kaplan have to land here, in my hotel?'

Billy rather liked it when Frank got his blood up. It happened so rarely – except when he was dancing, wild and unbridled, in the clubs. 'What I meant was – if Rosa wasn't in love with this

Kaplan fellow, she'd have been in love with somebody else. Just about anybody would have done. She's that kind of girl. She's in love with *love*. The brute truth is: she just wasn't in love with you, Frank, and the sooner you wrap your head around it, the sooner you can get on. There's Americans everywhere this Christmas. It's better just to get used to it. As a matter of fact, there'll be some waiting in Lambeth for me right now.'

Albert Yard in Lambeth: the Brogan family home, and lodgings for Max Allgood and his sister. They'd almost lost it in an air raid last Christmas – but, thanks to Billy's wile and guile, it had risen from the ashes.

'There's airmen coming back to Maida Vale as well,' said Frank, glumly.

'Well, there you go!' laughed Billy, and clapped him on the back as he hustled him out of the post-room door, then locked it behind them. 'It could have been worse, Frankie. Joel Kaplan could have been sent to your *house*.'

It wasn't that Billy was tired of consoling Frank. The boy needed to pull his socks up and embrace a bit of life – but Billy quite understood the vacuum Rosa had left behind. Frank had had two things in his life: dancing, and Rosa. Now he only had one, and he barely knew what to do with his time. The trick was to keep busy, thought Billy as he loped towards Regent Street to catch the omnibus back into Lambeth. Billy kept himself quite busy enough with his enterprises. He wouldn't have had time for romance, even if it came knocking.

The omnibus took Billy over the fortified bridge at Westminster, past the grand palaces of government, the silent clocktower of Big Ben, and underneath the flotilla of great barrage balloons that protected the river. London sat under a shroud of white this Christmas – but not even the snowfall could hide the marks of the last two years' devastation.

There was sadness in seeing it, but it filled Billy's imagination as well.

There were always *opportunities* in chaos, and Billy had found plenty of those since he returned from Dunkirk.

It was only a short walk from the south side of the river to Albert Yard. Billy's leg, obliterated at Dunkirk – but patched back together, like so much of London itself – still ached when it got cold, so it would be wrong to say there was a spring in his step. But there was certainly a twinkle in his eye as he approached the old house. The knapsack over his shoulder was packed with luxury soaps he'd taken from the Buckingham store rooms, a bottle of brandy courtesy of the turned backs at the Candlelight Club, candied greengages from the Queen Mary kitchens and a set of fine Romeo y Julieta shorts. They were a gift from one of the shopkeepers Billy 'helped out' with produce, and he was quite certain that they would impress whichever American servicemen had been allotted to the Brogans for Christmas. All across London, people were talking about how flashy the American GIs were. Well, Billy didn't intend to let them think the Brogans were in want. If his family was hosting them for Christmas, he wanted them to go away downright *impressed*.

The blackout was almost in place by the time Billy reached Albert Yard. From inside, he could hear the sounds of the old gramophone playing. Bing Crosby, thought Billy. 'White Christmas'. Was ever a song as timeless as this one, that was scarcely six months old? His ma had been playing it since the middle of November, when Billy – feeling flush after a round of deliveries to the shops he supplied in Camden – had brought it home for her.

He opened the door.

47

'And here he is,' beamed Billy's father, from the heart of the sitting room – where the table had been set for eight, flames crackled and danced in the grate, and glasses were already being clinked. 'Billy, get yourself in here before the heat gets out. Our guests have already arrived!'

So they had. Billy had hardly taken off his overcoat before the introductions were being made.

'Billy,' his father pronounced, 'allow me to introduce Private Ollie Newell and Private Kit McArthur.'

'That's Private *First Class*,' said the one named Kit, shambling forward to vigorously shake Billy's hand.

Billy felt himself suddenly at sea, shaken up and down by McArthur's greeting. By the time he wrestled free, he felt rather green around the gills.

'Billy was with the British Expeditionary Force,' said Mrs Brogan proudly, emerging from the kitchen with a basket of freshly baked bread. Each host family had been awarded extra rations in the run-up to Christmas – it was part of the reason so many had clamoured to be part of the programme – and, at Albert Yard, they had not gone to waste. 'Nine months in France, that first year – and then all the trouble at Dunkirk. He was lucky to get out alive.'

The infantrymen whistled. Billy supposed it was meant to be a sympathetic gesture. Kit McArthur clapped him on the back, which just staggered him against the hatstand in the corner. On the other side of the room, from her armchair by the fire, his younger sister Annie – herself a chambermaid at the Buckingham Hotel – sniggered.

Sniggering, thought Billy, *at a hero of the war.*

'You British boys have stood firm,' said Private Newell. 'It's been a hell of a thing. My folks and me, we've been eager to get over here and help since it started, sir.'

It took Billy a moment to realise that, when Private Newell had said 'sir', it was directed at him. *Sir*. He liked the sound of that. Annie could learn a little bit about respect from these Americans.

'Well, boys,' Billy began, 'it's just good to be having you. As a matter of fact, I brought a few gifts – things to welcome you to our home for Christmas.' And he strutted over to the dinner table to open up his knapsack and reveal the goodies he'd stashed inside.

'Oh, you don't need to worry about that!' Mrs Brogan laughed, slapping Billy playfully on the back of the hand. Then she lowered her voice. 'Our Bill can get hold of just about anything. It's all those contacts of his at the Buckingham Hotel. All the errands he runs. They reward a hard-working boy like my Bill.'

In the corner of the room, Annie bristled. Their parents thought the world of Billy, but they might think differently if they knew Billy didn't just profit from errands run and hard work; that, for two years now, he'd been stealing and selling – and, what was more, enlisting his sister in the 'family business', quite against her will.

'It's a fine gesture,' Kit McArthur grinned, 'but it really ain't necessary. We're just happy to be sharing your company this Christmas.'

'We brought some gifts of our own,' said Private Newell, nodding to the sideboard, where a treasure trove was piled up. Here were bars of American chocolate, two packets of nylon stockings, a case of American cigarettes, chewing gum and fine leather gloves.

'Courtesy of us, to you,' said Kit.

Billy could hardly believe his eyes. He'd heard it said that the American quartermasters had bottomless supplies, but the casual way they'd piled these goods up sent his mind racing. Billy's days and nights were spent conniving ways to add to his own supplies: soaps and lotions lifted from the Buckingham store rooms; Champagne stolen and traded with farmers and wholesalers; silk sheets and pillowcases, their Buckingham embroidery carefully teased out, to be swapped and sold. No fewer than seventeen different shops, stretching from Camden Town to Finchley, relied on Billy's wits in conjuring up off-ration supplies for their customers. And yet here stood two American lads, with all the bounty of the US Army at their fingertips.

He was marvelling over it when Annie sidled up to him and said, '*Real* chocolate, Billy. Do you remember?'

Billy had been able to get his hands on a lot of produce other people had stopped dreaming about, but not even the Buckingham Hotel traded in chocolate anymore.

'Maybe they can get more,' Billy whispered. He flashed a look round. Kit and Ollie were sitting at the dinner table now, complimenting Mrs Brogan on the scents coming out of the kitchen and discussing the matters of the day with Billy's father. At the head of the table, Mr Brogan brandished that day's copy of *The Times*, its headline screaming about the chaos in Italy – where Mr Mussolini had ordered a general evacuation. 'You might have to work hard on these two, Annie. Charm them with that smile of yours. Get them on side, then ask if there's a way they can help us out.'

Annie's face darkened.

She didn't like talking about Billy's 'enterprise' at home.

She hardly liked talking about it at the Buckingham Hotel either – but Billy could be very insistent.

'Can't we just have a lovely night, Bill? Not everything has to be business.'

'I can't help it, Annie.' He picked up a chocolate bar. HERSHEY'S TROPICAL CHOCOLATE read the packet. 'When I see an opportunity, it just grabs hold of me.'

Annie folded her arms across her chest and said, 'Just leave it, Billy. Leave it for *one night*.'

'There'd be plenty of families in London willing to pay extra for this. Just imagine the good it would do.'

'Oh Billy, do we have to talk about that today?'

If Billy noticed the disapproval in Annie's tone, he either ignored it, or simply didn't care. 'There's hundreds of families going to bed not worrying about where dinner's coming from the next day because of me, Annie.' He caught himself and added, 'Because of *us*. If a man makes a little for himself along the way, it's only fair. We're Brogans. We can't stay on the bottom rung of the ladder forever.' He put his arm around his little sister and squeezed her tight – and, for a moment, it was like they were children again, like nothing, no secrets or lies, had ever come between them. 'Just see what you can do, Annie. Imagine the kids who haven't had any chocolate since the beginning. By God, I've seen kids eating *carrot lollipops* on these streets. Carrots, Annie. And here's these two, with hands on great barrels of the stuff.' He gave her a cheery wink, completely at odds with the restlessness Annie felt inside. 'Let's just see. There's no harm in just *seeing*.'

Mrs Brogan had casseroled rabbit for dinner, with the extra rations of bacon to add flavour. She was just serving it up when the front door opened – and in waddled Mr Max Allgood, of the Buckingham Orchestra.

'It's bitter out there tonight,' Max huffed, swinging Lucille in her case as he took off the multitude of coats, scarves and hats that he wore. 'Not as bitter as a New York night, of course, but…'

Max turned, to find two infantrymen staring at him from the dining table.

'I quite forgot!' he exclaimed, and waddled over, reaching out his hand.

Billy and Annie both saw what happened next. The infantrymen's faces had creased, as if in incomprehension – and though they both took hold of Max's hand, there was enough hesitation beforehand to spread a strange discomfit around the room. The only person who didn't seem to acknowledge it was Max himself. He just kept talking: tomorrow he was meeting the new piano player, so he had to be up early; the dancers were up against it, with even Raymond vanishing that afternoon. Perhaps he hadn't noticed the infantrymen's confusion. Or perhaps he just better understood the way they did things in America.

'Mr Allgood and his sister Daisy lodge with us,' Mrs Brogan explained, dishing up the casserole.

'Daisy's gone to see her son,' Max said, darkly. 'Not that the blackguard wants much to do with us, not now he's ruling the roost at the Imperial Hotel.'

'How long has it been, Max, since you came?'

'Last Christmas, ma'am,' said Max – and the two American infantrymen shared a puzzled look at seeing him taking a seat at the head of the table, directly opposite Mr Brogan himself. 'And I'm still glad of it, every day.'

Perhaps, if Max had acknowledged the awkwardness, conversation might have taken a darker turn. There was always a chance he was oblivious to it, just swept up in all his talk of the Grand Ballroom and Alix Monet, the new pianist he'd been waiting for all year – but, as dinner was served and everyone tucked in, Billy rather thought he was just practised at stepping round the delicate subject of his skin colour. There were a good number of fêted Black musicians in London – an even greater number in the United States – and music seemed to have set Max apart, his talent opening doors in society through which men like him were not ordinarily invited. The same did not go for Black soldiers enlisted in the US Army. Even here in Great Britain, they were kept to their own barracks, handed duties in logistics and supplies, instead of being asked to lead in the charge.

It had not escaped Billy's notice that Black soldiers were not sent around the country to spend their Christmases 'home away from home'.

'Why don't you tell these good men about Dunkirk, Bill?' said Mrs Brogan, once the plates were being cleared and tidied away.

Billy looked about as uncomfortable, now, as the infantrymen had upon seeing Max. 'It's a long time ago, Ma.' And the truth was, he didn't like speaking of it. The whole country talked about the derring-do of Dunkirk, the heroism of fishermen and hobbyist sailors surging out to bring the BEF back home. But what Billy remembered was the feeling of being exposed upon the beaches, he and Raymond stranded in the open as the sky was filled with artillery fire.

Drowning in the English Channel, until the fishing boat pulled him aboard…

By good fortune, though, there was chocolate for dessert to dispel the nightmare.

'It tastes even better than I remember,' swooned Annie, as she let a piece dissolve on her tongue.

'Good Lord, it tastes like *home*,' beamed Max.

'And this is just standard ration pack stuff, is it?' asked Billy.

Annie shot him a warning glare.

Then, as if to head off a difficult conversation, she ventured, 'They're putting on such a spread in the Queen Mary restaurant – but even *they* don't have chocolate. Figgy pudding and brandy sauce, but not *chocolate*. Even if King George does take Christmas dinner at the hotel, they won't be able to feed him Hershey's Tropical.'

Private Newell guffawed. 'I tell you what – we'll send him a bar or two, how's about that?'

Billy cut in, 'You can really just get hold of it?'

That was when Annie kicked him, as suddenly and sharply as she could, underneath the table.

'Oh, there are ways and means,' laughed Kit McArthur. 'Hey, you don't mean to say that you'll *really* be cleaning the King's dishes on Christmas Day?'

'Not personally,' said Annie, 'but...'

'You rather get used to it, when you're working at the Buckingham Hotel,' cut in Billy, puffed up with pride. These Americans might have had chocolate and nylon stockings – but one thing they didn't have, and hadn't had for generations, were Kings and Queens. 'King Haakon will be at the ball – that I *do* know. And King Zog – he's from Albania – he stayed at the Buckingham for months. Queen Wilhemina... Oh, they come and go at the Buckingham Hotel!'

'I'd really like to catch a glimpse of the princesses, if they do come,' said Annie. 'Princess Elizabeth – she'll be Queen one day. The girls at the Buckingham think it's already been decided. They think they're bound to come – only they're keeping it under wraps, for security. And Victor says...'

'Victor's our Annie's sweetheart,' said Mrs Brogan.

Annie flushed at the word, but went on regardless, 'They're laying it on in the Queen Mary kitchens. They've got three dozen geese maturing in the larders, but there's one plumper than all the rest. A *kingly* goose, Victor reckons.'

The infantrymen grinned at that. 'A kingly goose,' said Private Newell. 'I reckon I could go for that, on Christmas Day!'

'I'd second that!' laughed McArthur, raising his glass as if in a toast.

By the head of the table, Mrs Brogan clutched her husband's hand. Billy saw a sudden worried look colouring her face. His ma was good at hiding her feelings, but Billy saw it plain as day: it was a flash of shame.

'I'm afraid there won't be a goose at this table, not this Christmas. More rabbit, I was thinking. But there'll be plenty of trimmings, and even some sausage-meat in the stuffing.' She stood up, eyes downcast, and started clearing away the plates. 'I hope you'll understand.'

'A nice eel pie,' added Mr Brogan – for he too had sensed his wife's unease. 'We'll give you a good meal, don't you worry.'

At last, the soldiers understood. 'We meant nothing by it, ma'am,' said Kit McArthur. 'It was just all this talk of Kings and princes – we're just a couple of Boston boys, here. Out of our depth in the old world and…'

That was when Billy got to his feet.

'You don't need to worry, Ma.'

He couldn't bear the shamed look on her face. He couldn't stand how hard she'd worked today, how eager she was to open her house up to guests, only to end up embarrassed in her own home. And maybe those American boys hadn't meant it, maybe they hadn't been thinking – but right there on the sideboard stood their pile of chocolate and nylons and cigarettes, all the things they'd brought into this house 'as a gift', as if to show how much better they had it than their hosts.

Mrs Brogan looked at him and gave a weak, half smile.

'Sit down Bill,' she said. Then, as if she needed to convince herself, she said, 'We'll do our best for Christmas Day. It mightn't be goose, but we've never gone hungry. Even when I had all seven of my children under this roof, we didn't go hungry.'

Mrs Brogan's voice caught, fraught with emotion. Perhaps it was only the mention of her children, all of Billy and Annie's brothers and sisters, scattered across Suffolk since the evacuation, and the fact they wouldn't be here for Christmas. Or perhaps it was the weight of everything else as well. All of a sudden, Billy truly understood the reason his mother threw the doors of their home open to any lodger who needed a roof – whether it was Max Allgood and his family, or American infantrymen in need of a home-cooked dinner at Christmas.

It was because the house felt so empty.

'I know we're not going to go hungry,' Billy declared. The eyes of the table were on him now. A little voice inside told him he ought to stop – but he was Billy Brogan, and Brogans didn't stop. 'Christmas dinner isn't going to be rabbit and gravy, not this year. It isn't going to be eel pie – lovely as your eels are, Pa. No, we've worked too hard for that. It's been a long year. It isn't just kings and princesses in the Queen Mary restaurant who deserve something special on Christmas Day.' Billy took a breath. 'Ma, I've been saving it as a surprise, but now seems as good a time as any. You're going to be cooking a goose on Christmas Day. No, you're going to be cooking the biggest, grandest goose you ever saw. What did they call it? A *kingly* goose, big enough to serve the whole house on Christmas Day and Boxing Day, right the way to New Year.'

There was silence at the dining table now.

Eyes were agog.

Only Annie's burnt with strange fire – for out of everyone, only she seemed to think Billy was lying.

'What do you mean, Bill?' asked Mrs Brogan, in wonder.

'Well, when have I let you down before?' Billy asked, eyes flashing between the Americans and that pile of goodies they'd brought. 'I've got us a goose, Ma.'

Mrs Brogan rushed around the dining table and threw her arms around him.

'Are you sure, Billy?'

'Sure as you're standing there, Ma.'

When his mother released him from her arms, Billy looked around.

The Americans were toasting *him* right now.

They looked suitably impressed.

Some moments later, as they helped their mother clear the table, Annie slid to Billy's side and said, 'What are you talking about, Billy? You don't have a goose at all. I can see it in your eyes.'

Billy took her by the arm and led her aside.

'Annie, haven't you learnt yet to have a little faith?' In the kitchen, as they scrubbed plates, Billy's voice dropped to a whisper. 'I've never let the family down before, have I? We damn near lost this whole house, and I gave it back to Ma and Pa. Well, didn't I? *Didn't* I?' Billy waited for Annie to nod. 'Then hold me in a little higher esteem, won't you? Those American boys aren't the only ones who can get hold of things. You mark my words – come Christmas Day, there'll be a big fat goose sitting on that table, golden and glistening, the toast of the whole of Albert Yard.' Billy grinned. 'Yes, Annie, I can see it now. Goose all the way into 1943 – and all because of *me*.'

Chapter Five

'Of course, I heard all sorts of music, that summer I was in New York City,' said Raymond. 'All these sounds I hadn't heard before! It felt like the world was opening up.'

Somehow, he'd managed to control the thunderous beating of his heart. Right now, he was lowering his Benny Goodman record onto the gramophone. He'd danced to these songs at a club in the Bowery in the summer of 1937, that journey he'd taken to win over John Hastings and bring his investment to the Buckingham Hotel. As the strains of 'Stompin' at the Savoy' picked up, he took a moment before turning back round. How was this going to work? Get them dancing, fill them with wine, lead them into some knotty conversation and make whichever one of them it was stumble? The sooner he got this over with, the sooner his wife and family would be safe. Excuses would have to be made, stories spun – lies, lies, yet more lies – but at least then there'd be Christmas and the Winter Ball to look forward to without shadow or blight.

He had to pretend he was simply hanging there, absorbing the music. He needed a moment to think. Two hours ago, all had been dance. Now, Maynard Charles lay fighting for life in a hospital bed, while a traitor stood in his sitting room.

He turned round, with a dashing smile.

'You must know this one, boys?'

'I can tell you're a dancing man, sir,' said Jonah Linden. 'I've never been much for it myself.' As if to prove the point, he started shuffling on the spot – more like a man whose trousers were falling down than somebody warming up for a dance.

'Oh come on, Jonah!' laughed Ellsworth March, propped up by the blackout blind with a glass in his hand. 'I've seen you at the soirées. Remember Camp Pendleton?'

Jonah hung his head, almost in shame. 'Hey Ellsworth, that was almost compulsory. The admiral expected it.'

'So do we all, old friend.'

While Jonah flushed red, reminded of some former embarrassment, Raymond made a mental note: Ellsworth March and Jonah Linden had known each other for years, attended the same functions, moved in the same circles. Perhaps that might mean something, further along the line.

'What about you, Mr McCord? You must have danced at some army functions along the way?'

Henry McCord had already drained his glass. 'No, sir. Not me, sir. As a matter of fact, I haven't served in the frontline military at all. I've been an embassy attaché since the start. It's Mr March and Mr Linden here who served.'

'You served?' asked Raymond, turning to Jonah and Ellsworth.

'As did you, Mr de Guise. Your housekeeper was just telling us, they invalided you back home?'

As the words came out of his mouth, Vivienne appeared in the sitting room doorway, another tray of drinks in her hands.

'Housekeeper sounds about right,' she said, but her eyes sparkled with levity.

'Vivienne is family,' Raymond intervened.

'I'm just grateful to hear a voice from back home,' smiled Ellsworth, taking a drink and winking at Vivienne. Stan – who had been stampeding around the kitchen in search of something to eat – appeared, and would have leapt into her arms if Ellsworth hadn't hoisted him up. 'It's just a shame this little scamp's growing up with a London accent. In another lifetime, young man, you could have been a New Yorker.'

As they set about talking about New York – and Vivienne started talking about the places she used to know, the Manhattan apartment she remembered, the townhouses on the corner of Washington Square where her socialite friends used to live – Raymond found it hard to believe that any of these men were enemies. The sitting room rang with laughter. The conversation flowed with memories – and the truth was, Raymond couldn't remember seeing Vivienne as energised in years, certainly not since that first terrible day of the war, when she'd both married his brother and watched him march off to battle.

Raymond looked at the clock on the wall.

Barely fifteen minutes had passed in conversation.

There was still time.

Still time to make them stumble before the evening was out.

Then he heard his son crying upstairs, and Nancy's voice rang out from the kitchen, 'Raymond, can you see to him?'

Raymond hated leaving Vivienne with the Americans, but perhaps the space would be useful to formulate a plan. Before striding upstairs, he looked in on Nancy. It didn't escape him that she'd been on her feet all day at the Buckingham Hotel, and that she was on her feet all evening now. She would need a rest soon. Raymond would give it to her, the very moment that he could. Unpick the problem of the embassy men, then find a way for Nancy to relax.

Arthur clearly knew that something more exciting than sleep was going on downstairs. When Raymond entered the room, he was up on his feet, fists wrapped around the bars of the crib like a prisoner protesting his sentence.

As Raymond picked Arthur up and danced him to the mirror that hung on the outer wall, his mind was scrambling. Perhaps this couldn't all be done in one evening. First, he had to learn about the Americans. Then, he had to define which one of them was capable of such a betrayal. Only then could he trick them into slipping up.

'Arthur,' he whispered, 'you've no idea what's going on tonight. Pray God you never will.'

'Sorry Raymond,' laughed Nancy from the nursery door, 'I didn't realise you hated dinner parties *quite* as much as that.'

Inwardly, Raymond winced – but, outwardly, he turned and grinned at Nancy. 'I didn't hear you there,' he said.

'Dinner's nearly ready. Maybe he should come down for it.'

Raymond wanted to say 'No' – anything to keep Arthur out of the Americans' arms – but just nodded instead. This was to be a battle of words and wits. He had to remind himself of that. Arthur wouldn't be in any more danger than he was already. Even when he did reveal the traitor, there was every chance the man himself would never know it had been Raymond who unmasked him. If he was going to do this, he'd have to keep up an impression of normality. And wasn't that what he'd been doing all year? Lying to his wife's face, and becoming so good at it that it was frightening?

'Those soldiers will have landed at the Buckingham today as well,' said Nancy, grateful for a quiet moment with her husband before the evening truly began. She rested her head upon his shoulder and sighed. 'Did it have to be Joel Kaplan? Right there in the Buckingham Hotel?'

'I saw them arriving. They were going up to their rooms.' Raymond hesitated. 'Kaplan looked a normal young man. It's hard to hate him.'

'No,' said Nancy, 'he doesn't deserve hate.'

'All's fair in love and war?'

Nancy shook her head. 'I've never liked that saying.'

'People get hurt in both,' said Raymond.

'It's not good for the girls, having Kaplan around. Ever since it was announced, it's all they've talked about. Rosa's got them all stoked up. She's got the others thinking that, if she's got a GI on her arm, then maybe they could too. I'm going to have to ban them from inviting those Yanks up to the chambermaids' kitchenette.'

'They'll think it's because you're protecting Frank, of course.'

At that moment, they heard the front door opening downstairs, and Frank's voice calling out a hello. Introductions were being made.

'I just can't have my department disrupted. It's playing with fire. Rosa's wild enough, without having her paramour under the same roof.'

Raymond neglected to remind Nancy that Frank and Rosa had been working under the same roof all of the time they were stepping out together, and just held on to her instead, gazing into the mirror. Father, mother and infant son – if you ignored what was going on downstairs, it might have been a perfect moment.

'I'm glad you're here, Raymond,' Nancy whispered.

Such a simple emotion, but sometimes these things needed to be said.

'Last Christmas was hard,' she went on, voice cracking as she remembered. 'You were so far away. Arthur was so small.'

'He still is,' said Raymond, holding his son aloft.

*

Downstairs, conversation rose and fell. Raymond could hear voices drifting up through the floorboards, ebbing and then flowing again. It was war talk, of that he was certain. Ellsworth March and Frank were talking about El-Alamein, where the second great battle had just been fought and won. If Maynard Charles hadn't summoned Raymond back to London, he would have been part of that campaign. This Christmas there was cause to rejoice: the Allies had secured the road to Baghdad; right now, the soldiers with whom Raymond had spent so long were sweeping across French North Africa. In Europe, the Nazis' stranglehold endured – but, across the world, the battlefield was being rearranged.

Then Jonah Linden piped up, 'I hate to be pessimistic at Christmas, but my instincts are what they are. There's a lot of work to do. Europe's a fortress. It would take something remarkable to change things quickly. Something new, something dazzling, something *dangerous*. Something nobody's seen before.'

Raymond placed Arthur in Nancy's arms and marched to the nursery door, the better to hear what Jonah was saying. 'We should join them,' he said. 'Nance?'

Nancy had remained by the mirror. 'I was enjoying a quiet little moment, just the three of us. The eye of the storm.'

Raymond laughed, 'Back to battle, Mrs de Guise,' and hurried to the top of the stairs.

From here he could hear the conversation even more clearly. From the advances of North Africa, they were suddenly at Pearl Harbour – and, unless Raymond was very much mistaken, Ellsworth March had been at the harbour on that day, little more than a year ago.

'Frankie,' he called out, sashaying into the kitchen where they were now all sitting around the dining table and grasping Frank by the hand. 'You're here just in time.'

Frank looked a little spent by the day, but he was very clearly grateful to be home. 'It's a full house tonight, Raymond.'

'Did I hear you say ... Pearl Harbour?' Raymond asked, eyes flashing around the room.

At the stove, where she'd just lifted the casserole dish out of the oven, Vivienne stopped dead. Behind her, Ellsworth March was beginning to spin the story for a second time – how he'd been stationed at the naval base in Honolulu on the day the Imperial Japanese aircraft appeared – and he certainly had a gift with words, for part of her felt as if she was there, watching the devastation alongside him. But her eyes were fixed on Raymond. Something in this didn't seem right.

Raymond had been upstairs, with Nancy and their child.

Had he really *heard* Ellsworth talking from up there?

'Of course, you'd know all about destruction, Mr de Guise. Weren't you there, at Dunkirk?'

Now it was Raymond's turn to look at Vivienne. He decided that that darkening look could mean only one thing: tonight was not the night to talk about Dunkirk, and all it had wrought for their family. He gave her the barest of nods, as if to acknowledge this unspoken thing. Then, as Nancy arrived to hand Arthur over to Frank and help dish out dinner, Raymond asked the only question he'd been able to formulate that might start them marching down a path to the truth.

'Sometimes this war just seems unending,' he shrugged, sitting down at the head of the table and breaking the bread Vivienne had spent the day baking. 'The tides of battle come in and the tides of battle go out. We lose Tobruk, then capture it again. We're on our knees, then on our feet, then on our knees again. I was talking to an old friend at the Buckingham Hotel today. He saw battle in the Great War. And he said: we're not dug into trenches, not this time, but is the feeling of it any different? The lives lost for no real gain? So ... *how* can it end? How do you go from just trading blows to ending it once and for all? What would it take?'

Ellsworth made a steeple of his fingers and gave a wearisome sigh. 'That, Mr de Guise, is the question on everyone's lips. The question President Roosevelt loses sleep over every night. And I daresay we're not going to solve it over this dinner table tonight!'

Raymond felt the laughter start ringing. But laughter would not do.

He seized the moment and pressed his point: 'The world's never seen war like this. There are warplanes. Tanks and submarines. A war that's being fought by engineers, scientists, inventors too. *Technology*. Who knows? Maybe it's *them* who'll win the war.'

Raymond waited, every sense alert to the imperceptible flickers on their faces.

He seemed to have unnerved Nancy, who was looking at him oddly.

He'd certainly unnerved Vivienne, whose eyes were narrowed and glaring.

The truth was, he'd almost unnerved himself. Vernon Fox's words kept ringing in his ears.

'Hey,' said Jonah, 'you're asking the wrong fellow. I'm just an army grunt turned embassy staffer. This is for higher minds than me. You want to ask Henry there.'

'Me?' laughed Henry McCord.

'Well, Henry here,' Jonah went on, 'might look a little green around the gills. He might look like he's fresh out of the academy. But the fact is, he's the most knowledgeable one of all of us. Ellsworth and me, we're good with people – you have to be, if you work in an embassy – but McCord's the one with the brains. He's our rising star. It'll be the Senate for Henry, by the time he's thirty. Where was it you studied, Henry?'

'MIT,' McCord replied proudly. 'That's the Massachusetts Institute of Technology, gentlemen. My father's alma mater too.'

'Our very own intelligence analyst,' Jonah said. 'The boy looks twelve, but he's a prodigy.'

'Hey, I'm only a stats man. I crunch numbers. I analyse data. I'm not a philosopher. But, listen, if you want to know what I think's going to stop this war – I say … *this*.' McCord spread his arms open to the table. 'Good people,' he declared, 'from different corners of the world – people who wouldn't be sharing Christmas dinner if they weren't being thrown together, but who can find common ground, who can work for the common good. Doors thrown open to neighbours, strangers becoming friends, allies coming together. Yeah, I reckon *that's* what'll win this thing.'

'Hear, hear,' said Nancy, passing the plates around.

But Raymond was not finished. 'People are dying out there. We lost too many people in France. I said too many goodbyes at Tripoli and Tobruk.'

Nancy touched his shoulder, as if to console him. 'We almost lost Raymond on the road out there.'

Taking her seat with Stan, Vivienne looked at Raymond closely. That was the story, of course – that Raymond had been injured in an attack and lost his hearing, shipped off home when the medics decided he could no longer serve. But he'd certainly heard the conversations in this kitchen from the nursery above. And now he was hosting a welcome dinner for his house guests, while simultaneously pressing them – fiercely, almost viciously – for their thoughts about the war. This was meant to be a cheery occasion. This was meant to be the preamble to Christmas Day.

It didn't seem right.

'Ellsworth,' Raymond went on, 'I'm sure you lost friends at Pearl Harbour.'

Red-headed Ellsworth looked suddenly pale. 'More than I care to mention, sir. And I take your point. Wickedness like that can't be defeated with magical thinking. Bullets and bombs don't know about optimism and hope. But I like to think Henry has a point, regardless. I think what you're trying to say, Henry – and forgive me if I'm wrong – is that you've got to know what you're fighting for. To make sense of the madness, you need to dream about what's on the other side.'

'What *I'm* saying,' said Raymond, and his eyes turned from Ellsworth back to Henry McCord, 'is that innocence is gone. It's going to take something sudden, something decisive, to win this war. I don't know what – some new development, a new technology, a new kind of warfare. Something to force wickedness's hand…'

There was a ghostly silence around the table. Raymond tried to keep his eyes from fixing on Henry McCord, but some inexorable force seemed to be dragging them that way.

He looked as innocent as apple pie – wasn't that what the Americans said?

And yet who among them would be better placed to come into possession of military secrets, than a man who studied at the Massachusetts Institute of Technology, the one bona fide intelligence analyst among them?

Raymond felt his hand trembling under the table.

He breathed deep to keep it under control.

Then Frank's voice piped up: 'This conversation is terribly dark for Christmas, isn't it? Raymond, why don't you tell everyone about the Royal Dansant last summer?'

'I was there!' Ellsworth exclaimed. 'The whole embassy were invited.'

The Royal Dansant: a day of dance and music, held in honour of the Americans flocking into London, and the turning of the tide in this long, bitter war. Raymond remembered it vividly, for he'd reigned victorious and danced in the arms of both King George's daughters as the night reached its end.

He wished he could feel a little of that joy right now.

But the air in that little house on Blomfield Road was throbbing with secrets.

As Raymond watched Henry McCord, Vivienne watched *him*.

'A toast,' said Nancy at last, 'to new friends, new beginnings and new hope for the New Year!'

Raymond lifted his glass.

'To new friends,' he cheered.

But all throughout dinner, he couldn't stop staring at Henry McCord.

Day Two:

Thursday, 17 December 1942

Chapter Six

Throughout the long night, snow dusted the rooftops of London.

When Max Allgood awoke, it seemed as if the world had been started anew.

It was not often that Max was the first to stir at Albert Yard. Ordinarily, he slept late, exhausted by the efforts of the night before. But last night, sleep had come only fitfully. Scarcely two days separated the Max Allgood Orchestra from the moment when they would have to hold the entire Grand Ballroom – and perhaps even the King himself – in their thrall, and in that time he would have to induct a new pianist to their ranks. Most piano players knew the standards well enough, but Max had spent all year making sure that the Orchestra was anything *but* standard.

Already dressed in his crushed velvet jacket and necktie, Max waited in the attic window – lovingly polishing Lucille with a square of green silk – until he saw the taxicab arrive. Then, mumbling something to himself about putting on a show, he shambled down the attic stairs and through the silent house.

Or, at least, he *thought* it was silent. When Max reached the sitting room, one of the American soldiers was sitting in front of the embers of the fire – with a slightly haggard look that seemed to suggest he had been there all night. 'Just couldn't sleep, Mr Allgood,' said the soldier, as Max stole past. In return, Max only doffed an imaginary cap. He'd seen the way the servicemen had looked at him at dinner last night, the way this one was looking at him right now – not with malice, nor with the disdain he used to feel in Chicago, but almost with *curiosity*. Part of him wondered if this was worse than disdain. 'Why would *you*,' they seemed to be saying, 'be so lauded that you might lead an orchestra for the King?'

'Buckingham Hotel, sir?' said the driver, when Max lowered Lucille into the back seat and settled down beside her.'

'But take me the long way, won't you?' Max asked.

The driver looked back. 'Long way?'

'Don't worry. I'll direct you.'

Dawn was beginning to show itself when the taxicab slid along Knightsbridge, into view of the Imperial Hotel.

'We're a long way from home,' smiled the driver.

But Max just asked him to idle for a while, as the curtain of snow came down and London woke up.

Sure enough, after a frigid hour in the taxicab, Max saw what he was looking for.

'You see that young man?' he asked the driver.

'Sure as day, Mr Allgood.'

'That's my nephew.'

Nelson Allgood: Max hadn't lain eyes on him since he'd moved out of the Brogan house. Nelson – and his perennial problem of causing friction with just about anybody who gave him a chance – had been the reason Max and his sister crossed the Atlantic. They'd found him a home, got him work in the clubs of London, even cleared the path so that one day – once he'd proven himself – he might become part of the Orchestra at the Buckingham Hotel. But when that chance did not come soon enough for his liking, Nelson had strutted off in his own direction, accepted the hand of an enemy orchestra, and – or so it seemed to Max – lifted two crooked fingers at everything his family had done. In doing so, he'd damn near broken his mother's heart.

Max understood that the boy's benefactors at the Imperial Hotel had found him lodgings in Knightsbridge, quarters from which he could even see the Royal Albert Hall. Now, though he didn't lead the Orchestra there, he was considered their prize asset: something a little different, something a little wild, something to draw the eye of society.

Something, if the whirlpool of rumours were right, that might even draw the King to the Imperial Hotel this Christmas.

'Are you getting out, sir?'

Max said nothing, for he was too lost in thought.

'Sir, he's almost at the hotel.'

Max reached for the door handle, but at the last moment he relented. He'd thought he might confront the boy. He'd thought he might make some impassioned plea, ask him to come home for Christmas. For all the torment he'd given her, his mother would have liked that. But some fire in him failed, for his eyes had seen the three-day-old newspaper the cabman had tossed on the back seat. There a grainy image showed the entirety of the Imperial Orchestra – and, in the middle of the sea of faces, one stood out: Nelson himself, the only Black musician in the band. Not even the Orchestra's esteemed bandleader, Bob Holloway – portly and Scottish, brandishing his trumpet with the broadest of grins on his face – drew attention away from Nelson.

'CHARITABLE BONANZA,' read the headline, 'FOR HEROES, PAST AND FUTURE, OF THE WAR.'

A charitable concert was held last night at Wellington Barracks, where a host of general infantrymen from the United States came together with veterans of the miracle at

Dunkirk to raise money for families in need. In attendance was the Imperial Orchestra and their esteemed bandleader Bob Holloway. After a long career in the clubs of London, Mr Holloway is enjoying a resurgence in popularity and fame, thanks to a startling young pianist who joined his Orchestra this summer. The event was praised by Buckingham Palace as a 'symbol of unity and strength, and everything that is great about our two nations', and received special commendation from the US Ambassador. 'We at the Imperial Hotel have always held our duties to the citizens of our proud nation dear – and now to these we add the love and honour of our American cousins. In times like these, we all need a little light – and the Imperial Orchestra has been proud to provide it.'

Max couldn't read more. He averted his eyes from Nelson and said to the driver, 'I suppose you must know a bit about momentum?'

'Aye sir,' said the driver, 'like when your car gets going on an icy road – and there's not a thing you can do to stop it.'

Mr Hastings said there was still hope for the royal party appearing at the Grand Ballroom on Saturday night, but in his heart Max knew the battle was lost. When one star is rising, another must fall. And in a game like this, there could be only one winner.

'To the Buckingham then,' he said, sombrely. 'As directly as you like this time, sir.'

The dark feeling sloughed off Max as the taxicab drew around Berkeley Square. If he was right, and they'd already lost the battle for the royal party, well, there was still a show to put on. The Grand Ballroom would still be thronged with the great and the good; there was still wonder to conjure up, magic to be wrought. The moment he started waddling up the steep marble stairs, he felt the fire again. Nelson was a comet: right now, he was hurtling skyward, but some time soon he would come crashing back to earth. It was the habit of his lifetime to sow chaos wherever he trod. Perhaps all Max really needed to do was tend his own garden. One day, Nelson's would be turned to cinders – while Max's was in full bloom.

Max Allgood wasn't much of a wordsmith – it was only through Lucille that he ever got to the heart of an emotion – but, as he slipped through the bronze revolving door, he was rather pleased with this image.

He was halfway across the reception hall, passing into the glittering shadow of the fir tree, when Mr Hastings called his name.

'Mr Allgood, I'm glad I caught you.'

Max's heart had been on a rollercoaster this morning; hearing the hotel director's tone it plunged again.

'I'm sorry, Mr Hastings, but I promise we'll make magic on Saturday night. I don't know what happened to Mr de Guise yesterday, but we were just about pulling it together. I tell you, even if we haven't won the King, we'll win *hearts*.'

'Well, that's rather what we need to talk about, Max.'

Max didn't like it when the Hotel Director used his Christian name. Perhaps he did it because they were both American men and, in that way, brothers – but he always feared it presaged some terrible dressing-down.

'Your new pianist has arrived a little early. I had the pleasure of introducing the Grand Ballroom just now.' Mr Hastings paused, his expression inscrutable. 'Listen, old boy. I know we asked you to cause a *conversation*. I know we asked you to make headlines with the Orchestra, but I didn't expect *this*.'

At once, Max felt lost at sea. 'Mr Hastings?'

'Listen out, Max.'

While they'd been talking, Mr Hastings had gently been shepherding Max towards the archway that led down to the Grand Ballroom. As they stepped away from the hubbub of the hotel reception, he could hear the tinkling sounds of a piano echoing in the Grand.

'It sounds good to me, sir,' said Max, as they approached the ornate ballroom doors. 'By my reckoning, we've had a lucky break. I've got a friend out in the clubs to thank for it. He'd heard Alix had been in London since the fall of France. Hadn't been playing much – too busy working with the Free French, so music had to be forgotten about for a while. But I got hold of some old recordings sir, and . . .' Max paused, just outside the doors of the Grand. 'Just *listen* to it. It's exactly how I thought it would be, Mr Hastings.'

Mr Hastings adjusted his spectacles and said, 'Not *exactly*, Max.'

He pushed open the doors.

Max was the first to step through.

There was nobody else in the Grand Ballroom, nobody but the piano player up on stage.

Music filled the cavernous hall.

But Max stopped dead.

'Good Lord,' he said, under his breath.

He'd known from the recordings that Alix Monet was a pianist of rare talent and flair.

He just hadn't known that she was a woman.

At the Imperial Hotel, Nelson Allgood threw open the doors to the ballroom and beamed.

For four months he'd been causing beautiful chaos in this ballroom. Across eighteen Saturday nights he'd summoned up devils for the lords and ladies to dance to. But this weekend would be the first ball he'd played for his new employer, and every fibre in his body was ready for it. The Imperial Orchestra's opening number, 'Nobody But You', had been reworked so much that it almost belonged to him. Whenever he played it, he fancied that it had been written exclusively for him.

'Well boys,' Nelson began as he loped into the dressing room behind the stage to find Bob Holloway and the other musicians already preparing for the day, 'I make it fifty-eight hours until we're on that stage. Tick tock, boys. *Tick tock.*'

The Imperial Orchestra were used to Nelson's bravado by now. At the beginning it was something they'd been instructed – by no less than the Hotel Director, Mr Hubert Gove – to make allowances for. There'd been much disgruntlement, a good number of disagreements – and at least one occasion when one of the trumpeters threatened to break Nelson's fingers. But when that trumpeter had been summarily jettisoned from his post, the message to the rest of the Orchestra was loud and clear: this year, the Imperial meant to challenge the Buckingham, the Savoy, the Dorchester and Ritz for the right to rule London; any man who hindered them – notably, for instance, by breaking Nelson Allgood's fingers – would find himself without a home.

This morning, however, a raft of blank faces greeted Nelson. Even Bob Holloway – who quite understood the pact they'd made, and did his utmost to keep peace in the band – looked impassively on and told him he might consider sitting down.

'Sit down?' Nelson baulked, strutting across the dressing room to the trolley the service maid had left behind, then pouring himself a hot coffee. There was so little of the stuff left in London that Nelson felt like a prince with every cup. 'I've got ants in my pants, boys. I can't sit. By God, I'll hardly be able to sit all Saturday night. I can feel it – I'll be standing at that piano, making her *howl*.'

'Nelson, it's Mr Gove,' Bob intervened, in his sturdiest Scottish brogue. 'He's got an announcement to make.'

Perhaps for the first time in his life, Nelson became distinctly aware of the atmosphere in the room. Ordinarily this was something he was quite immune to, for it involved thinking about what another human being might be feeling – but right now he saw their sallow expressions, their downcast eyes, and thought he understood. 'We *lost*? The royal party? They made their announcement?'

The musicians started grumbling, leaving it to Bob Holloway to say, 'What else can it be? I just pray to God they haven't declared for the Buckingham.'

'If they have, I'll drag the King here myself,' Nelson suddenly snarled.

The musicians fell silent.

It wasn't often that they heard Nelson Allgood do anything other than blow his own trumpet. They had certainly never heard him genuinely snap – not even when disagreements got heated or, in those early days, when half the Orchestra wanted him gone. He seemed to weather every storm with the same insouciant grin. But now, his eyes had narrowed, and the coffee cup was trembling in his hand.

'Whatever it is,' Bob Holloway announced, 'we've got a show to put on – and if those bastards at the Buckingham take the prize, well, it's our job to show London that they didn't deserve it. Christmas is a battle, gentlemen. It isn't the whole war.'

Nelson almost spat out his coffee. 'Good Lord, Mr Holloway, if you don't win the battles, you don't win the war. I didn't come to the Imperial to play second fiddle. I came to the Imperial to cause waves – and stick it to my uncle Max. I could have been playing over there by now. You better hope and pray we've won this or...'

One of the trumpeters was on his feet – apparently willing to break the edict never to challenge Nelson Allgood – but on this day his career would survive, for at that moment the dressing-room doors opened and the Imperial's director, the tall and willowy, white-whiskered Hubert Gove, walked in with his personal valet just behind.

For some reason, he was carrying a record in his hands.

'Gentlemen,' Mr Gove began, 'I won't keep you long.'

Nelson watched as Mr Gove parted the musicians with an airy wave of the hand, then crossed the dressing room to put the record onto the gramophone. Some moments later, the gentle sounds of a piano filled the air. It was elegant, stately playing – nothing at all like the riot Nelson conjured up – but, just when Nelson was ready to dismiss it as an irrelevance, the player started pounding the bass, and the song turned into a stampede.

When the piece finished, leaving Bob Holloway's Orchestra largely perplexed at its significance, Mr Gove instructed his valet to lift the needle from the gramophone.

'This was recorded by one Alix Monet,' he announced, 'a French pianist who has latterly landed in London. Gentlemen, *this* is your new competition.'

A multitude of murmurs and whispers spread around the dressing room.

'This is who they hired at the Buckingham Hotel?'

'So my sources say,' said Mr Gove. 'What do we think? Is it enough to challenge us?'

There were yet more murmurings, until at last Nelson intervened: 'It's a good sound, but that's all it is. Does it have character? Does it have passion? Does it have drama? That's the kind of thing it's hard to say from a recording.' He paused. 'But what does it matter? Uncle Max doesn't have a chance of stirring up interest in it, not by Saturday night. Half of society's already decided where they're going. It's the King we're waiting on.'

Mr Gove was exceedingly tolerant of Nelson, but his brow darkened at the way the uncouth American used the King's name so flippantly.

'Well, gentlemen, I'm here to tell you that Alix Monet will, indeed, cause a stir. Nelson, your Uncle Max has hired himself a woman.'

Some of Bob Holloway's Orchestra were stunned into silence. Others shared hurried looks and sniggered.

Even Mr Gove, Nelson saw, was wearing a wry grin.

'Gentlemen, I have spent all year utilising this hotel's resources to undermine the Buckingham Hotel's efforts to hire a permanent piano player. Every time they identified somebody they wanted, that person was mysteriously approached for slots at this very hotel. It has cost me a great deal of time, energy and effort to keep the Max Allgood Orchestra on the back foot. But I did not foresee this. I thought it would be a fight until the end – but it seems they've submitted.' He paused. 'They got desperate, gentlemen. They scraped the barrel.'

A deep sigh of relief had spread around the dressing room.

Bob Holloway stepped up to shake Mr Gove's hand. 'It's ours, then. The spoils of the night belong to us.' He paused. 'No word of the royal party?'

'That,' Gove replied, 'is something I'm still working on.' Then he opened his arms and added, 'I just thought you might like to know: the Max Allgood Orchestra have rather lost the plot. Saturday night is going to be fun, gentlemen.'

While the disbelief turned to laughter in the dressing room, Mr Gove took his leave.

'Well boys,' Bob Holloway ventured, 'I wasn't expecting *that*. But let's make the most of it. If the Max Allgood Orchestra are going to make fools of themselves, let them. By God, I thought we were preparing for battle. Now I think—'

'You're being a fool.'

Nelson's voice rang out across the dressing room.

All eyes turned back to him.

'Is that so, Allgood?' smirked one of the trumpeters. 'Listen, boy, there's no love lost between you and your uncle. You snipe about him almost every hour of the day. If he's determined to make a fool of himself – to make a fool of the Buckingham Hotel – I say give him the rope to hang himself.'

'It would have been nice to beat them fair and square,' said one of the percussionists. 'I didn't expect them to throw in the towel.'

Nelson shook himself angrily, like a dog rising out of a river. 'My uncle's cannier than you think. Don't you see? He hasn't thrown in the towel. He hasn't miscalculated. He's ... daring to *try*.'

'Yeah,' laughed the trumpeter, 'he's trying to rubbish the reputation of the whole hotel. This couldn't have gone better if we'd planned it.'

'You old fools are stuck in the past,' snapped Nelson. 'Haven't you ever heard of Hazel Scott? She's been playing with the Count Basie Orchestra back home for years. She was all over the Cotton Club Revue the year I left New York. And ... Billie Rogers? By God, she plays the trumpet better than anyone here. Hell, the whole line-up of the Sweethearts of Rhythm are women, and they're playing for bigger crowds than we do out there. I'm not saying it's *normal*, and I'm not saying there aren't folks like you grumbling about it back home – but, where I come from, lady musicians are seizing the stage wherever they can.' Nelson kicked at a chair, sending it flying. 'And there you are, you old dogs, kicking back and laughing. No, Mr Gove doesn't know what he's talking about. He's stuck in the eighteenth century. This isn't something to *dismiss*. This is something to … start panicking about.'

'Panicking?' quizzed Bob Holloway. 'Now, hold your horses there, Nelson, we've—'

'There's no point holding the blinkin' horses!' Nelson sighed. 'The bastards have already bolted.' Then he shook his head, as if in weary admiration of his uncle. 'God, the old man must be getting sharper in his old age.' He surveyed the room with darkness in his eyes. 'We better think fast, because the Max Allgood Orchestra just took the headlines from us. This is the sort of thing they'll write about in the Society Pages. And yes, maybe they're as stuffy and old-fashioned as old Gove out there – maybe they'll snort and scoff and laugh about it. Or maybe, *just maybe* it's all anyone will talk about until Christmas and beyond.' Nelson could tell, by now, that his words had pierced the smug veneer of the rest of the band. 'We have to roll our sleeves up, boys. This fight has been dirty from the beginning – but, by God, it just got *ugly*.'

In the same moment that Nelson Allgood was parading himself in front of the rest of the Imperial Orchestra, Max Allgood was standing flabbergasted in the Grand.

At his side Mr Hastings said, 'She's good, Max.'

Yes, thought Max, but *she's …*

'How many piano players have you had in and out of this ballroom since summer? Six? Seven? Eight?'

'Seven, sir.'

'Was any one of them as talented as this?'

On the stage, Alix Monet looked up from the grand white piano and realised she had an audience. A lesser player might have stumbled, but it only seemed to embolden her. She'd been elegant before, but now her playing attained a kind of grandeur Max had rarely heard in a solo instrumentalist. Alix did not rise from her stool onto the balls of her feet and hunch over the piano as Nelson did when the music took hold of him, but still she seemed to melt into the piano. Yes, thought Max, she was *very* different to Nelson: when Nelson was at his best, it was like he and the piano were in a boxing ring, trading blows, a battle being fought; Alix treated the piano more like a partner who had taken her in hold. It felt very much as if Alix and the piano were *dancing*.

She was a tall woman, with jet-black hair cut almost as short as a boy's, a sun-kissed complexion – even in the middle of December – and was wearing a white blouse decorated in frills like a dress shirt and a pair of loose-fitting black trousers that put Max in mind of the pants the workmen wore when they were remedying the fixtures and fittings around the hotel. If Max had seen her striding across the hotel reception, she would have looked striking enough; rolling her wrists across the piano to conjure up this constantly cascading storm, she was more striking still.

'Excuse me, Mr Hastings,' said Max.

Then he took Lucille to one of the tables at the dance-floor balustrade, lifted her from the velveteen lining of her case and – having first adjusted her slide – waddled out to the middle of the dance floor.

He started to play.

Lucille's wild, swooping song sailed up to join with the piano. Soon, he could feel her diving through the wild breakers of Alix's melody. Piano chased trombone; trombone darted playfully around and chased the piano in return.

Then they came together, spiralling round and round – until, unable to outdo each other, they collided in a chaotic explosion of sound.

Max stepped back from Lucille, beaming.

Up on stage, Alix Monet had risen from the piano to take a bow.

On the other side of the ballroom, John Hastings put his hands together in applause. 'I'll leave you two to get acquainted,' he said. 'Max, I'll see you in my office later today.'

After Mr Hastings was gone, Alix vaulted from the edge of the stage to land (rather inelegantly, it had to be said) on the sprung dance floor, then loped over to Max and took his hand. 'Mr Allgood, I'm devilishly pleased to meet you. I've listened to so many of your recordings.'

'Devilishly, is it?' laughed Max. She had a strong English accent, though the cadence of her mother tongue had not been completely overridden. 'Well, Miss Monet – it is Miss, isn't it?'

'The proper term would be Mademoiselle,' said Alix. 'But *Miss* will do.'

'You weren't nearly what I was expecting, Miss Monet.'

A look ghosted across Alix's face, which seemed to suggest she knew *exactly* what Max had meant. Regardless, she said, 'I'm a little rusty, Monsieur. I haven't played since Paris – not in any real way. They have a piano at the French House. Sometimes, late at night, I played for de Gaulle and the rest. But a palace as magnificent as *this*?'

Together, she and Max gazed around the empty Grand.

'It's quite something, isn't it?'

'*Mai oui.*'

'It'll be something else altogether on Saturday night.'

Alix had her hands deep in her trouser pockets, but now she brought them out. Her fingers dazzled with rings. Opals and ambers shone upon each knuckle.

'Do you doubt I'm ready for it, Mr Allgood?'

Max was silent, ruminative, lost in thought. The morning had been discombobulating enough, and it hadn't truly begun.

He didn't doubt her talent. What he doubted was the reaction of the rest of the Orchestra; the reaction of society. There were fêted female musicians back in the United States, but no woman had ever played in the Orchestra of the Grand Ballroom. This was a place of tradition and decorum – and yes, traditions and decorums changed; Max himself was evidence of that. But only two days separated them from the Winter Ball. Nelson and the Imperial were already in the ascendant. How did the woman in front of him change the future? Did she upset the equation? Did she balance the scales? Did she make the Max Allgood Orchestra a mockery or a sensation?

Alix seemed to sense his hesitation.

She screwed up her eyes and said, 'Has there been some mistake, Monsieur? You did write to *me*, did you not?'

The doors of the Grand were opening. Max looked over his shoulder to see the other members of the Orchestra starting to appear. Among them, James Heath – for decades the Orchestra's eminent percussionist – looked curiously on, his jowly face pursed in confusion. Beneath the fat grey slug of his moustache, Heath's face might either have been smile or scowl.

And Max thought: that's exactly how I'm feeling as well.

The rest of the Orchestra were assembling; Max knew of only one way he would be able to convince them to go together on this adventure.

'Miss Monet, we've two days to go. Nerves are shredded. There's a mountain to climb. I need them all to *believe* we can still create something special.' He paused and pointed Lucille to the stage. 'Alix, let's play.'

Chapter Seven

When Nancy awoke, Raymond was no longer there.

It was strange how quickly you could get used to a warm body beside you again. All those long months when Raymond was away at war seemed unimaginable the moment he was back where he belonged. All year Nancy had been waking in the blackest hours of morning to make her way to the Buckingham Hotel, kissing her sleeping husband on the brow before she left. But now, as she pulled on her day clothes and fixed her hair in the mirror, he was nowhere to be found.

The three Americans were soundly sleeping behind the spare bedroom door. As Nancy stole down the stairs, she saw the shadow of Frank's fidgeting form, curled up like an infant, on the settee by the hearthfire. The sound of a soft footfall drew her along the hall, into the kitchen.

There was Raymond, pacing up and down. He looked as though he'd hardly slept a wink. Nancy had seen him less lined with exhaustion – or could it be *worry*? – on those nights when he used to walk patrols with the fire-watch and ARP.

'Raymond, what's wrong?'

But Raymond just said, 'I couldn't sleep last night, Nance,' and, when she asked if it was about the Winter Ball, he only nodded vaguely, as if to say he didn't want to speak about it. This made Nancy falter. There were few times in life when Raymond had doubted his talent in the ballroom – and even fewer when, late at night, he hadn't wanted to confide in her.

'You can do this, Raymond,' she said, crossing the kitchen to fold her arms around him. Her husband was so much taller than she was, his body so taut and strong – conditioned not just by his years in the army, but by a lifetime in the ballroom. 'I know it's been swift. I know Marcus left in a hurry. But you're where you belong. You do *know* that, don't you?'

Raymond nodded, but he would not look her in the eye. 'I wanted this Christmas to be peaceful,' was all he would whisper.

Then – because he always knew the right moment – Arthur started crying upstairs, and Nancy left Raymond with nothing but a kiss on the cheek.

By the time she reached the nursery, Vivienne, bleary-eyed, was lifting Arthur to her shoulder.

'Well, here's Mama,' Vivienne said, as Nancy crept in. 'Don't cry on her uniform, kid. Mama's got a big day ahead of her.'

Arthur was reaching for his mother, so Nancy took him and danced him around the nursery. 'Viv,' she ventured, when the crying ebbed away, 'Raymond's already awake. He's down in the kitchen, like he hasn't slept one wink. Did you think, perhaps... he wasn't *himself* last night?'

Vivienne had clearly noticed it too. Raymond had seemed on edge from the moment he stepped through the door, almost belligerent throughout dinner – almost *unwelcoming*.

'I think, perhaps, it's to do with the ball.'

Vivienne suddenly staggered forward, catching herself against the side of the crib. As was his wont, Stan had woken, discovered his mother gone and charged headlong out of the bedroom, colliding with the back of her legs like a runaway freight train.

To Stan this was a more entertaining sight than anything he'd seen since the circus last summer.

'He hasn't been himself for a while,' said Vivienne.

'You really think so?'

Vivienne wasn't certain how much she should say. How could you articulate such a diffuse, ambiguous feeling? Certainly there was no way of doing it that didn't provoke more concern. 'I'll fix him a proper breakfast before he follows you to the Buckingham. That ought to set him up for the day.'

Vivienne had just started shooing Stan to the stairs when she looked back and realised that Ellsworth March had emerged from the spare room where the soldiers were sleeping. It had been a late night and he looked about as dishevelled as Vivienne felt – but his eyes were luminous, and he didn't seem irritated by his rude awakening. If anything, he seemed entertained.

'Is this the way of things in this house?' laughed Ellsworth. 'No need for alarm clocks, when you've got young Stan?'

Stan stopped dead and fixed Ellsworth with a stare. Then he strode in front of his mother, like a dog protecting its pup from a predator, and said, 'Back to bed!'

'Stanley Cohen!' Vivienne gasped, and swept him up. 'I'm sorry,' she said to Ellsworth.

'You've got a fierce protector there,' he laughed. 'A true warrior. You do right, Stan – you look after your mama,' he said, and slipped back inside the bedroom.

For a moment, Vivienne's eyes lingered on the space where Ellsworth had been. He had a warmth about him that she admired. Perhaps there were young children in his family – nephews and nieces, from whom the war had taken him far away. She would have to remember to ask him. In the meantime, she prodded Stan with a finger. 'You can't speak to guests like that, Stan,' she laughed, carting him to the top of the stairs.

Nancy was already halfway down, carrying Arthur.

'Are you going to be all right hosting them today, Viv?'

Vivienne took a breath. 'They'll be *busy*, won't they, Nance? I'll have dinner ready later ... but I'm not really expected to *entertain* them, am I?'

'Good Lord, no!' came Ellsworth's voice. Apparently the man had a habit of appearing at the most inopportune times. In Vivienne's arms, Stan threw him a demented salute. 'In fact, I think you might consider letting us entertain you. I've seen the way you run this house. I think, perhaps, you might deserve a day off.'

Vivienne rather liked the idea, but the truth was there was so much to do – how could she ever indulge herself, this close to Christmas? 'There is one thing you can do to help,' she ventured – and promptly turned round to launch Stan into his arms. 'He's always at his wildest first thing on a morning. But there's fresh snow out there in the garden. Run some of the wildness out of him, while I get on with breakfast.'

Ellsworth had been a military man. He was used to taking orders – just not from a petite New Yorker, still dressed in her red flannel nightgown.

Nevertheless, like a good soldier, he understood his calling.

'Come on then, young man,' he declared, opening the back door. 'Hat and scarves, and off to battle.'

'I thought we were hosting soldiers,' Nancy called from the kitchen, where she was settling Arthur, 'not babysitters.'

Vivienne remained at the foot of the stairs, half bewildered.

Perhaps a day hosting the men from the American embassy mightn't be such hard work after all.

She suddenly became aware of movement behind her. In the darkness by the front door, Raymond was hovering at the hall table, the telephone receiver in his hand. The moment he saw her looking, he clattered it back into its cradle and breathed a deep sigh.

'Sorry Vivienne, I didn't mean to startle you.'

The sounds of Stan waging war in the garden could be heard through the kitchen walls. Vivienne felt a rush of such warmth for her son (warmth for Ellsworth too, who had thrown himself into the game so wholeheartedly), but crept closer to Raymond and whispered, 'What's going on, Raymond? You look... *haunted.*'

At least he smiled at that. 'I just couldn't sleep, Viv. Two days – that's all we've got. There are demonstration dances this afternoon – and tonight, the full rehearsal. Hélène's coming, and we haven't rehearsed a thing.' Hélène Marchmont – Raymond's old partner in the ballroom, and former Queen of the Grand. She'd been dipping her toes back into the world of dance of late, taking on private students at her manor house in Rye. On Saturday night, she'd return to the ballroom that had made her a star. 'Don't worry about me, Vivienne. This Christmas just seems... a test.'

'A test?' Vivienne whispered.

Raymond nodded. 'What with Marcus gone, and everything happening with the Imperial Hotel – and the royal party, and...' He lowered his voice. 'I was just thinking it would have been nice to have had a quiet few days at home.'

'Nancy's worried about you.'

Raymond hated to hear it. He squeezed Vivienne's hand. 'Just a couple of days, and it will be done. We just need to get through it.'

Then he marched past her, as if to join Nancy in the kitchen.

'Raymond?'

Vivienne had whispered the word, but still Raymond turned round.

She looked at him now, like a fortune-teller might look at tea leaves in the bottom of a cup. 'There's something you're not telling. What is it?'

Raymond hesitated before he said, 'I just need everything to go according to plan.'

Vivienne watched him go. Moments later, he entered the kitchen – and it felt very much as if he had stepped from some rehearsal area into the full glaring lights of the stage, for immediately his tone changed, his aura lightened, and Vivienne heard him conjuring whoops of laughter from his infant son, while he regaled Nancy with plans for the day. At least that would assuage Nancy's fears, thought Vivienne – but she couldn't help thinking that it was all a lie, all the act of an expert showman. She'd seen the grave lines on his face. Raymond de Guise was a champion of hope and optimism in the ballroom – but sometimes it seemed that the war was sapping it out of him, bit by bit.

Vivienne was about to follow him into the kitchen when she heard a dull buzzing at her side.

She looked down.

The telephone receiver hadn't been put down properly in its cradle.

A tinny voice was crackling down the line.

Slowly, stealthily, with one eye on the kitchen door – for something told her she really shouldn't be doing this – Vivienne went to the table and picked up the phone.

'Hello?' she ventured.

The voice on the other end of the line faltered. 'Sorry, I lost you there. I'm afraid there's neither good news nor bad. Mr Charles remains in a critical condition. St Thomas's ordinarily makes allowances for family and friends, but the Sister says they'll accept no visitors – not unless Maynard wakes. I'm sorry, sir. I know it isn't the news that you wanted.'

Vivienne was silent.

'Sir?' came the voice. 'Sir, have I lost you again?'

At once, Vivienne replaced the receiver in its cradle, terminating the call.

Maynard Charles. She hadn't heard the name in years. There'd been a time, though it seemed entire lifetimes ago, when Vivienne had been a permanent resident of the Buckingham Hotel – exiled there by her stepfather when her mother brought her across the Atlantic to take his hand. Those were days she didn't like to think about, and she had long since parted ways with the unfettered, debauched girl she was back then. But in those days, Maynard Charles had been the Hotel Director, and she remembered him fondly. Taciturn, sullen, silent – but possessed of unparalleled patience, and (she had come to learn) a heart of immeasurable depth. She couldn't say that she'd thought of him often in the years that had passed, but when she did it was a reminder that good people existed in this world.

So why was he lying in critical condition in St Thomas's Hospital?

Why was Raymond calling the hospital before dawn to check on him?

And furthermore, why was he being so secretive about it?

Those thoughts were tumbling through Vivienne's mind as she joined the family in the kitchen. Nancy was almost ready to head to the hotel, steeling herself with tea and toast, while Raymond entertained Arthur at the table. Vivienne fixed her eyes on him. At least, now, she knew one thing he was hiding: the curious fate of Maynard Charles. But why he chose to hide it, or even *how* he knew about it, she could not say.

As Vivienne went to the window to watch her son gambolling in the snow – Ellsworth March was being a good sport, allowing himself to be peppered with a veritable hailstorm of snowballs – she heard the other two Americans clattering down the stairs.

Vivienne started warming a pan to scramble what eggs they had left, as Nancy bowed to Raymond and Arthur to kiss them goodbye. 'I'll see you at the hotel,' she whispered to Raymond – and Vivienne noticed a flicker of unease in him as she left, as if he was in some way dreading that day's trip to the Buckingham.

It couldn't really be that the weight of the ball was affecting him, could it?

It had to be something else.

Maynard Charles...

'I trust you young men have busy days ahead?' Raymond ventured, once Nancy had gone and Ellsworth March was tramping back in from the cold. Stan looked ruddy and red, but at least some of the boundless energy had been run out of him. 'All of London to explore?'

'We rather know London by now,' joked Jonah Linden, taking tea at the table.

'And a week off duties at the office,' added Ellsworth, stamping the snow from his boots.

'Lots of boys being barracked outside London are pouring into the city for Christmas,' Henry McCord began, 'and I'm sure they're flocking out to see the sights – but us three? Well, we're almost Londoners ourselves.'

Vivienne watched Raymond's eyes narrow guardedly.

'I think what the man of the house is saying,' said Ellsworth, finally taking his own seat at the table, 'is that we're guests in this fine home, and perhaps we oughtn't be kicking around here all day, while the family's hard at work? Is that right, sir?'

The hollow look in Raymond's eyes vanished in a second. Vivienne was quite sure, now, that he was putting on another show.

'We'll reconvene for dinner,' he grinned, 'but Vivienne here has so much to attend to, with these two scamps.' He winked at Stan. 'I'm sure a little peace and quiet will be most welcome.'

So that was it, thought Vivienne. For some reason she could not yet fathom, Raymond wanted the Americans out of his house.

'Actually,' said Ellsworth, 'I was thinking a little ... *adventure.*'

The other two Americans looked at him quizzically.

'We're guests in this home, boys, but we're not guests at this Buckingham Hotel of theirs. And I say, when you're guests in somebody's home, when they've opened their doors to you for Christmas, you better show how grateful you are.' He looked at Vivienne. 'Ma'am, the boys and I would very much like to take you and your boys shopping today. We want to contribute – not be waited upon. You've already got two little boys to wait on. You don't need another three.'

Vivienne couldn't help it: her face brightened.

Shopping?

The days of indulging herself in the Regent Street arcades were over even before she vacated her suite at the Buckingham Hotel – but the thought of leaving these four walls, of venturing out into London and seeing *something*, seeing *anything* to remind her of what life used to be like, was welcome.

'Well, ma'am,' said Ellsworth, 'what do you say?'

There was a strange look flickering on Raymond's face. It seemed to be hovering somewhere between outrage and relief. Could it be that he wanted Vivienne to stay? Could it really be that he wanted her to remain here, chained to the kitchen, as if she really *was* just his house servant?

He did not seem to want her to seize this opportunity, to head out into London in the company of these bright young men.

Perhaps it was her honour he was worried for.

Perhaps it was the memory of his brother.

Or perhaps...

Perhaps he didn't trust the motives of the men he'd invited into his house?

She fixed him with a questioning look. The moment he noticed she was staring, his features suddenly softened. 'I'd come with you if I could,' he smiled, 'but the Buckingham needs me and...' What was wrong with him? He seemed to be floundering as he searched for the words. 'It's cold out there today. Keep the boys safe – and Vivienne, don't let them out of your sight.'

Chapter Eight

'I thought London was hungry,' said Private Newell, at the dining table in Albert Yard, 'but it seems to me you're living like Kings!'

'That's all courtesy of our Billy,' said Mrs Brogan proudly. She had just dished up her second pan of eggs (they were turkey eggs, courtesy of a farmer Billy did business with – but they tasted as good as chicken, and they stretched much further), and tousled her son's hair as she passed. Billy didn't mind; his mother's pride always reminded him of why he'd got into this business in the first place.

'There's food for them that needs it,' said Billy, as he readied to leave. 'Sometimes it just takes a bit of ingenuity. I happen to have a knack for finding the finer things.' He grinned as he reached the door; it felt good that these American boys knew they weren't the only ones who could get their hands on some goodies. 'Which is exactly how we'll be feeding you goose come Christmas Day.'

Any other man who had set himself this challenge might have ventured into London feeling the unbearable weight of the endeavour. But not Billy Brogan. Something about the impossibility of the challenge titillated him. He felt like a dog after a scent.

By the time he reached the hotel, his leg aching from the old injury, the Buckingham was coming to life. He made his way directly to the Housekeeping Lounge, where the chambermaids always gathered to receive their duties for the day – but not a soul was to be found. Soon enough he was standing at the backstage doors of the Grand Ballroom, watching as Nancy de Guise marshalled her girls to polish every golden fixture in the hall. Workmen were already on ladders, lowering the great chandeliers to the dance floor – where Rosa, Mary-Louise, Annie and the other girls waited with their polishes and vinegar solutions.

He used to admire the chambermaids – they worked so hard for such little thanks, the invisible agents of the Buckingham Hotel – but latterly he had begun to wonder why they cared so much. There had to be easier, better ways to make a living than scrubbing some debauched lord's bedsheets. Not for the first time, Billy wondered idly about his own future – and how he might one day spread his wings beyond the Buckingham Hotel.

But that was for another day.

First off, there was the small matter of a Christmas goose.

Mrs de Guise had just finished delivering her instructions when Annie caught Billy's eye. He whistled, half under his breath. Her face turning crimson with apologies, Annie shuffled away from the girls and skittered to Billy's side. 'What is it, Bill? I'm in the middle of a shift.'

'I'm going to need you to fetch Victor and meet me after your shift ends. You hear me?'

Annie flashed a look over her shoulder, fearful somebody had heard.

'You never used to be frightened of your own shadow, Annie.'

'I never used to do anything wrong,' Annie returned.

This wasn't quite true – Annie had been accident-prone since she first turned up at the Buckingham Hotel, responsible for more breakages in her first month than the other girls were in a year – but Billy decided not to press her on it. Annie singularly failed to see the virtue in what Billy did. It wasn't her fault; it was simply a lack of imagination. He'd hoped she might have begun to see the world for what it truly was by now – but she still seemed enamoured of the Buckingham Hotel, blinded by its riches. By this point, Billy thought, it was a kind of wilful blindness. She just didn't *want* to see, because it would upset her simple black-and-white, right-and-wrong view of the world.

'This is about that goose, isn't it?' she whispered. 'Billy, nobody *needed* a goose for Christmas dinner. We'd have been quite all right going without. It would still have been special.' She folded her arms across her breast. 'You've made a promise you can't keep.'

'Who says I can't keep it?' Billy grinned. 'I don't know how you dare doubt me. Just find Victor and meet me in the post room.'

From the middle of the ballroom, Rosa started calling Annie's name. She had the condescending lilt to her voice that meant she was thoroughly enjoying doling out orders, and enjoying the opportunity to lord it over Annie.

'I've got to get back,' Annie muttered.

'But you'll come?' Billy saw Annie drifting away without answer, so reached out for her arm. 'I've never let you down, little sister. I've never put you in harm's way. But this is for the family. Don't you want us putting on a good show for these Yanks?'

'I think they're very nice people.'

'And they'll think *we're* even nicer if they've got a big fat goose leg to get their chops around. Look, Annie, I'm not suggesting anything too risky. Nothing we haven't done already. I've got too many folks counting on me to risk our position in this hotel.'

Position. There he went again. Sometimes it seemed as if Billy thought he was politicking in some medieval court – not just fencing stolen goods to a few wily shopkeepers.

'If I lost my job at the hotel, I'd lose everything. My suppliers trust me *because* I'm a Buckingham man. I'm nothing without it.' He paused. 'Annie, I wouldn't let you get into trouble. I swear it.'

Sooner or later, Mrs de Guise was going to notice how many soaps, lotions, bath sponges and silk pillowcases went missing from the Housekeeping stores. It couldn't all be put down to greedy guests. One day, Annie was going to come a cropper, and all the work she'd been putting into building a good reputation in the department would be ruined.

It was on the tip of her tongue to say 'No'. She could feel the words rising up her gorge: 'Do your own dirty work, Billy Brogan.' And yet, every time the moment came to give them voice, some memory would smash into her – some recollection from long ago, long before the war, long before any of this began. It was always like this. She'd summon the courage to tell Billy he had to stop, but then she'd think of the time he picked her up from the gutter at the bottom of the Archbishop's Gardens; the time she'd been lost, wandering back from the schoolhouse, and Billy had been the one to find her; the night, before the evacuation, when he'd gathered Annie and all the rest of the younger Brogans in the bedroom at Albert Yard and filled them all with courage, conviction, and the certain knowledge that, no matter how scattered they were, they would still be Brogans together. 'Brogans together, from now until the end!' Billy had said, wrapping his arms around all his brothers and sisters, big and small.

'I'll be there,' Annie said, conflictedly.

Her uncertainty was immediately counterbalanced by Billy's glee. Dazzling her with a smile, he said, 'I can always rely on you, Annie!' and turned to leave – with such a spring in his step that, unless you knew it was there, you wouldn't have noticed he was limping at all.

As she returned to the other girls they were all chirruping about the wonder of the Grand Ballroom, but now Annie couldn't feel the splendour at all.

'Joel's going to be here this afternoon,' said Rosa proudly, 'right in this very spot.' She was down on her knees with her vinegar solution, moving in gentle circles around the chandelier. 'Dressed up in his uniform and watching them dance.'

The other girls seemed as pleased with this as Rosa. 'Nobody said he can't take a guest,' Mary-Louise grinned. 'Mr Hastings might have said he can't go to the Winter Ball, but he didn't say anything about taking his sweetheart to the demonstrations.'

Rosa blushed, but Annie could tell she was enjoying the attention. 'Oh, give over!' Then she paused in polishing, with a dreamy look on her face. 'Mr Hastings has already told him – no soldiers at the ball. Can you imagine it, though? *Me*, dancing in here?'

'Ah, but what did he say about the *demonstrations*? That's just watching the troupe. You might get away with it, Rosa.' Mary-Louise shrugged. 'They're guests here. They ought to get privileges.'

This idea seemed to please Rosa very much. 'I suppose, if nobody actually *banned* it . . .'

The girls started hooting.

'Joel took me to the Ambergris the other weekend. We were turning and kicking, and he had his hands on my hips and . . . We'd have to do it differently in here, of course.'

The other girls were blushing too. 'I'm sure he could put his hands on your waist, Rosa. He'd have to take you in hold.'

'It's where his hands went *after that* that would get tongues wagging,' laughed one of the other girls.

Rosa's eyes opened wide. She looked either mortified or excited. Perhaps a bit of both.

'You can't come in for the demonstrations anyway,' Annie blurted out, quite without meaning to. 'You're not thinking about Frank.'

The eyes of the other girls shot towards Annie.

'Here comes little Miss Brogan to pour vinegar on everything,' tutted Mary-Louise. 'We're having a laugh, Annie. You could use a bit of a laugh. You've got a face like a smacked backside.'

Annie couldn't help it; her eyes darted to the backstage door. There, just inside the dressing rooms, Billy was chatting away with Mrs de Guise, as if he didn't have a care in the world. Why did it have to be Annie who carried the guilt over Billy's enterprise?

'I'm just saying – this is Frank's ballroom too. He'll be demon-strating the dances later today. How do you think he'd feel, if Rosa comes in here with Joel?'

'Give it a rest, Annie,' one of the chambermaids groaned. 'Rosa and Frank were only stepping out together. They wasn't engaged to be married.' Suddenly, she stopped. 'Was you, Rosa?'

Rosa seemed a little abashed. 'It was just a fantasy, Annie. Just a bit of playing. I wouldn't want to upset Frank.'

Annie was about to snap, 'You upset him *already*', but managed to corral the words before they slipped out. Instead, she just shrugged and bowed down to start polishing.

'It *would* be something special,' Mary-Louise went on. 'Rosa, you ought to just *ask*. You don't get anything by not asking. Just imagine it! You can't let a chance like this go begging. Fate's been good to you, Rosa. The way I see it, you're honour-bound to see where it goes.' She paused, 'It isn't like any of us are going to get a chance like this, is it? So, in a way, aren't you doing it for us?'

Annie tried not to listen any more, throwing herself into her work instead. Two hours later, when Mrs de Guise returned to dispatch half of the girls back to their suites, Annie was grateful to be shot of them all.

Frank deserved better than Rosa anyway.

She'd been good to him once – but, of late, all she'd talked about was herself.

Working the suites helped Annie blot out all other thoughts, but the moment the last rooms were done, she felt the mounting dread once again. The only silver lining was that she would get to see Victor. It had been a few days since they last went on a stroll – Victor seemed perennially locked inside the Queen Mary kitchen, helping with all of the extra Christmas preparation, and she'd missed him.

He'd grown wirier this year, losing some of the puppy fat of youth. His jawline had become more pronounced, and he looked altogether stronger. Now that he'd come of age, it was only his Italian heritage that had been keeping the Board from sweeping him off to war. Annie was glad of it. Rosa might have spent day and night swooning over her soldier, but Annie would rather take tea and toast with her kitchen hand any day.

'I don't want to see Billy, not today,' Victor said, when Annie explained. 'Just ignore him. Whatever it is, let Billy take care of it himself.'

But when Annie said, 'You know I can't do that,' Victor relented. Sometimes he hated the way Annie still doted on her brother, even after everything Billy had been asking them to do, but he knew it came from her very core: Annie and Billy were Brogans together, and through thick and thin, good times and lean, darkness and light, that mattered.

It was with some weariness, and not a little trepidation, then, that Victor followed Annie down to the post room.

Billy had been diligently completing his Buckingham duties, but as soon as Annie and Victor arrived, he sprang up.

'It's very simple,' he pronounced. 'One Christmas goose, for Christmas dinner. And Victor, you're going to help me get it.'

Victor's eyes darted around. It was true that he often lifted goods from the kitchens for Billy. It was true that he'd even done it willingly, happy to take the money Billy paid him home to his mother. So it wasn't the idea itself that stirred such venom in Victor; it was the way he'd simply *assumed* Victor could make it happen.

'Look, I'm not a fool,' Billy began, when he saw Victor's face pale. 'I wouldn't have got as far as I've got if I didn't have a brain up here.' He tapped the side of his head, throwing Victor a wink. 'So let's just talk about it. What are the problems? What are the risks? I don't want any of us in trouble. But we can do it cleanly and efficiently – I'm sure of it.'

'The orders are already done, Billy.'

Billy clapped his hands. 'Perfect! So it's just like it always is. The same as skimming a few rashers of bacon off the package. You'll be there when the geese are delivered. You'll tick them off the manifest. You'll smuggle one off, then tell your butchers they delivered one fewer than asked. Everyone wins.'

This was precisely how Victor had been pillaging the Queen Mary all year. He'd lost count of the number of pheasants, partridge and grouse destined for the plates of the Buckingham's guests that had actually ended up in Billy's network – although, almost certainly, Billy had the details in that ledger he kept. His business might have been illegitimate, but he was fastidious at keeping records.

'You don't understand,' Victor went on. 'The geese are already here. We've got them hanging in the larder – it ages the meat, ripens the flavour. Before long, they'll be taken down and brined, ready for Christmas Day. If you wanted me to nab you a goose, you ought to have put your order in weeks ago – just like the guests did. And just like *we* did to the butchers. Maybe I could have worked it. Maybe there'd have been a way. But not now.'

'Then one just flies away in the dead of night,' remarked Billy.

Victor groaned. 'And who flies with it? Me, I suppose? It's more than my job's worth.'

A look of the utmost displeasure crossed Billy's face. Annie feared he was about to start throwing demands around, but then he softened and said, 'We've done it for pheasants. A goose is just a bit bigger, that's all.'

'Then find a fat pheasant for Christmas Day,' Victor snapped, and turned on his heel as if to leave.

'Victor, do I have to remind you that we're in this together? That you've been taking payment for harvesting the kitchens all year?'

Annie took a breath.

Here it came: the confrontation she'd been dreading.

But Victor seemed to have learnt patience in the last few months; instead of biting back, he just sighed, 'A goose isn't just a bird, Bill. It's a *prize*. It's pure Christmas on a plate. It's rich and it's indulgent and it makes *memories*. We've had the reservations since October. Every goose has a guest's name on it. M. Laurent's been planning Christmas dinner every bit as passionately as Mr Allgood and Mr de Guise have been planning the Winter Ball. We can't just make one disappear.'

'We'll write it off to rats,' declared Billy, proud of his imaginative flourish.

'There hasn't been a rat in that kitchen in months.'

Billy grinned. This, he decided, was a rather unlikely story. Even the grandest kitchens in London had to guard against rats – and their numbers had only got stronger since the war began.

'A rat could never drag a whole goose away, Billy. You're just not thinking straight.'

Billy rose from his seat. This time, Annie really did see a dark look in his eyes. 'No, Victor, it's *you* who aren't thinking straight. You've been helping me make my *donations* to good causes for a long time now. You've been instrumental, in fact. I'm sure you wouldn't want M. Laurent knowing what you're really up to in those kitchens.'

'I've told you before, Billy – threats won't work. You rat on me, and you're only ratting on yourself.'

'Just stop it!' Annie exclaimed. 'We don't need to fight. We're family, aren't we? All three of us.' And she reached for Victor's hand.

Victor drew her near. 'Dry your eyes, Annie,' he whispered.

'Listen to him, Annie,' Billy intervened. 'Dry your eyes, or someone's bound to ask why you're upset.'

Holding Annie tight, Victor said, 'What do you want me to do, Billy? It's no use asking my opinion, not when you don't want to hear it. Why keep pretending we're working together? I work *for* you. That's just the way it is.'

Billy considered this quietly. 'I'm glad to hear it,' he finally said. 'So here's how we'll do it. Tonight, after the dinner service, you'll make sure you're the last one there – make sure there's some extra pan that needs scrubbing, make an unholy mess if you need, but make sure M. Laurent lets you stay behind to finish up and lock down. Tell him he needs some rest – he'll need all his strength for Christmas week. Then, once you're sure that you're alone, go into the larder, take one of those geese and wrap it in wax paper. Put it in the trash, and out the chute onto Michaelmas Mews. Me and Annie, we'll be out there – we'll dig it out before it gets taken away.'

Victor hated everything about this plan.

'You're going to serve your family rubbish for Christmas Dinner?' he asked, with a taunting air.

Billy prodded him sharply in the chest. 'Just be there, Victor. After everything I've done for you and your mother, it's the least you can do.'

Bile rose up Victor's gorge once more. It was the way Billy had so casually dropped his mother's name into things that did it. But no sooner had he opened his mouth to spit out some retort, than he sensed Annie straining on his hand, imploring him to leave – and all the fire in him died. Billy was still Annie's brother. To bite back now was to make things worse for her, and that was the last thing he wanted.

'A goose,' Victor snapped, as he marched away from the post room, Annie scurrying at his side. 'By God, Annie, a *goose*. He's no idea how much thought and planning M. Laurent's put into that dinner. It isn't like a few rashers of bacon. It isn't like fiddling the manifests. He'll *notice*. The head chef will *notice*.'

As they reached the Housekeeping hall, Annie begged Victor to keep his voice down. Though quieter, Victor's voice was dripping with disdain as he went on, 'I don't want to, Annie. I don't want to do any of it anymore. Your brother stopped making sense a long time ago. All of that talk about honour and fairness, about helping out the little folks, it's all *gone*. A goose? For his own Christmas dinner? It's just theft.'

Annie whispered, 'It's always been theft,' and immediately felt a strange twinge of guilt for saying it so brazenly.

Victor broiled. He'd been denying it to himself for so long, pretending he believed Billy's rationale, that to hear it spoken so plainly by the girl he loved hit him hard. But the truth was, he'd always known. Billy had come to him two weeks before, offering a little ivory pendant as a thank-you for everything Victor had been doing. He'd planned on making a gift of it to Annie, but the moment his fingers closed around it he'd felt the cruel, sharp stab of guilt.

'At least, at the start, there were good people benefiting,' Victor whispered. 'Taking a few crumbs off a prince's table, to feed some paupers – you might go to prison for it, but you'd get into Heaven.'

Annie dried her eyes. All along, she'd been silently crying.

'But Billy lost sight of it a long time ago. And now we're to risk everything, just so he can show off to some Americans?' Victor kicked at the wall. 'Was your brother ever a good man?'

Annie stuttered in response. Every time Billy had coerced her, every time she'd felt bullied and compelled, a dozen memories from when they were children sprang to mind. It was the gravity of those memories that kept her thinking Billy was still decent. The problem was, Victor had none of those good times to anchor him.

'The worst thing is, I can't say it's love that's made me help him,' said Victor. 'At least you've had that excuse.'

'You've done it for your mother, Victor. You've *helped* her.'

'But at what cost? I'm trapped in Billy's enterprise. I'm stuck, waiting for my next command. Your brother could tell me to burn down the hotel, and I'd have to do it. He's like a spider – and you and me, we're the flies.' Furiously, Victor thrust his hand into his pocket and brought out a crumpled piece of paper. 'Here, read it,' he said, and passed it blindly to Annie.

Annie was expecting some missive from Billy, but the crimson lettering at the top of the paper read 'IMPERIAL HOTEL', and suddenly she didn't understand.

'A few of us got them,' Victor muttered. 'The Continental Kitchen at the Imperial Hotel's looking for staff. Just potboys and kitchen hands. I'd be back on the bottom rung of the ladder, back having to prove myself again. But at least I wouldn't be *this*.' Annie realised, all of a sudden, that Victor didn't reserve his disdain for Billy alone; right now, it was directed at himself.

'The other boys threw their letters in the fire. They reckon the Imperial's just playing games with us, turning us into part of the battle with the Buckingham – the battle to win Christmas. Probably they're right. But when Billy talks to me like that – well, I'd rather be a pawn in that battle, than Billy's right-hand man.'

For perhaps the first time in her life, Annie realised she didn't have the words. She just kept reading the letter, over and over, until at last she said, 'You wouldn't... leave?'

'I love the Buckingham – and Annie, I...'

Victor started stuttering. There was something he wanted to add to that sentiment – but now *he* didn't have the words.

Annie threw her arms around him.

'It's all right,' she said. 'I do too.'

Victor nodded, though suddenly he felt a fool. Why was it easy to say you loved the Buckingham Hotel, but impossible to say you loved Annie Brogan?

'Come with me,' he said quietly, still holding her tight. 'There are bound to be chambermaid jobs – girls always come and go. It could be a fresh start for both of us. A new beginning.'

Annie could hardly believe it. One hour ago, she'd known what her future looked like. Right now, nothing felt certain,

'Just think about it,' said Victor, kissing her gently on the corner of her lips as he drew away. 'We can be good people, if we start again. We don't have to be in his web. We don't have to play Billy's game. I'm getting out of here, Annie. I'll be gone by tonight – so if your brother thinks I'll be waiting for him at the Queen Mary kitchen, he's going to get the surprise of his life.'

Chapter Nine

Alix Monet had come to London at the invitation of an old music hall friend, only to discover that it had been made in the hope of romance and, though he'd been good enough to offer her a roof for the first weeks, Alix had spent too many nights locked in an Anderson shelter with him, while the German bombs rained down, not to know that, sooner or later, he was going to try to take her hand, tell her Fate had thrown them together and invite her to his bed. Alix would never submit to a man she did not desire, not for something as flimsy as a roof above her head. So she soon struck out on her own. Since then, she hadn't slept in the same place for more than three weeks at a time. She'd rallied to the Free French – they'd called themselves the France Combattante since summer – taking secretarial duties with one of the ministers of that Government in Exile, and made it her business to bring together as many of her scattered countrymen as possible. Music had all but been forgotten. She was damn good at it as well, slotting into Mr de Gaulle's army of administrators with ease. But every now and then, after midnight at the French House – where de Gaulle and his government so often gathered – she could be seen eyeing up the rickety old upright piano in the corner; and sometimes, if enough wine had been poured, she would stretch her beringed knuckles over it, and lean into a song.

The letter from Mr Max Allgood had gone unnoticed for some days. The idea that somebody as esteemed as Max might pluck her out of her new life and summon her back into music and dance – well, it was beyond the limits of Alix Monet's imagination. By the time she'd finally opened it, read it and replied, she feared the opportunity had gone.

Still, she'd thought about refusing the summons. France remained in the hands of General Pétain and his cabinet of traitors. Perhaps song and dance had to wait until France was returned to its rightful heirs and the Continent was free. She'd wondered if her associates in government might think less of her – but no; even Mr de Gaulle himself had instructed her to go and let the music of old Paris ring out.

That was exactly what she intended to do.

Even if it lasted only one night, she would know that she was weaving magic for a ballroom full of men fighting for freedom.

Christmas was coming.

She would make them dance.

She had just finished inscribing the kohl around her eyes, dreaming her dream of old Paris restored, when a knock came at the door of the suite Mr Hastings had generously provided for her.

'One moment,' she announced.

Max had told her that the Buckingham delivered the most beautiful luncheons to their rooms, and she was eager to fortify herself for the day. Straightening her hair, she went to answer the door. There stood one of the hotel porters – but he had not come with a room service trolley; instead, a bouquet of flowers, a rainbow of two dozen different hues, hung in his arms.

Alix had rarely seen such colour, certainly not in the depths of winter. 'For me?' she queried.

The porter just inclined his head in acknowledgement and gently placed the bouquet in her arms. Then he took his leave.

As the door fell shut, Alix carried the bouquet to the bed – and, burying her face in the blossoms, luxuriated in the scent. She'd known that places of plenty still existed in London, but here was the evidence of it. You didn't get flowers on the bombed-out streets of London.

It was sweet of Max to send her the bouquet. She felt certain it could only be him, welcoming her to the Orchestra that bore his name. In only a couple of hours, she'd be playing with them for the first time – the demonstration dances were not strictly a rehearsal for Saturday night, but it would certainly feel like one. Then, later today, the full dress rehearsal would begin. The flowers, she supposed, were as much a good luck charm as a welcome. Max had put a lot of faith in her. She would have to repay it before the night was out.

There was a little card attached to the bouquet.

Crimson letters at the top of the card read: FROM THE SPLENDOUR OF THE IMPERIAL HOTEL.

And underneath that, in spidery, slanting handwriting:

'Perhaps a guest slot on Saturday night? A lady like you deserves to play for the King…'

The message ended only with a name, NELSON ALLGOOD – signed with a flourish, like some Hollywood star bestowing an autograph.

Alix looked back at the bouquet of flowers.

What had seemed such a beautiful gesture suddenly felt like something of a… taunt.

Quite what it all meant, she didn't understand.

But for the first time she wondered if her appearance at the Buckingham Hotel mightn't be just about music and dance at all.

*

The chambermaids had finally vacated the Grand Ballroom, and in the middle of the dance floor, Nancy de Guise was overseeing the workmen as they hoisted the chandeliers back into place. Up on stage, Max Allgood surveyed it all and ran his hands along Lucille. He was beginning to believe that everything would work out. For a fleeting moment, he even believed that, on Saturday night, the doors of the marble arch might open to reveal King George and his retinue.

Up on the stage, the percussionist James Heath was setting up. 'It's really going to be something,' he said, twirling his drumsticks over his hi-hat cymbals.

In the same moment that Heath started warming up, the backstage doors flew open – and there, dressed head to toe in black, stood Alix Monet. Even without music, she was striking. Max had detected some hints of doubt in the rest of the Orchestra when she'd first been presented to them, but those had largely melted away when they'd heard her play. Now, as she strode towards the stage, she seemed even more striking still. She had a sort of defiance about her – and well she might, for it had taken courage to escape France. Max knew what it took to leave your old world behind, and be rescued by music in the new.

He imagined she was heading straight for the piano. She seemed to have the single-mindedness of a musician with a point to prove. Yet, when she got close to Max, she threaded her arm into his, took him to the side of the stage and pulled out a little card with crimson letters from her pocket.

Upon reading it, Max's heart sank.

'What does it mean, Mr Allgood?'

But Max could tell, by the tone of her voice – flinty and hard, as if perhaps she'd been duped somehow and was only just beginning to realise it – that she already had an inkling.

'I'm not some maiden to be wrestled over. I didn't agree to be in the middle of a fight. If I was interested in battle, I might have stayed where I was, fighting for my country.'

Max thrust the card into his pocket, then drew from it his silver pocket-watch. Two hours separated him from the first number of the demonstration dances. That ought to be enough.

'It's a situation,' Max grumbled. 'A family affair.'

'I know what it is. He's your... nephew.'

'And somebody ought to have boxed his ears a little more, when he was a boy.' Although Max had to admit: there'd been quite a lot of that, and it never seemed to do much good. Some boys were born with a devil in them. It was Nelson's good fortune that his particular devil could play piano so well; were it not for that, he'd have spent his life on a chain gang. 'Miss Monet, you have my promise – the Buckingham's proud to call you its own. We're about the music here, not about my nephew's silly little *games*.'

'And yet it strikes me, now, that you're two days away from the Winter Ball. Two days away, if the rumours are true, from playing for the King himself. And yet... you're only just hiring a piano player.'

Max could tell the eyes of the rest of the Orchestra were on him. It hadn't been easy getting them on side this year; he'd made many stumbles, but somehow, he'd managed to retain some modicum of respect. But all men had their limits – and he fancied he could detect a hint of exasperation now, as if Nelson and all his childish stunts were in some way Max's doing. 'The Great Appeaser,' he'd heard James Heath calling him once. 'Nelson's invaded the Sudetenland, and Max has signed his very own Munich Agreement.'

'A good number of our pianists have been tempted by guest spots at the Imperial,' Max murmured. 'But I wouldn't want you thinking that's why you're here, Alix. I wouldn't want you thinking you're bottom of some list. When I heard your recordings…'

Alix shook her head ruefully. 'Let's just play.'

Alix was gravitating to the piano stool when Max raised his voice to the assembled musicians, 'Get warming up, boys.' Then he caught himself and added, 'You too, Miss Monet.'

Some moments later, he was in another taxicab, sailing along the bombed-out ruin of Oxford Street.

By the time he emerged into the snow, he'd just about ordered his thoughts. He'd brought Lucille with him for luck – only another musician would understand; Lucille gave him courage, off stage and on – but still he was beset by nerves as he looked at the hotel's grand façade. It was true that the Imperial was smaller than the Buckingham, but it was also true that its history was longer, that it had been hosting foreign princes and tsars since long before the Buckingham's founders broke ground.

Max ignored the doorman dressed in royal blue as he shuffled inside. Some of the concierges watched him closely – but it wasn't until he'd crossed the reception hall, following the sounds of music from the Imperial Ballroom, that one of them accosted him.

'Might I help you, sir?' came the concierge's simpering voice.

'You can point me to the ballroom,' Max barked back, shaking off the man's hand.

The concierge looked at him through narrowed eyes. 'Might I ask in which room the gentleman is currently residing?'

Max looked around. Still uncertain from which direction the music was coming, he turned on the spot. 'The ballroom, sir. I have an appointment to keep.'

He said it so brusquely that the concierge was quite certain it was a lie – but then Max held Lucille aloft, and, in a conciliatory tone, he said, 'Are you with the Orchestra?'

This was the opening Max needed. 'And it rather sounds like I'm late,' he snapped.

The concierge relented. Huffing to himself, Max followed him through a fringe of fir trees bedecked in silver baubles, and into an atrium with the air of a winter grotto.

'Sir, the afternoon Show Dance is in session. I might have to suggest you wait until its intermission – but perhaps you might make yourself comfortable in the dressing rooms?'

Max barely acknowledged him. Grunting, 'I'm sure I'll be very comfortable through here,' he bouldered to the doors, and directly into the Imperial Ballroom.

He'd heard tell of this place. Mathilde had entertained dancing here once before, and the way she'd described it was perfect: only a fraction smaller than the Grand, no expense had been spared in making it seem just as ostentatious. It was only midday, and yet the chandeliers glittered. No natural light could reach the Imperial Ballroom; the effect was such that it seemed to be cut off from the rest of the world – cut off from time itself, so that only the music and dance could ever exist within its walls.

On the sprung dance floor, the Imperial troupe were performing a wild waltz to the music on the stage above. The dancers moved in perfect synchronicity – this was more like something for a stage, thought Max, than a dance floor – while guests gathered at the balustrade, applauding every move. Max could easily imagine how wonderful this would seem on Saturday night, the Imperial's Yuletide Ball in full flow, princes and lords raising their Champagne flutes to every song.

Up on stage, Nelson hunkered over the piano. He had always had the faint air of a witch stirring her cauldron when he played – up on the balls of his feet, attacking the piano as if it was his enemy. They'd done something to refine him – and Max had to admit he looked superb in a suit of jet-black gabardine (though what he was doing, wearing a trilby hat indoors, Max had no idea) – but he still had the *feel* of a devil about him. This was in stark contrast to the elegance and stateliness of the rest of the band. Bob Holloway, the Orchestra's leader, was a solid pair of hands, a trumpeter of decent (if unspectacular) renown – but evidently he'd accomplished what Max himself never could: he'd harnessed and directed Nelson's wildness. If Max had been able to corral Nelson like this, Nelson might have been the centrepiece of his own orchestra by now. The story of the last year might have been so different.

All of these thoughts were cascading through his head when he felt a tap on the shoulder and turned round to see a tall, lithe gentlemen with white hair like thistledown standing behind him.

'Mr Max Allgood, I presume,' intoned the elder man, his voice as feathery as his hair. 'And this, I imagine, is Lucille?'

Max turned his attention back to his nephew, up on stage. This was hardly ballroom music, he thought. Max had been embellishing each waltz and intensifying every foxtrot with his own Orchestra, but Nelson seemed to be disregarding the rules of elegance and restraint almost entirely.

'That's right,' he said, 'and who in hell are you?'

Max hadn't meant to speak out of turn, but his blood was boiling – and, for a moment, he'd quite forgotten he was in the gilded old world, imagining himself back in the cut-and-thrust of New York instead. The look on the gentleman's face suggested he had never been spoken to so improperly.

'My name is Mr Hubert Gove, and I happen to be the director of the Imperial Hotel. Mr Allgood, you're trespassing on my property.'

'I'm sorry about that, sir, but it's a matter of some urgency. I need to speak to my nephew.'

Mr Gove didn't disguise his distaste as he turned to the concierge and whispered his instructions. The concierge nodded and weaved his way through the dance troupe and leant up to the stage to deliver Nelson a message. Max watched as the pianist's eyes goggled; then as he turned to survey the crowd from under the shadow of his trilby.

Their eyes met.

Nelson smiled.

And when the concierge returned, it was with a simple message for Max Allgood: 'He'd love to speak with you, sir, but he couldn't possibly interrupt proceedings. You'll just have to wait.'

Max would have done the same. Nothing, neither family argument nor military bombardment, could interrupt a set in full flow. All he could do was look at Mr Gove, mutter, 'I'm sorry for cursing, sir. It's just family business. I hope you understand,' and wait.

Mr Gove gave him a smirk and exited the ballroom with his hands folded behind his back, and Max was left alone to watch the rest of the Imperial Show Dance play out.

It was hard to be impartial. Max's heart was torn: he'd half-raised Nelson, and wanted him to succeed; but he'd sworn himself to the Buckingham Hotel, and *needed* the Winter Ball to be the toast of society. Nelson was unscripted and loose, but he still seemed to be as one with Bob Holloway and the rest. He wasn't forsaking all others and striking out alone – which had always been his fatal weakness in the past. He was keeping better time, more aware of the room than he'd ever been. Quite simply, he was *better*, and it made Max feel uneasy in the pit of his stomach.

He checked his pocket-watch.

In another hour, he himself was due on stage.

The Show Dance seemed to be coming to an end. On the dance floor, the Imperial troupe were taking their bows. The ballroom filled with applause.

Max steadied himself. He'd say what he had to say to Nelson and then get out of here. He'd seen what the enemy were creating; now he knew what he had to do to beat them.

Then, just as the Orchestra were taking their own bows and preparing to depart, Nelson flashed a smile at his uncle, cast himself back at the piano – and started to play.

This one truly was *wild*. Almost immediately, Max recanted his thoughts of moments before and saw that, bridled as he was, the Nelson of old still remained.

He still had his old power too. By the force of his playing – a rambunctious forest fire of a song – he dragged the other players back into their seats. By the urgency of his left hand – pumping like a train piston until the song took off – he compelled the dancers back onto the dance floor. Max felt his heart do somersaults. By God, his nephew was good. But, by God, the thing that made him good was his complete and total disregard for the rules of civilised society. These ballrooms were no place for Nelson Allgood.

The song just kept going. Twice, Max was certain it was about to end – but twice it soared to new heights, keeping the dancers moving. The next time it peaked, Max knew that Nelson could go no further – but still, onward he ploughed, until even his bandmates were looking at him askance. But, by then, Nelson was too wrapped up in the music to notice that anything but the piano even existed.

The dancers stopped dancing.

The other musicians fell away.

Nelson played on alone – until, at last, the song was set free, hurtling ahead of him, out of control – and, with one final triumphant run, he threw open his arms, beamed at the ballroom and declared, 'Get ready for Saturday night!'

As he left the stage he singled out Max in the crowd and winked again.

If Max's fury had been fading, fresh flames of it grew in him now. He scythed his way across the ballroom and followed the last of the dancers through the backstage door.

He entered the dressing room and found Nelson with his jacket ripped off and his trilby cast aside, clinking brandy glasses with some of his bewildered band.

'Uncle Max!' Nelson exclaimed, as if he couldn't have been more delighted to see him. 'It's a pleasure to see you – but I'm afraid we already have a trombonist, and he's not going anywhere. We couldn't make room for you, even if we tried.'

But Max wasn't laughing. He took out the ivory card from Alix's flowers and thrust it at his nephew.

'What the devil do you think you're doing?'

Nelson's act ended as suddenly as his song. Catching the ivory card, he straightened it out, kissed it once for good luck, then slipped it in his pocket.

'Alix Monet, Uncle Max. She's a good player. But is she a... *Buckingham* player?'

'I won't stand for it, Nelson. I've been trying to hire a piano player ever since summer – and every time, they get an approach.'

Nelson just shrugged. 'I don't run the Orchestra, Uncle Max. You'd have to take it up with Mr Holloway.'

The mere mention of his name seemed to bring Bob Holloway out of the crowd. 'This is a respectable establishment, Mr Allgood. I'm not sure this is the time or place to be airing family grievances,' he said.

'Family grievances can wait,' Max snapped. Part of him wanted to brush Bob Holloway aside – but he summoned a little restraint; it was infinitely more than Nelson had ever shown. 'This is professional. This is pride. Mr Holloway, if you want to compete with us for the spoils this winter, then do it with your music. Do it with your dance. By God, you're good enough. I've seen it with my own two eyes. But I've got a pianist now, and she's a damn good one.'

The moment Max said the word 'she', some of the musicians started smiling, or shaking their heads.

'Uncle Max, I was just wishing her good luck,' Nelson opined. 'Two days until the Grand opens its doors. She's got enough problems without worrying about us. A little musical camaraderie, that's all it is.'

Max could have lunged for him. 'I'll tell you what it is. It's skulduggery, plain and simple. You never could let your music do the talking for you, boy. You always had to open your mouth. Well, it got you in trouble in New York – and I don't give a damn if it gets you in trouble here in London, not anymore. But you leave my ballroom out of this.'

'I hear you, Uncle Max. We're all friends here. It's just a bit of friendly rivalry, that's all it is.'

'Friendly, by God? Is that what it is? Coming after my musicians? Trying to undermine everything I've done? You know how I had to fight to take my place in the Grand. Now, you've got your home and I've got mine – isn't that enough?'

Nelson grabbed his hand, even though Max tried to resist. 'Uncle Max, it *isn't* enough. We ought to be friends.'

Max just glared, incandescent. How could anyone, confronted with such anger, react with a smile?

'Look, old man, why don't you sit down? Why don't you have a drink with me? It's Christmas, ain't it? A time for families, right? I can get some drinks sent down. Maybe even some food. Hey, maybe we ought to be playing some music together, just for old times' sake? Just to show there's no hard feelings?' Nelson paused – and the smirk that twisted his face was even more pointed than the one Mr Gove had been wearing as the Show Dance began. 'Or … is there somewhere else you're meant to be?'

Nelson pointed at the clock up on the dressing-room wall.

Its hands were ticking down towards two o'clock.

There were barely fifteen minutes to go.

In the Buckingham ballroom, the demonstration dancers were waiting to begin.

'You never play fair, boy,' Max bawled, and – quite without meaning to – bustled Bob Holloway out of the way as he swung round to leave. 'You can't just be talented, can you? You can't just be *good*? You'd be on top of the world, boy, with your music alone. But instead, you have to …' By now, Max had reached the dressing-room doors. All the frustrations of the last six months were getting ready to erupt.

Then, a preternatural calmness came over him.

He turned round.

'Your mother misses you, boy,' he said, through gritted teeth – for, despite it all, he couldn't forget the times when Nelson was but a small boy, sitting on his lap, tinkling at the keys of whatever pianos sat in the bars back home. 'You're still her son. You're still family. And … she's laying a place on Christmas Day.'

Max's gaze met Nelson's across the dressing room, so suddenly silent.

The boy's eyes seemed to glow.

Perhaps it mattered to him as well.

But then he grinned and said, 'Goddamn it, Uncle Max, I've got a finer place right here than I ever had in Lambeth – and I'm damn sure Christmas dinner's going to be finer as well. Uncle Max, they're treating us like royalty. They're serving us *goose!*'

Max tore himself away.

Whatever love he'd once had for the boy hadn't just withered on the vine.

It had been deliberately crushed.

Backstage, the Orchestra was waiting. Raymond de Guise and his dancers were waiting too, their faces etched in lines of concern as Max blustered in, drenched in sweat and mopping his brow.

'Mr Allgood, we thought we'd lost you,' remarked Raymond, rallying his dancers – but Max just swatted him away and, ripping off his overcoat, carried Lucille to the dance-floor doors. Somehow, he had to douse the fire in his belly. Somehow, he had to make it count.

Alix appeared at his side. 'You vanished, Mr Allgood. I thought, for a moment, it was because of me.'

'Never you, Miss Monet,' muttered Max. He caught himself before he said more, caressing Lucille until he was calm again. 'My family is, and always has been, an unholy mess. But it's sorted now. My nephew's always going to get under my skin, Alix, but if you ever hear from him again, there'll be hell to pay. The Buckingham's your home. You don't need to doubt it. It's yours until the war is over and France reclaimed. Let's just give them the music.'

He opened the doors.

Out marched the musicians.

Perhaps it wouldn't be as free and adventurous as the Imperial Show Dance, but at least it would be their own.

Up on stage, Max signalled to the Orchestra – and the music began.

Chapter Ten

The moment the band struck up, Raymond turned to the troupe.

At least, now, music would focus his mind. The rest of the dressing room might have been fretting at Max's sudden disappearance, but Raymond was beset by worries of his own. He was grateful Ellsworth had suggested taking Vivienne out into London – it somehow seemed she'd be safer out there, in the ruined city, than alone with a serpent – but it would have been altogether better if they'd just left her at home and headed out themselves. However, there was every chance Vivienne might pick up on something that could help him identify the errant embassy worker. Perhaps he'd drop his guard and let something slide. Vivienne might not know it, but right now she could be picking up information that would help him avert this disaster.

But Raymond knew he ought to have been there.

And that was what had been weighing on him the most.

Now, however, with Lucille's music soaring, somehow he found the presence of mind to begin:

'These aren't just demonstration dances. Not today.'

Those aren't just American embassy men, out about town with my sister-in-law and my son.

'This is the start of an occasion like no other.'

Because three men are in my house, and one of them wicked.

'This is something only we can do.'

Maynard Charles lies dying in a hospital bed. He gave this task to me alone. Either I will succeed, or nobody will.

Raymond tried to blot out the insidious thoughts and went on:

'When we go through those doors, we might not be dancing for lords and kings – but we are representatives of the Buckingham Hotel, and to the Buckingham Hotel, every guest is a king. When we take our first steps, they are not just the first steps of a demonstration. They're the first steps of a journey that will not end until midnight on Saturday, until all the magic and splendour of the Winter Ball has been spun and we have given our guests a night like no other.' Raymond paused. He could hear, in the triumphant music, that it was almost time to sally out.

The clock is ticking, Mr de Guise.

Every moment one closer to the betrayal.

Do you know how much chaos one man can sow?

The last face he saw, before he turned to the ballroom doors, was Frank Nettleton's. The young dancer had slept soundly last night, completely oblivious to the fact that he was sharing a house with a man who meant to damn them all. And yet here he stood, more rigid than Raymond had ever seen him, tormented at the thought of who was in the ballroom right now.

'We dance for the Buckingham,' Raymond announced.

You tell lies for your country, tolled the voice of Maynard Charles.

Pivoting on his heel, he held out his arm for Karina – and together they passed through the great dance-floor doors, to the waves of applause already crashing over the Grand.

As the doors rolled back and forth and the other couples sallied through, Frank stood in line with Mathilde.

'He's just a man, Frank,' Mathilde said. 'And so are you. Just look at me.'

So Frank did.

'*I'm* your partner today, Frank Nettleton. You're letting yourself rot, still thinking about her. She doesn't deserve a single one of your thoughts – and neither does he.' It was nearly their time to pass through the doors. Mathilde held on to him fiercely. 'I want us to be spectacular out there. By Saturday night, I want people saying – Raymond de Guise and Hélène Marchmont, well, they *used* to be the King and Queen of this ballroom... but look at these two; they're the *future*. You remember what Marcus said this summer, don't you? Once the war is over and everyone wakes from this dream, you and I can start *competing* again. The Grand Ballroom isn't the end of our journey, Frank. It's the beginning. But you can't dance, holding this in your heart. You're too heavy. You need to be *light*.' She poked him in the ribs. 'It isn't as if he'll be there on Saturday night. And it isn't as if he's even going to be dancing this afternoon. It's just a demonstration.'

'Oh much better,' grinned Frank, ruefully shaking his head. 'He's just going to be *watching* my every move.'

The doors opened.

Out skipped Frank and Mathilde, sliding into the heart of the dance floor in the same moment that the first grand foxtrot began.

'There you are Frank,' Mathilde whispered, 'just let it all go. Just dance!'

Frank knew she was right. He could even feel it – the music rushing into him and driving all the bad feelings away, like light chasing out the darkness.

But the moment they made their first turn, and all the spectators crowding the balustrade wheeled around him, his blood ran cold.

His eyes scanned the soldiers: first Buxton May, then Eugene Tuck. Then, inevitably, they found Joel himself.

There he stood, proud and dignified in his military uniform, a representative of his homeland.

And on his arm, wearing a dress of lemon yellow with flowers embroidered at its neckline, stood Rosa.

Her lips were painted scarlet red.

Her eyes dazzled at the sights and sounds.

Frank missed a beat, scrambled his footing, had to be righted by Mathilde.

'Just dance,' she told him. 'Frankie, just dance.'

By the balustrade, Rosa marvelled at the lights.

She'd been in this ballroom only hours ago, down on her knees with a scrubbing brush in hand – but that seemed like a distant aeon now. It was the girls who'd encouraged it. If it hadn't been for Mary-Louise and the others, Rosa might never have dared to ask. But in the end, all it had taken was for Joel to put in a request to Mr Hastings. 'Might I bring my girl to the demonstrations, sir?' He hadn't expected Mr Hastings to oblige – but Mr Hastings, it seemed, was committed to making sure the Americans enjoyed every moment of their stay in the Buckingham Hotel. Now here she stood, with her soldier on her arm, and the Orchestra filling the cavernous Grand with music.

Then she saw Frank, sailing past on the dance floor below.

She'd often seen him in his elegant suit of midnight blue, but she'd never before seen him on the dance floor of the Grand. Through countless nights they'd jived in the clubs of Soho – but that was always the untutored, carefree dancing Frank loved so much. He looked *different* this afternoon. He looked studied and poised.

She felt a pang, and forced herself to look away.

Damn Annie Brogan and that high-mindedness of hers.

Rosa was allowed to live her life as well, wasn't she?

'I wish we *could* dance,' said Rosa, leaning into Joel.

Joel Kaplan smiled, 'Perhaps tonight, then – somewhere out in London?'

Thursday night dancing – well, there was bound to be a place. But Rosa had to be loading the Housekeeping trolleys by six o'clock in the morning, so perhaps this perfect moment would have to do.

Sometimes the stars aligned. Now was one of those moments.

Joel bowed down to Rosa and said, 'I wish you could dine with us in the Queen Mary too. Us there, at the hotel director's table. Now, *that* would be a Christmas to remember.' He paused, for something had suddenly told him that Rosa wasn't listening. He followed her eyes. There, on the dance floor below, Frank had just spun Mathilde around, caught her again and leant back into the dance. 'Rosa?' he whispered. 'Are you there?'

Rosa tore her eyes away from Frank and melted into Joel.

Guilt was a terrible thing – but love was the elixir.

'I'm going to wait for you after your Queen Mary dinner tomorrow night,' she said. 'That, *Corporal Kaplan*, that's when we'll dance.'

By the end of the opening foxtrot, Frank had found his rhythm again. By the second number, he was having to fight away a vague feeling of embarrassment – for if Rosa cared so little that she'd accompanied Joel Kaplan to watch him dance, why should he feel anything at all? The problem with feelings was that you couldn't command them to just go away. But the music helped. So too did Mathilde's touch.

The Grand Ballroom didn't often host a tango – but Max Allgood had been leading the Orchestra towards one ever since he'd arrived in the hotel. Now, the sounds of his 'Ten Steps to Tango' rang out. Frank had only ever heard it with Max himself at the piano, but with him freed to bring Lucille into the music, the song had a new, unearthly dimension. Alix was clearly a committed student of the tango and, along with Max, she conjured an atmosphere so unlike anything the Grand had known that the hairs stood up on the back of Frank's neck.

'See, Frank?' whispered Mathilde, as the last song of the demonstrations reached its heights and the dancers fanned apart to take their bows. 'What does it matter who's in the ballroom, when we've got music like *that*? What does it matter, when you and I dance?'

Around the balustrade, the spectators were on their feet.

If it felt as wonderful as this, what might it feel like on Saturday night?

What might it feel like if the King truly did come? If, perhaps, Frank Nettleton danced with one of his daughters? Turned a waltz with a future queen?

At the head of the dance floor, Raymond presented Karina to the crowd. Then, with open arms and a winsome smile, he ushered his dancers up from the dance floor to fraternise with the guests.

'Come on Frankie, we're not finished yet.'

But Frank remained rooted to the spot. Part of the purpose of the demonstration dances, especially at times like these, was to tantalise the Buckingham's residents. A guest who'd seen a dancer they liked at a demonstration might reserve a foxtrot, a tango, a waltz for the ball on Saturday night. That, any good hotel dancer knew, was how reputation was built.

But as Mathilde skipped off to romance the guests, Frank felt gravity drawing him back towards the dressing-room doors.

'Frank, we've got to,' Mathilde said, looking back across the emptying dance floor. 'Frank, it's your *job*.'

But suddenly all of the freedom and lightness he felt as he danced abandoned Frank.

He took one last look at the ballroom, heard Rosa's distinctive laugh rising through the hubbub and turned to leave.

Mathilde's heart sank. Frank would receive a dressing-down for leaving the job half-finished, and without Marcus here, it would come from Raymond. That was going to smart. But, right now, Mathilde had duties of her own to attend to. Painting the smile back across her face, she skipped up the steps, through the balustrade and entered the throng.

Raymond de Guise was already in deep conversation with one of the spectators, a middle-aged lady in fine blue silks, pearls at her wrists, ears and neck. Mathilde hoped dearly that, once this war was over, there would come a time when she and Frank travelled the Continent, dancing in the same palaces, ballrooms and summer gardens that had once hosted Raymond and Hélène – but, if Frank didn't pull his socks up and do what had to be done, Mathilde was in no doubt: she would do it with somebody else, somebody who matched her commitment both on the dance floor and off.

Her eyes landed, at last, on Mr Hastings and two of the American infantrymen. At least Rosa and her sweetheart were somewhere else, thought Mathilde as she felt herself drawn into the group.

There was no point fraternising with the infantrymen – they would not be here on Saturday night – but Mathilde made nice as Mr Hastings introduced them nonetheless. The benediction of the Hotel Director mattered. One day, there might be a space for lead dancer in this troupe – and, if Mathilde wasn't already competing on the international stage, she intended to take it.

'Miss Bourchier has been dancing with us for some years,' Hastings explained. 'Truth be told, it's the war that's given her to us. I'm quite sure she's one of our silver linings. We might have lost her to Paris or Milan.'

'Vienna,' Mathilde smiled, demurely. 'That's been my dream.'

Eugene Tuck drew a breath. 'That's enemy territory, ma'am,' he said, with a smile.

'And the sooner we free them, the sooner we can dance,' said Mathilde.

'It's a real spectacle, ma'am,' ventured the other, the man named Buxton May. 'It's nothing like the dance halls back home.'

'Where Buxton comes from, the dance halls double up as cowsheds.'

Buxton May groaned. 'Eugene here wouldn't dare to dance, even if it *was* a cowshed. The boy can march, but he sure can't dance. Me, Miss Bourchier, I'd like to get on that dance floor and show all these lords and ladies a little something about good old American dancing. As for Eugene here ...'

And Buxton started clomping around, doing his very best impersonation of a farm boy stamping on a nest of mice.

Eugene Tuck just rolled his eyes. 'Give me half a chance, and I'd show you a move or two.' He gazed upwards. 'I'd sure like to see it on Saturday night.'

At this point, John Hastings – who had been listening with curiosity – seemed to come to attention. 'Let me brood on this, gentlemen. I wonder if, perhaps, the Board has been a little hasty. I must take this under consideration.' Then he stepped backwards, proclaimed, 'Gentlemen, I leave you in Miss Bourchier's very capable hands,' and turned into the crowd. John Hastings was, perhaps, the most consummate fraterniser in the ballroom, eclipsing even Raymond de Guise; mere moments later, he was in the depths of conversation with one of the Cornish lords from the second-storey suites.

'I have to say, this is already a Christmas to remember,' said Eugene. 'I wasn't looking forward to Christmas in the barracks. Christmas dinner on a tin tray in the mess.'

'When we heard about Home Away From Home, we thought we'd get stuck in one of those little cottages we pass by.'

Eugene added, 'It was a bind, missing Thanksgiving. You limeys haven't even heard of pecan pie. But, by God, if the folks back home could see us now.' He grinned at Buxton. 'Wait'll I tell Peggy about this. She'll think I'm blowin' smoke. She'll think I'm putting it on, just to get her to say *yes*.'

'Peggy's your girl back home?'

Buxton May snorted. 'Don't let him tell you that. He'll say any old thing – he reckons, if he imagines it hard enough, it might just about come true. Peggy's a girl he's sweet on. A girl he's been sweet on for far too long, if you catch my meaning.'

'She puts up a good fight,' Eugene remarked, 'but if she thought this was the sort of dance hall I could take her – well, *then* you might see a ring on her finger.'

'What about you, Private May?' Mathilde asked. She was rather enjoying hearing these two infantrymen gibing at each other.

Buxton May shrugged. 'Matter of fact, I was engaged to be married.'

'*Was?*' Mathilde asked, gently.

'Oh, there's no need to be shy about it, ma'am. Georgie and I had set a date for this spring. But then along come our Japanese friends to drop their bombs on Pearl Harbour – and well, off

I go, with a rifle and a rucksack, to answer the calling. Some girls will wait for you. Some just won't. And I guess you know, of the two, who it's worth spending your life with and who it ain't.' He paused, for Mathilde had reached out to touch him on the forearm. 'You don't need to feel sorry for me, ma'am. I certainly don't feel sorry for myself. Who knows how long we'll be at this war? It's probably for the best that Georgette finds some farm boy who isn't about to get drafted, and it's probably for the best I'm free to live my life as well. Otherwise, you get all tangled up, just like our friend Kaplan over there.'

Mathilde followed their gaze. She could only fleetingly see Rosa and Joel in the crowd – they didn't seem to care for fraternising with others; they just stood together at the balustrade, soaking in the atmosphere of the Grand – but the ballroom seemed to shift underneath her, Buxton's words ringing in her ears.

'Tangled up?' she asked.

Eugene and Buxton shared a look. 'Well, naturally, it's not for us to say,' Buxton went on, 'but Joel's always been a popular guy with the fairer sex. That hotel girl's wrapped around his little finger.'

'Oh she's a wild one,' laughed Eugene.

'But to be honest, Joel really needs a girl who matches him right – Michelle might have matched him once, but they were just kids. It hasn't been the same for them, not since they got married.'

Now, the ballroom wasn't just shifting. It positively seemed to be spinning, out of control.

'Married?' Mathilde stuttered.

'Now I don't want to speak bad of the lady. But, by the sounds of it, I reckon she frogmarched him down to the chapel, the moment they came of age.' Buxton just rolled his eyes with a smile. 'It's like I was saying – sometimes, you're better off being free. On the whole, it makes life a lot less complicated.'

Mathilde turned to look at Joel and Rosa one more time, but what she saw was Raymond de Guise, cutting through the crowd to meet her.

'Mathilde, where's young Frank?'

Mathilde's heart started hammering. She could no longer see Rosa, but she could hear her laughter ringing. What joyful, carefree laughter it was – the laughter of a girl with nothing in the world but the man that she loved. It was hard not to feel envious of that joy – for wasn't this the most magical afternoon of Rosa's life? Yet, at the same time, Mathilde felt a strange sinking sensation.

Her mouth was suddenly dry.

A secret like this couldn't be kept, not without becoming part of it.

Sooner or later, she was going to have to tell Frank.

'He's – he's backstage,' Mathilde stuttered.

Raymond arched an eyebrow in enquiry.

'Don't be too hard on him, Mr de Guise. He just needed a moment. He knows what his job is. He just couldn't summon up the …'

Rosa's laughter rang out again; this time Raymond too seemed to hear it.

'Go and find him,' Raymond told her. 'Tell him he has a duty out here.'

Mathilde nodded, 'Yes, Mr de Guise,' and bade goodbye to the infantrymen.

And, as she crossed the dance floor, wondering if she ought to tell Frank now or wait for some better moment, she wondered if Raymond, too, was weighed down by some secret. He looked almost ashen. In truth, he looked as if there was anywhere in the world he'd rather be than gallivanting around the Grand, making niceties with guests.

In fact, thought Mathilde as she pushed through the dressing-room doors, he looked rather like Frank Nettleton himself.

Chapter Eleven

There'd been a time when the Regent Street arcades were like a second home to Vivienne. In the days when she was a permanent resident of the Buckingham Hotel, living on a stipend from her stepfather – on the strict instruction that, barring holidays and special invitations, she not frequent the Suffolk manor house where he and Vivienne's mother had set up home – she had accounts at all the fabulous dressmakers between Piccadilly and Oxford Circus. At McCardell's in the Quadrant Arcade, they called her 'madam' – which, in those days, had tickled Vivienne. In Liberty's department store there was a personal steward who knew her by name. She had credit accounts at Jackson & Livingstone's, Lady Ettingham's and Salisbury's Evening Wear – and, as a consequence, she was treated like royalty every Friday afternoon, when she set out to find a new gown to wear in the Grand that Saturday night. New York loved money, and back home it bought you an awful lot of love – but it never bought you *class*. For the younger Vivienne, exiled to the Buckingham Hotel, that had been London's saving grace.

Now, however, she walked past the ornate edifice of Liberty's department store with Stan straining on one hand, Arthur grizzling in his pram, and barely a penny to her name.

She supposed the younger Vivienne would have got a thrill out of walking the streets of London with three strapping American servicemen at her side. And at least she had this in common with her younger self. It had been so long since she ventured into the West End that it almost felt *new*.

So much time had flown by since her wild days. To be reminded of the vastness of London, to parade it in the company of three of her own countrymen – well, Vivienne had quite forgotten it was possible to feel like this.

If only the small matter of Raymond's secrecy hadn't been dogging her, if only the voice of the attendant at St Thomas's Hospital wasn't still buzzing in her mind, she might have been enjoying this.

She was thinking of this when she caught Ellsworth March's eye. Ellsworth, it seemed, had something on his mind as well. He winked at her and said, 'It's nothing like a New York winter though, is it?'

New York winters could be bitter, but what Vivienne remembered was skating in Central Park.

It seemed they were both thinking the same thing: New York a dream, from times gone by.

They lingered a moment too long, basking in the shared recollection.

Then Ellsworth, perhaps mitigating some embarrassment, said, 'Some nice candles, that's the thing for a Christmas night. I suppose candles aren't rationed yet?'

Vivienne said, 'Not rationed – but just walk into a chandlers and see the price on one of them.'

'That'll be all the paraffin, taken by the armies. It forces up manufacturing costs. You pick up on these things, when you go to enough meetings. You'd be surprised how much of our work at the embassy is industrial.'

Vivienne ruminated on it, while she was wrangling Stan to keep on his scarf and gloves. 'The thing about rationing, though, is ... if you've got money, almost nothing's off limits.'

Ellsworth could see she was struggling with Stan. In a moment, he swept in, had the little boy saluting and slipped on his gloves. 'I've a family of brothers. I was the eldest. I'm good with little ones, ma'am. As a matter of fact, I rather miss it.' He paused. 'But what do you mean ... if you've got money, nothing's off limits?'

Vivienne could not ignore the effect Ellsworth had had on Stan. The boy seemed to respond to a man in a different way to how he responded to his mother. Something instinctive seemed to tell him he was his mother's boss. Right now, against all the odds, Stan was behaving like a perfect cherubic child.

'Oh come now, Mr March,' she said, returning to the question at hand. 'You're not so naive. At the Winter Ball on Saturday night, they'll be dancing in silks and chiffon, won't they? At the Queen Mary restaurant, they'll be eating goose and all the trimmings. Rationing's for those that have to stand in bread queues, or count their pennies at the grocers. It isn't for *everybody*. Here, I'll show you.'

This felt good too: to be the one leading the charge. As Vivienne took the Americans down Regent Street she got a surge of another old feeling: what it was like to feel as if *you* were the one driving forward your own life. Of all the many casualties of war, the one that went unremarked upon was *ambition*. If there'd been a time when Vivienne was an indulged debutante with a penchant for Moët and Benzedrine, there'd been another time when she dreamt of accomplishing great things. It was good to be reminded.

The Beagles' Chandlery by the Quadrant gates was not a place that cared much for privation or the perils of rationing.

Its windows proudly stated that, in accordance with its Royal Warrant, the candles on sale within were produced with beeswax courtesy of the apiarists who worked the Royal Parks – which was a longwinded way of saying these were *kingly* candles. 'Just the thing,' Ellsworth remarked, before he slipped inside. 'My grandaddy worked at a candle factory back in Pittsburgh,' he said when he re-emerged, a bundle of sculpted beeswax candles wrapped in cloth under his arm. 'He fought in the war – a Union man, I'm proud to say – but, after that, he just wanted a quiet life. By God, he wouldn't recognise these candles. He sat on a production line and trimmed wicks. I reckon he'd consider these things works of art.'

'And your father,' Vivienne asked, 'was he a candle man too?'

Vivienne could see her reflection in the window: she and Ellsworth standing abreast of each other, she fitting neatly alongside his left arm. Ellsworth's expression changed. For a second he was quieter, more ruminative, faltering before he said, 'My father was a military man, ma'am. An ambitious one at that. He came over here after the *Lusitania* went down, when the American Expeditionary were sent into France.'

'Back in New York, we had a houseboy whose father was with the same. He didn't come back home.'

'Mine did,' said Ellsworth, 'but he came back different, that's for sure. I was twelve years old when he went away. Fifteen by the time he got demobbed and back to the States. It wasn't the same after that.'

'The war changed him, you mean?'

'I figure it was just the years. When he left I was a boy. When he came back, suddenly he had a young man in the house.' Ellsworth grinned. 'It's fair to say, we didn't see eye to eye.'

'Oh, but he must be proud now? To see you in his footsteps?'

Ellsworth touched her shoulder gently, as he turned away. Perhaps she was wrong, but it seemed he was avoiding the question. 'Hey, I was thinking – we need to get something for these two scamps.' He indicated the boys. 'Christmas is coming.'

Vivienne was about to object – she couldn't possibly allow their houseguests to indulge the children – but quite suddenly she stopped and thought: why the devil not? The Vivienne of old would have welcomed indulgence, especially at Christmastime. That was the New York way. Sometimes, when she thought of Stan's childhood and compared it to her own, she was filled with a cocktail of emotions. Stan had love and the busyness of a warm family home; but he didn't have the riches of Madison Square Garden and Times Square. A little indulgence never hurt.

'Hamley's is back that way,' McCord began. 'What do you think, young man? I reckon there's a toy train with your name on it.'

'Do little boys play at cowboys and Indians in England?' Jonah asked.

'You're forgetting, *this* little boy has the blood of New York in him,' Vivienne smiled. She so rarely thought of Stan as inheriting anything from her family line – he looked so much like his father – but this brought a rush of good feeling as well.

'I don't remember any cowboys in New York,' Ellsworth joked, seemingly forgetting the sombreness of just moments before, 'but we can always pretend.'

Vivienne looked at her son. Though he seemed to understand something of what was being discussed, his cheeks had acquired a certain ruddiness and his lips were tinged in blue. She tightened the scarf around him and hoisted him up. 'Perhaps a café first.' Stan's eyes lit up. Then Vivienne flashed a look around. 'Nothing's rationed in cafés. The boy doesn't need toy cowboys – but he could do with cocoa and cake. You can still find a decent cocoa, if you know where to go.'

Before they set out, McCord looked at his wristwatch and said, 'I'll bow out before lunch, Mrs Cohen. I have a few errands of my own to run.'

Ellsworth and Jonah seemed to be expecting this. 'No rest for the wicked,' Ellsworth remarked. 'We'll meet you back at the house, Henry. Stay safe out there.'

After McCord took his leave, Vivienne flashed looks around and asked, 'What was that about?'

Ellsworth laughed, 'Young McCord takes his job very seriously indeed. His father expects great things. As a matter of fact, we all do.'

Soon the party had crossed the grand thoroughfare of Regent Street and vanished between the townhouses of Mayfair. When they reached Berkeley Square and the Buckingham Hotel, Vivienne paused. It remained such a large part of her life, dictating the rhythms of the family she'd made her own, but it seemed forever since she'd last laid eyes on it. The feeling was not altogether pleasurable.

'I could buy us all lunch in the restaurant,' Ellsworth said.

Evidently he was keen to impress Vivienne. Jonah had noticed it and ventured, 'I could take a stroll, if you two want to get acquainted?'

At that moment, Vivienne caught Ellsworth's eye once more. They remained, locked together, for fractionally too long. Either Vivienne was waiting for Ellsworth to say something, or Ellsworth was waiting for her.

Only the snow curling between them saved Vivienne from being momentarily lost in his eyes.

Ellsworth broke the silence: 'I'm just aware we're spending this Christmas on your charity, ma'am. It doesn't seem right. So if you'd allow me?'

Vivienne's face crumpled. 'I rather think the Buckingham isn't the place for two babes.' But really her mind was on other things. 'My stepfather used to be the Head of the Hotel Board,' she carried on. 'That is, until they locked him up. He's sitting in some internment camp now, waiting out the war. I'm afraid, boys, he'd have been one of the first to shake Mr Hitler's hand, if the Wehrmacht were billeting at the Buckingham.' She shook her head ruefully; by the looks on their faces, she could tell that she'd sombred the mood. 'I think, perhaps, somewhere else?'

Ellsworth clasped her shoulder. 'I should have enjoyed seeing the finery in this place. The Ambassador speaks so highly of it. But... where to, my lady?'

Vivienne was trying to picture all of the restaurants and cafés she'd frequented, back in her Buckingham days – really, she ought to take these Americans somewhere a little more special than the Lyons Corner House on Piccadilly – when the memory of that morning resurfaced.

Maynard Charles, who'd once presided over this hotel with such dignity and poise...

Maynard Charles, fighting for his life in a hospital bed.

'I wonder,' she blurted out, 'if you might want to take a walk along the river?'

It was further than she wanted to go – further than Stan wanted to go too, but soon he'd submitted to being carried by Ellsworth, and this seemed to lift the young boy's spirits. It lifted Vivienne's spirits too: Stan seemed to respond so well to the presence of the Americans. It wasn't that he'd been missing a man in his life this year, because Raymond had been there, and Frank too – but Stan had never really known a father. The idea that he might become so captivated by a new man was a revelation to Vivienne.

There were cafés much closer, but now that she'd set her mind on it, Vivienne felt a force like gravity dragging her through St James and towards the river. By the time they reached it, to see the barrage balloons above Westminster occluded by snow, and the Thames itself trembling beneath the constantly twirling winter haze, she was cold to the bone and in need of hot cocoa herself. But, just a little upriver of the Westminster Pier, she settled them into the condensation-fogged window of a café bustling with government clerks from the nearby palaces, and gazed across the busy river at the ghostly outline of St Thomas's Hospital.

Somewhere in there lay the answer to the mystery of the morning call.

Right now, however, she was too cold – and too concerned with the wellbeing of the boys – to contemplate it.

Jonah ordered cocoas, hot buttered teacakes and sandwiches of genuine mustard and ham. Within moments of them arriving, Stan had painted his face with a chocolatey smile and devoured his sandwich, crust and all.

'You can tell he's going to be fearless,' remarked Ellsworth. 'You have an interesting future ahead, Mrs Cohen.'

Vivienne blurted out, 'You may call me Vivienne.'

'Viv,' Ellsworth said, with a gentle incline of his head.

Viv. She liked the sound of that. Yes, it was familiar – far too familiar, perhaps – but it rolled off his tongue. 'Viv it is,' she said. 'It's been some time since I felt like Mrs Cohen. And if you're anything like me, you don't think a lot about the future. You know it's coming, and you do your best to avoid it.'

Ellsworth rather enjoyed this back-to-front logic. 'The future is waiting for us all, as soon as this damn war's won.'

Stan's eyes bugged out at the curse word, but Vivienne ignored it and went on, 'Do you think this war *can* be won?'

'It must,' Linden intervened, 'but, as for how and when, well, you'd have to ask McCord that. But I'm quite sure,' his eyes twinkled, 'if he told you, he'd have to…'

Vivienne's eyes flared. 'Yes, that's quite enough of that,' she grinned – and, as she took her next sip of cocoa, her gaze returned to the river and, across the water, to the hospital's floating ghost.

'Right, that's it. That's decided,' Ellsworth announced, when the silence had gone on too long. 'War talk must end, and talk of Christmas must begin.' He directed his gaze to Stan. 'What are you thinking, Stan? Some toy soldiers? An airplane? I've heard Hamley's is a kind of temple to these things. A grand cathedral.'

Stan was babbling out an answer when Jonah said, 'Why not one of everything?'

'And something for the other little soldier too. Some dancing shoes, so he can waltz like his father?'

In his pram, Arthur just gurgled.

'Let's hop to this,' Ellsworth announced, rising to his feet and offering her his arm. 'We can be back home by dark, with more to show for our hosts than a few candles. Very *kingly* candles though they are.'

Stan's eyes had lit up: a trip to Hamley's, Vivienne thought, might be one of those memories that stayed with him through all the days of his life. But she could hear again the buzzing voice of the hospital attendant, see again the shadowy, secretive look upon Raymond as he skulked by the sitting-room door.

'I think, perhaps, we're not quite ready,' she ventured. Then, when Ellsworth looked about to retake his seat, she blustered on, 'But perhaps… Stan might like a surprise?' She lowered her voice, cupping hands around Stan's ears. 'You've no idea the mayhem he might cause in a shop like Hamley's. But a surprise... for Christmas morning?'

The truth was, she was torn. She rather liked sitting here in Ellsworth's company, and for a split second, part of her hoped Jonah might disappear up to Hamley's on his own. But here was her opportunity to find out what the devil had happened to Charles Maynard. It took considerable effort to resist the temptation to remain in the café, but Vivienne was no stranger to difficult decisions 'You don't have to, of course. You're meant to be our guests.'

'Viv,' Ellsworth laughed, 'it would be our honour.'

Now Jonah stood too. 'You better hope we got taste, kid,' he grinned. 'We'll meet you back here, Mrs Cohen.'

Ellsworth looked back as the two Americans crossed the café floor and winked at Vivienne across the bustling hall.

And though Vivienne was already warm through from the cocoa, she had to admit that another rush of warmth spread through her. Later, she would start to wonder if this was the start of some betrayal – for here, right here in her lap, sat the spitting image of her fallen husband, his own flesh and bone, reincarnate.

But that feeling could wait.

Now what Vivienne had to think about was Maynard Charles.

It would be cold upon the river, the winter wind raging up from the Thames across Westminster Bridge, but Stan had a belly full of cocoa and, if she found space for him alongside Arthur in the pram, he wouldn't feel the worst.

Westminster Bridge was a veritable fortification of barricades, barbed wire and soldiers standing guard – but the barrage balloons overhead seemed to absorb the worst of the wind, and the cold wasn't as ferocious as Vivienne had feared. Vivienne's teeth were chattering as she reached the doors of St Thomas's

Hospital – but this was less from the cold than it was the sense of anticipation and dread that had been mounting in her since morning. Whatever secret Raymond held would be revealed through these doors.

Just like the bridge, the hospital had a military air. Vivienne had never before stepped through these doors, but she supposed it had not been the same during peacetime. A pair of soldiers stood at a counter, where an attendant was flicking through paper files. Another attendant put down one telephone receiver and immediately picked up another. Deeper in the hospital, trolleys wheeled past and a collection of dour-looking patients waited anxiously in a great horseshoe of seating.

Vivienne trembled with impatience as she waited at the counter for the soldiers to move on. Right now, Ellsworth and Jonah were probably stepping through the doors of Hamley's. Perhaps they'd spend a little time marvelling over the toy shop's splendid creations, but before long, they would be on their way back to the café to join her. Vivienne didn't want to face any awkward questions; she meant to be there when they returned.

'I'm here to visit my ... godfather,' she ventured, when her turn at the counter finally came. She didn't know she was going to spin this lie, but something about it felt true; she'd infuriated and sorely tested Maynard Charles on occasion, but she had often felt his guiding hand on her shoulder.

'His name?' the attendant asked.

'Charles,' Vivienne replied. 'Mr Maynard Charles.'

It took the attendant some time to sort through the cascade of cards on the shelf behind her, then to cross-reference it with the thick admissions book which dominated the desk. When she eventually looked up, she said, 'I'm afraid Mr Charles in a critical condition, madam. He's in the King James ward, but I'm not certain if—'

'That's quite all right,' she said, cutting off the attendant mid-flow. 'I'm sure I can make my own way.'

That was easier said than done. Hospitals were like labyrinths, and she made a multitude of wrong turnings and hit several dead ends before she finally came to the doors of the King James ward.

The corridor here was eerily silent. She was grateful that Stan and Arthur were asleep in the pram, for a single noise would have echoed interminably in these halls.

Vivienne wasn't sure why, but the sense that she was trespassing grew stronger the moment she pushed through the door – and realised, suddenly, that this was no ordinary hospital ward. No vast room spread out in front of her, with nurses clucking back and forth, doctors making their rounds or hospital porters rearranging trolleys and beds. Instead, Vivienne was faced with a single long corridor, flanked by a dozen doors on either side. The first was marked 'WARD SISTER', but thereafter they led into private rooms.

At the uttermost end of the corridor, two soldiers stood outside a door.

Vivienne checked the names of the rooms as she approached.

The squeaking of the pram wheels echoed, filling the air.

Names she did not recognise flickered by, but Vivienne was not yet halfway when the inevitability of what she was seeing hit her: the soldiers at the end of the row were guarding the door behind which Maynard Charles fought for his life. She didn't need to see the name to know it. She was as certain as she had been of anything in her life.

No wonder Raymond's face had been etched in concern.

Somewhere behind her, the ward sister's door opened up. 'Excuse me?' came a voice, following her down the hall. But Vivienne did not turn round. She knew, now, that she was

walking where she had no right to be – and that, if she acknowledged the voice, she would swiftly be escorted out of the
ward. Instead, she quickened her pace, wheeling Stan and Arthur
until they were in the shadow of the soldiers standing sentry
at the door.

In chalk upon a slate hung just outside the room, someone
had scrawled the words MAYNARD CHARLES.

Vivienne saw him fleetingly through the glass.

He didn't look like the Hotel Director she remembered.

He looked like a shrunken bundle, trussed up in bed, his
body attached by lines to bags of fluid, to machines whose uses
Vivienne did not understand. A mask had been strapped over
his face, trailing a bag that kept inflating and deflating with
every assisted breath.

Footsteps tolled behind her: the ward sister.

The soldier at the door screwed up his eyes in disbelief.

'I – I wanted to see my g-godfather,' Vivienne stuttered.

'You shouldn't be here, ma'am,' the soldier intoned.

Vivienne turned round. The ward sister was almost upon her,
her face like thunder.

'I just wanted to know if he was . . .' She stalled. What, she
wondered, had she hoped to discover? That Maynard Charles
was in hospital was one thing; that he was in hospital under
armed guard, the only man on this ward with soldiers stationed
at his door, was something else altogether.

'Madam,' the ward sister exploded, 'I'm afraid I must ask you
to leave. This is a closed ward. No visitors allowed.'

So that was what the attendant at the front desk had been
trying to tell her.

'This is absolutely no place for children. You ought be
ashamed.' As Vivienne started retreating along the hall, she

scurried after. 'I shall need your name, madam. These are matters of national security.'

But Vivienne was already at the door – and, in the confusion, Stan had woken and started clamouring to get out of the pram. In the sudden explosion of voices and crying, Vivienne burst back through the doors and started running along the corridor, the pram surging in front of her. She didn't look back at all, not until she was out in the cold London air and once again bound for the riverbank.

The coldness brought a clarity back to her thinking.

The problem was: none of this felt very clear at all.

Maynard Charles was just a retired Hotel Director, wasn't he?

So... what had he become, that he deserved the honour of a military guard? Or... what had he *done*, that, loitering around the doors of death as he was, he still needed guarding? Which was he – hero being protected, or villain being jailed? What had happened that had left him fighting for his life?

And, above all other things, what had this got to do with Raymond de Guise?

Chapter Twelve

One by one, the lights went out across London. In the grand townhouses of Berkeley Square, blackout blinds were drawn into place, cocooning families for another dark December night.

But at the Buckingham Hotel, the evening was about to begin.

As the darkness hardened, a taxicab wheeled around Berkeley Square and drew to a halt beneath the hotel's grand colonnade. Ordinarily a driver depositing a guest at this fine establishment would step out of his taxicab to help his guest alight – but on this occasion, the back door simply opened and an elegant lady dressed in a silver fur stole, with white hair framing her face like a veil, stepped out. It had been many years since Hélène Marchmont last graced the Buckingham Hotel, but this week all of that was going to change.

Raymond de Guise stood in his midnight-blue evening suit, just outside the bronze revolving door.

'You'll catch your death of cold,' Hélène said, by way of greeting.

Raymond smiled. 'You're a sight for sore eyes, Hélène.'

'Raymond, you look quite frazzled. This is only a rehearsal. You must leave yourself some space to grow truly distressed before Saturday night.'

Hélène's upper-crust tones had been settling Raymond's nerves since their earliest days as dancers together. Her departure from the Grand on the eve of war had left him rudderless – but they'd danced together at the Albert Hall this summer, and the knowledge that they'd dance together in the Grand this Saturday night had been filling Raymond's heart ever since it was agreed. She even calmed his frayed nerves now, as his mind trilled and buzzed with thoughts of the Americans back home. Dancers so often slipped back into old patterns, and Raymond needed that tonight. He took her by the arm and steered her into the hotel.

'Does it feel strange?' Raymond whispered, as they walked across the bustling reception hall, down towards the Grand. 'Or does it feel like ... home?'

'Perhaps not *home*,' said Hélène.

But then they stepped through the marble arch, into the ballroom, where the musicians were setting up on stage, and Hélène had to catch her breath.

'No,' she whispered, 'how could it ever feel like *home*? I'd quite forgotten, Raymond. You can dance here every Saturday night, and every time it feels like your first.'

The words had a spellbinding effect upon Raymond. His own return to the Grand Ballroom had come with so many secrets, caveats and lies, that he had quite forgotten the honour it was to lead here.

Backstage, the troupe were assembling. Many of them remembered Hélène from her days in the Grand – but there were new faces here too, and to Hélène everything felt just a little off kilter. Raymond took her hand and began:

'The meeting of old world and new ...'

He'd been rehearsing this speech for some days. 'Isn't that what this year's been about? Old world and new, coming together? That's what Saturday night is for. That's the hope we're meant to embody out there. And this evening is our final chance to prove to ourselves that we're ready to do battle.' He stepped aside, as if introducing Hélène for the first time. 'For almost a decade, Hélène and I led the troupe in the Grand. On Saturday night, I shall be proud to reintroduce the ballroom to the lady who taught me so much about dance. But this is about more than us. It's about the guests. It's about the hotel. My friends, it's about the war. Let us treat this evening as if the ballroom is already full.' Momentarily, Raymond's eyes landed on Frank, and Frank seemed to sense some gentle admonition in his tone. He nodded fiercely, as if to show that, no matter what private turmoils flooded his mind, he was ready to dance. 'In fact,' Raymond pronounced, 'let's treat tonight as if the King and his retinue really are in attendance. Our guests will deserve nothing less.' He turned on his heel. 'How long have we got, Mr Allgood?'

Max started bumbling, and turned to Alix Monet. 'Are you ready, Miss Monet?'

Alix said, 'Let's find out,' and flashed him a grin.

Hélène caught sight of her and thought: Well, things really *have* changed in the Grand. 'Raymond,' she whispered, 'it *feels* different here. It feels like we're back at the beginning, when the Grand was only just opening its doors. When Archie Adams took up residence and nobody knew how we were going to fare. Whether we'd still be there in six months – or go down as a noble failure. Raymond, it's … exciting.'

It was just like Hélène, to raise the mood. While his mind raced with thoughts of the American's betrayal, Hélène saw only promise and hope.

As Hélène joined Max, Alix and the Orchestra to see the set lists, the dressing-room doors opened and two porters wheeled in the racks of gowns just delivered from the hotel laundries. The laundry seamstress was on hand for any last-minute adjustments, and soon the troupe were donning gowns of chiffon, silk and lace; Mathilde stood striking in scarlet, and Karina in crimson red. Startling colours for a startling Saturday night. Hélène approached the rack and saw the very same ivory gown that she'd worn on her final night dancing in the Grand. She'd left here, thinking she'd never wear it again. Indeed, she'd left here, thinking she might never dance.

How the wheel of history turned…

She reached out and ran a finger around its neckline.

Then, suddenly, Frank Nettleton was beside her.

'Miss Marchmont,' he ventured.

'Look at you, Mr Nettleton,' Hélène smiled. 'It's on the tip of my tongue to say, my, how you've grown. But I'm afraid that might make me sound like your mother.'

'We're all just so thrilled to see you again,' Frank ventured.

'I'm not sure I'm ready,' Hélène said, quietly.

Frank cast a look around, fearful Raymond might overhear when he said, 'I'm not sure I'm ready either. I suppose you never quite know, not until the band strikes up. I've had things playing on my mind, Miss Marchmont. I find them creeping in, even while I dance.'

Hélène lowered her voice. 'Do you remember coming down to Rye, and everything I said to you?'

Frank nodded. He'd taken tuition with Hélène that first springtime of the war.

'Life is full of pitfalls and traps, Frank. It's full of things to fear and worry over. But when we're out there, it's our job to give the world something to treasure as well. Just remember that. Give the guests – no, give *yourself* – something to truly cherish.'

As Frank watched Hélène lift her gown from the rack, he dwelled on those words. He was dwelling on them still when Mathilde drew near.

'I know what you're thinking,' Frank said at last. 'But I'll be OK. I won't let you down – not this evening, and not on Saturday night. It's done now. It's over. Rosa isn't here, and I can concentrate on what really matters. It was only romance. Let her live her life. I've got to live mine – and mine's … dance.' Frank paused. Mathilde had a pained expression. 'Mathilde, is everything OK? I know I let you down at the demonstrations, but it'll be different this time. I promise.'

Mathilde let out a breath; if there had been something she wanted to say, now it seemed to sail away. 'Let's show them, Frankie. Let's show them what we can do.'

Perhaps it was fine to hold on to a secret, for just another few days.

When you worked in the Buckingham Hotel, you got used to its rhythms. The porters and pages, the concierges and kitchen hands all felt it: the Buckingham, they said, was like a great living creature, and if you cared to listen you could hear what it was saying as it moved through the rhythms of its day. Now, while London readied itself for another night behind the black-out blinds, the nocturnal corners of the Buckingham Hotel came to life. In the Queen Mary restaurant the head chef rallied his staff for the dinner service to come. In the Candlelight Club, the first cocktails of the evening were about to be served. Guests returned to their suites from the business of the day, to change clothes and freshen themselves for whatever their evenings had in store. And, though the Grand Ballroom was closed tonight for rehearsals, the music of the Max Allgood Orchestra rippled out from the stage, touching every corner of the hotel. As

Mr Hastings marched past on his way to meet the Comte de Renesse, staying this Christmas in the Trafalgar suite while Nazi warmongers ravaged his estates, the swooping sound of Lucille, dovetailing with the music of their startling new pianist, put a fresh spring in his step.

But there was one person in the Buckingham Hotel who remained unmoved.

In the dark caverns of the Queen Mary kitchen, the head chef, M. Henri Laurent, stalked from counter to counter, muttering darkly under his breath. A kitchen like this was a well-oiled machine – it needed every piece in good working order, and today he was one man down. He'd never put much stock in Victor – just another kitchen whelp, good for chopping and gutting and scrubbing out pans – but nor had he imagined him the sort who'd march in with a hastily scribbled note to announce his departure on the eve of their year's biggest night. Sweat beaded on his brow. Tonight there would be three hundred diners in the main restaurant, and thirty-eight more in the private dining rooms that opened onto the Queen Mary. Running a kitchen one man down felt like running a race uphill.

And in her attic bedchamber at the very top of the hotel, Annie Brogan paced up and down, wondering if she ought to follow where her sweetheart had gone.

The music emanating from the Grand Ballroom did not reach the far-flung corner of the hotel where its chambermaids were housed, but the music that Rosa and the others were playing in the kitchenette was so loud it rattled through the walls of Annie's bedchamber. These were old records, ones Frank had bought for Rosa – Benny Goodman and Fats Waller, Tommy Dorsey and Bunny Berigan – and Annie was quite sure there was dancing going on as well. Every now and again a gale of laughter rung up. Annie was also quite sure Mrs de Guise would have disapproved. Nobody minded the hotel staff gathering for a good time, away from the prying eyes of guests. The problem was when the guests were *invited*. And when Annie had finally dried her eyes enough to venture out of her bedroom, that was exactly what she saw: Joel Kaplan and the other GIs, twirling Rosa, Mary-Louise and the others around between the sofas as the music played. A bottle of gin, Rosa's favourite tipple, was stacked on the countertop between the toaster and teapot.

'Annie,' came Rosa's shrill voice, as Annie tried to steal past. 'What the devil have you been doing in there?'

'She looks like she's been *crying*,' said Mary-Louise, peering out into the dark hallway where Annie stood. 'Hey Annie, what's got into you? It's Christmas! Come and have a drink.'

'Is it that kitchen boy?' Rosa asked, sliding out of Joel's arms to join Mary-Louise in the door. 'What's he done to you this time?'

This time? thought Annie. That was just like Rosa – she loved to stir up a bit of fuss.

'Get yourself in here, girl. There's enough tea in that pot for one more. Enough gin in that bottle too!' Rosa lowered her voice. 'I'm sure one of Joel's friends will give you a dance.' She craned over her shoulder, but Annie reached for her hand, imploring her to stop. 'Oh Victor won't mind!' Rosa laughed. 'You need a bit of fun, Annie.'

'I c-can't,' Annie stuttered.

The girls didn't need to know it, but it wasn't really Victor she was thinking about.

'I've got to go.'

Rosa started booing, but Annie just retreated along the attic corridor, bound for the rickety stairs leading below.

'Oh, Annie!' Mary-Louise called after her.

'Just leave her to it,' Rosa sighed. 'Her loss, isn't it?'

And the last thing Annie heard, before she hurried down the stairs, was Rosa adding, 'She's such a stick in the mud. Honestly, she isn't going to last. You've got to take your joys. Annie Brogan just can't take her joys.'

The truth was, Annie would have loved to have taken a little joy tonight. Billy's request had been playing on her all day. Part of her still couldn't believe Victor was gone. It was all so sudden, all so abrupt. Yet another part of her was ashamed she hadn't gone with him. It was the first big thing he'd ever asked her. Oh, he'd asked her out for walks and picnicking in Hyde Park, but he'd never before asked her for something that really, truly mattered – not until this very day. And when he had, she'd let him down.

Billy was waiting in the hotel post room, just like he'd promised. Billy was *always* waiting. You could set your pocket-watch by him. 'Right then, Annie,' he announced, when Annie slipped inside and closed the door behind her. Evidently he'd been hard at work, on both legitimate Buckingham business and not, for papers were strewn around his desk. 'The dinner service ought to be over by now. Victor ought to be scrubbing down. We'll just let the lights go dark and...'

Annie hadn't even bothered rehearsing the words, because she knew they'd just burst out anyway. 'Victor's not—'

'Oh, I *know* he's not happy about it,' Billy groaned, levering himself to his feet. 'But we've all got to do things we're not happy about. Who does he think he is, that he can go through life not doing things he's not happy about? I went to the blinkin' war. I went to do my bit, and look how it's left me.' He tapped his bad leg with a smile. 'Let's just have a lovely Christmas. A proper Brogan Christmas, just like they used to be.'

The will had been sapped out of Annie.

'We've never had a goose before,' she muttered. 'Never needed one.'

'No, but we always talked about it. It was always a dream. And now, *now* we've got a chance to make a dream come true.'

Annie knew she ought to tell him, but summoning the courage was proving too much. Billy had already brushed past her, was already halfway to the post-room door, when she realised every step he took was just making it worse.

His hand fell on the door handle.

She felt a shiver as it turned.

Billy looked over his shoulder. 'Come on,' he grinned. 'Annie, this is for you too!'

And it was those words, as illogical and implausible as they seemed, that finally made up her mind. It was the look of magic in his eyes, the way he puffed up with pride at the gift he was about to make the whole Brogan clan. Later she would wonder at how *silly* it had been – but right now, it almost felt like it wasn't *fair* on him.

'Victor's not there,' she blurted out, before Billy went through the door.

Billy looked over his shoulder, his face a puzzled mask. 'What do you mean, he's not *there*? Old Laurent would serve him up for breakfast if he wasn't there.'

Annie shook her head. Tears were prickling her eyes again, now that she had to say it. 'Victor left the hotel. Right after you told him about the goose. I've been trying to work out a way to tell you all day.' Now the tears flowed, bejewelling her face as they came. 'He couldn't stand it anymore, Bill. He just wanted it to end. And he had a letter in his pocket, an offer from the Imperial – and he's gone, and ... and he wants me to go with him!'

Billy's nostrils flared. His eyes darted up the post-room corridor until he was certain nobody was out there lurking. Then he slammed the door shut. 'Annie Brogan, keep your voice down!'

She couldn't help it. There were no more words to say – just the flood of tears she'd been repressing all day.

'You drove him away, Billy. You made up his mind.'

Billy rushed to her side. Through her tears, Annie saw his face pitched somewhere between confusion and disappointment. Lord help her, she hated the feeling of letting Billy down. She felt six years old again, gazing up at Billy – her proud, confident, cocksure big brother – and eager to join in with whatever mischief he had planned.

'It'll be all right, Annie,' said Billy, trying in vain to dry her tears. 'You'll just have to go to him. You're the only one that can make him see sense. Walk out on the Buckingham Hotel? Walk out on our endeavours? He's had a panic, that's all it is. He *knows* how good he's got it around here.'

'But that's exactly the point, Billy – he knows what it's like and he can't do it anymore.'

Billy's tone darkened.

'I'll bet he wants paying more. That's what it is.'

Annie sobbed, 'He doesn't want paying at all.'

'Annie, you have to trust me on this. Have a bit of faith in your big brother, can't you? Victor's a nice lad, but he's simple. He's got spooked. But it's only a *goose*. It's nothing he hasn't done before – it's just a bit more ambitious. And, well ...' Billy pulled her near and held her tight, like he used to when they were tiny and the world seemed so unyielding and vast. 'All he's done is guarantee *he'll* be missing out on Christmas Day. He could have shared in that goose, Annie, but now it'll just be us Brogans.'

Annie had already been so cold, but now a different kind of chill ran through her.

'What do you mean, Billy? If Victor can't get that goose for us, nobody can.'

'Oh Annie, that's just defeatism! You don't win wars like that. No – *you'll* just need to slip into the kitchens before they're closing down. You know the lay of things in there, Annie. I know you do. You and Victor, with your little midnight meet-ups. It doesn't have to take long. Just pass it out down the chute, and I'll do the rest.'

Annie just stared, but Billy's eyes were so insistent that, moments later, she found herself nodding.

'That's a good girl, Annie. That's a brave, bold Brogan!'

It almost seemed like a dream – and, in the dream, she felt Billy shepherding her through the post-room door, through the Buckingham and up to the reception hall, where the doors of the Queen Mary restaurant awaited. The last strains of the Orchestra's finale rippled out of the Grand, and that was the only thing that brought her any cheer as Billy patted her on the shoulder and said, 'Just make your excuses. Slide on into the kitchens. I'll be waiting in the mews. It's only this one time, Annie. And don't worry – I'll tell Ma that this goose was as much down to you as it is me! Oh Annie, she's going to be so proud.'

It was the damnedest thing, but when Billy left her, as full of expectation as he was, she felt suddenly more lonely still. She didn't like to admit it, not when Rosa was glorying in it so much, but she would have *loved* to have caught a sight of the dancers in the Grand today, even if it was just a demonstration. The rules had been bent for Rosa this afternoon – but they would never have been bent for somebody like Annie.

The doors of the restaurant fluttered. Out came one of the waiting staff, finished for the evening.

Billy's words echoed in her as she stole across the reception hall. It was the way his eyes had been so brimming with expectation and excitement that unnerved her the most. It was the way he seemed to *believe*. Billy had always been an optimist. But lately there had seemed something stubborn, something wilful, about the way he ignored the dangers of his business. The way he ignored the dangers for *her*.

He said he was doing it for his family.

But here his family was, sent to commit a crime in his name.

On the far side of the reception hall, the lights of the Queen Mary restaurant snuffed out.

It wouldn't be easy, but there were ways.

No doubt somebody was in there, scrubbing down the surfaces, but that would only make it easier to slip within. Then – hide, perhaps? Find a spot in the darkness of the larder to lay low and bide her time before...

'*No.*'

It wasn't just the word that sprang out of her lips. Her whole body seemed to be saying it too: every muscle suddenly rigid, refusing to let her walk on.

She wouldn't do it.

She couldn't.

She turned to take flight, back to the chambermaids and whatever party was still happening above – but her eyes were still clouded by tears, and as she turned she crashed directly into a tall, lithe figure dressed in a silver fur stole who had just emerged from the Grand.

'I'm – I'm sorry miss,' Annie blathered, gathering her own skirts to run. 'I wasn't watching. I'll do better.' And she started curtseying like some crazed palace retainer, grovelling as she staggered backwards. 'I'm sorry. I truly am.'

Then she turned and fled.

Billy would be furious.

Perhaps he'd even come looking for her.

But she'd worry about that later.

After Annie had vanished, Hélène Marchmont turned to see two figures following her through the marble arch that led up from the Grand. Moments later, Raymond de Guise and Alix Monet entered the reception hall's glittering light.

'She had the unmistakeable look of a Brogan about her,' Hélène remarked.

'It's like we always said,' smiled Raymond. 'The Buckingham's a *family*. No doubt we'll have half a dozen Brogans here before the war ends.' He paused. 'Good night, ladies. I think we might just about be ready for Saturday – whether the King walks through these doors or not.'

Raymond watched as Hélène and Alix sailed towards the golden elevator. They were bound for the Candlelight Club to take part in the evening's last drinks – Hélène was staying in one of the staff suites, just as in days of old – but Raymond had declined to join them. Though he'd managed to keep his thoughts about home at bay while they danced, the moment the music ended the fears surged up in him again. There wasn't a moment to lose.

Out on Berkeley Square, the taxicabs were waiting. Navigating the blackout was not easy, but in the snowbound city there was still light enough to drive. For the first time that night, true exhaustion weighed down upon him – but images of Nancy and Arthur, Vivienne and Stan sliced across him, driving all weariness away.

He was just bowing into the taxicab, instructing the driver to Maida Vale, when he became aware that a dark figure was lurking in the shadows of Michaelmas Mews. Raymond lingered by the open taxi door, trying to make out the angular figure in the alley.

Moonlight scudded over the Buckingham Hotel, revealing none other than Billy Brogan by the refuse chute at the mouth of the alley. Raymond had seen Billy unnerved before – they'd stood together on the beaches at Dunkirk, wondering if this was where their life stories came to an end – but he'd never seen him looking quite as impatient, nor as disgruntled, as he did tonight. It was almost as if he was waiting for somebody, thought Raymond.

Their eyes met.

Billy raised his hand in greeting, then slunk backwards into the darkness of the mews.

'Are you ready, sir?' came the voice of the cab driver.

Raymond slid inside, then heaved the door shut.

'As quickly as you can, please.'

'I'll do my best, Mr de Guise. Want to get home for the little one, do you?'

'Indeed,' Raymond replied, hoping his laughter buried his rising nerves. 'Him, and everyone else.'

Chapter Thirteen

Midnight in Maida Vale: above the rooftops, silver starlight spilt across a dark figure stalking up Blomfield Road.

Raymond left the taxi at the end of the road and approached his house by foot. He wasn't sure why, but somehow it felt important – something to do with the tradecraft they'd taught him when he came home from Cairo. At the bottom of his garden, he stopped and looked up at the house. The blackout blinds were closed, betraying no light from within – but that didn't mean that the house was asleep. Perhaps Nancy was in the nursery, tending to his infant son. Perhaps Vivienne still ran around after Stan.

Or perhaps the American traitor was awake, brooding over his next move.

The gate creaked as Raymond slipped within. If the American was practised at espionage, if he suspected he was being surveilled, that might have piqued his attention. But, so far, Raymond had no reason to think it was so. By Vernon Fox's reckoning, he was just an opportunist operating under the aegis of his own warped conscience. A man like that didn't have to be dangerous – not unless he was cornered.

This was Raymond's own house. He had to approach this as naturally as he could.

All the magic of the Grand had vanished by the time he reached the front door. The thought of what was happening at home hadn't quite left him, but there'd been moments – just a few, fleeting moments – when the magic of the song, the sensation of Hélène in his arms, the memories of the dancer he'd once been, had eclipsed his fears. Now, however, he had quite forgotten the sounds, the sights, the touch of the Grand. He slipped his house-key into the lock and thought: tomorrow, I won't have to leave them alone. Tomorrow, my only duty at the Buckingham Hotel is Mr Hastings' dinner for the soldiers in the Queen Mary.

The key turned in the lock.

The door slipped open.

Immediately, he knew he wasn't alone.

The lamp in the sitting room was snuffed out – Frank was at the hotel tonight, taking his turn on the observation post – but, at the end of the hall, a low light glowed in the kitchen. Raymond hung up his overcoat, took off his shoes and stole down the hall. Of course, whoever it was knew he was here already. There was no need to creep around his own household.

But not one of the Americans lurked in his kitchen tonight. They were all upstairs, sound asleep in their beds.

It was Vivienne who stood in the kitchen, an inscrutable look on her face.

She looked at him blankly as he appeared.

'Vivienne, you startled me,' Raymond began, summoning his most genteel laughter. 'I didn't think to find you awake. I rather expected you'd had an exhausting day.'

As he was speaking, Raymond ventured to the tin sink and took a draught of water from the tap. He and his brother had forever been being told off about this as boys. 'We didn't spend our money on cups just to have you slurping from the tap!' his mother had been known to shriek. For all the airs and graces he'd developed in the ballroom world, Raymond still liked his boyhood rebellions.

'Exhausting is only half of it,' said Vivienne. She'd seemed brittle, somehow, but now she softened. 'It floored the boys. They've been asleep since six, and not a peep out of either one.'

'If that's the case, you'll have to do it more often!' Raymond caught her reflection in the sink. A distorted Vivienne looked back at him from the ridges in the draining board. She seemed to be staring at him so intently, thought Raymond. Was she cross with him? Seething, that she'd been left to entertain the Americans all day? Or ... was it possible that one of them had let something slip? That she was carrying information of her own? 'Tell me,' he said, as jovially as he could muster, 'what are our house guests *really* like?'

'Generous,' she said, 'to an absolute fault. Come with me, Raymond.' And she led him into the sitting room – where the small fir tree they'd decorated the weekend before was now the host to two fat presents wrapped in silver paper and ribbon. 'Ellsworth and Jonah took themselves off to Hamley's. They wouldn't take no for an answer. McCord had errands to run, but the others trekked around all day, picking up things for Christmas. Beeswax candles from Beagles. Chocolates, Raymond – actual chocolates – from a place on the Strand.'

'It sounds like you marched around most of London!'

Then Vivienne said, 'Oh, not me. The boys did, but I was happy being left behind. We found a little place by the Westminster Pier for some sandwiches. You know, just opposite St Thomas's Hospital.'

Raymond paused. His thoughts fractured. His mind whirled. *St Thomas's Hospital.* Was this just paranoia? Was it just his natural suspicion bubbling to the surface? Or was there something pointed about the way she had said it?

How many other, more natural ways were there to describe that café, without picturing the hulk of the hospital looming over the river?

The silence had gone on too long.

Raymond waded directly into it, without thinking again. 'McCord went off on his own, running errands today? Did he say what for?'

Vivienne just shrugged. 'Embassy business, I should think.' And she tapped the side of her nose, as if to suggest he was doing something secretive, into which mere civilians had no right to intrude. 'It was nice in the café, but I couldn't help thinking – that hospital, it's where so many of the wounded end up, isn't it? If they make it back from the front? St Thomas's has whole wards devoted to them.'

She seemed to be searching his face, searching his eyes, searching his soul for some sign. Raymond just looked at her blankly, urging her on.

'Aren't you due a hospital visit soon, Raymond? You've been home nearly a year. They can't have forgotten about their veterans already?'

Raymond clasped her hand, summoning his warmest smile. 'I'm coping, Vivienne. I just,' and he shrugged softly, 'don't like speaking of it. It worries Nancy. She's got enough to worry about.' His eyes drifted upward, through the ceiling tiles, to where his sleeping wife lay. 'Good night, Vivienne. I promise I'll be more use around here tomorrow.'

Raymond turned from her, with a gentle caress of the hand, and breathed a deep sigh of relief as he reached the hallway. He'd known he was coming back to a house riven with tension; he just hadn't expected to get it from his sister-in-law as well.

Then Vivienne's whispered voice rang out, and Raymond stopped dead.

'Raymond, have you ever heard from Maynard Charles since he left the Buckingham Hotel?'

Raymond looked over his shoulder. 'What did you say?'

Vivienne's eyes opened fractionally.

A look like realisation coursed across her.

Then Raymond realised too: by rights, he oughtn't to have heard her whispered voice while his back was turned.

He took a step toward her.

'Now, Vivienne,' he began, all pretence melting away.

'I knew it,' she whispered. 'Raymond de Guise, I *knew* it. I think I've known it all along. Or some part of me has. You're...'

Raymond marched towards her purposefully. Perhaps she thought he was going to close his hand around her mouth, for she staggered backwards into the sitting room. Then she remembered who she was, and slammed the flat of her palm against his chest.

'You're a terrible liar, Raymond. But I didn't know for sure, not until this morning – not until you left the telephone hanging, after you called the King James ward. Maynard Charles works for the government now, doesn't he? Why else would he have a military guard, lying in his hospital bed? And I know for sure he hasn't come back from fighting at the front. Not a man of his age. Not a man in his condition. He isn't fit to be a general.' Raymond could see her joining the dots, leaping to conclusions, *knowing* she was right. 'And if he isn't waging the war out there on the battlefield, that means he's waging the war right here in London. *That* means he's in military intelligence.' She gripped him hard, stared into his dark, deceitful eyes. 'Which can only mean *you're* in military intelligence too.'

Raymond flashed a look back into the hallway, fearful of her voice being heard up above.

'Did that accident in the convoy even happen, Raymond, or was it all just *lies*? Are you injured at all, or is it all just a story? They brought you home to work for Maynard Charles. To put you back in that hotel and spy on the guests. It's true, isn't it? I'm right?'

Raymond had held his silence too long. The gears of his mind were thrashing, but in his gut he knew it was already too late. 'Keep your voice down, Vivienne,' he said, his voice verging on a growl. 'The Americans will hear.'

'The Americans?' Vivienne baulked. 'Don't you mean Nancy? Aren't you worried about what happens when Nancy finds out you've been lying all along...' She stopped. Her face paled – and, at once, Raymond realised he'd let yet another secret slip. 'Raymond, what's going on? What's this got to do with the Americans?'

Raymond took her by the wrist. 'We can't talk here,' he whispered, and bundled her bodily into the hall, past the darkened well of the stairs and across the kitchen. Moments later, the lights were snuffed, the back door was open, and Raymond was frogmarching Vivienne across the garden to the Anderson shelter half buried at its bottom.

Inside the frigid tin shell, he lit the storm lantern, illuminating the cramped interior where his family had spent so many nights cowering from the bombs.

'Well go on,' said Vivienne at last, 'tell me I've got it wrong. Tell me I've lost my mind.'

'You haven't lost your mind, but you'll lose your head if you can't keep a secret. You'll lose mine too. Vivienne, this isn't a game.'

Where to begin? The summons in Cairo, that seemed so long ago? The moment, only yesterday afternoon, when everything had changed?

Vivienne's face was wide open with expectation.

Her eyes weren't just asking. They were *demanding* to know.

So he did the only thing he could think of.

He said, 'I've sworn to such secrecy that I'm sure even saying this makes me a traitor. But we've got real traitors to deal with, Vivienne. Real flesh and blood traitors, trying to sell the country from under our feet.'

Then he told her it all.

About his duties in the ballroom. How they'd concocted a story for him, to bring him home from war. How he reported to Maynard Charles, and how Maynard Charles was now fighting for his life – but how, just before the gunman found him, he'd commissioned Raymond with a quite specific task.

'One of them's a danger, Vivienne. Ellsworth, Jonah or McCord – I don't know which. But one of them holds a secret, and he plans to trade it to the enemy. I can't tell you what. I scarcely know myself. I don't believe he's acting out of wickedness. I don't even believe he wants the enemy to win. He's trapped himself in some twisted logic, and decided this is for the greater good. But…'

Vivienne's anger had melted away. Now she looked pale. Raymond was not without sympathy for her. He'd just told her there was a traitor only a wall's breadth away from her sleeping son. Vivienne knew there was a war being fought; she just never expected to discover it under her own roof.

'You're going to have to keep my secret, Vivienne. It isn't just for me. It's for King and Country. It's for everything that's holy and good.'

'Are we in danger, Raymond?'

Raymond was silent. 'Vivienne, I honestly don't know. Do you take any of them as violent men? I don't. But I've seen things you haven't. Vivienne, I've killed men.' Raymond looked at his hands. The same ones that had just taken Hélène Marchmont in hold, had wielded the Bren gun that cut through the enemy at Tobruk. 'I don't know what a man like that could do if he's exposed.'

'Raymond, the children…'

He grabbed her hand. 'I know. They're my children too. My family.'

'You have to tell Nancy.'

Raymond tensed. 'I'll do no such thing, and neither will you. Don't you see? A secret shared too widely always slips out. I need to get these men out of my house as quickly as possible – and without any of them ever knowing what we've done.'

'*We?*' Vivienne asked.

Raymond nodded. Suddenly it seemed so simple. 'You'll have to help me now, Vivienne. I'll be here as much as I can, but it's *you* who'll get to know them. It's you who can lure him out. You'll have to plumb their minds. Search their rooms. Search their cases, their packs if you can. You can start by finding out where Henry McCord went today. Off in the city, running errands of his own? A man might easily pass it off as Christmas shopping, but if McCord's our man then he might already have made the transaction.'

It wasn't the cold that was making Vivienne tremble now. It was the weight of everything she'd just heard.

'I've got to go to Stan,' she announced – and, before Raymond could say otherwise, she pushed past him, bursting out of the shelter into the garden.

In one of the windows above, the blackout blind trembled.

A silhouetted face peered down.

Raymond reached for Vivienne and drew her near.

'Vivienne, promise me.'

Up above, the figure shifted, watching the ballet being played out on the snow-shrouded lawn. A tiny cigarillo light flared – and, if either Vivienne or Raymond had cared to look up, they would have seen the face of Ellsworth March flickering, for just a second, in the fiery glow.

'This isn't about us,' Raymond said. 'It's about the war. It could change the course of things.'

'I won't have him in harm's way.'

Raymond shuddered, 'You *have* to. The country's counting on it. Counting on *us*. And the sooner we get it done, the sooner we lure him out and make a report, the sooner it can be over. Do you hear me, Vivienne? You *have* to hear me – because there's no other way.'

Her eyes had grown full with tears. Whether they were tears of terror, or just the release of some wild, pent-up emotion, Raymond could not say. 'Let's get in from the cold,' he whispered. 'I'm with you, Vivienne. I'm with you all of the way. I'm just ... so sorry. I should have handled it better. You never needed to know what danger we're in.'

He folded his arms around her, pinning her in – as if, by doing so, he might bind them in the secret.

Up above, Ellsworth March saw Raymond's arms locked around Vivienne, and inwardly he sighed. 'Go into a family home for Christmas,' they'd told him. 'Experience Christmas at the hearth of a good old English family.' But what they'd failed to say was that all families had their secrets – and here was one, right now, as the man of the house cradled his sister-in-law in the garden at midnight, while behind the blackout blinds his wife slept soundly on.

A family man and his brother's widow ...

Ellsworth snorted, in disappointment as much as disdain.

In the garden, Raymond looked up.

But Ellsworth March had already retreated into the bed-chamber, his cigarillo light snuffed out at last.

Raymond's heart was beating madly as he led Vivienne back inside.

But it beat more fiercely yet when he took off his clothes, donned his nightshirt and slipped into bed beside Nancy.

She stirred, rolled against him and purred into his ear, 'You're cold, Raymond. Let me warm you.'

No number of kisses, no amount of cuddling, would warm him tonight.

He held her until she slept in his arms, and listened to the seconds flickering past in the carriage clock out in the hall.

Day Three:

Friday, 18 December 1942

Chapter Fourteen

Dawn had not yet broken when Billy Brogan left his childhood bedroom and stole along the empty hallway at No 62 Albert Yard. Some moments later, having swaddled himself in his old army greatcoat, he was tramping out into the snow. The little grocery van he kept for deliveries was sitting under a tarpaulin by the construction works at the bottom of the yard. Billy cranked it to life, then sat shivering inside while the engine warmed him through. His mind had been fizzing all night. To be left standing alone and empty-handed in Michaelmas Mews was humiliation, but it wasn't defeat. Annie might have forgotten what promises meant to the Brogans, but Billy had not.

The snow had fallen in great drifts through the night, so it took some time for Billy to guide the grocery van to the corner of Knightsbridge and Lowndes Square, where the Imperial Hotel sat waiting. Still, he was certain he'd made good time. The doormen had not yet changed shift, and the blackouts were still in place in the hotel windows, making it look sorrowful, almost abandoned. At least the Buckingham Hotel still looked resplendent and *royal* in shadow. Looking at it now, Billy was quite certain the King's party would not choose this place over the Buckingham by the time tomorrow night came.

Tomorrow...

In little more than a day, society would convene to celebrate the season. The Grand Ballroom would become the very centre of London's social firmament – while, in all the hidden corners of the hotel, the chambermaids, concierges, porters and pages would convene for spectacular shindigs of their own. Billy had never been the sort of boy who relished a party, but of late he had started wondering if he might acquire the taste. If he had that goose in his hands, of course, there'd be something to celebrate.

He didn't have to wait long.

Within half an hour of him arriving, the Imperial's day workers – those who weren't quartered on site – started arriving at the hotel. There among them, kicking through the deep piles of snow, was Victor.

Billy watched him approaching in the wing mirror of his van. He was just a shambling silhouette, but Billy would recognise that gait anywhere. It was, he decided, the gait of a guilty man.

The moment Victor drew alongside the grocery van, Billy opened the door, directly into his path.

Then he stepped out to meet him.

'Don't look so startled, Victor,' said Billy, when the boy reeled back – apparently thinking he was about to be robbed. 'We're pals, aren't we? I just want a talk. A quiet word, for old time's sake?' When Victor said nothing, Billy added, 'You've upset my sister. I think you ought to know. I've seen Annie emotional before, but not like this. She thinks she's lost you.'

Having debated it for little more than a second, Victor shouldered past Billy and said, 'Stuff a sock in it, Billy. I've got to get to work.'

'Well, that's what I wanted to talk about,' Billy called after him.

Victor just shambled on, until at last Billy called out, 'You're forgetting, Victor. We work *together*. You can throw away your position at the Buckingham Hotel if you like – seems a strange thing to do, to walk out on the Buckingham for a dump like this, but that's your *prerogative*. But you can't just walk out on me. That's not fair. That's not right. We're meant to be friends.'

'Stuff another sock in it, Bill. Your mouth's too big for just one.'

'I reckon your new employer probably wants a reference, do they?'

Victor seemed to have had every intention of just marching on and pretending Billy didn't exist, but at this he turned round, marched directly up to Billy and prodded him firmly in the breast. 'You used to be a decent sort. You used to have some charm about you. Everybody liked Billy Brogan, didn't they?'

'Everybody still does,' Billy said, straightening the folds of his coat – and pretending Victor didn't just do something as inconceivable as *poke* him. 'As a matter of fact, there's plenty more families who like me now than ever did before. It just so happens that not many of them know my name.'

'Yeah,' said Victor. 'So nobody lets it slip, and you wind up in a prison cell.'

'See, that's what we've got to talk about, Victor. People letting things slip.'

Victor softened. Now, at last, he thought he understood the purpose of Billy's visit. 'You don't need to spell it out, Billy. I'm not going to go around blabbering about what you get up to. It's none of my business. Not anymore.'

And Billy smiled as he said, 'Yes it is.'

Victor stared, dumbly.

'Get in the van, Victor. Let's just have a chat.'

As Victor relented, sliding into the passenger seat, Billy stopped to gather his thoughts. The truth was, he'd never enjoyed strongarming Victor and Annie into helping in his enterprise. The deeper truth was, he'd never properly understood why they were so reluctant to help.

He climbed into the van alongside Victor and said, 'I don't want to cause trouble for you, Victor. I've been treating you like family for so long now – and, as a matter of fact, I hope one day you'll do the noble thing and make it proper. Annie would be the one taking your name, of course, but we can all live with that. You'd be a Brogan in spirit, and that's what matters.' He paused. 'But, if you're family, then you've got to start acting like it. And walking out like that – it just isn't right.'

'You're talking horseshit, Billy. You're trying to run me in circles. Well, it isn't going to work.'

'The Buckingham needs you. Poor old Henri Laurent can't just click his fingers and replace you, not in time for the next service. It isn't just me you're letting down. You're letting down the Queen Mary. You're letting down Annie. And, more than that, Victor, you're letting down yourself. You don't really think the Imperial Hotel's home for a lifetime, do you? They've just hoiked you out of the Buckingham as part of this game they play. The Buckingham's where your heart is. The Buckingham's where your bread's best buttered. So here's what you're going to do. You're going to turn up for shift today, at the Buckingham Hotel, as if nothing ever happened. M. Laurent's going to play hell with you, but you're going to feed him a sob story. Tell him something about your mother. He'll grizzle at you, of course. He'll call you a blackguard and a crook. But he won't be able to turn you away – not now, not with Christmas coming. By tonight's dinner service, you'll have won back his trust. And then, Victor, *then* we can get on with the job at hand. We can keep on helping out those folks through our deliveries.' Billy's voice darkened. 'And Victor, you can get me my goose.'

Throughout it all, Victor had been listening with mounting surprise. Now, at last, he spluttered, 'Are you pulling my leg, Billy? I'm not going back to the Buckingham Hotel. I'm sorry Annie's upset – but, if she knows what's good for her, she'll be here by the New Year as well.' Victor reached for the door handle, but paused before erupting back onto Knightsbridge. 'I don't care if the Imperial's just using me to rile up the Buckingham Hotel. I'm using them as well. You know, Billy, you've been saying you're bending the rules, pillaging the hotel to help people, for such a long time that I truly think you believe it. And maybe it was so, back at the beginning. Maybe you really did feel it. But...' Victor thrust the door open. '...somewhere along the way, you lost sight of it. It isn't just this silly goose. Something got dislodged, inside your mind. You started out seeing what good you could do, if you just broke a few little rules. But you've ended up breaking the rules just for the *fun* of it. By God, Billy, a *goose*.'

Victor meant to slam the door behind him as he clambered out, but Billy was fast. He tumbled after Victor, into the snow. 'We've been through it a hundred times. There's families with empty bellies all across London, while they gorge on foie gras at the Buckingham Hotel. I'm not the one who rigged the system, Victor. I'm the one who sees it for what it really is. There are people, *real* people like my ma and yours, grubbing around from day to day – while lords and ladies think nothing of their Christmas goose.'

But Victor was impervious to Billy's words. He'd heard them too often. For a fleeting moment he felt guilt – Billy was a veteran of Dunkirk – but it was easy enough to rid himself of the feeling. All he had to do was think of Annie. 'You know, of all the scurrilous things you've done, the worst is what you've done to her. When I met Annie, she was like … like sunshine. Sunshine on a windy day! Bright and breezy, and wonderful and chaotic and …' Victor took a breath. 'Now she's none of that. Now she's anxious and afraid. Looking over her shoulder all of the time. Forever wondering if she's got a good heart or bad – plagued, Billy, *plagued* by it, because the truth is, she knows what we're doing is wrong; she just can't admit it. You want to know why?'

'I'm sure you're about to tell me, up on that high horse of yours.'

Victor faced Billy through the veil of swirling snow. 'Because if she said it out loud, for even a second, it would mean admitting that the brother she loves, more than anyone else in the world, is a downright villain.'

There was enough power in Victor's words to silence Billy.

He loved Annie too.

He'd looked after her all of their lives, hadn't he?

He was looking after her still.

She just couldn't see it.

'If you're not going to come back to the Buckingham Hotel, Victor, you know what you'll have to do.'

Victor just marched on.

'You'll just have to get me a goose from here instead.'

Victor turned over his shoulder. 'It's too late, you damn fool. The geese are already hanging. I can no more fudge the order book here than I could at the Queen Mary. You want a goose, Billy, go out into one of the Royal Parks, look over your shoulder to make sure no warden's watching, and strangle one.'

Billy reached for his arm. 'Victor. You *know* me. Remember what I said about references? I'll tell the head chef in here. I'll tell him what you've been doing in the Queen Mary kitchens.

Then you'll be out on your ear, and no job at all. How's your ma going to get through Christmas like that?'

Victor just shook him off. 'You do that, Billy, and I'll have no reason not to rat on you as well.'

But Billy just said, 'And bring Annie into it? Have her disgraced as well? Don't you love her, Victor?'

Victor barely wasted a breath before he said, 'I do – and, Lord help me, I believe you do as well. You've betrayed your sister, Billy, but there's some part of you wouldn't land her in handcuffs for all the trouble you've caused.' He shook his head. 'So I reckon neither one of us is going to rat on the other. And I reckon neither one of us is going to do what the other one wants. We're finished here, Billy.'

Billy stood bereft in the snow.

Victor just smiled and turned to walk away.

Then he stopped, for a thought had just popped into his head, one it was impossible to ignore.

'I want you to leave Annie out of this now, Billy. We understand each other, don't we? They can hang you for all I care, but I want the old Annie back.'

Billy wrestled with it. 'I need help, Victor. If you're not coming back, Annie's all I've got.'

'What if I could make you a trade?'

Billy muttered, 'Go on.'

'Tomorrow afternoon, right before the ball...' Victor tipped his chin at the Imperial Hotel. 'The Continental Kitchen's putting on dinner for the Orchestra, right there in the ballroom. All the dancers, all the musicians, they're to be seated at a long table to toast the night ahead. It's something of a tradition in these parts.' He stopped. 'There's goose on that menu.'

Billy closed the gap between them, but Victor lifted a hand, ordering him to stop.

'Taking a goose off some guest's plate – well, I can't see how it would be done. But taking a goose off the Orchestra's own menu? Carving up one too few and squirrelling the other away? Well, I reckon *that* could be done. Throw on a few more lamb cutlets for them. Once they're in their spirits, nobody's going to care.' Victor paused. 'Of course, it doesn't come without risk. So I'd want something in return. I'd want Annie, out of your shadow. And Billy, I'd want those ledgerbooks you keep. It's a damn silly thing, keeping records like that. I want them shredded and burnt, right in front of my eyes. At the end of the day, you'll be chomping on goose – and me and Annie, we'd be clean, to start again.' Again, he paused; Billy's eyes seemed to be darting, as if trying to comprehend. 'That's a deal, isn't it, Brogan? A goose for my future? A goose for Annie's life?'

Billy said nothing.

His fingers flickered, as if he might reach out to shake Victor's hand, but then he was rigid again.

'Think on it, Bill,' said Victor. 'But you best let me know what you want by tomorrow morning – or it'll already be too late.'

There was a moment in which both young men's stances softened; a moment in which, to any passerby, they might have looked like the close confidants, genuine friends, that they used to be.

Before he turned to go, Victor added, 'You know, Billy, you ought to think about a fresh start as well. You've got away with it this long. You won't get away with it forever. Maybe it's time. Maybe you've done your bit. The tides are turning in this war. It isn't going to last forever. Maybe you ought to start thinking about where you want to be at the end of all this – on the up, at the Buckingham Hotel . . . or rotting away at Pentonville prison? All for the sake of a blinkin' goose?'

Billy stood there dumbly as Victor marched away.

All the memories of his young life rushed past.

Victor was right in one thing and one thing alone: Billy never wanted Annie to get into trouble. She was still his sister. A thorn in his side she might have been, but she was still a Brogan.

And Brogans deserved the best.

They didn't deserve to be grubbing around in the gutter, one generation after the next.

Brogans were every bit as good as the lords and ladies of the Buckingham Hotel.

No, damn it, they were *better* – because they'd had to work for every penny they had.

Didn't they deserve their goose?

With Victor's offer still ringing in his ears, Billy tramped back to the grocery van and started the engine.

He didn't know why, but tears were prickling in his eyes as he started to drive.

Chapter Fifteen

John Hastings had grown accustomed to getting very little sleep. He prided himself on being a punctual, efficient man, an excellent judge of character – and an even more excellent judge of opportunity. But one year ago, he had made a catastrophic misjudgement: not until he'd been in post did he properly appreciate that being the director of the Buckingham Hotel was about so much more than finances and staffing, profit and loss. All of the problems of his previous business career could be solved mathematically. But the challenges of the Buckingham Hotel relied on charm, wit and reputation.

It had been a long year, filled with hard lessons.

This morning, another one was hoving into view.

Hastings had barely been in his office ten minutes when his personal secretary appeared, bringing his morning pot of coffee. It had caused quite a stir when Mr Hastings became director and eschewed the traditional morning tea for a pot of coffee – for was ever a symbol more potent than American coffee usurping good old British tea? Along with the coffee, his secretary had brought a selection of the morning newspapers, the night manager's briefing on events of the previous twelve hours and a single ivory envelope, sealed in red wax.

Upon seeing it, Hastings stalled.

His secretary was running through the affairs of the day – first, a breakfast with the Earl of Harrowby and his wife, the patrons of the Ethelred Suite; next, a meeting with the contractors due to begin work on upgrading the hotel's air raid shelters; later, dinner in the Queen Mary with the Hotel Board and their Home Away From Home guests – but Hastings hardly noticed, for his eyes were lingering on the letter.

'Hand delivered, no doubt?'

'I believe so, sir,' said his secretary.

'By the Palace equerry?'

The secretary nodded. 'I'll leave you to your deliberations, sir. You've an hour until the Earl of Harrowby.'

The John Hastings of old would have ripped the letter open in a second. Men of finance did not fear the unknown; to them, if one trade floundered, there was always another to be made. But it was different at the Buckingham Hotel. Here, it was *story* that mattered. Was the Buckingham Hotel still the playground of the rich and royal? Or, in the hunt for American money, had it sacrificed something of its old-world lustre, its princely charm?

The answer was surely in this envelope.

He looked at the royal seal.

This was the missive he'd been waiting on for weeks.

The single word that would make, or break, his Winter Ball.

He was about to open it when a knock came at the door.

'One moment,' he announced.

He slid his finger into the lip of the envelope, breaking its seal.

John Hastings was not given to prayer – but, had he not been alone in this moment, he would have been observed whispering a petition to God up above. Right now, it felt as if the message in this envelope was about so much more than the Winter Ball. It felt like a judgement on his directorship itself.

Every business instinct he'd developed had told him he was right to hunt American money. After Pearl Harbour so much of it had flooded into London that every Hotel Director in the city had made it his mission – and John Hastings liked to *win*. He'd hired a fêted American bandleader, even instructed M. Laurent to tailor the Queen Mary's menu to cater for American tastes (their steak and eggs at the breakfast service was simply *divine*). But the other members of the Hotel Board, British industrialists with deep-seated connections to the English gentry had made their doubts perfectly clear. They didn't hold the shares to sway him from his mission, but at innumerable meetings, their voices had been raised as one: the Buckingham was a British institution; it was the proud bearer of a Royal Warrant; its connection to all that was good and grand about Great Britain ought not to be squandered for cheap, short-term gain.

Old money mattered more than new...

The knock came at the door again.

Again, John Hastings called out, 'One moment!' this time with a little more force than the last.

He'd known he was nervous; he just hadn't known he was quite as nervous as this.

He wasn't the only one chasing American money, was he? The Imperial Hotel had hired Nelson Allgood – their wild American star. Yes, their bandleader was a Scotsman and had performed for the King on more than one occasion – but how much did that count? Where did a businessman draw the line between profits and reputation?

For a third time, knuckles rapped on the door.

The letter was trembling in John Hastings' hands. With a start, he thrust it into one of his open desk drawers, slammed it shut and called out, 'Come in.'

The office door opened, and in tramped Monsieur Henri Laurent.

Laurent was a big man. A veteran of Parisian kitchens since he was a boy, he was thick-set, brawny, with a ruddy face and hands as big as hams. A storybook ogre, his underlings in the kitchen often said – yet none could utter a word of complaint against the delicacies those enormous hands concocted, nor the sheer inventiveness and imagination that had conjured up the Queen Mary's delectable menus, even during the blockades.

Most men presented themselves to the Hotel Director at their smartest, but Laurent was wearing his kitchen whites and apron. Nobody in the Buckingham Hotel questioned the personal grooming of a man with talents like his.

'M. Laurent, I wasn't expecting you.'

'No sir,' Laurent grunted, 'and please take no offence when I say: I should rather be any other place than here. I should much rather be in my kitchen, envisioning the day. But we need to talk.'

Hastings' thoughts flashed back to that letter in the drawer. Laurent was wise enough not to have given it voice, but he was certainly one of the heads of department who disliked the hotel's focus on American money. Laurent had done precisely as he was asked, reorienting the Queen Mary menus to American tastes, but it had been done under some duress.

As Laurent stared at him, Hastings found his mind flitting back to the soldiers they were hosting in the Queen Mary tonight. Yes, he thought, they did seem to be enjoying the old-world splendour of the hotel. As a matter of fact, they'd seemed rather overwhelmed by the magnificence of the Grand. Few places in the Americas compared; it was a shame they wouldn't see the grandeur and flair of Saturday night. Yet how was he to invite them to the very same event at which the King and his retinue might appear? Were paupers really to dance with princes at the Buckingham Hotel?

'Talk about what, M. Laurent?' he asked. Laurent might have been demanding his attention, but the letter seemed to be calling out to him, whispering of all its promise and potential. It was almost as if he could hear it fluttering around, trapped in the darkness of the drawer.

'It's my kitchen, Mr Hastings. I'm two men down in less than a week. It just won't do.'

Hastings drew a breath. 'Two, M. Laurent?'

'The potboy last weekend, and my kitchen hand Victor just yesterday. He's nothing special, sir, but it's not special I need – it's dependability, and that grunt had it in spades. But yesterday he just marched in, grovelled around for a few moments, and handed me a letter. It's those dogs at the Imperial, sir. Undermining us at every opportunity! Kitchen boys come and go. Some of them can stand the heat and some of them can't, and you have to make peace with that. But I can't tolerate it so close to Christmas. You wouldn't put up with the Grand being two dancers down. You wouldn't let the Orchestra lose two trumpeters. But as for my kitchen?'

Hastings nodded. 'I take your point, M. Laurent.'

'I'm not sure you do. Last night's service was on a knife's edge. We've got the Board in tonight, and all the heads of department – we're meant to put on a show for those infantrymen. Then, tomorrow night, it's all the great and good of London, to dine before the Winter Ball. And sir, all of this is before I've even broached Christmas Eve. Before I've even dreamt about Christmas Day.'

Hastings felt fresh fire in his belly. The tactics of the Imperial Hotel were, indeed, deplorable – but he had known backstabbing just as bad in the business world. 'I'll hire you new staff. We'll get the word out.'

'Getting the word out isn't going to help, sir. This isn't happening next week. It's happening right now. I need staff by the lunchtime service. If I don't have them by dinner...'

'What would you have me do, M. Laurent?'

The letter had started fluttering again, cavorting around inside the drawer.

'Drag me some underlings from somewhere else in the hotel. Damn it, a chambermaid would do. I don't need them talented at anything other than scrubbing pots and mopping floors. I'll promote one of my potboys for chopping and kneading – but somebody will have to do the jobs he leaves behind. Somebody who can stand the heat. It's all hands on deck, sir. I need your help.'

Hastings reached across the table to shake Laurent's hand.

'I'll make you a promise, Monsieur. You'll have your extra hands by the end of the breakfast service – or I'll come and scrub plates myself.'

Laurent had been ready to argue further, but at this he simply muttered beneath his breath and retreated to the door. 'Thank you, sir,' he said as he departed.

The moment he was gone, Hastings opened the drawer. There lay the letter, staring up at him, as if begging him to reach down. He supposed he'd have to deal with Laurent's problem soon, but a few minutes wouldn't hurt. A few minutes in which he'd learn his fate.

He peeled back the seal and slipped out the letter.

His eyes took it in.

A whole year had been spent building to this moment. Every wager he'd placed on the fate of the Buckingham Hotel, every gamble he'd made with its reputation, was about to be revealed.

For some time he sat in silence, absorbing every word.

Then, primly folding the letter and slipping it back inside its envelope, he reached for the telephone sitting on his desk and lifted the receiver.

'It's John Hastings here,' he announced to the attendant on the other line. 'I need you to place me an outside call.'

'Yes sir,' buzzed a voice in return. 'To whom are we calling?'

Hastings took a breath. 'Get me Raymond de Guise, and make it quick.'

Chapter Sixteen

It would be wrong to say that Vivienne woke early that morning.

In truth, she hadn't slept a wink.

Now, as the pale light of dawn spilt over the snowscape of Maida Vale, she peeled back the blackout blinds of her bedroom and begged the day not to arrive. In the bed behind her, Stan kicked and grizzled and she silently pleaded with him to sleep on. In the sleeping world, none of this existed. The Americans were good men, beyond intrigue, beyond suspicion. Here, in the waking world, everything felt amiss.

At least there were a few blessed moments of silence before the day properly began. She'd wondered, yesterday, if having the Americans here was a godsend; wandering along Regent Street, listening to the hubbub of American voices, it had felt as if the world was sending her a signal, telling her not to forget from whence she came. Yet now everything felt corrupted. She didn't know how she was going to face them this morning. Raymond was a gifted liar – but it had been many years since Vivienne had practised that particular skill. At least Raymond would be here, for a while.

Stan opened his eyes.

It was time to face the day.

Downstairs, she lit the fire in the grate, set water boiling for the morning tea, brought out the oats she'd been soaking overnight and set about making porridge. The ordinary rhythms of the day calmed her.

But then she heard footsteps on the stairs, and almost jumped out of her skin when a figure appeared suddenly in the kitchen.

Nancy was already dressed. She looked at Vivienne curiously as she caught her breath.

'You look like you've seen a ghost,' Nancy grinned, tousling Stan's hair.

Vivienne faltered before she spoke – because now the lying had to begin. 'It was a rotten night, Nancy. This one kept me awake all hours.'

Stan's face darkened. If even he seemed to know when a lie was being told, what hope did Vivienne have against the Americans?

'Vivienne,' Nancy ventured, 'you really don't look well.' Then she sashayed over, lifting the back of her hand as if to feel for a fever on Vivienne's brow. 'You're white as snow. You've caught a chill, I shouldn't wonder, out all day yesterday.'

Vivienne reeled back from Nancy's touch, and was about to put up a protest, when – another godsend? – the telephone started ringing out in the hall.

Nancy froze. 'At this time of day?'

They looked at each other: one of them bewildered, the other mortified beyond measure. 'I'll go,' Vivienne said, and hurried past, grateful for the excuse to escape Nancy's scrutiny.

As she bustled down the hall, it occurred to her that this could only be the ward sister at St Thomas's, to tell Raymond that Maynard Charles had died. The thought chilled her as she reached for the receiver. She had to stop the infernal trembling of that hand. She wasn't some damsel in distress; she was

Vivienne Cohen, a woman unbowed. She'd have to find some steel soon.

She picked up the receiver.

But it wasn't the ward sister at all.

It was the telephone exchange at the Buckingham Hotel.

'I have Mr Hastings for Mr de Guise,' came the voice. 'Mr John Hastings for Mr Raymond de Guise.'

'One moment please.'

Vivienne laid the receiver beside its cradle, straightened her skirts and marched to the stairs.

As luck would have it, Raymond was already stirring behind his bedroom door. Vivienne called through, then waited for the door to open.

But it wasn't Raymond's door that opened.

At the end of the hall, from the spare bedroom, Ellsworth appeared. He looked at her oddly, as if he found something to suspect in Vivienne knocking at Raymond's door. He was wearing a strange, almost sad sort of smile. 'Good morning, ma'am,' he said.

The warmth and camaraderie of yesterday's shopping expedition was gone. A part of her she couldn't deny was disappointed. Perhaps it was the idea that Ellsworth, who'd joked and laughed with her, might be under suspicion that discombobulated her the most.

She was about to stutter a reply, when Raymond revealed himself. 'It's the Buckingham Hotel, on the telephone,' Vivienne explained.

Raymond looked up and down the corridor. It seemed that he, too, had seen Ellsworth's interrogating eye. He arched an eyebrow at Vivienne; then, rather too breezily, he said, 'I'll be down directly,' and slipped back inside to change out of his robe.

Alone in the hallway, Vivienne felt herself compelled to look at Ellsworth.

'You sure are a close family here,' Ellsworth remarked, with a certain understated sadness.

Vivienne's eyes flashed back to Raymond's door. She felt sure there was some insinuation behind Ellsworth's words, but her mind was still racing. 'Breakfast's a little time away,' she murmured, hurrying back to the stairs. 'There's hot coffee and toast. We've even some eggs.'

Vivienne's heart stilled as she began cooking. She could hear Raymond out in the hall, conversing with Mr Hastings.

'You should take it easy today, Vivienne. Tell these American boys to clear out so you can take a breath. Christmas is still a week away.' Nancy was stirring the oats, but she turned and took Vivienne's hand. 'You're not our housekeeper, Viv. I've two days off after the ball, and...'

Out in the hall, Raymond put down the receiver.

His footsteps approached the kitchen.

Vivienne whipped back her hand. The way that Nancy really, truly seemed to care was like a knife in her side. How Raymond had spent a whole year repaying Nancy's kindness with lies, Vivienne would never know.

But then Raymond appeared, and the look of steel in his eyes made her remember. 'It's for King and Country,' he'd said. 'It's for everything that's holy and good.'

Fear had no place here – not today.

If what Raymond had been told was true, if one of these Americans really was carrying a secret to upend the course of this war, then wasn't it *her* duty as well? She thought of her husband Artie, buried forever in some lonely foreign field. Yes, damn it. It was time she started remembering Artie again, instead of Ellsworth's long, lingering looks. How ardently he'd marched off to sign up on the day war was declared. She remembered him regaling her, long into the night, on the beating he'd taken on Cable Street in '36, when the fascist mob had marched against the barricades that he, and people just like him, had thrown up in their path. Artie had had his run-ins with the law – he'd bent the rules so much that they very often broke – but he'd always known how to stand up to a bully. He'd always wanted to do his bit.

Well, perhaps Vivienne would too.

'I'm OK, Nancy,' she said, as Raymond strode across the kitchen. 'As a matter of fact, I'm looking forward to spending some time with our guests. I thought Raymond and I might really get to know them this morning. Isn't that so, Raymond?'

Raymond stared at her, the merest of twitches in his eye.

'I'm afraid not, Vivienne,' he began. 'Mr Hastings has asked me to the hotel. He says it's quite urgent.'

Vivienne's face blanched. Through a tightly clenched jaw she said, 'But Raymond—'

'Nance, we can go together.'

If Nancy perceived something was wrong, she paid it no mind. Vivienne watched her take one last bite of the toast she'd been eating, then hurry out to the hatstand in the hall.

'Raymond, you promised,' Vivienne began.

Raymond's face contorted. 'Keep your voice down,' he said. Then he took a step closer. 'It can't be helped. I can't change it now. I can't stop the tide. Just … find out what you can. I want to know what errands McCord was running yesterday. I want to know where he went.'

'Raymond, I'm not sure I can.'

Raymond took her by the shoulders. 'It isn't about whether you can. The fact is: you *must*.' Then he bowed close to her and whispered, 'I'm sorry, Vivienne. If I can get back, I will. And if you learn anything at all, you leave a message for me at the Buckingham Hotel. Do you hear?'

Vivienne nodded.

Their eyes locked together.

And, behind them, in the kitchen door, Ellsworth appeared.

His eyes lingered on Vivienne and Raymond – and, at last, Vivienne thought she understood the insinuation of the hallway above. *You sure are a close family here.*

She stepped out of Raymond's arms, flushing red.

'Breakfast isn't quite ready,' she beamed, eyes flashing between Raymond and the American, 'but it'll be any minute soon!'

On the other side of London, among the close streets and alleys of Camden Town, Billy Brogan tried desperately to swallow his irritation as he unloaded the grocery van in front of SELLERS AND SONS, purveyors of all north London's finest off-ration goods.

Taking deliveries from Billy Brogan was often fraught – but today it seemed more fraught than ever. Today, as he watched Billy lifting crates out of his van, he didn't only have the ordinary illegality of life to contend with. He had Billy Brogan's ire as well.

'It's like they just can't *see*, Mr Sellers. It's almost like they *want* to be blind. If you sat them down and said, "Don't you know, there's hungry people in London?," they'd all nod along and yap. *Of course we know.* That's what they'd say. *Do you take us for fools?* But the second you try and do anything about it, they look at you like you've got a devil sitting on your shoulder, whispering in your ear.' Billy heaved off a tray filled with sugar cubes, courtesy of the Buckingham Hotel. 'These people are meant to be my friends. You'd think you could count on your own damn friends.'

Mr Sellers didn't mind listening to Billy's ranting. The boy gave him good prices, and Mr Sellers liked him for that. Of course, there'd been a time when Billy's prices were non-existent – so perhaps these friends of his had a point. Somewhere along the way, altruism had surely given way to avarice in Billy's heart.

'You don't need a goose for Christmas dinner, Billy. Who do you think you are? You work at the Buckingham Hotel. You don't *dine* there. You don't have the taste for it, lad.'

'I don't need the taste for it,' Billy spat. 'I just need the goose. All I want is a bit of thanks. I reckon I deserve that, don't you? I've been doing so much for everyone else, all so they can have a nice Christmas. Well, why can't my family have a nice Christmas too? But *nobody* thinks of that, do they? They think I do this for fun? I'm a man of the people!'

Mr Sellers said, 'Those GIs at your house, they're not expecting goose. It's turkeys they eat over there.'

'Maybe I want to show them a bit of old Brittania,' Billy groaned.

'You'd do just as good with a big Cornish hen. Roast that in a bit of goose fat, and who's going to tell the difference?'

'A Cornish hen?'

'They're nice birds, if you can get one. They'd feed a family, that's for sure.'

Billy hesitated over this idea. He paused in his unloading.

'That would be cheating, Mr Sellers,' he remarked, as he handed over the last of his crates and waited for the envelope Mr Sellers had prepared, already stuffed with his payment.

But all the way back to the Buckingham Hotel, the idea remained lodged in his brain.

A Cornish hen, drenched in goose fat, and a little white lie? Mightn't that be better than accepting Victor's terms? Better than losing Annie? Better, at the end, than losing *face*?

At the Buckingham Hotel, he threw open the post-room door, sat in his chair and slumped.

Sometimes, this enterprise was like being back in France, marching along the road to Dunkirk: enemies on the left of you; enemies on the right.

The difference was, back then, at least you could count on your friends.

In the same moment that Billy Brogan slammed the post-room door and set about sifting through the morning delivery, a taxicab wheeled round Berkeley Square, and out stepped Raymond de Guise. Moments later, he was helping Nancy out into the snow.

Raymond had been curiously quiet on the journey to the hotel. Nancy supposed it was the thought of the next two days preying on him. Funny – he'd never been nervous before. When she'd met him, in that long-ago age before the war, he'd been a colossus at the Buckingham Hotel: King of the Grand. He'd never before shown a flicker of apprehension at the thought of a ball.

It was the injury that had changed him. Nancy was sure of that. It was coming back from war, trying to slide back into the old life, but finding nothing quite the same. He so rarely talked about it – he never, ever complained – but Nancy had observed the differences in him this year. It was as if he was set apart, as if a veil existed around him. She'd long since stopped asking, but she could only imagine what it might feel like, to be dancing in the ballroom and not be able to hear the music as once you could.

She took his hand.

'A cup of tea, before my girls start appearing.'

Raymond demurred, 'I really must find Mr Hastings.'

Nancy chided him with a soulful look. 'One cup of tea won't hurt.'

But Nancy didn't have a chance to make that tea, because when she opened the door to the Housekeeping Lounge, it was to discover Mr Hastings already waiting, looking strangely downcast.

He couldn't possibly have been here for Raymond – so, as she hung up her hat, scarf and coat, she realised he must be here for her.

What was it with the men in the Buckingham Hotel this Christmas? They all seemed to have forgotten that Christmas was a time of magic and light.

'Ah, Mrs de Guise,' he began. His eyes lingered on Raymond for a moment, but he seemed to pause that particular thought, and went on, 'I'm afraid I need a little indulgence.'

'An indulgence, Mr Hastings?'

'As you know, things are not always straightforward with staffing over a Christmas period, so I'll just come out and say it: the Queen Mary is in need of help. I'd like to borrow one of your girls, from the end of the morning rota. She'll be scrubbing pots, washing plates, that kind of thing. She'd be paid her overtime, of course. I imagine you must have a girl who'd like a little extra in her pay packet, the week before Christmas?'

Nancy marched into the office at the end of the lounge, consulted the rota up on the wall, then craned back out and said, 'I'll put the word out at breakfast, Mr Hastings. My girls are rather run off their feet – but I've some hard workers here.'

Hastings nodded. 'Well then, to business,' and he pivoted on his heel to grasp Raymond's hand. 'A private word, Mr de Guise?'

Raymond looked at Nancy and just shrugged; that cup of tea would have to wait.

'I'll need word by 10.30,' Hastings called back, as he led Raymond away, and Nancy was left alone to face the day.

She wasn't alone for long – just about long enough to settle down with her paperwork and the first cup of tea of the day. This seemed to be some kind of natural law: the moment Nancy took her first sip, somebody would blunder into the Lounge and the day would begin. This morning it was Annie Brogan.

For a moment, Nancy remained in the quiet of her office while Annie rattled around the Lounge, laying the table for breakfast. It occurred to her that the girl must really have been trying to put on a good show – Annie was so rarely the first to appear in the morning – so, for a time, she endured the sounds of tumbling and crashing. Then, unable to bear it a second longer, she called out and waited for the startled chambermaid to appear in the office door.

'Y-yes, Mrs de Guise?'

'Annie,' Nancy said, inviting her to sit down with a second cup from the pot, 'I have an opportunity for you. A way you might make a little extra in your wages this Christmas.'

Annie started. To her ears, this seemed frighteningly like something Billy might have said. Even the tone Nancy was using was nearly the same.

'They're missing a pot washer in the Queen Mary kitchens. Mr Hastings has put out an "all hands" call, looking for a volunteer. I'm given to believe it will pay a handsome rate – if you can stand the heat of the...'

'No, Mrs de Guise!' Annie declared, suddenly rearing from the chair and spilling the tea she'd just been served. 'I – I don't want to work in the k-kitchens. I can't. No – I – I *won't*. It's not for me, Mrs de Guise. I'm a chambermaid, through and through. That's what I'm good at. Which is to say – I know I'm not *always* good at it. But I can't work in the kitchens, Mrs de

Guise. It would land me in all sorts of bother. I'm quite sure of it.' Then she turned round, curtseyed as if presenting herself to a princess and returned to the Lounge.

Nancy had grown used to Annie's skittishness over the year, but this was something new. After mopping up the tea, she took her own cup to the office door and watched the girl feverishly laying the table, scattering knives, forks and breakfast spoons as if she was haphazardly decorating a cake. There was something wrong with Annie, thought Nancy. And it occurred to her then that she really ought to have asked Mr Hastings quite *why* the Queen Mary was suddenly in need of staff – for she had a sudden inkling that perhaps the member it was missing might have gone by the name of 'Victor', the boy with whom Annie had been stepping out since summer.

Nancy was watching her still when the Lounge door opened and the other girls poured through.

She could tell, almost immediately, that they'd been up long past midnight.

Her girls weren't meant to go out dancing on nights when they were working the next morning – but Nancy had done it often enough, back when she was a chambermaid living in quarters above, so she had often turned a blind eye to it. This morning, however, she took one look at their long, drawn faces, the sallow bags under their eyes, and gritted her teeth.

'Get a good night's sleep, Rosa?' she asked, when Rosa tramped through the doors, looking more dishevelled than them all.

Across the Housekeeping Lounge, the other girls bowed their heads and tittered. Whispers ricocheted from one end of the Lounge to another.

'It was a bit sleepless, Mrs de Guise,' Rosa said, scurrying to the table.

Mary-Louise looked at Rosa and grinned.

That was when Nancy knew for sure: the girls hadn't gone out dancing at all; they'd been up there in the kitchenette, hosting a shindig – and no doubt the infantrymen had been there too.

'Rosa,' she announced, 'my office *now.*'

A dressing-down wouldn't work, thought Nancy.

It never did with Rosa – and, besides, she'd only think it was done in defence of Frank.

So today it would have to be a different punishment.

Something that really made her recognise the importance of a good night's sleep when you were working somewhere as prestigious as the Buckingham Hotel.

'Rosa,' she said, after she'd gently closed the office door, 'have you ever considered a career in the hotel kitchens?'

Chapter Seventeen

Alix Monet had lived in so many different places since she came to London that she had expected her first night at the Buckingham Hotel to feel just like any other. Yet when she woke the next morning, to pull back the blackout blinds and see Berkeley Square resplendent in fresh snow, she got an altogether different feeling. Out there, the world was falling apart – Paris was lost, perhaps never to be recovered – but sometimes, just *sometimes*, you felt like you were winning.

Not even that bouquet of flowers and the note from the Imperial Hotel upended her this morning. A day full of music and dance, performing in the demonstration dances and then the full dress rehearsal, had made her forget the ill-feeling of Nelson's note. The two cocktails she'd shared with Hélène Marchmont, and all her talk of the hotel's glory days had helped as well. High on the spirits of the season, she had gone to bed with the feeling that war was for the rest of the world; Alix Monet had been gifted a perfect Christmas, and she meant to make the most of it.

Now, as she sashayed through the hotel as it stirred – the first guests flocking to the restaurants for the breakfast service, the porters and pages and chambermaids all fanning through the hotel to stoke its engines for the day ahead – she could feel the anticipation in the air. Tomorrow night, the Grand would open its doors – perhaps, even, to the King himself. She'd known special occasions – the Paris Opera in '37 had truly opened her eyes – but never before had she sensed it rippling through a whole establishment like this. From on high to down low, the Buckingham's eyes were fixed upon Saturday night.

As she reached the reception hall, Raymond de Guise appeared from Housekeeping, walking in step with the Hotel Director. Both men inclined their heads in greeting, but they seemed locked in a sombre conversation. Whatever was troubling them, however, was not Alix's concern. She approached the Grand by the dressing-room doors, slipped into the little rehearsal studio behind and found Max Allgood already at the piano.

Max looked as if he'd been here all night. His necktie, ordinarily bunched tight around his collar, was hanging loose, and a dark stubble covered his jaw. He would have to smarten himself by tomorrow, thought Alix wryly.

The kitchens had already brought through a succession of silver breakfast trolleys. A scattering of other musicians, and several dancers, were picking over their plates, talking about the day ahead. Last night's rehearsal had gone well, but it was not without fault.

'Mr Allgood, did you not sleep?'

'I should like to play the end of our first set again, Alix. I should like to get it right.'

Max was clinging to Lucille like a distraught mother does her child.

Alix flashed a look around the room. By now, Frank Nettleton had appeared. He, too, seemed to acknowledge Mr Allgood's scattered state of mind – but, knowing better than to wade in, he hurried to the breakfast trolleys and waited for Mathilde. Last night, their tango was executed to technical perfection – but

Frank still felt as if he was missing some passionate beat; today was the very last chance to make it sublime.

'Is something wrong?' asked Alix. The way she remembered it, the song that was to finish tomorrow's first act, a composition of Max's own named 'Sentimental Man', had come together perfectly. It was a slow song at first, a song that invited curiosity, reflection and deep thought; then, just when the listeners thought they had its number, just when the dancers were settling into a slow, emotional waltz to end proceedings, it broke – like a skipping record – and turned into a riot. Within three short bars, the music transformed. If they got it right, at the moment of the song's transformation, the technicians would darken the lights in the chandeliers, and the whole atmosphere of the Grand would change. From that point on, for two riotous minutes, the Grand would feel more like a dance club than the elegant institution it was.

It was an act of daring.

A moment of drama and excitement.

And, with the show only a day away, it had started to scare Max senseless.

'I think we need to tame it. I think, perhaps, I've been carried away. It's my nephew that's doing it to me. I don't even have to see him for him to torment me. It's like he's goaded me somehow – made me push things too far. This is the Grand Ballroom.' And he seized Alix by the hand, marching her out of the rehearsal studio, across the dressing rooms and through the dance-floor doors. There it was: the cavernous interior of the Grand; the place that, in less than thirty-six hours, would dazzle and delight all the great and good of London town. 'Maybe we don't need to chase the kind of performance Nelson's doing at the Imperial. Maybe we need to remember who we are.'

As if in reply, a voice hailed him across the ballroom:

'Mr Allgood!'

Max looked up. Crossing the great empty vault of the Grand, limping through the place where so many lords and ladies would soon be standing, was the hotel postmaster, Billy Brogan. A bundle of ivory envelopes were in his hands.

'It's going to be quite an evening, Mr Allgood,' said Billy, upon handing them over.

Max took the letters. There were often missives directed to the Orchestra at the hotel – often from admirers, who might be looking to hire them for a private event (only ever undertaken with the express permission of the Hotel Board) – but Max couldn't spare a thought for them today. In fact, he might have asked Billy to retain them until after the ball, if the young man hadn't immediately started limping on to his other duties.

Billy Brogan was a curious fellow: he'd been with the hotel for so long, and in so many different guises, that Max sometimes thought he acted like he owned the place. Even with his war injury, he achieved a certain swagger as he left the Grand.

'Sometimes, M. Allgood, a little bit of the unexpected works wonders for a piece.'

'The unexpected can go awry,' said Max, still beset by nerves as he opened the first letter.

'At the Paris Opera, we called it *"Le chaos contrôlé"*.' Alix paused, searching for the right translation. 'The Controlled Chaos. Perhaps the Orchestra gets a little carried away. Perhaps everything's a tiny fraction after the beat. It's like a horse bolting under its rider. It could throw you any minute – but, after it's done, you look back and think: *I want to do that again.*'

'It's *controlling* the chaos that I'm worried about,' said Max, opening the second letter, then the third. Most of these were just the ordinary well wishes that guests sent to the Orchestra on the eve of a night as significant as this. 'We're all musicians,

Alix. We all like a little chaos. It keeps the music alive. I just worry that…'

Max opened the last letter.

His heart skipped beat.

Dear Mr Allgood:

I regret to inform you that my client, Miss Francesca May, will be unable to perform at the Grand Ballroom on Saturday 19th December.

While I understand the inconvenience this will cause, please be assured that my client was left with no other choice and deeply laments letting you and your estimable Orchestra down.

I have written separately to the Hotel Board to assure them of the return of Miss May's fee.

Yours in good health and with Christmas tidings,

Mr Brian Walsh

At first Alix didn't understand why the paper crumpled in Max's hand. She watched his face crease yet further – and only then did she dare lean in and read the letter. 'It isn't so bad, Monsieur. How many guest singers have we? Three? Four? Five?'

'Seven,' Max said, 'but that isn't the point.'

No one would ever have accused Max Allgood of being 'fire and brimstone', but he seemed to be driven by some sort of righteousness as he stomped directly across the ballroom floor and up through the marble arch.

Alix felt compelled to follow. It felt rather unseemly exiting the ballroom by the guest entrance, but the look on Max's face was more unseemly still. She was quite certain some of the guests had seen it as she hurried after him, under the boughs of the giant fir tree, and past the check-in desks. At least, in the warren of hallways behind, he wasn't to be noticed. Moments later, huffing and puffing, he had bludgeoned his way into the empty night manager's office, picked up the telephone receiver from its cradle and asked the hotel exchange to put him through to the Imperial Hotel.

'M. Allgood,' Alix ventured, 'do you think that—'

Max held up a hand, commanding silence. The act was so unusual – for a bandleader, Max had never been very 'commanding' – that Alix immediately obeyed. Then she watched curiously as Max began, 'It's Olson here. Jack Olson. Yes, my master's attending the ball on Saturday night. He's asked me to make a little enquiry.'

The expression Max was wearing made it very clear that he didn't consider this a laughing matter, but the princely English accent he was adopting was so mangled, so far-fetched, that Alix couldn't help but smirk. She had always known of Max Allgood as a virtuoso performer – but it turned out that the talents he had with the trombone were in no way matched by his talents as an actor. This character he was putting on – quite where he'd got the name 'Jack Olson' from, Alix didn't know – sounded about as English as an Eskimo.

'Yes sir,' Max went on, 'might I ask about your guest singers for the evening? My master is very particular.'

All Alix could hear was a tinny buzzing as the gentleman from the Imperial regaled Max with a list of names.

Max's hand tightened so fiercely round the telephone receiver that Alix was certain it would crumple.

He slammed it down and turned on his heel.

Alix reached for his arm – but she didn't need to ask to understand what had happened.

'She's gone to sing for them, hasn't she?'

Max reached for the office door handle.

'Monsieur?'

'It's a dirty trick,' Max seethed. 'Another dirty, cheap trick – just like those flowers he sent you. He can't play fair. He can't just throw himself into the music. He's got to set fire to things instead.' Max paused. 'He's breaking his mother's heart, and he doesn't give a damn.'

In the bitter silence that followed, Alix said, 'I think, perhaps, he is breaking another heart as well.'

'Well, that's as may be,' said Max, and flung open the door. 'But I can deal with a broken heart. I just can't deal with attacks on my Orchestra.'

Max started tramping back towards the Grand, Alix at his heels. Before they returned to the reception hall, she asked, 'What can you do about it, M. Allgood?'

'Do about it? I can't *do* anything. Nelson's the wildfire, and I've got to be the ditch the panicked villagers dig to keep it from spreading. Nelson's the battering ram, and I'm the fortress wall. Nelson's the ... the bullet, and I'm the armour.' Some of the guests lined up at check-in had heard Max snapping; when he saw them staring, he had enough sense to quieten his tone. 'I can't do a damn thing, Miss Monet. He's family.'

'Monsieur,' she ventured, 'I think you're wrong.'

'With all due respect, ma'am, you don't know what it's like. It's personal.'

'I know a little bit about war, Monsieur.'

Max felt suddenly chastened. Before they breached the Grand doors, he stopped. 'I know you do, Alix. But this ain't a war, not like that.'

'It's a war exactly like that,' Alix returned. 'One person attacks; the other defends. The first launches his salvo; the other puts up his shield. And it doesn't stop, M. Allgood – it doesn't stop until one side wins.' She sighed. 'It takes two to tango, but one alone can make a war.'

Max seemed to have calmed, but still he rocked on his heels. His fingers had started fidgeting. He needed Lucille. A few moments alone with her would calm him. The fury could come out of him in one long, uncontrolled melody.

'I left my husband in Paris,' Alix declared.

The improbability of it quelled some of Max's anger. He looked at her curiously. He'd never wondered, before, if Alix was betrothed – but then, not long ago, he hadn't known a thing about her, and since then his mind had been swamped with other things.

'Valentin wouldn't come with me when I escaped. He decided to stay.'

'And help the resistance,' Max nodded, recalling Alix's commitment to the Free French.

'Oh no, Monsieur. The man I used to love is a committed collaborator. He plays for German generals at their soirées now.' Her voice had grown darker, assuming a sharp, flinty edge.

'I thought about staying with him, at first. All this war, all this *politics*...' Her diction was dripping in disdain as she said the word, '...it wasn't for us. All I ever wanted was music. But then...'

'War,' said Max.

'War changes everything. Suddenly, there were Nazis all over France. Plush functions with German officers and treacherous French – even right in the heart of Paris. Well, it turned out that Valentin would rather bury his head in the sand than risk our lifestyle. What did it matter to us, he used to say? We're above all this. We're *musicians*. And, to my shame, I went along with him – for a time. I looked the other way, pretended I could get through without ever having to think of it. In the end, M.

Allgood, it tore me apart.' She paused. 'I didn't want a war with my husband. I wanted to *pretend* that we were still what we once were. And the longer I pretended, the more difficult it got. The longer I acted as if I didn't care, the closer he got to *them*. Do you see?'

Max was silent.

'I didn't challenge him on it. I didn't want to fight. So every day got darker than the last. By the time I ran away, all the good things I had with Valentin had just rotted away. M. Allgood, just because you turn the other cheek to something, doesn't mean it stops happening. Just because you're not firing back at Nelson, it doesn't mean there isn't a battle raging on. It's like you're sitting in an air raid shelter, bombs raining down, just weathering every blast, pretending there isn't a war.'

'So what should I do?' Max asked.

Somewhere along the way, it was Alix Monet who'd found the 'fire and brimstone'.

'You can't win a war by simply putting up a good defence, Monsieur.' Alix threw open the doors of the Grand and strode through. 'Sooner or later, you've got to fire back.'

By the time Max and Alix returned to the Grand, Frank and Mathilde were running through the final sections of 'Cubana Moonlight'.

From the middle of the dance floor, Frank looked up.

'Mr Allgood looks like he's carrying the weight of the world,' he said, watching the bandleader locked in conversation with Miss Monet.

'He isn't the only one,' remarked Mathilde.

Frank knew what Mathilde meant. He was about to assure her that he really wasn't thinking about Rosa, that every ounce of him was focused on the dance, when he saw that Mathilde was, in fact, indicating Raymond de Guise, who was standing just beyond the open dance-floor doors, greeting Hélène. Raymond looked dour, though he was evidently putting on an act for Hélène. Frank was uncertain if he'd seen Raymond looking quite as taut since the days after he'd returned from France, when he joined the air raid patrols each and every night.

'I didn't know Raymond was here this morning. I thought he wasn't due until evening.'

'Perhaps he and Hélène needed some extra rehearsal too?'

Knowing that this was Mathilde's way of prompting him, Frank opened his arms, ready to take her in hold.

But still her eyes focused on him intently.

Still she seemed to lack some element of belief.

'Mathilde, I know I let you down. I know I wasn't on form. But it was only a demonstration, wasn't it? We can do this. I know we can.' Frank looked from left to right: on one side of the Grand, Max looked embattled; through the dressing-room doors, so did Raymond. What use was there in joining in? 'Let's just dance?'

Still wearing that inscrutable expression, Mathilde stepped into his arms.

But, after scarcely ten steps, Frank whispered 'stop' and released her from his arms.

'It's like *you're* carrying the weight of the world as well,' he laughed. 'Mathilde, please? The ball's tomorrow night. It has to be … special. Is it something I've done? What's on your mind?'

Frank saw her draw a deep breath, as if she was about to tell him – but, at that moment, he heard the click of footsteps, and turned to see Nancy at the balustrade, beckoning him over.

'I'll be back,' he said, squeezing Mathilde's hand. He flashed her a sheepish smile. 'We're going to tango like *we're* the King and Queen of this place!'

Frank could hardly believe it when he reached the balustrade – it seemed as if Nancy was carrying some deep-seated frustration as well. 'Nance, what is it? What's happening today? Everywhere I look,' and he flashed his eyes around, 'people are acting like the world's caving in.'

'I need a favour, Frank.'

'A favour?'

'I know you should be focusing on your dancing today.'

Frank shrugged. 'I think Mathilde's just about given up on me. She thinks I'm a lost cause.'

He was pleased to see Nancy smiling at that, rolling her eyes at him in the way she always did when he'd caused some mischief at home.

'It's the Queen Mary. They need extra hands. I've strong-armed Rosa into taking the lunchtime service, scrubbing pots and plates – but they need someone this evening.' She paused. 'I know it's the big night tomorrow, but you're not on shift tonight, are you?'

Frank cast his mind back to last night, the long and lonely shift on the hotel rooftop. There'd been a time when the fire-watch felt like a sacred duty, for every night some new conflagration rose up on the city skyline – but those days had long gone, and with them the fervour that carried him through those evenings. Last night had left him dog-tired and anticipating a rest.

'It's extra money, Frankie. Mr Hastings is paying a double rate to fill the gap.'

Still Frank hesitated. He had never really known how to say 'No' to his big sister.

'Come on Frankie,' Nancy grinned, 'it's not like you'd get much rest at home, is it? Not with the Americans...'

At last, Frank relented. 'Tell M. Laurent I'll be there.'

Nancy bowed down to kiss him on the cheek. 'You never let anyone down, Frank.'

Then she watched as he returned to Mathilde, to take her in his arms.

She was watching them still when, in the corner of her eye, she saw Raymond emerging from the dance-floor doors, Hélène at his side.

Nancy couldn't help it – her mind cartwheeled back in time, back to the very first moment she'd stepped into the Grand.

She shouldn't have done it, of course. Her first season at the Buckingham Hotel, desperate to catch a glimpse of society, desperate to understand the magic of the ballroom, she'd donned her mother's old gown and slipped through the doors: a chambermaid, breaking every rule to experience the magic.

It was here that she'd first met Raymond.

They'd crashed into one another, only a few steps away from where she was standing.

And her whole life had changed.

Now, gazing upon Hélène and Raymond, it was like none of the intervening years had happened.

She was enjoying the spectacle when she heard Frank exclaim, 'That's impossible, Mathilde. It's just impossible!' and looked down to see him tumbling over his own feet as he retreated from the dance. What could possibly have happened to break up the rehearsal – Frank was looking at Mathilde with mounting horror. Mathilde reached for him. 'Frankie, I didn't know what else to do. I *had* to tell you.' But Frank didn't want to hear. He'd reeled round and run for the steps leading up from the dance floor. He looked back and said, 'Just let me take a breath. I'll be back. I just want some air.' He stalled. 'You shouldn't have told me. I was ready for the dance. You shouldn't have said.'

Then Frank was gone, up and out of the Grand.

Nancy would have followed, for she'd rarely seen Frank over-come with emotion – even when Rosa declared their romance dead, he'd sat quietly with himself, barely breathing a word about what she'd done – but Mathilde was approaching, eyes glistening with tears.

'He's right,' Mathilde said, gravitating to where Nancy stood above, 'I should have kept it to myself. At least until after the ball. But he's been so ... quiet. So distant. Yesterday that American boy was here in the ballroom with Rosa and ...' Mathilde wiped her eyes. 'I thought it might make him feel better. That he'd lost Rosa, but she was going to regret it.'

Nancy marvelled at how little Mathilde actually knew Frank, to think he might want bad things for Rosa, even after every-thing she'd done.

'Mathilde, precisely *what* did you tell Frank?'

Mathilde felt a rush of shame. 'He's married, Mrs de Guise. The American boy she left Frank for, he's got a wife back home. And I thought ... she's stuffing up her life. Frank ought to know. She made the biggest mistake, and it's going to undo her.'

Nancy was silent.

She closed her eyes.

'Are you sure about this?' she said wearily, when she opened them again.

'I heard it from the other Americans. They told me, plain as day.'

Nancy reached down and caressed Mathilde's shoulder. 'You did the right thing,' she whispered. 'The truth always comes out.' Then, in the corner of her eye, she caught sight of Raymond, turning on his heel to spin Hélène around. It was in moments like these that she was grateful she had him; there wasn't a thing she couldn't tell Raymond, and there wasn't a thing he wouldn't tell her. She was, she knew, one of the lucky ones: it was with dishonesty that the rot so often set in.

Her mind flashed back to the Housekeeping Lounge just one short hour ago: Rosa's dishevelled look, the tittering of the other girls.

It wasn't going to be easy, but she was going to have to handle this.

It seemed that everyone in the Buckingham Hotel was holding a ticking time bomb this week.

Nancy had just found hers.

Chapter Eighteen

There was music playing in the sitting room at Blomfield Road. While Vivienne scrubbed at plates in the kitchen sink, she could hear the refrain of 'It Don't Mean A Thing' blasting out while Jonah Linden and Ellsworth talked.

There was laughter too, coming through the walls.

It set her teeth on edge.

Vivienne drained the sink, dried her hands – and, lifting Arthur from his seat at the table, where Stan remained scribbling on the backs of old envelopes, she stole down the hall.

On any other morning, it would have been a sight to lift the soul: two of her countrymen, sitting by the morning fire, their conversation alive with memories of New York. This morning, however, there was no room for sentimentality. No space for joy.

This morning she had a job to do.

The sooner she knew the truth about these men, the sooner she could report it to Raymond, the sooner the house would be hers again. The sooner Christmas could return.

She stepped into the room.

One of the Americans was missing.

'McCord?' she whispered to herself.

At that moment, Vivienne turned to see the hulking figure of Henry McCord lumbering down the hallway. He must have returned to the bedroom above after breakfast. Now, when his eyes locked with Vivienne's, he seemed to be wearing a glassy smile. Inwardly, she cringed. Was *any* smile to be real, ever again? Now that she knew her own household swirled with subterfuge and secrets, could she ever trust the look in someone's eyes?

McCord was holding a black leather briefcase in one hand – and, in the other, a dog-eared notebook fastened with rubber bands. Vivienne's gaze was drawn instinctively towards it, and McCord seemed to register it too; when he saw her staring, he covered the notebook with his hands, and slid it into the briefcase.

'Jump to it, Jonah!' McCord said, reaching for the black woollen coat on the stand. 'You're not on vacation quite yet.'

Jonah Linden emerged from the sitting room, brushing past Vivienne and flashing a smile (was it real? was it fake?) at baby Arthur as he came.

'I'm afraid duty calls today, ma'am,' said Jonah, pulling on his boots.

McCord nodded. 'You'll have a bit more peace today, Mrs Cohen.' He lifted an imaginary cap to her. 'And don't worry about dinner tonight, ma'am. You leave that to us. They're throwing a luncheon at the embassy. Now, I can't say for what – national secrets, and all – but I *can* say, without a doubt, that there'll be leftovers. Tonight, Mrs Cohen, you can dine on Uncle Sam.'

Vivienne's mind was racing. Part of her was grateful that the Americans seemed to be shipping out for the day, but the other part wondered if it might be better if they stayed. How was she to plumb the backroads of their mind, like Raymond had said, if they weren't here?

Soon, Jonah and McCord had opened the front door and stepped out into the world. A fresh wind blew across Maida Vale, turning the gardens to a maelstrom of white.

They turned to salute Vivienne.

She took a breath.

If the Americans were gone for the day, then she was free – free to go into their room; free to search through their packs, just like Raymond had said. Free to find something, *anything*, that might bring this to a head.

It was only then that she realised Ellsworth was standing beside her: no boots upon his feet, no scarf around his neck. He was waving McCord and Jonah goodbye, just the same as her.

The moment the door was closed, he put a hand upon her shoulder.

'I know what you're thinking,' Ellsworth began. In the sitting room, the Duke Ellington recording came to its end. 'You're thinking: couldn't March have marched off as well?'

'Oh nothing of the sort,' Vivienne blathered, still trying to make sense of all this. 'I wasn't expecting any of you to leave. I wondered what the day had in store.'

'What the day has in store, ma'am, is rest and relaxation.' Ellsworth reached for his own coat. Then, Vivienne realised, he was lifting her green lambswool from the coat rack as well. 'The truth is, I asked the boys to make themselves scarce today. I wondered if you and I might get a little more acquainted?'

This time yesterday, she might have had the idea herself. This time yesterday, she might have been battling the guilt about Artie, just to spend a few hours in this man's company. Right now, however, she just tightened. 'Acquainted?'

Her mind was still racing through all that she had to do. If the key to this lay upstairs in the houseguests' room, today was her chance.

'It was all that talk yesterday that got me thinking,' Ellsworth went on. 'It seems, to me, that you've lived a whole lifetime – and you're still so young. Exiled, disowned, married, widowed...' He paused. 'I should like to indulge you for a day. In fact, I made us reservations.'

Vivienne's eyes flashed to the stairs, then back to Ellsworth. 'Reservations?'

'I'm not ashamed to say that I pulled some strings at the embassy. Just a few hours, Vivienne. Let me take you out, for just a few hours.'

'But the children,' Vivienne ventured, 'and...'

Ellsworth laughed. 'Now, I love children – just as much as the next man. Matter of fact, I rather like the idea of having some scamps to call me Daddy one day. But today? Well, you might have to pull some strings of your own there.' He stroked Arthur's brow. 'There must be a neighbour you might ask for some help?'

There was: Mrs Fitzwilliam, from three doors down. She was tantamount to a grandmother to the boys.

And suddenly, Vivienne was thinking: if I'm to miss my chance searching the bedroom above, then why not take this one? I can't sift through their suitcases, excavate their packs, but there's an opportunity right here, isn't there? Perhaps Ellsworth knows where McCord sneaks off to. Perhaps he himself might let something slip.

Vivienne looked into Ellsworth's eyes.

Today, it seemed, there was no other choice.

The taxicab took some time in arriving, but at least that gave Vivienne the opportunity to speak with Mrs Fitzwilliam, to pack a bag for the boys – and make pre-emptive apologies for how unruly Stan was bound to become. Mrs Fitzwilliam was only too happy to open her house to children as Christmas approached. The tree in her sitting room was festooned with baubles, and presents of all shapes and sizes were arranged in the hearth. These would have to be carefully guarded from Stan,

Vivienne warned – though she got the feeling that, by the time she returned, Stan might have been gifted one or two.

And so, with her heart thumping – and her mind racing with thoughts of what the day might bring – Vivienne slid into a taxicab beside Ellsworth.

Let it be over by day's end, she told herself.

'I hope I'm not being presumptuous,' Ellsworth said. 'It isn't on me to judge – but I know what it takes to run a household. You're a battler, Vivienne. The truth is, I rather feel bad that we've added to your workload.'

It was on Vivienne's mind to agree – all things told, this Christmas would have been a lot easier without three house guests to cater for – but very quickly she buried the thought. There was a duty here: if it hadn't fallen to her, it would have fallen to somebody else. She would need to lead him into the questions she needed to ask. Treat Ellsworth like a key, she thought – let him unlock the mystery. And wasn't she better placed to do this than Raymond? A woman could unearth secrets that remained forever hidden from a man.

Through the frosted windows, she realised that they were sailing along the edge of Hyde Park. Army wagons sat cloaked in snow beneath the trees. Soldiers stood sentry around the moorings of the great barrage balloons.

'Where are we going, Ellsworth?'

She had a sudden thought that he was taking her to the Buckingham Hotel – but, very quickly, he disabused her of the notion. 'I wasn't sure what your feelings were about the hotel, not after what you said yesterday. The place of your exile.'

Vivienne feigned a laugh: 'There are worse places to be exiled. I was young. I was carefree. I was ... wild.'

Ellsworth arched an eyebrow. 'So how does a wild girl end up a suburban housekeeper?'

I'm much more than that, thought Vivienne.

Today, I'm a servant of the Crown.

She just laughed, 'Where *are* we going?'

'I know it isn't the Buckingham Hotel,' said Ellsworth, as he helped Vivienne out moments later, 'but it was the grandest place I could find. The Continental Kitchen,' he declared – for, up above them, hung the baroque edifice of the Imperial Hotel.

Vivienne gazed at its turrets. 'I'm not sure I'm dressed for high society.'

'Nonsense, Vivienne – you'll fit right in. There's even an afternoon show dance to watch, after we've lunched.'

Ellsworth was already striding towards the sweeping stairs of the hotel entrance. Strafed by the wind, he looked back and held out his arm.

Get him on side, Vivienne.

Work your way in . . .

Vivienne summoned a smile, threaded her arm into his and entered the hotel.

People often spoke of the Imperial as a mere pretender to the Buckingham's throne – but the truth was that its opulence and lavishness matched the Buckingham's in every way. As Vivienne stepped through the doors, to a gracious bow from the doorman and the warm hello of a concierge, it felt like she was stepping into a palace. A wave of warmth enveloped her, dragging her into a reception hall fit for a king, where men in long tailcoats gathered by check-in desks that glistened like gold, and the Christmas tree which dominated the area was decorated in simple silver stars.

It had been some time since she'd stepped into the Buckingham. She remembered it as a little less sparkly than this, perhaps a little more reserved. No reasonable soul would have called the Imperial's reception hall 'gaudy', but it was evident that no expense had been spared in making it stand out.

The hubbub of the hotel brought back a rush of memories. If it had been Ellsworth's intention to remind her of the days before Stan, before the de Guises, before the responsibilities of hearth and home, he had chosen perfectly. But Ellsworth could not have known how lonely those days had been – nor how destructive.

The Continental Kitchen sat on the far side of the reception hall. Vivienne waited while Ellsworth caught the maître d's attention, then followed him across the bustling restaurant floor, the smells of salt, sage, chestnut and cinnamon wafting through the air. Though it was the middle of the day, candles illuminated every table. Dessert wine flowed. Somewhere, a cork popped from a bottle of Champagne – and, for the first time in years, Vivienne felt a sudden *thirst* for it. It was nice to be reminded of her carefree years, but with it came the familiar prickles of shame.

The maître d' left Vivienne and Ellsworth at a table in the corner, and promised he'd be back soon. 'I'm afraid it's the only table I could get. I believe some *earl* took the tables in the window.'

Vivienne rather liked the way he rolled his eyes upon saying the word 'earl'. She'd lived in London long enough to get used to it, but for an American the very idea of aristocracy was absurd. In America, a man earned his greatness – either on the battle-field, or in the boardroom. Even now this seemed, to Vivienne, a much more honourable way of ordering the world.

'Wherever we sit,' Vivienne ventured, 'I'm sure we're going to be dining better here than Henry and Jonah are.'

'Don't be so sure,' Ellsworth replied. 'The embassy kitchen is quite spectacular. You don't think the ambassador would serve up slop at his receptions, do you?'

'You've been there long, have you? All three of you?'

As he perused the menu, Ellsworth said, 'McCord's the veteran. He mightn't look it – why, sometimes I look at him and want to send him back to kindergarten – but he's the longest serving. I was happy sunning myself in Hawaii, until the Japanese came along. I never once thought I'd be posted somewhere as *cold* as London.' He shrugged. 'But here I am.'

'And here was I thinking your father would be proud of you, following in his footsteps.'

Ellsworth shook his head. 'He'd have been prouder if I was still a soldier, ma'am. All this embassy work, he thinks it's just paper pushing. You know, I only signed up to make the old man happy. I'd have been content just making candles, like my grandaddy. But...' He sighed. 'Here I am.'

'You'd rather be somewhere else?'

Ellsworth sighed. 'Wouldn't we all?'

'I'm not sure where I would go,' said Vivienne.

It was, she realised, her first genuine admission of the day.

From across the restaurant floor, there came a clattering of pots and pans in the kitchen.

The waiter gave them a wry smile. 'A new kitchen hand joined us, only yesterday. He's still finding his feet. Might I recommend the quail, my lady? And, for the gentleman, terrine of duckling and cauliflower vinaigrette?'

'Hey,' Ellsworth laughed, and snapped shut the menu, 'if it's good for the lords and ladies, it's good for us.'

'As you like, sir,' said the waiter, and beat his retreat.

'If Mr McCord's the veteran among you,' Vivienne ventured, 'why is he so young?'

'Well, that's a question,' Ellsworth replied. 'You see, me and Jonah cut our teeth in the military. We've done our postings. Now, I can't say we ever went into battle, but we know our way around the military. But, hey, sometimes life takes you on an unexpected path. You ever read Robert Frost?'

Vivienne couldn't say she had.

'My father's favourite poet. "Two roads diverge in a forest…"'

Vivienne just gazed, urging him to go on.

'Well, after Pearl Harbour, I figured there was a way of making better use of myself than taking a command. I've got family in Australia. I was going to take a diplomatic post there – but destiny decided I looked better in a hat and scarf than I did in a pair of shorts.' Ellsworth laughed. 'Now, Jonah – he's security. He would make a fine soldier, but he makes a finer security officer. There isn't anyone I'd rather have my back in a gunfight. Who's the fellow the English tell stories about? The guy with the apple?'

'William Tell,' Vivienne laughed.

'Could shoot an apple off his friend's head from a hundred yards? Well, that's our Jonah.'

'With a bow and arrow?'

'A Smith & Wesson, but I reckon he'd do just as good with a bow.'

'You're saying you wouldn't trust Mr McCord?' grinned Vivienne. It felt important, somehow, that she steer the conversation back towards McCord.

'Well, different folks have different talents. I've never seen Henry shoot – though he looks the solid type.' Ellsworth paused. 'But McCord's not an army boy. He wasn't raised on it. He hasn't done his basic training. Between you and me, the US State Department can be a bit like a royal house – you know, if your grandfather was born to it, and your father was born into it, then, likely as not, you'll be born into it as well. That's what Henry's life's been like. What do they call it, around here? The Divine Right of Kings?'

'Something like that,' laughed Vivienne.

Their drinks had arrived: two glasses of dry white wine, to ease into lunch.

'McCord's father was on staff at the embassy in Berlin. You can imagine he's had a rotten time of it. Incarcerated for most of this year – locked up as soon as the US joined the war. I believe he's made it back home at last, but one wonders what it's done to him.'

'Good Lord,' whispered Vivienne.

'It's him who got Henry into this world. I'm not saying Henry wouldn't have succeeded on merit alone, but ...' A waiter was approaching with their food. Ellsworth waited as it settled, then gazed at Vivienne through the rising steam. 'McCord will end up ambassador one day – you mark my words. He's got an air of *ambition* about him, don't you think?'

Vivienne thought she understood. 'Are they priming him for it, at the embassy?'

'The US State Department moves in mysterious ways.'

Vivienne laughed.

Then, without thinking too deeply about it – because to think too deeply was to unearth reasons *not* to say it – she blurted out, 'If the American Embassy in Berlin lasted as long as it did, does that mean Henry's father ... worked with Nazis?'

'I'm not sure you would call it *work*. It's diplomacy, ma'am. It's what we do.'

Now was her chance.

'And are there *still* ways of talking? While we're dropping bombs on each other and razing each other's cities to the ground, do the diplomats still *talk*?'

She'd tried to make the question as innocent as she could, just an incredulous woman asking an incredulous question in this incredulous world, but she sensed some flicker of hesitation in Ellsworth – and immediately she knew she'd pushed it too far.

He pondered the terrine on his plate, stabbed a piece with his fork and brought it to his lips, before he said, 'It sounds to me, Viv, as if you're asking for trade secrets.'

Vivienne tensed.

She felt a rush of blood, coursing up her neck, colouring her cheeks.

The silence had gone on too long. She started to stammer out a response, but Ellsworth laughed and said, 'None of us are writing postcards to Nazis, ma'am – but you'd be surprised what whispers get passed around. How do you think McCord's father got out of that camp? We have to talk. It's how we get things done.' Ellsworth paused, then tasted his terrine. 'There's wickedness over there, but there's goodness too. The worst thing about knowing the enemy is knowing that some of them are *just like us.*'

Vivienne felt her flush retreating.

The way Ellsworth laughed, he couldn't possibly have known why she asked.

And yet...

Here was something she could report to Raymond. McCord's father had been in Berlin when the Americans declared war. They'd rounded him up, incarcerated him in a camp – until some deal was struck for his release. What if McCord could use his father's contacts? If McCord was carrying a secret he meant to deliver to the enemy, wasn't this *how*?

After that, Vivienne dared not ask anymore. For a time they talked about almost anything else – about home, and the time before the war, Stan's temper tantrums and Christmases from times gone by.

'I remember Times Square in the snow,' said Vivienne. 'Some time between Thanksgiving and Christmas. My friends and I, out in the night when we really oughtn't to be...'

'I'm beginning to sense where Stan gets his wildness.'

'Oh, *that* was his father,' said Vivienne – and for the first time that day, a pall of sadness settled over the couple, as if they had strayed into a conversation where they really shouldn't be.

Their eyes lingered on each other.

And, for a brief few moments, Vivienne rather forgot that she was now working for military intelligence.

And perhaps those thoughts would have gone on, but suddenly Ellsworth was on his feet. 'It looks like we'll have to forsake dessert, ma'am,' he said. Next moment, with thanks to the maître d', he was leading Vivienne across the restaurant floor.

The doors to the Imperial Ballroom stood open on the other side of the reception hall, a flight of broad stairs leading down into the underground vault where the ballroom was lit up as if Saturday night had already come. By the time Ellsworth and Vivienne arrived, quite a crowd had already assembled. It was a darker vault than the Grand, slightly smaller too, but no less opulent for that. Silver chandeliers spilt radiant light across a sprung dance floor of interlocking black boards. Sprigs of holly, glistening with fat red berries, adorned the tables that surrounded its edge. Candleflames set in ostentatious candelabra flickered and danced.

Ellsworth navigated the crowd with aplomb, finding a space close to the balustrade. 'How long since you were in a ballroom, ma'am?'

Vivienne had a shiver of recollection. 'It was a different age.'

Her mind was wheeling back again, back to those tempestuous days when she used to disgrace herself nightly in the Grand.

'Look,' said Ellsworth, 'here they come.'

There was a stage beyond the dance floor, and a set of ornate, sculpted doors led directly onto it. As Vivienne watched, the doors opened and the Imperial Orchestra filed out to take their seats. First came the trumpeters, the trombonist, the saxophonist bearing his instrument aloft. Then came a pair of percussionists; twin brothers, bringing out their clarinet and bassoon. The bandleader was a thickset man, but he wasn't the last to emerge. To the crowd's delight, a tall Black man, lean and angular as a scarecrow, strutted out. To the bewilderment of those gathered at the balustrade, he marched up and down the edge of the stage, taking the spectators in, before he settled at the piano, cracked his knuckles and gave the ballroom the strangest of smiles. It was almost a leer, thought Vivienne. Whoever he was, he had a very odd kind of charm. Things had evidently changed since Vivienne had moved in these circles. When she used to go to the Grand, Archie Adams and his Orchestra had been the very height of elegance and respectability.

'An American man,' Ellsworth noted.

'How do you know?'

Ellsworth laughed. 'Sometimes you can just *tell!*' Then he paused. A riot of voices sounded around them, but Ellsworth's voice cut through. 'Vivienne, do you ever think about going back home?'

Something in his tone told her this wasn't merely an offhand comment.

Suddenly, she felt his hand on her waist.

'I don't want to speak out of turn, Vivienne. Please don't take offence. But I simply have to say it. As a matter of fact, it's the reason I wanted to take you out today. I've just been trying to find the words.'

The show dance was about to begin.

A taste, the whispered voices said, of Saturday night.

'What do you mean?'

Ellsworth was struggling to summon any words. Was this, she wondered, related to Raymond's mission?

'I've only been at Blomfield Road a very short time, Viv. But you get good at noticing things, when you're in my world. And...' He paused again. He took her hand – and, to her surprise, Vivienne let him. 'I can see how you're stuck. I can see what the world's done to you. You've been dealt a rotten hand, and... I suppose, what I'm trying to say is, Vivienne, you deserve so much more.'

Vivienne couldn't help it. She felt a rush of warmth. He was still holding her hand, but now Vivienne started clasping his as well.

'I don't know how to say this,' Ellsworth laughed. 'Words are failing me! These things aren't easy, but they can be done. You're still a citizen of the United States. I could pull some strings. I could put you and your son on a diplomatic flight. You could be back in New York City in the New Year – about as far away from this damn war as it's possible to be.' He stopped. 'I want to help you, Vivienne. I can see how you're pinned. And... it's not that I'd expect anything. I'd not want anything in return. I just can't sit and see you and your boy, stuck in that situation, and not lift a hand.'

It felt as if a sudden gust of wind had stolen away Vivienne's breath. They'd spoken so much of New York, of the old times in Central Park and Washington Square – but it had been nostalgia. Fantasy. Yet here Ellsworth was, telling her he could make it come true.

She hadn't thought of going home in years.

Not once since Stan was born.

Now, however, the possibility lit her up.

But there was something else in Ellsworth's words, something she didn't quite understand.

'What situation?' she asked. 'Raymond and Nancy are my family. They might not be my blood, but they're *Stan's*. My own family were only too eager to forget about me. But this? This is the family I chose.'

Ellsworth took a breath.

'I'm really sorry, Viv. I didn't mean to – but last night, I couldn't sleep, and I was sitting in the window, smoking my cigarillo and ... I *saw*.'

Vivienne could only stare.

'I don't want to cast aspersions,' Ellsworth stuttered. 'I'm a guest in your house. But I saw you and Mr de Guise coming out of the air raid shelter in the dead of night and ...'

A hot burst of fire prickled across Vivienne. Was Ellsworth really suggesting what she thought he was suggesting? Did he really think she and *Raymond* were conducting some affair, right there, in the house where they lived?

She knew she ought to tell him no, she knew she ought to protest in no uncertain terms – but then a thought struck her: what was she to say she was doing, out there in the air raid shelter at night? How could she possibly tell him the truth, that Raymond was commissioning her to spy on his house guests, and all in the King's name?

'Ellsworth, it really isn't what you think. You've jumped to conclusions. You've—'

'You're still young, ma'am. You're still worth so much. Life's been rotten to you so far, but it doesn't have to be like this.'

Vivienne felt twisted inside. If he'd seen her creeping into the air raid shelter with Raymond, what else had he seen? What had he *heard*? If he'd told the others, there was every chance the whispers would reach Nancy. And what might happen then?

What was it that Benjamin Franklin, the old American president, had said?

Three may keep a secret, so long as two of them are dead.

'Ellsworth,' she said, brooking no argument, 'you've got it wrong. I was married to Raymond's brother.'

'I know that, ma'am.'

'He swore an oath to look after me.'

Ellsworth smiled, sadly. 'He swore a vow to his wife as well.'

Vivienne couldn't help it. She tore her hand away.

'Ellsworth, please.'

'I didn't want to think it, Viv. But why else would you be sneaking into an air raid shelter with him, in the small hours of night?' Ellsworth tried to take her hand once again. 'Don't think too badly of me. I don't of you. I look at you and I think . . .'

Vivienne tried to hold on to some good feeling, in the middle of it all. His eyes were brimming with compassion. That was something. And . . . America. Perhaps he was suggesting it because of some untoward assumption, but the offer was *real*, wasn't it?

'What, Ellsworth? What do you think?'

'I think you could have a different world. A different life. One where – where you're the lady of the manor, not the housemaid. I think America is waiting. All you'd have to do is say. I could start making the calls.'

The band struck up.

The pianist rolled his hands over the keys.

The dance troupe stamped their feet in time, then spun into their dance.

Applause spread like wildfire, from one side of the ballroom to the other.

And Vivienne was lost in the middle of it all, for she'd come here to mine Ellsworth for secrets – and ended up being faced with the biggest question in all of her life.

Chapter Nineteen

Raymond threw open the door of the taxicab, told the driver – in far too brusque a tone – to wait, and flailed up Blomfield Road until he reached the garden gate. The moment he stepped through, he got a sinking feeling – for no smoke trailed from his chimney, and even from without the house looked curiously uninhabited. He'd meant to come back hours ago, to be here to challenge these Americans himself – but now not even a footprint marred his garden path. By the time he opened the door, he already knew what he would find: not one soul.

'Vivienne?' he called out. 'Vivienne, are you here?'

No music, no footsteps, no quiet conversation or squalling children. As he reached the foot of the stairs, Raymond realised that he'd never before been alone in this house.

Where were they?

Outside, the afternoon dark was drawing near. Raymond had spent the morning buffeted between the Grand and the Benefactors Study, where Mr Hastings was preparing to meet the Hotel Board – dancing alternately with Karina and Hélène, watching Frank and Mathilde fine-tune their tango, joining long discussions with the Orchestra about tweaks to the set. But there was yet time before he was due to take dinner in the Queen Mary. The taxicab would wait just a little longer.

Raymond felt like an intruder as he strode up his own stair-case, along the hall and into the bedroom where the Americans were staying.

Like good soldiers, they had kept it in pristine condition. Three beds, one pressed to each wall, were perfectly turned down, with suitcases and haversacks stowed neatly underneath.

Raymond rushed to the window. The blackout blind was still in place from the night before, but now he peeled it back. From this vantage there was no seeing anyone approaching along the street, for the window looked down only upon his snowbound backyard and the Anderson shelter dominating the bottom lawn. Perhaps they'd be back any moment. Perhaps Vivienne and the Americans were waltzing up the garden path right now. If so, he wouldn't know until he heard them entering the house – and, with that in mind, he got to work straight away.

On Raymond's return from North Africa he'd spent several days being tutored in tradecraft by Maynard Charles's depart-ment. The first rule was to always go unobserved. That was why, when Raymond opened Ellsworth's packs, then Jonah's, then McCord's, he paused over each one, memorising exactly how it was laid out, before he proceeded to lift out every garment, searching for whatever was hidden underneath.

He worked quickly and confidently, replacing each suitcase exactly as he had found it.

What he'd been looking for, he wasn't sure – but whatever it was, he didn't find it. There was nothing suspicious in neatly folded shirts and balls of socks.

From downstairs, he heard the turn of a latch.

Raymond was still running his hands under Jonah's mattress, wondering if the American might have been foolish enough to hide something there, when he heard the noise. Immediately, he wrenched himself free, steadying himself with breaths as he pivoted and skipped to the bedroom door. If this was the Americans, it was of paramount importance they not catch him snooping – but, he reminded himself, he did not have to be ashamed of sloping around his own house.

He straightened himself, practised a smile and glided to the top of the stairs.

Halfway down, he realised it wasn't the Americans at all.

It was the cab driver.

'My engine's going to freeze if I don't keep moving, Mr de Guise. Are you likely to want a lift back to the hotel?'

Raymond reached the bottom of the stairs and looked at the carriage clock in the hall. Darkness was falling. The clock was ticking. In a few short hours, he needed to be the King of the Ballroom again, romancing the hotel's own American guests for dinner.

'Let's drive,' he said.

The Hotel Board had arrived at the Buckingham Hotel at 4 p.m., just as the last of the day's sun was disappearing, but by now the blackout was in place – and yet, for some reason none of them could fathom, they were still waiting.

By half past the hour, their muted looks were turning to open discontent. Uriah Bell, the longest-standing investor on the Board, looked particularly cantankerous, as he paced the Benefactors Study and said, 'It wasn't like this in Edgerton's day. In Edgerton's day, we were all valued members of the Board – majority stakeholders or not.'

The Benefactors Study was dominated by a big circular table, designed specifically to stop any one member from sitting at its head.

'And yet the man thinks he's a king,' said Peter Merriweather, shifting his not inconsiderable gut into a more comfortable position. Merriweather owned extensive estates across Yorkshire, and was one of the few people in Great Britain to have actually gained weight under rationing. His jowls wobbled as he said, 'He's been treating us like second-rank lieutenants for too long. All I'll say is: he better have good news today.'

The door opened.

John Hastings appeared, unflustered and unfussy, with a sheaf of papers in one hand and a set of Christmas cards in the other. Though it would have been far-fetched to believe he hadn't heard Bell and Merriweather griping, he began handing out the cards with a smile and said, 'My Sarah wouldn't leave any of you out, gentlemen. Seasons greetings, from my family to yours.'

The door of the study closed.

All eyes fell upon Mr Hastings.

The Hotel Board did not often meet en masse. Five men strong, including Hastings himself, it comprised Bell, Merriweather, Lloyd and Fletcher – the latter two being pettier investors than the first – and a coterie of silent investors on the side. Lord Bartholomew Edgerton's share was considered defunct, on account of the fact that he was now interned at His Majesty's Pleasure as a seditionist and potential collaborator with the enemy.

Hastings looked on the men around his table and smiled.

'Gentlemen, I'm glad you could join us tonight. I'm sure you'll see, soon enough, that the Home Away From Home programme has been a roaring success for this hotel. The boys we've got staying here are the best my nation has to offer.'

'Yes, yes, enough of the preamble, Hastings,' Uriah Bell said, finally retaking his seat. 'Playing host to some infantry is all well and good. Jolly well done, you boys, off to kill the Boche! It's playing host to King George that we want to hear about. You do have news, I take it? You *have* heard from the Palace?'

Hastings straightened his papers and surveyed the room.

He'd forgotten that it wasn't just a matter of business to these men.

Too often he overlooked what the King actually meant to the Board.

'Sirs, we heard from the Palace this morning.' He took a breath. 'I'm afraid I don't have good news.'

At that moment, before the invective could be muttered and the demands for an explanation be made, he unfurled the letter delivered by the Palace equerry and started to read.

'Dear Mr Hastings, it is with some regret that I write to inform you that His Majesty King George VI and the royal party will not be accepting your invitation to attend the Winter Ball on Saturday 19th December. Please be assured that the King holds the Buckingham Hotel in the highest of regards and looks forward to his next opportunity to visit this finest establishment.'

Hastings slowed as he read the last sentence. Though he knew it would be no consolation to the Board, he felt like a few extra seconds might dampen the ire.

He was wrong.

Uriah Bell was already on his feet. 'Mr Hastings, time and again this Board tried to impress upon you: American is not the only money in London. Time and again, we tried to make you understand the importance of tradition to an establishment like this. All you see are numbers, sir! You've no idea the cost to reputation we've just suffered!'

Merriweather stood as well. 'I have to agree, sir. The responsibility for this lies at your feet alone. Chasing American money was all well and good – but at the expense of what makes the Buckingham so pure? Shredding our reputation to chase American gold? Sir, it was uncouth from the beginning – and just look what it's wrought.'

Uriah Bell could hardly keep the sneer from his face. 'An American at the head of the Board. An American to lead our Orchestra. An American to lead our hotel. Good Lord, man, this is Great Britain. This is *London*. You know nothing about history, sir. This would never have happened, had Lord Edgerton still—'

Hastings was a quiet man. He was able to bear almost every attack with a simple stony face – but, at this one, he baulked. Lifting a single finger, he said, 'If Lord Edgerton were still head of this Board, the King would never grace the establishment again – for Lord Edgerton is a traitor to his name.'

His words silenced the Board.

'I remain the majority shareholder of this hotel, gentlemen. None of your slings and arrows will change that. Whatever reputation we have, right now, is far better than the reputation we would have had were Lord Edgerton still leading you all. Or is that what you'd prefer? In my world, the Buckingham is a home away from home for simple American soldiers, eager to do their bit. In yours, it seems, the hotel would be a home away from home for Nazi sympathisers.'

'Now, listen here,' Merriweather intervened. 'I believe our objections hold more merit than that.'

'King George might not grace us tomorrow evening, sirs, but the Grand Ballroom will still be alive. King George has taken nothing from us. Check your profit and loss accounts, gentlemen, and see what we've accomplished this year. Hold you breath just a little longer, and see what we'll accomplish next.'

Hastings slammed his fist on the table and scoured the room with his eyes.

'Take your investment to the Imperial Hotel, sirs, if you must. I'll have your paperwork on my desk by Christmas night. Do not believe, for even one second, that my fund doesn't have the resources to replace you. Then, perhaps, we could see what the Buckingham Hotel becomes.'

It took a lot to startle Uriah Bell, Peter Merriweather and the rest of the Board, but this barely bridled threat, coming from a man normally so taciturn, shocked them to the core.

'I didn't get where I am today by simpering, gentlemen. I believe in treating others with basic human decency. But I believe in getting what I want as well. And right now, what I want, is for us to all sally out together into the Queen Mary and take dinner with our American guests – to put on a welcoming face for them, and tell them how proud we are to call them our allies.' Hastings drew himself up, and marched to the door. 'If you can do that, gentlemen, then follow me – and let us enjoy the evening.' Then he looked over his shoulder. 'If you cannot, then I invite you to leave the hotel post-haste.'

Hastings didn't wait to see who followed.

He simply opened the door, strode into the corridor – and kept on striding.

Only after several paces did he take the handkerchief out of his breast pocket and dab at the sweat beading on his brow.

On balance, that hadn't gone quite as badly as he'd expected.

The problem was: Bell and Merriweather were right.

That letter from the Palace was a downright disaster.

But, as he'd said to Raymond de Guise when he summoned him this morning, the ball had to go on.

And it had to be *spectacular*.

'They're coming,' boomed the voice of Henri Laurent.

For the first time, Frank understood why the kitchen hands had always said that the head chef made them quake in their boots. Frank had never had the privilege of serving in the armed forces, not like Billy Brogan and so many of the rest, but working for M. Laurent was rather like he imagined serving under some grizzled old general would be.

He'd arrived at 3 p.m., when the lunchtime service was over and the kitchen was being cleaned down, stripped back and prepared for the dinner service to come.

'You're the latest lamb to the slaughter, are you?' asked Henri Laurent, inspecting Frank from head to toe. 'That chambermaid needed some telling at lunchtime. I trust you're made of sterner stuff.'

Frank gulped. 'That' chambermaid was, of course, Rosa, and he was only glad he hadn't been assigned to the same shift as her.

'I'll do you proud, M. Laurent,' said Frank. He meant it too; after a morning spent with Mathilde, he needed something mindless, something physical, to get lost in. If it hadn't been for his shift in the kitchen, he might have spent the day brooding, wondering what to do.

Rosa had made her decision, hadn't she?

Was it any of Frank's business if the choice she'd made was a duff one? People had their hearts broken all the time. Rosa had taken his and cast it aside. Mathilde seemed to think he ought to be *pleased* that she was going to get her comeuppance – but the thought was needling at Frank that he could spare her the humiliation, save her from embarrassing herself...

'In this kitchen,' M. Laurent barked, 'you'll call me Chef. Is that understood?'

'Yes, M. Laurent.'

Henri Laurent glared, with all the anger of the fires flickering in his range.

'Yes, Chef,' Frank corrected himself, and trudged on to find his station.

The Queen Mary restaurant was a brightly lit palace of elegance and refinement – but the kitchens that served it seemed, to Frank, more like a Victorian prison or workhouse. In here the lights were low, the air was stiflingly hot, thick with smoke and steam and the crackle of fires. This was not like the ballroom, where sensation and feeling counted for so much; this was like a battleship, where men followed orders to the letter or found themselves cast overboard.

Frank was grateful that he was to be on the lowest rung of this particular ladder. A pot washer did not have to engage directly with M. Laurent – and the vast pot wash, with tin troughs full of scalding soapy water and racks where pots, pans and crockery were left to dry, was like a prison within a prison, locked away from the rest of the kitchen. Consequently, though Frank quickly found himself sweating, straining and gasping for air, he was, at least, left alone to do his job. In here, scouring grime from cooking pans, he didn't have to think about Rosa.

His duty wasn't to her.

His duty was only to fat and grease.

'SERVICE!' boomed a voice through the kitchen beyond. 'TABLE SEVEN UP!'

Then, most terrifyingly of all – for three words had never been uttered with more vindictiveness, not in Frank Nettleton's experience – came the incandescent order: 'DO IT AGAIN!'

'I'll bet that's Jackson,' snorted one of the other pot washers, to whom Frank was expected to pay deference. 'He fancied he'd got himself a promotion when Victor left. Now I reckon he'd rather have stayed here scrubbing dishes! Old Laurent'll have roasted him by the end of the night.'

'CLEAR!'

The other pot washer, a ratty little man with a pencil mous-tache and lank hair beneath his cap, jabbed a finger at Frank. 'That's our order. Go and round up,' he said, indicating the trolley. 'Then you'll get a taste of this kitchen!'

Frank wasn't sure he wanted a taste of this kitchen, but he ventured out all the same. Through reefs of steam he came, up and down the ranges and countertops, collecting every dirty bowl, utensil and chopping board he could find.

He wondered how Rosa had fared in this job.

No doubt she was lamenting her lot with the other chambermaids right now.

Frank was passing the service hatch – where chefs were plating up food, and waiters were gathering in a throng, ready to take it out – when, quite without meaning to, he caught a glimpse of the restaurant floor. This must have been the same feeling prisoners in Pentonville prison got: staring through the bars, glimpsing a brighter, better world.

Across the bustling Queen Mary, he saw Mr Hastings leading the Hotel Board to their tables.

There, ready to greet them, were the American GIs.

Frank stared.

Joel Kaplan had gripped Mr Hastings' hand, shaking it eagerly as the other infantrymen were introduced to the Board.

The smile on his face was so broad that he looked quite deranged.

There he stood, a simple infantryman, being hosted in the greatest hotel in London town, sharing his Christmas with lords and ladies, dining at the Buckingham's expense…

…and all while lying to Rosa through his teeth.

'Max, are you ready? Mr Allgood, it's time.'

Upon his return to the hotel, Raymond had found Max, Alix and a small band of other musicians rehearsing with the guest singers in the Grand – but it had seemed to Raymond that it was Alix leading the sessions. Max himself seemed on a different plane, half-removed from the goings on in the ballroom.

Raymond had seen stage fright beset performers before, and it was true that Max only became a genuine showman when he had Lucille pressed up to his lips – but he'd never before seen the bandleader so distracted.

It was Hélène who told him about the guest singer who'd abandoned the show for a stint at the Imperial.

'Archie Adams was never as riled as this, not on the eve of a ball,' Hélène whispered.

'Archie Adams didn't have a nephew trying to undermine him at every turn,' Raymond returned – though, in truth, with his own mind a whirlwind, it was difficult to think of Max's troubles as anything other than a sideshow. From the middle of the dance floor, he looked up and declared, 'Mr Allgood, the Board will be waiting.'

From the other side of the piano, Max just scowled. 'You go ahead, Mr de Guise. I'll be with you shortly.'

Raymond declined to say that the Board were unlikely to look kindly upon their bandleader dragging himself into their soirée late, and instead escorted Hélène out of the Grand, across the reception hall and into the Queen Mary. It would, he reflected, be hypocritical of him to lecture Max on focusing on the ball and forgetting his private woes, when Raymond himself could hardly think of the dance for his fears about what was happening back home.

'Mr de Guise,' John Hastings declared, standing to receive Raymond. 'Miss Marchmont.'

The Queen Mary was a bustling hive of activity, a dozen contrasting smells combining to make a tantalising aroma. The Board and their guests had been afforded the most palatial of tables, in windows that would have looked out across snowbound Berkeley Square had it not been for the blackout blinds. No expense had been spared in hiring an expert artiste to decorate the inside of the shutters; this Christmas, Berkeley Square was rendered in oil paints.

The Board stood to receive Raymond warmly. Hélène was greeted with significantly less warmth, and smiles painted on – it had been the members of this very Board that terminated her employment at the hotel, some years before – but Mr Hastings didn't seem to notice. His good lady wife, bedecked in pearls and a simple cream dress, was immediately on her feet and fawning over Hélène's gown. 'Oh, it isn't nearly as ostentatious as the gown for tomorrow night, Mrs Hastings,' Hélène laughed. 'I'm to wear the very gown I wore on my first performance at the Grand. Ivory chiffon and lace. Silver thread, that sparkles in the lights.'

Waiters fluttered about, pouring Champagne. A cork exploded, describing a perfect arc across the restaurant floor.

'Ladies and gentlemen,' Hastings began, raising his glass. Raymond tried hard not to glare at Joel Kaplan and gazed, instead, at the other faces. He got the uneasy feeling that the Benefactors Study had just hosted an outburst of bitterness among the Board, for Bell and Merriweather were fighting hard not to scowl. There could only be one reason for this, and it was the one Mr Hastings had divulged when he summoned Raymond to the hotel this morning: the royal party had declined to attend tomorrow night's ball. 'I am proud beyond measure to have welcomed three fine examples of my countrymen to the Buckingham Hotel this week. In dark times, it is our duty to bring light. And we at the Buckingham Hotel consider it our sacred duty, as standard bearers for this proud nation, to welcome you, our allies, to the table. Corporal Kaplan, Private May, Private Tuck – the Buckingham Hotel is yours for the week. We thank you for your service.'

The American boys looked half-embarrassed and half filled with wonder.

'As you know, the Buckingham Hotel hosts notable members of society from all four corners of the world among its guests, but none are more important to me than...'

Mr Hastings stalled in the middle of his speech, for Max Allgood had suddenly appeared at the table, still cradling Lucille in his arms. Raymond's heart sank for the man, for he could see the excoriating looks on the faces of the Hotel Board. They had never wholly approved of Max – to hire an American to lead the Orchestra in the Grand felt like a treachery; to hire a Black American was, perhaps, even worse – but today their disdain was understandable. Max looked about as dishevelled as a musician did after a wild night playing in one of the Soho dance halls. He might, Raymond thought, at least have tucked his shirt in and refastened his necktie.

'I'm sorry, Mr Hastings.' Max settled himself, then hastily stood and shook each of the American soldiers' hands. They looked on him with some surprise as he said, 'Like Mr Hastings said, boys, I'm proud as hell that we're hosting you. I hope you enjoyed the demonstrations yesterday? I reckon I saw one or two of you tapping your feet?'

The Board seemed to be bristling at Max's interruption, but Mr Hastings just laughed and prepared to resume.

That was when Max said, 'Could we have a quiet word, Mr Hastings? After dinner, perhaps?'

Raymond watched intently. This could only be something to do with the singer stolen by the Imperial Hotel. Max hadn't yet been told about the royal party; Raymond rather doubted that, after that news, Mr Hastings would care about a single singer being poached.

Mr Hastings nodded to Max, and went on, 'A toast to our allies!' He raised his glass. 'A toast to my countrymen!'

'This is strong stuff, sir,' said Joel Kaplan, having tasted his Champagne. 'I don't know if I ever tasted Champagne.'

A thought entered Raymond's head: perhaps *this* was how he lured Henry McCord into the open and tricked him into exposing his secret. One glass of Champagne too many might catch him out. A crude tactic, perhaps – but he was running out of ideas.

'Well, drink up, corporal, because I have another invitation to make – and I'm quite sure it's deserving of another glass.' Hastings steeled himself with a breath. 'I'm afraid that, contrary to popular rumours, the Buckingham Hotel will not be playing host to King George and his royal party tomorrow night.'

Raymond watched eyes flicker and dart around the table. The Board must have been apprised of this before they came to the Queen Mary, for it wasn't shock on their faces; they were each trying hard to hide their fury and indignation.

Max Allgood just started mopping his brow, lips moving without making a sound – as if he was muttering silent curses to himself. Raymond tried to catch his eye with a defiant, consoling look – but it was no use; Max was lost in his blackest thoughts, imagining Nelson playing for the King.

'The Buckingham Hotel would have been proud to host the royal party at our Winter Ball – but it will be no less lavish, no less magical, no less *perfect* without them.' He paused. 'And, of course, without the presence of the King and the security implications his party's presence would require, it leaves open other opportunities.' Joel Kaplan lifted himself, commanding Buxton May and Eugene Tuck to pay careful attention. 'Let this be a Christmas to remember, my friends. I should like it very much if you were to attend the ball tomorrow evening.' His eyes flashed around the table, pointedly ignoring the looks of ire on the faces of Uriah Bell and Peter Merriweather. 'The night will belong to you as well, my friends. Who knows – you might even reserve a dance with Miss Marchmont here?'

Hélène smiled. 'It would be my pleasure, gentlemen.'

'Raise your glasses, gentlemen. This shall be a night like no other!'

As the toast was made and the chattering began, the three Americans filled with wonder and expectation, Max shifted uneasily in his seat, snagged Mr Hastings by the sleeve and drew him down to talk.

'I'm sorry, sir. I'm just so damn sorry.'

'Mr Allgood, whatever for?'

'You can lay it at my feet, sir. I'm damn sure of it. It's *him*, Mr Hastings. My nephew. They've been playing dirty from the beginning. And, by God, they won.'

'Mr Allgood, the battle might be lost – but there are more battles to come. I still expect spectacle tomorrow night.' He lowered his voice to a whisper, bringing Raymond and Hélène into the conversation as well. 'I still expect magic. We must make a virtue of our situation. This is the year that will change the course of the war. Let us welcome it, in splendour and light – and the company of our allies.' He gripped Max's hand, but gazed at Raymond as well. 'Your mission, gentlemen, is to make sure the royal party rue the day they didn't side with the Buckingham Hotel. But we must be noble in defeat. It was a fair fight, after all.'

Max didn't mean to; he opened his mouth and the words just rushed out. 'It wasn't a fair fight at all, sir. It's the ugliest, bitterest fight there is. Those blackguards at the Imperial, they poached my nephew this summer. He would have been playing for us, but they got inside his head. But it's more than that, sir.

247

They took our guest singer. They tried to take Alix, when she was barely through our door. They've been chipping away at me since summer.' Max's voice was rising, attracting the attention of the other members of the Board. It was Alix's counsel that was playing on him. She'd been right in everything she said.

Mr Hastings tried to quell him with a look, but Max blathered on: 'They declared war on us, sir. A war for the spoils of Christmas, and they've been using every dirty, underhand tactic they can find. Well, it's true. Isn't it?'

At this point, Mr Hastings paused, and Raymond saw his eyes flit momentarily to the service hatch across the restaurant floor, and the kitchen beyond.

'They took a number of our kitchen hands as well.'

'So what's next?' Max snapped. 'Come for our dancers? And we just let them?' Feverish now, Max clung to Lucille. 'There are only twenty-four hours until the band strikes up. Don't you get the feeling, Mr Hastings, that they're not finished with us yet? You want us to make magic. Well, how in hell are we to do it when they're coming after us, one by one? We should be saddling up for the adventure of a lifetime – but, by God, I can't do it, not when they've got their pistols trained on me all the time.' Defeated, Max slumped into his seat.

Mr Hastings would have responded that he would deal with it, that if the Imperial Hotel had started a war, then the Buckingham would end it, but at this moment, Joel Kaplan raised his voice and confidently ventured:

'Sir, me and the boys were wondering – and, of course, it might be that this is us pushing our luck too far, and I'd be happy to hear it if that's so – but me and the boys, we got to thinking... what are the chances we could invite guests to the ball?

*

248

In the kitchen, Frank Nettleton froze. It was difficult to make out much of what was being said at the hotel director's table from here, but enough of the conversation had reached him that he was beginning to understand.

Joel Kaplan's voice cut through the hubbub.

So did Mr Hastings', in return:

'Do you know what, boys, I think that's a fine idea. The Buckingham Hotel is your "Home Away From Home" – this is *your* Winter Ball as well.'

Frank heard M. Laurent bawling in the background, but all he could see was Joel Kaplan and the other infantrymen clasping hands in celebration.

'And Mr de Guise,' John Hastings went on, pivoting from the soldiers to his star dancer, 'I'm right in thinking, am I not, that you're hosting our allies at home as well? Well, let me say it loud and clear: this invitation is extended to them as well. Let this be our New World Winter. Let this be our New World Symphony! Embrace our allies, and hold them dear, for all the Christmases to come.'

Frank saw a look of horror flicker on Raymond's face – something to do with that invitation, perhaps? – but it was nothing to the horror that was yawning open inside of him.

There was only one reason Joel Kaplan had asked that question.

Only one girl he had in mind.

A plate slipped from Frank's hand, shattering into a hundred pieces on the cold stone ground of the kitchens.

'NETTLETON!' bawled Henri Laurent.

But Frank didn't care.

The head chef could rant all he wanted.

Because the worst thing that could possibly happen had already come to pass – and suddenly every assurance he'd made

Mathilde, telling her he would dance unfettered and free, crumbled to dust.

Joel Kaplan was about to invite Rosa to the ball.

And there was only one thing Frank could think of doing that would possibly stop it.

There and then, Frank Nettleton made a decision.

He was going to do what was *right*.

Rosa deserved to know.

Chapter Twenty

The blackout was already in place by the time Nancy left the Buckingham Hotel – where Raymond was now dining in the Queen Mary – and climbed in a taxicab back for Maida Vale. Because the hand of fate is playful and capricious, the driver who took her along that long, frozen road was the very same who had ferried Raymond back and forth some hours ago. 'It's a busy route, this one,' he said, smiling at Nancy in the fogged-up rear-view mirror. 'Not that I'm complaining – but you might think of hiring me as the family's personal chauffeur.'

'Do you mean to say my husband came back and forth today?'

The driver paused, sensing that he had, perhaps, broken some confidence. 'I expect he's planning a nice Christmas surprise for you, ma'am. A solid, dependable gentleman like that. An upstanding hero of the war. Yes, now I come to think of it, that's exactly what he was doing. You'll have to pretend I didn't say a thing. Mum's the word.'

After that, apparently afraid he might let some other secret slip, the driver said nothing until, arriving on Blomfield Road, he scurried round the taxi to help Nancy onto the frozen pavement and said, 'No fare tonight, Mrs de Guise. You just get into the warm now, won't you? And have a happy Christmas with that little'n of yours.'

Nancy didn't like the creeping feeling of unease that prickled in her as the taxicab wheeled away. She'd bumped into Raymond twice at the hotel; neither time had he mentioned that he'd made a mad dash back home in the middle of the day.

The house looked empty, as it always did hidden behind its blackout blinds, but she could hear music playing inside. Vivienne was doing a sterling job entertaining the Americans – but it was only one more day before Nancy's allotted leave from the hotel. She had so much to deal with by then, not least confronting this issue of Rosa and her infantryman, but a few days at home would change everything.

As Nancy reached the front door, it opened in front of her. There stood Henry McCord, his face banked in shadow beneath a Homburg hat, half hidden by scarves. In his gloved hand, he carried the briefcase he seemed to take everywhere with him.

'Excuse me, Mrs de Guise,' he ventured, striding past. 'I almost didn't see you there.'

'I would have walked straight into you!' laughed Nancy. The warmth of home was rushing out to hold her, just as winter was stealing within. 'Is everything OK, Mr McCord?'

Henry just lifted his hat to her and smiled. 'I just need some air, ma'am. I won't be long. I'm sure glad of your hospitality.'

Then he sloped off down the path.

Nancy watched until he was gone, then slipped inside the house. She was still shaking the snow from her boots when Vivienne appeared from the sitting room, cradling Stan. 'Arthur's sleeping upstairs,' she said. 'The boys have had quite a day.'

Nancy was beginning to realise how unusual the day had been – for there, in her sitting room, enjoying glasses of brandy with Ellsworth and Jonah, was Mrs Fitzwilliam from down the road. 'I see you're embracing your role as host,' Nancy grinned.

Was Nancy imagining things, or did Vivienne's laughter seem just a little *forced*? It rang out, but it didn't seem to reach her eyes – which was exactly how Raymond seemed, to anyone who knew him well, when he was adopting his role as 'King of the Grand'.

'I'll tell you everything,' said Vivienne. 'But here, let me help with your coat.'

This was unusual too: Vivienne was Nancy's friend, and yet suddenly she was acting as if she really was the housekeeper.

Moments later, having said her hellos, Nancy hurried upstairs to look in on Arthur, who reached out to her with loving arms. Rocking him tenderly, Nancy gravitated to the nursery windows – and, having first put out the light, pulled back the blackout blinds.

'Showing him the snowfall?' Vivienne whispered.

Nancy started; she hadn't realised Vivienne was standing in the nursery door.

'He loves watching it fall,' Vivienne went on.

'I was rather looking for...' Nancy paused. 'Vivienne, come here.'

Vivienne joined her in the window.

'You see the shadow, at the edge of the green? The silhouette, underneath the streetlamp?'

Of course the streetlamp stood in darkness, as did the whole of Blomfield Road, but even so Vivienne could make out the hulking shape of a man standing on the corner, where the street swept westwards, round the curve of the Regent's Canal.

'Henry McCord was going out to get some air. Is that *him*?' asked Nancy.

She didn't see the way Vivienne started, just stared more intently as Vivienne said, 'Perhaps he didn't like the atmosphere.'

253

There was that laughter again. 'Did he happen to say where he was going? I thought he was just freshening up.'

Nancy let the blackout blind fall. 'I'm sure he'll be back soon. Better pour me a glass of that brandy, Viv. It's been a long day.'

Frank hardly noticed when the last order had been fulfilled, for the deliveries of fully laden trollies to the pot wash seemed unending. He was deep in a trough of scalding water, scrubbing grease from roasting pans, when Henri Laurent appeared through the steam, clapped him on the back with a meaty fist and said, 'One smashed plate aside, you've done a fine job, Nettleton. If you ever get sick of dancing, there's a place for you in my kitchen.'

Frank smiled weakly in reply, then returned to his scrubbing.

The truth was, he'd been flagging, exhaustion overcoming him, by the time he was halfway through his shift. Nevertheless, he'd kept on scrubbing with brio.

There was one reason, and one reason alone, why he had become such an efficient pot washer.

It turned out that attacking dirty broiling pans, and even dirtier skillets, was a perfect way to scourge himself of the fury he'd been feeling ever since Mr Hastings made his announcement.

'They'll be poaching you from the Grand if you're not careful!' laughed one of the sous-chefs, wheeling the last of the trolleys through.

Frank just grumbled in reply.

At least the end was coming. And his mind was made up. Frank was one of the last to remain in the kitchens after the service had ended, but eventually his fellow pot washer dismissed him from service. 'You'll need to shower all that grease out of your hair, or you'll be looking like a sewer rat for those lords and ladies tomorrow night.'

Frank didn't really care, not until he caught sight of his reflection in one of the tin work surfaces as he crossed the kitchen. Tomorrow night, he was expected to be a debonair representative of the Buckingham Hotel; right now, he looked like one of the vermin the kitchens were constantly battling to keep at bay.

Having taken just a few moments to make himself look presentable, Frank emerged from the Queen Mary by the back exit and took to the lesser, unseen halls of the hotel. One shift in the kitchen had been more tiring than twenty-four hours in the Grand, but he discovered fresh fire as he made for the service elevator. He was just pulling the lever for the attic quarters when he heard somebody calling his name and looked up to see Billy Brogan limping towards the closing grille.

'I can't stop, Billy,' said Frank. 'I'll see you soon.'

'Hold there!' Billy exclaimed – and, sticking out the crutch he'd been using, managed to waylay the elevator. 'I heard you took a shift in the Queen Mary tonight. That's right, is it?'

'Look at the state of me, Bill. You don't look quite as ragged, dancing in the Grand.'

'See, that's what we need to talk about. Frank, let me get you a drink? A stiff brandy, to celebrate the night?'

Frank liked Billy, but tonight his patience had all been used up. 'I'm flat out exhausted, Bill. That drink will have to wait.' Then, ignoring Billy's further protests, he gently moved aside Billy's crutch, heaved shut the elevator grille and rode the rattling contraption up through the heart of the hotel.

Some moments later, he was heaving back the grille and climbing the last flight of rickety stairs, into the attics where the chambermaids lived.

It was a strange feeling, venturing back here – for so long, the kitchenette at the end of this hall had been a second home to him – but he kept his head down, passed the narrow stair leading to the observation post on the hotel roof and rounded the corner, hurrying past the girls' bedrooms. By now he fully expected to hear music blaring from the kitchenette – but only silence greeted him as he approached the door. He knew somebody had to be here, for a lamp was on inside, but of the usual raucous ribaldry of the chambermaids, there was not one peep.

Frank took a breath and marched into the kitchenette.

Rosa was nowhere in sight. Nor, indeed, did a gaggle of chambermaids fill the kitchenette tonight.

Only Annie Brogan, curled up in one of the threadbare old armchairs, a pile of magazines in her lap – and looking about as forlorn as Frank had ever seen her.

She started when Frank appeared, upending the plate of hot buttered toast which had been precariously balanced upon the armrest. 'Frankie?' she ventured.

Frank decided he must still have looked haggard, because Annie seemed mortified to see him here.

'Sorry, Annie – I was looking for …'

Annie didn't let him say her name. She picked up her toast, dusted it down to put back on the plate and said, 'They went dancing. As soon as the Americans were finished in the Queen Mary. Corporal Kaplan was up here. He said he had some news and he wanted to …'

Frank shook his head, telling Annie not to go on. He knew what that news was.

But he also knew the news he was carrying, and what it would do to her.

'Do you want some tea, Frank?'

Frank sauntered further into the room. 'I'd like that, Annie,' he whispered.

The fire that had propelled him up here was fading now.

The girls were probably out at the Midnight Rooms, or the Ambergris, perhaps even the Starlight Lounge – those places of feverish, frenetic dance which Frank and Rosa used to hold so dear. It was funny how quickly a person could shed their memories. To Frank, those dance halls would always be places that reminded him of Rosa; to Rosa, it seemed, they carried no fond memories at all – they were just places to take Joel.

'How about a splash of this instead?' came a voice from the door.

Frank and Annie turned. There stood Billy, his crutch in one hand and a bottle of Cles des Ducs Armagnac in the other.

Billy seemed to sense the stilted sadness in the room and seized his opportunity to march in.

'Frankie, this ought to warm your cockles,' he said, finding three teacups and pouring full measures. 'It can't have been easy, a night working for old Henri Laurent. But that's exactly what I want to talk to you about. Frankie, I've got a bit of a proposition…'

The night had grown old. Exhaustion had dragged Nancy under. The truth was, she'd rather enjoyed an evening drink with Vivienne, Ellsworth and Jonah – but what she'd enjoyed even more was the moment when, having heard Arthur cry out, she'd come upstairs with her nightcap, settled herself in the rocking chair by his crib and held his hand as he went back to sleep.

Only now did she realise that she too had fallen asleep – for she awoke, still in the rocking chair, to the front door opening downstairs, and the tread of footsteps in the hall.

No more music played. The clock on the wall said midnight was already on the approach. Perhaps this was McCord, returning from his nocturnal wanderings?

She crept to the top of the stairs and looked down.

A shadow crossed the bottom of the stairs.

Vivienne…

'Raymond,' she whispered, 'we've got to talk.'

Nancy froze. A woman always knows when something is wrong in her own house, and suddenly her senses tingled.

She heard her husband's voice, as he took off his boots, hung up his coat and came down the hall. 'We can't talk here,' he said, his voice a low whisper. 'To the shelter?'

'We can't do that either,' Vivienne returned. 'Ellsworth *knows*. He saw us out there last night. He thinks—'

Nancy had rarely heard Raymond so commanding when he said, 'Thinks what, Vivienne?'

'That I love you,' she said. 'That we're betraying Nancy.'

'Good Lord,' Raymond seethed. 'Is there no end to this?'

'Raymond, he told me he could take me away from you – as if you're a scoundrel, keeping a mistress under your own roof. He said he could take me back to New York. That there are diplomatic flights he could put me on. Take me and Stan away from the war. I don't know what to do.'

'The only thing we can do. Get them out of our house, Vivienne, as quickly as possible.'

There was some bridled fury inside Raymond. It unnerved Nancy, for she'd never known him cling on to real fury before. Something must have shifted in her weight, because at that moment the floorboard creaked underneath her, and Raymond's silhouette appeared suddenly at the bottom of the stairs.

'Nance, I'm so sorry,' he whispered, 'did I wake you?'

Behind her, Arthur was crying out. She walked slowly back to him, mindful of Raymond following her into the nursery.

'I'm sorry Nancy,' he said, masking the fury of moments before, running his hand around her waist as she reached the crib. 'It's been a rather testing day. We lost the King. The royal party aren't attending, and—'

'Vivienne never told *me* all that, Raymond. She never told me what Ellsworth thought.'

Raymond tensed. 'I'm sure she didn't want to upset you.'

Nancy had to turn this thought over, inspecting it from every angle. She was sure it made sense, but the unease wouldn't leave her. She felt Raymond reach for her hand; part of her thought to draw away, but the other part told her to keep on pretending. Suddenly, it felt like there was a lot of *pretending* going on in her house.

'He said that he'd seen you with Vivienne, out in the air raid shelter.'

She could feel Raymond's hand start to tremble.

'I want to give you the best Christmas,' he said. 'We were planning your gift, that's all.'

Raymond sensed some hesitation in Nancy. For the first time, he felt a chasm opening between them. 'Let him think what he wants,' said Raymond. 'It isn't true. You *know* it isn't true.'

Nancy did. Why, then, did this still feel so *awry*?

Raymond could see the concern still etched into her face. 'I don't care what he thinks, Nancy. But I do care if he's making Vivienne offers. Take her back to America? Put her on a diplomatic flight? The man thinks he's a knight in shining armour.'

This, it seemed, was enough to divert Nancy from any ideas of indiscretion in the air raid shelter last night. 'It wouldn't be such a terrible thing for Viv. It would get her away from the war.'

'And take Stan with her?'

'It would take him from the war as well. They'd be safe in New York. Safer than we are, right here.'

That much was true, thought Raymond. Right now, just about anywhere would be safer than his own house.

'Raymond,' Nancy whispered, 'if she wants to go, she should go.'

'Nancy, let's just get some sleep.'

'I'm going to talk to her about it in the morning. Get to the bottom of it. It would change everything for us, Raymond. I couldn't keep up at the Buckingham without Vivienne. But it's her life we're talking about. It's her future. It's…'

'It's not going to happen,' said Raymond, flatly.

'And why not?' Nancy demanded. 'Why not, if we love her?'

How to put this into words, without spilling his own story? 'She's part of the family,' he said, softly. 'She wouldn't leave us, any more than we would leave her. We rely on each other!' He forced a laugh. 'This is all my fault. It's all just misconstrued. I just wanted to make this a Christmas to remember. I missed you last year. That's all.' Now, when he reached out to brush the hair from Nancy's brow, she didn't resist. 'I'm sorry, Nancy. It seems I'm terrible at keeping secrets.'

But *was* he? thought Nancy, as she let him go and reached for Arthur instead. Or was one secret burying another? She had a sudden flash of what Mathilde had told her about Joel Kaplan's secret bride. Perhaps her day was so filled with rumours and lies that she was seeing them everywhere she looked, but something told her there was something else here, something she didn't understand.

She was thinking it still, as they lay Arthur back in his crib and retired to their room together.

She was thinking it as the lights went out and Raymond slid in beside her.

It was almost as if she could *hear* him thinking.

Almost as if, even in the absolute blackness of that room, she could see his eyes wide open, staring at the ceiling, contemplating whatever came next.

*

'A proposition?' Frank said, puzzlement drawing deep lines on his face.

'Drink up, Frank,' said Billy. 'It'll do you some good.'

It'll do me some good too, thought Billy, *if Frank's got a nice brandy in him before I ask . . .*

The moment Billy had breathed the word 'proposition', Annie started glaring at him – but Billy didn't mind. Tonight, fate had offered him a second chance. Victor might have absconded, but destiny had sent him Frank Nettleton. It was too good an opportunity to miss.

'Oh leave Frank out of it, Billy!' Annie groaned.

Billy pitched forward, making a steeple of his fingers. He tried to dazzle Frank with a grin, but Frank barely responded. Never mind, thought Billy – Frank was a good sort; and, of course, he owed the Brogans a thing or two. When he'd first come to London, back in the days before Nancy and Raymond were married, Frank had lodged at Albert Yard. In all likelihood, he still felt like he owed the Brogan family a debt. To Billy's mind, that almost *guaranteed* he'd help.

'You see, Frank, I made my ma a promise I'm struggling to keep. Now, you know my ma – she's a proud woman, and she's had a tough life. But she's generous to a fault – she opens her home to every old waif and stray, as I'm sure you remember! – and I think she deserves something in return. Something to make this Christmas extra special for her.' Billy paused. 'I've promised her a goose.'

'A goose?' Frank uttered. This night was like a runaway train, teetering on the tracks; it seemed to lurch from one extremity to another.

'What's wrong with that?' Billy said, trying to disguise how truly affronted he was. 'You don't think the Brogans deserve a nice goose?'

'It's not that Billy,' said Frank, verging on laughter. 'It's just – a ... goose?'

'Well, I'm having a hell of a time getting hold of one, actually. I've tried all over. Do you know how rare goose is these days? You'd think they've got them rationed, the difficulty I'm having.'

Frank felt as if he'd been sucked, somehow, into an absurdist vaudeville act. He looked for some flicker of mirth on Billy's face, but found none.

'Well, you do know *one* place where there are geese, don't you?' Billy went on.

Annie rose suddenly from her armchair, spilling yet more tea – and depositing her toast, for a second time, on the floor. This time, she didn't stoop to pick it up. Instead she said, 'Billy, leave Frank out of it. He's having a hard enough time as it is. All this business with Rosa and the American, and the ball tomorrow night, and—'

'Well, precisely!' Billy went on. 'Frank's got talent. He's a stalwart. He took that shift in the kitchen today because he knew he couldn't let down folks who need him. And that's what *I* am right now. Hear me out, Frank. What I'm thinking of is a gentle bend of the rules, and it's all in a good cause. I've been looking at this problem from just about every angle – and I think I've got a solution. An associate of mine – you don't need to know who, Frank,' and Billy tapped the side of his nose, a great pantomime gesture that just had Frank more puzzled still, 'told me I should forget about the goose altogether, that a big Cornish hen ought to do the trick – if I roasted him with a bit of goose fat. Well, to begin with I thought this was a fine idea. But then I realised – Ma would know. You couldn't just give her a hen and tell her it's a goose, and she'd get suspicious if, suddenly, I told her *I* was going to be doing the cooking.

She'd take it as a barefaced insult, and I'm meant to be doing something special. So *then* I got thinking...'

'Oh, spit it out, Bill!' Annie bleated.

Billy just grinned. 'What I need, Frank, is a favour. I've got myself a promise on a hen. One of my associates has sworn he'll deliver it, if I get hold of a bottle of the hotel's finest Champagne for him. He's got a particular taste, this friend of mine. Veuve Clicquot. Ponsardin. He wants a '32 vintage, but reckons '37 was a good year as well. Anyway, I'm meeting him tomorrow morning to get my hands on this hen – which is where *you* come in.' Billy rolled his eyes – another big pantomime performance. 'Oh, don't look at me like that, Annie! I can hardly go into the kitchens and make the swap myself.'

'S-swap?' stuttered Frank. By now, he was completely bewildered.

'Well, exactly!' Billy exclaimed, and pitched across the cluttered coffee table to pour Frank some more brandy. 'What I need you to do, Frank, is take another shift in the kitchen. You'll sneak my Cornish hen in, and pop one of those geese from the larder down the rubbish chute for me to collect. It won't be spotted, not for a couple of days when they start the preparation for Christmas Day, and when it is – well, M. Laurent can duke it out with the suppliers. How *dare* they send him a hen instead of a goose? What kind of enterprise do they think they're running?'

There was silence in the kitchenette.

Annie held her head in her hands.

Frank just stared, as his bewilderment turned into disbelief.

'You want me to help you *steal* a goose from the larders, Billy?'

Billy shook his head. 'I hate it when people use that word. *Steal*, as if the Buckingham Hotel hasn't been stealing from the common man ever since it was founded.' He paused. 'Look, Frankie, we've all pinched a few things from the hotel over the years, haven't we? Half a bar of soap. A heel of bread. Don't tell me you haven't had a scrap of bacon off the room service trolleys, Frank, 'cause I know you have.'

'Billy, it's hardly the same thing.' Then another thought occurred to him. 'Billy, you said *Champagne*. You're swapping Champagne for a Cornish hen. Since when can you lay your hands on Veuve Clicquot?'

Billy shook his head ruefully. 'This hotel fritters away good things, while families out there starve. You and me, Frank, we get to stop a bit of the rot. There's got to be some perks about working here.'

'Oh, Bill!' Annie snapped, kneading her eyes. 'I saw Victor for a stroll this afternoon. He told me what he offered. Can't you just take him up on it? Can't we just be done with this?'

Billy didn't have time to answer because, suddenly, Frank was on his feet. His eyes darted at Billy, then at Annie and back again. 'I can't believe I'm hearing this.'

Then, all of a sudden, there was something else he couldn't believe he was hearing.

Out in the hallway, the service elevator had ground to a cantankerous halt, and half a dozen sets of feet were clattering up the final narrow flight of stairs.

Frank braced himself.

He got to his feet and wheeled round.

'I've got to go,' said Frank – and, at that moment, the chambermaids burst, cackling and clucking, back into the kitchenette.

They fell silent when they saw Frank. 'How do, Frankie,' said the one called Vera, not looking him in the eye. 'Nice to see you, Frank,' said Mary-Louise – while simultaneously shooting venomous looks at Annie, as if Annie had invited him here just to cause trouble.

'I'm not staying,' said Frank, sheepishly. Head down, he barrelled through the chambermaids, with Billy hoisting himself up to follow. 'I just needed a quiet word, but... Just tell her I came asking after her. Tell her I'll find her tomorrow.'

Frank had already set off along the hall when Mary-Louise's voice called out, 'She's just taking a stroll, Frank. Just a nice snowy stroll.'

He was pulling back the elevator grille when Billy caught up with him.

'Frank,' Billy said, sliding inside the elevator, 'try and see it from my perspective. I made a promise. You wouldn't want me to break a promise?'

Frank didn't know what possessed him. As Billy slid inside the elevator, Frank jumped out, heaved the grille shut and pulled the lever to send it down through the hotel. 'Don't make promises you can't keep,' he snapped – though, whether he was thinking of Billy, or whether he was thinking of Rosa and Joel, he couldn't say.

A midnight stroll, thought Frank as he clattered down the stairs.

Rosa used to like a moonlit stroll.

Hand in hand, down by the river...

And now she was out there with a man who was lying to her with every breath that he took.

Frank reached the sixth-floor landing, then the fifth, then the fourth. By now, another voice was whispering inside him – telling him to let it go, that it didn't matter, that Rosa would have to find out in her own time. Frank's duty was to himself. To his family. To the hotel. In less than twenty-four hours, he would be performing in the Grand. What might Mathilde say to him, if he couldn't corral all these thoughts and feelings and focus on what really mattered?

Then he remembered: Joel Kaplan was going to be in the Grand.

He would have Rosa on his arm.

And Frank would have to dance around them, every pivot and turn weighed down by the secret.

He burst onto the third-storey landing and hurried along the hallway, past the doors of the Candlelight Club, where the evening's last cocktails were still being savoured. If he didn't tell Rosa before she stepped through the doors of the Grand, he'd have to dance through the deception. And he wasn't sure he could.

He'd do it tomorrow.

Find her in the Housekeeping Lounge and break her heart.

It was the only good thing.

Then two American voices sallied out through the doors of the Candlelight Club and he froze.

Something told Frank he ought to march on, but instead temptation drew him back to the doors and he peered through. Few guests remained at the tables. In the distance, by the potted palms of the closed terrace, he saw Hélène Marchmont taking a drink with Alix Monet – but there, at a table just inside the doors, sat two of the American infantrymen who'd just been out dancing with the girls.

Buxton May, Frank remembered.

Eugene Tuck.

They each had a martini glass in hand, clearly flying high on the feeling of their spectacular evening – but, of Joel Kaplan, there was no sign.

The knot in Frank's stomach hardened.

Perhaps Rosa really was out on a midnight stroll with Corporal Kaplan. Perhaps, having returned to the hotel and parted ways with the chambermaids, Tuck and May had simply decided to enjoy one last drink together before bedtime beckoned.

Or perhaps there was another reason they hadn't retired to their suite.

Perhaps they were keeping their distance, making themselves scarce, as a Christmas present for their friend.

Frank's hand had started shaking. He willed it to be untrue, just the product of his fevered imagination, but when one of the cocktail waiters approached the infantrymen and told them no more drinks were being served, he heard them asking if they could simply sit here a while, enjoying the atmosphere – and suddenly he *knew*.

Rosa hadn't gone on a midnight stroll at all. The girls all knew it; they were just lying for her, lying like Joel Kaplan was lying – and if Frank didn't stop it, if Frank didn't tell her the truth, there was every chance she'd make the biggest mistake of her life.

The 'Home Away From Home' suite wasn't far – down the next stairs, along the hall, through the double doors at the passage-way's uttermost end. Frank started running. Somewhere along that hall, he heard Billy Brogan calling his name – but not an ounce of him cared about that right now; he didn't even turn round. Instead, he just kept running – until, at last, he burst onto the corridor where the hotel's grandest suites gave way to their less lavish cousins, and – tumbling over his own feet, in the way no good dancer should – he reached the infantrymen's door.

There was a moment in which, braced against the wall and panting for breath, Frank still hoped it was all in his imagination.

But then he heard the laughter through the wall.

There was no doubt about it.

It was Rosa.

She was there, in the suite with Joel Kaplan.

She was giving herself to him, enveloped in his arms, enveloped in his bedsheets, enveloped in all the lies he'd been spinning ever since they met.

The worst had already come to pass.

There was no way in the world Frank could face them now.

Day Four:

Saturday, 19 December 1942

Chapter Twenty-One

They say the blackest hour is always before the dawn.

In the King James ward at St Thomas's Hospital, the security officer stationed outside Maynard Charles's private ward was deep into the seventh hour of his shift when he heard a rasping sound from within the room.

Immediately, his instincts drove him to action. Throwing open the door of the frigid chamber, he hurried to the bedside.

Maynard Charles – for too long lost in the depths of his own subconscious, his body raging with fever as the doctors kept him alive with saline, fresh blood and oxygen – was suddenly bucking in bed.

The officer had watched men die before. He himself had lain in a field hospital at Arras, convalescing for many long weeks. The gunshot he'd taken on the battlefield had spared him deployment at Passchendaele – he sometimes reflected that one stray shot from a German sniper had, in fact, saved his life – but he'd seen plenty of his brothers succumb. At first, he felt certain that this was what was happening right now: that Maynard Charles's body, having staved off death so valiantly for so long, was at last accepting defeat.

He reached for the old man's hand.

But then he *saw* ...

Maynard Charles's eyes were open.

They were darting in panic, with the look of a man lost overboard, who has just breached the surface of the sea trying to drag him down.

'Nurse!' the security officer cried, leaving Maynard momentarily to charge back to the corridor. 'Sister!'

A cavalcade of footsteps approached through the dark of the ward.

Soon, the ward sister and her nurses were gathered at the bedside.

'Somebody fetch a doctor,' the ward sister demanded. 'Mr Charles is alive!'

At last, the day had come.

Sleep had been fitful, when sleep came at all. Sometimes, Raymond had awoken, to find Nancy thrashing beside him, tormented by some dream. Other times, it had been Nancy who opened her eyes, only to discover her husband muttering darkly in his sleep.

Behind her own bedroom door, a chair pressed up against the handle to keep out any unwanted guests, Vivienne prowled back and forth, turning the events of the day over in her mind – catching herself, almost against her will, dreaming of New York.

And, at the end of the hall, where three Americans ought to be sleeping, one lay with his eyes wide open, staring into the impenetrable darkness of the room, imagining a future every bit as black: the world in ruins, the natural order destroyed, the war won at such terrible cost that it laid waste to the surface of the Earth...

On Raymond's bedside table, an alarm went off.

Not that he needed it. For some time he'd lain there, trapped somewhere between sleeping and wakefulness, and watched as

Nancy picked herself up, dressed behind her screen and emerged to face the day. He said nothing, just lay there pretending, as she left the room. She'd been stiff last night, distant and untrusting, and he sensed it in her still. Raymond couldn't remember another time in their lives when she'd looked at him in suspicion and fear. The guilt of it stabbed at him, but compared to the fear that had been coursing through him all night it was nothing. It had now been three nights since he'd been summoned to the Deacon Club. Three nights since he'd accepted – quite against his own wishes – his mission. Yet the truth of it felt as far away as ever.

And tonight, he was going to have to take them to the Grand.

Raymond sat bolt upright in bed.

The Grand…

Yes, he thought, that was it. Every disaster presented an opportunity. When the Americans were in the Grand, Vivienne could be searching their room, stripping it bare without fear of being discovered, unearthing whatever it was Raymond had missed.

In the Grand, there would be Champagne.

Cocktails, too many to mention.

He'd fill them with Christmas spirit, hit them hard with his questions, expose them right there on the dance floor, if it's what he had to do.

Downstairs, Nancy and Vivienne were working in the kitchen, readying breakfast for the Americans as they emerged. Frank – who'd crawled in even later than Raymond, then slept fitfully in the armchair by the fire – looked ragged as he dragged himself to the kitchen and sat, with the children, at the breakfast table. Nancy tousled his hair, though she still hadn't looked Raymond in the eye. 'Maybe I shouldn't have sent you to that kitchen, Frank. You look exhausted.'

'I've got all day to recover, Nance,' Frank smiled.

This time, when Nancy bowed to kiss him on the forehead, her eyes met with Raymond's.

He thought he saw ice in them.

He certainly saw distrust.

This had to end soon.

He waited in silence, reading the morning paper, and pretended he was still interested in what was happening in Africa, until the Americans arrived. Ellsworth seemed full of his usual bonhomie, even flashing a grin at Raymond, in spite of everything he'd said to Vivienne the day before. McCord was more reserved, accepting the newspaper from Raymond – 'Looks like they're being routed all the way back to Tunis!' he remarked – but it was Jonah who'd seemed to have slept most restlessly of all. 'Thank goodness for Christmas,' he laughed, accepting coffee from Vivienne's pot. 'We're not due back at the embassy now until after the big day. I intend to embrace the rest.'

This was Raymond's chance.

'Gentlemen,' he beamed – and hated the way Nancy creased her eyes when he adopted his princely air, 'I'm afraid there will be precious little rest today – though, perhaps, you'll have earned it by tomorrow. Gentlemen, I have news.'

Nancy froze.

So did Vivienne.

Around the table, the Americans shared a strange, expectant look.

'Last night I took dinner with the Board of the Buckingham Hotel. It is their express wish that the three of you join us, tonight, in the Grand Ballroom for the Buckingham's Winter Ball.'

The atmosphere changed in an instant. Jonah Linden seemed to shed his weariness in a single breath. 'Well, *that's* unexpected.'

'I trust you'll all be accepting the invitation?' Raymond beamed.

'To dance in the Grand?' mused Ellsworth. 'The way you talk about it, Mr de Guise, it sounds like we'd be fools not to.'

It was only McCord who looked unsure. 'Now, Mr de Guise, I hope you're not expecting us to do all your fancy waltzes and foxtrots?'

'Mr McCord!' Raymond exclaimed – and saw, again, Nancy's look of distrust at the act he was putting on. 'You can hardly enter the most splendid ballroom in London and not take to the dance floor.'

'I'm not sure I'm cut out for it, that's all!'

Raymond beamed. 'I'll let you in on a secret, Mr McCord – a good number of our guests have two left feet. It's the job of my troupe – and Frank can attest to this – to make them feel like champions regardless.'

'It's true,' Frank chipped in. 'It helps if you can box step a little though. It helps if you know the basics.'

'And that,' Raymond went on, 'is precisely what Frank and I are going to help you with.'

Frank looked at him quizzically; at least it was a better look than the one colouring Nancy's face right now.

'We don't have to be at the Buckingham until this afternoon,' Raymond remarked. 'So, after we've finished up in here, perhaps we make the sitting room our rehearsal studio? A few records, a little light tuition – how does that sound?'

And a little light interrogation, thought Raymond, eyes flickering from one to the other.

'What do you say, Vivienne?' Ellsworth ventured. 'Want to be my partner?'

Raymond tensed. It was true that Mr Hastings had told Corporal Kaplan and the 'Home Away From Home' guests that they could bring partners to the ball – and this, in all likelihood, meant that Ellsworth, Jonah and McCord were welcome to bring partners too – but there was nothing he wanted less than Ellsworth taking Vivienne to the Grand. Vivienne was needed here tonight. She was the only weapon he had left.

It was fortunate, then, that Vivienne feigned a laugh of her own and said, 'I'm afraid I've made a fool of myself in the Grand too many times. Besides – the boys need me at home tonight.'

There was a moment of silence.

It stretched on too long.

Ellsworth's eyes strayed from Vivienne to Raymond, then his gaze turned to Nancy – and suddenly it was brimming with sympathy. Nancy seemed to recognise it too. Without a word, she swept up Arthur and marched him off to get changed.

Frank and Raymond might have been able to spend the morning dancing – but Nancy had work to do. Whether it was the day of the Winter Ball or not, beds still needed changing, suites still needed cleaning.

'To dance, then!' declared Raymond. In the ballroom, you could make up for any uncomfortable moment by simply waltzing on; it seemed he meant to take the same approach here. 'The waltz first. Then some rudiments of the quickstep and foxtrot. If we get time, perhaps we'll even turn to the tango – the *forbidden* dance. We'll make fine dancers of you yet. Then, gentlemen, you *shall* go to the ball!'

John Hastings prided himself on arriving at the Buckingham Hotel long before the establishment awoke, but this morning it would have to wake without him, for just as dawn was breaking, he stepped out of a taxicab and marched with purpose to the doors of the Imperial Hotel.

Hastings held no particular enmity towards the Imperial. He was a man of numbers, letters and facts and, before his family fund had taken a minority share in the Buckingham Hotel, they'd scoped out a good number of other opportunities across London. The Imperial had been one of these. It was a solid establishment, with a loyal coterie of well-regarded guests. It was only the influence of Raymond de Guise, and the magic of the ballroom, that had brought him to the Buckingham. Had history been ever so slightly different, Hastings himself might have been the one fighting to take away the Buckingham's crown. Right now, he might have been celebrating his successful gambit, bringing the King and his party to the Imperial Ball.

But history was not different.

It was the Imperial Hotel who had spent the year chipping away at the Buckingham, undermining it at every turn.

And today that would end.

Hastings entered the hotel and crossed the barren reception hall, where an estimable gentleman of some considerable years greeted him in a rich baritone.

'I have an appointment with Mr Gove,' Hastings began. 'He's expecting me.'

'Might I take a name, sir?'

'Tell him it's Hastings, and I should appreciate it if I wasn't kept waiting.'

Hastings had sent his secretary last night to parlay with Mr Gove's office, thinking that arranging a sudden meeting might prove difficult – but Gove, it turned out, was eager to look Hastings in the eye and, consequently, the details were very quickly thrashed out. It was, Hastings later realised, the gloater's prerogative: the desperate need of a victor to look his loser in the eye and smile.

Naturally, Hastings had arrived half an hour earlier than the appointed time – and, just as naturally, Mr Gove kept him waiting until the allotted hour had come, passed and faded away. In New York, it was considered the height of ill manners to keep a business associate waiting, but in England they did things differently – being late, then pretending that you weren't, was (apparently) a legitimate tactic. For a time, Hastings took a seat in the reception hall and, when that grew tiresome, he ambled around the reception hall.

As guests began flocking into the reception hall, he followed the sloping hall down to the doors of the Imperial Ballroom, and into the dark, cavernous vault.

In twelve hours, the King would be here – but for now there was only darkness, and the hollow echoing of his footsteps as he walked along the dance-floor's edge.

He was standing there, lost in thought, wondering at everything the year had wrought, when the electric lights at the bar flared. When he turned, he realised that Mr Gove himself had appeared. Now he stood, like the most insouciant barkeeper, at the bar, a decanter of rich, auburn whisky in his hand.

'I was told you were waiting for me by the reception desks,' Gove smiled. Hastings had met him only once before; he was long and lithe, his noble face framed in white whiskers. 'But I had a feeling I might find you in here. I do hope you haven't come down here to flagellate yourself?'

Hastings instinctively hated the way the man could say such provocative things while retaining an air of absolute propriety. This, he had learnt, was another very English trait.

'I'm glad you've condescended to meet me at last,' said Hastings, walking methodically towards the bar. 'I'm afraid it's a little early for a drink for me – but, of course, you must indulge yourself, if that's what you need.'

Mr Gove smiled. 'I think a day like this should begin with a celebration, do you not?' And he poured himself a finger of whisky and inhaled its aroma.

'I'll start, shall I?' Hastings began. Then, before Mr Gove could intervene, he declared, 'This has to end, and it has to end now. Mr Gove, for many months, you and your retinue have been waging open war on the Buckingham Hotel. You poached the pianist my bandleader was lining up for the Orchestra this summer, and you didn't stop there. You've taken our kitchen staff. You've disrupted every appointment my Orchestra has tried to make. Now, I discover, you've taken singers we had under direct contract to perform in the Grand tonight.'

Mr Gove opened his hands, as if to show he was carrying no weapon. 'Ours is a competitive world, but I think it a tad hysterical to call it a *war*.'

'No, sir,' Hastings went on. 'It's very much a war, and … you've won.'

Of all the things Mr Hastings might have said, this was the only one that could actually bring Gove to silence. It even wiped some of the smugness off his face.

'I know that the royal party has declared for you, Mr Gove.' Hastings started pacing up and down, his hands folded in the small of his back. 'We received a missive from the Palace equerry, just the same as you. There is nothing, not one thing, that we at the Buckingham can do to change that. This evening, King George and his party will step through those doors. His princesses will dance with your dancers, to music performed by a pianist who, by rights, should have been ours. Long into the New Year, the Society Pages will thrill with it. And all of your staff – no, all of London itself – will carry the memories made this evening through the rest of their lives.' He stopped. At least, so far, he had what he wanted: Mr Gove looked astounded at how much ground he had given away. 'So what I need to say to you, sir, is: it stops here. You've already won. The spoils go to you, sir.' He paused. 'But my own ball still matters. The Buckingham's night is in jeopardy, because of what you've done. Accept your victory with good grace, Mr Gove. Give my Orchestra back its guest singer, and let's call this a truce.'

Mr Gove took a moment to deliberate.

Then, though the breakfast service was only just beginning in the Continental Kitchen, he drank his whisky and said: 'We don't need any truce, sir. All this talk of war is pure hysteria. If the Palace deems our offering better than yours – well, that is just the way of things. We at the Imperial Hotel have done nothing wrong. We have broken no moral code. What we have won, fair and square, we won't be relinquishing.'

For the first time, Hastings felt himself broiling. He had been able to withstand the smugness – he could even appreciate the gusto with which Mr Gove and his associates had worked to make sure their offering succeeded – but what he couldn't tolerate was the lie.

Then the doors of the ballroom opened.

In walked Bob Holloway, the rotund bandleader – and, at his side, a face Mr Hastings recognised only too well.

James Heath was clean-shaven, and dressed in his evening wear despite the hour of day, but it was unrecognisably him: the percussionist from the Max Allgood Orchestra. His warm and friendly manner towards Bob Holloway left little doubt in Hastings' mind as to what he was witnessing.

Mr Gove gave him a conciliatory look. 'I did ask you to wait in the hotel reception, Mr Hastings. You've only yourself to blame, for seeing things you weren't meant to see.' His elderly eyes sparkled over the rim of his crystal glass.

At least Heath had the good grace to look sheepish. The moment he saw Mr Hastings, he murmured, 'It's nothing personal, sir. I just – I want to play for the King, and when the offer came ...'

Hastings was silent.

He remained silent for a beat too long.

He remained silent, even as Bob Holloway led James Heath onward, to introduce him to the dressing rooms behind the ballroom.

Now that he and Mr Gove were alone, Hastings poured a measure of the whisky into his own crystal glass and studied it in the bar's low light.

'I am a patient man, Mr Gove.'

'Too patient by far,' Gove snorted. 'I thought you Americans were all gusto and brio, *carpe diem* types of men. You've been so patient you've been left behind – but you don't need me to tell you that. I'm sure the members of your Board will make it very plain.'

Hastings didn't waver. As he drained his glass, he held Gove's gaze.

'Just remember, when all is said and done: I came here to be a reasonable man. I was prepared to be magnanimous in defeat – but you, Mr Gove? You weren't prepared to be graceful in victory.' Crashing the glass onto the bar, he turned to leave. 'When you look back on this, please remember: it was you who took the gloves off, Mr Gove. I shan't speak to you again.'

'A shame,' Gove laughed, as Hastings left the ballroom.

Mr Hastings sank into contemplative silence as he crossed the reception hall and left the hotel.

He folded his hands behind his back and started walking.

He supposed it would be he who had to tell Max Allgood that the Orchestra would be missing a percussionist tonight.

Every man had his limits.

Mr Hastings hailed a passing taxicab and waited in the slush at the side of the road for it to approach. An omnibus appeared, crawling through the deep drifts of Knightsbridge to come to a halt on the opposite side of the road. Out of its fogged-up interior there tumbled a dozen passengers.

There, among them, was yet another face that he knew.

The kitchen boy Victor, wrapped in scarves and mittens, no doubt making his way to the Imperial Hotel.

'Where to, sir?' said the cabman, gliding alongside him.

'Start your meter, good man,' Hastings began. 'I shan't be a moment.'

Victor was crossing the road to reach the hotel, so he was easy to intercept. At first, the kitchen boy had no idea who had just stepped into his path. John Hastings had to introduce himself before he understood. Even then, his face screwed up in confusion – for why would a man with such high and mighty concerns as Mr Hastings be condescending to speak to a kitchen hand? It couldn't possibly be that he'd come here for this very reason – could it?

'Mr Hastings, sir,' Victor stammered, upon learning who this was, 'I'm sorry, sir, but I – I've got to go to work.'

Hastings was not the sort of director who enjoyed belittling his inferiors, but he had to suppress some ire before replying. 'Can you answer me a question, young man?'

Victor looked like a rabbit trapped in headlights as he said, 'Y-yes, sir.'

'Might I ask you why, exactly, you decided to leave the Buckingham's employ?'

Victor shuddered. This made no sense. It was like a king asking a peasant why he tilled one field over another. 'I'm sorry, sir. I know I let people down. But...' His mind was hurtling at a hundred miles an hour, certain that he'd been exposed, certain that something of Billy's enterprise had come to light, that the only reason a man as esteemed as Hastings could have come here to confront him was because his crimes had come to light. 'They made me an offer, sir.'

Hastings brooded, 'So you go where the best offer is, do you?'

Victor whispered, lamely: 'I've got a family, sir.'

'Indeed you do, boy,' said Hastings, and slapped him on the back. 'Your family is the Buckingham Hotel, and it's where you are needed. Whatever they're paying you in there, I'll double it.'

Victor was astounded. One moment he was certain he was about to be slapped in handcuffs; the next: benediction from above. 'Sir?' Then he looked crestfallen. 'I'm due on shift right now. They'll *kill* me if I walk out now.'

Hastings' face darkened, if only for a moment. 'And yet you walked out on us?'

'That was different, sir.'

'How so?'

Once again, Victor was in freefall. The truth was, he had no idea what was going on – not why Mr Hastings was here, nor what he should say to avoid telling him the truth: *I had to run, sir; I had to run to get away from Billy Brogan.*

In want of anything better to say, he ventured, 'I'm doing prep work today, sir. They're throwing a luncheon for the Orchestra and dancers, to ready them for the ball. Sir, they say the *King* is coming.'

The boy said it with so much wonder – and well he might – but this was not the part of his sentence that caught Hastings' imagination.

'What did you say, young man? For whom are you cooking?'

'The Orchestra, sir. The dancers. They need the ballast before this evening. It's what the Imperial does – they put on a banquet, right there in the ballroom, in the middle of the afternoon. They do it every year. It's tradition.' Victor's voice quietened. 'I've been trusted with the prep work, sir.'

Hastings looked back at the face of the Imperial Hotel.

And suddenly he saw a ray of light breaking through the clouds.

'Young man, you made a very poor decision, leaving the Buckingham Hotel. And I was serious when I said I'd double your pay to come back with me this very moment. But I have another proposition for you, one that might serve us both even better. There must be something you want? There must be some-thing you *need*? Christmas is coming. There must be some wish I could grant, to make you come back?'

Victor wondered if he was still dreaming.

The fact was, one thing really did spring to mind.

One thing that might solve all his problems in one fell swoop.

One thing to pay off Billy Brogan and free him and Annie forever.

'Well, yes sir,' he answered, 'but what would you want me to do?'

Hastings clapped him on the shoulder.

'Nothing more than change the destiny of our Winter Ball,' he smiled – and, turning again to the Imperial's implacable face, added, 'and help me show these underhanded bastards that there is no adversary more formidable than a reasonable man.'

Chapter Twenty-Two

At Blomfield Road, the sounds of the American bandleader Fletcher Henderson rang out.

'It's about as close to the Max Allgood sound as I can get,' Raymond said, browsing through his extensive collection of gramophone recordings. 'Enough to put us in the right frame of mind, anyway. Vivienne, I'm going to need your help. Nancy, you too.'

Nancy had been standing in the sitting-room doorway, watching as Raymond struck up the music and marshalled his unexpected students. The Americans looked intrigued, perhaps even energised, at the idea of their morning tuition. Frank, though he still carried the weariness of the day before, was already taking an imaginary partner in hold, then box-stepping lightly around the hearth, as if to illustrate the perfect frame. Vivienne, having declined her invitation to the Grand, had nevertheless allowed Ellsworth to take her in hold as the dancing began.

But when Raymond called Nancy's name, dazzling her with one of his smiles, Nancy just froze. 'I can't, Raymond. You know I have to go.'

Then she turned and started marching up the hall.

Raymond caught her before she reached the bottom of the stairs. There was yet a whole hour before Nancy needed to be at the hotel. The girls would be breakfasting, the rotas already worked out; Nancy could have stayed and danced if that was what she'd wanted – and yet here she was, beating a retreat.

'You're still angry with me,' Raymond said, quietly.

Even now, thought Nancy, she could tell he was dancing round the lies. It was the way he acted so innocently, as if she had no right to be angry – as if nothing had happened to cause distress.

'I'm not angry, Raymond,' she said, wearily. This, she supposed, was another lie of her own. 'I'm confused. I'm ... disappointed. What business is it of Ellsworth to say those things? And you and Vivienne, whispering about it, not sharing it, and ...'

The silence between them was punctuated by music and laughter from the sitting room.

Even Vivienne seemed to be laughing.

Into the vacuum, Raymond said, 'I love you, Nancy.'

'Why do you want them out of our house?' she asked, sudden and forthright.

It struck them both that Nancy had not returned the love, just pierced him with a question instead.

'I heard it with my own ears, Raymond. *Get them out of our house, as quickly as possible.* That's what you said.'

Raymond gripped her wrist. 'He's decided I'm a scoundrel. Just decided I'm an adulterous cad, keeping my wife and mistress under the same roof. Oughtn't the question be why I'd want him to *stay* here at all?'

Nancy's eyes were like glass. 'And yet you bluster down this morning and declare you're taking him to the Grand Ballroom? Does that sound like the act of an outraged man?

'I always loved your act in the ballroom, Raymond. The King of the Grand, sweeping around his estate, lord and master of it all. It's an act you've played to perfection. I just hate it in my own home. If a prince insults your honour in the hotel, Raymond, you *have* to turn the other cheek. If a man you've invited into your own home insults your honour – insults your wife – the same rules don't apply.'

'Nancy,' Raymond whispered, half following her up the stairs, 'it's for the war.'

She looked back at him with an excoriating gaze. 'For King and Country,' she said – and Raymond had never heard her sound as sardonic. 'All very honourable, Raymond.'

After she was gone, Raymond remained, bracing himself against the banisters, for just one moment. His falsity had been stinging him since he'd returned from Africa, but right now it stung him more than ever. He wanted to canter up the stairs, lock the bedroom door behind them and tell her everything he knew. By the standards of Maynard Charles, Vernon Fox and every other man at the Office, it would be treachery. But did that matter? Right now, it was as if he was committing treachery in his own home.

A voice sailed out of the sitting room.

It was Jonah Linden, evidently eager to learn a thing or two about dance.

'Are you ready, Mr de Guise?'

So Raymond took a deep breath, summoned whatever reserves of forbearance he had left and returned to the fray.

Some moments later, when Nancy breezed past the doorway – putting on an act of her own as she leant in to say farewell and wish them good fortune for the Winter Ball – he was to be seen dancing with Vivienne in his arms, illustrating to the Americans the finer arts of the foxtrot.

The carriage clock was ticking.

In ten hours, the ball would begin.

*

By the time Nancy arrived at the Buckingham Hotel, the Housekeeping girls were already finished with breakfast – and, having gathered around the rota pinned to the wall in the Housekeeping Lounge, were loading trolleys for their first assignments of the day.

'Girls,' Nancy began, the moment she marched into Housekeeping. Almost immediately, the chambermaids ceased what they were doing and gathered to face her. It was not often that Mrs de Guise displayed this kind of bold authority – the girls knew her as a sisterly presence, more inclined to lead them through friendship than brute force – but it seemed something had riled her. Her face was a stern mask as she said, 'You have a long day ahead. A hard day, just like every other at this hotel. But at the end of this hard day comes the night of the Winter Ball – and, as is customary, a night of celebration for all those who work unseen to make the Buckingham Hotel the glorious establishment that it is.

'Some of you will remember that, not so very long ago, the party to be hosted right here in the Lounge was my own favourite night of the year. It isn't just lords and ladies who deserve a little celebration at Christmas. You girls work harder than anyone in this hotel ever recognises. So too do the porters and pages, and everyone who'll be enjoying a drink here tonight.' She paused. 'But because I remember those nights so vividly, I also remember how easily a little merriment turns into wildness – so I am giving you all fair warning. Enjoy yourselves tonight, girls – but, while you are under this roof, you remain representatives of the Buckingham Hotel; and, more particularly, you remain representatives of my department. *Do not let me down.*'

Then she took a moment, allowing her eyes to linger on each of the girls in turn before she announced, 'Right then, off to your assignments. Oh, and Rosa?'

'Yes, Nance?'

'That's *Mrs de Guise*,' Nancy told her, for the umpteenth time. 'A quiet word, please?'

The other girls gave Rosa consoling looks as they took hold of their trolleys and departed. Mary-Louise looked horrified – perhaps suspecting that, somehow, Nancy had discovered where Rosa had slipped off to last night, after the dancing was done. Nancy, meanwhile, simply turned on her heel and went into the office. There she fussed around, turning on the lamps and shuffling papers, until Rosa arrived.

'Rosa, I don't want to cause any awkwardness between us – and I'm distinctly aware that, as a department head, my duty is to the hotel, and not to my family relationships.'

Rosa's face darkened. 'Mrs de Guise, I never meant to hurt Frank. I didn't want to.'

'I'll stop you there, Rosa.' Nancy hated saying what came next, but it was her duty – and no sooner had she thought that, than her mind was whirling back to Raymond and the way she'd castigated him for being so generous and kind to Ellsworth March this morning. That, she supposed, was Raymond's duty. 'I love Frank as only a sister could, and I'm sad beyond measure for the pain he's been through this year. But I also recognise that you're both young, and that young love doesn't always survive. That isn't what I want to talk to you about.'

'It isn't, Nancy?' Rosa caught herself. 'I mean … Mrs de Guise?'

'I understand that Corporal Kaplan has been invited to this evening's ball.'

'That's right, Mrs de Guise.'

'And I further understand that he has been permitted to invite a partner.'

Rosa couldn't suppress her smile, even though it seemed to irritate Nancy.

'Rosa, you have been afforded the most extraordinary invitation. To behold the Grand Ballroom on the night of the Winter Ball will be something you treasure for the rest of your life. But it behoves me to give you a warning, as well. You must treat it with the respect it deserves. Rosa, you must treat yourself with the same respect. This isn't the Midnight Rooms. It is not the place for a chambermaid – and take it from one who knows. You would be better served treating this evening as the most incredible theatrical show – something to be observed and admired, for one night and for always.'

Rosa ventured, 'Are you telling me I can't dance, Nance?'

Nancy glowered.

'I mean… Mrs de Guise.'

'I'm telling you to act with dignity and reverence. It isn't a sideshow. What you do in that ballroom matters.'

'Is it because of Frank, Mrs de Guise?'

Nancy glowered yet further. The truth was, the fact that Rosa was going to enter the Grand Ballroom tonight was about so much more than Frank – it was about what she meant to this department, how the other girls might look on her (with reverence or jealousy? admiration… or spite?), about the reputation of both the girl and the ballroom itself. But yes, she privately admitted, it was about Frank as well. Frank had worked as hard as anyone she'd ever known to earn his place in that ballroom; that Rosa should simply get to waltz in there stuck in her throat.

'Be aware of yourself in there, Rosa. And no more than one glass of Champagne. Do you hear? If you want wildness, come down to the Lounge after hours. The Grand Ballroom is for decorum.'

Rosa understood, then, that Nancy's lecture was coming to an end. 'Yes, Mrs de Guise,' she said, not entirely without irritation, and went back to the office door.

'Rosa,' Nancy called out, 'how much do you really know Corporal Kaplan?'

'I should think I know him rather well, Nancy. We've been stepping out for six months.'

It was on the tip of Nancy's tongue to ask her about what Mathilde had said, yesterday in the ballroom. But the moment passed, and instead, having first dismissed Rosa, she simply sat in the office lamplight, warming her hands around the teapot.

One moment of introspection was enough.

Nancy de Guise had work to do.

And the clock continued to count down.

The clock was counting down at the Imperial Hotel as well.

Nelson Allgood had arrived early that morning, though not early enough to catch John Hastings attempting to castigate Mr Gove, right there in the ballroom. By the time he arrived, however, the rumour had spread around the hotel: the Buckingham were roundly beaten, their Hotel Director had come in person to grovel at the feet of Mr Gove, and the night belonged to them. Now all there was to do was sit back and luxuriate in the victory.

The morning wore on. The anticipation rose. A gaggle of chambermaids, coming off shift, lingered in the lobby to watch the Palace's security officers arrive to make plans for the evening ahead. Meanwhile, backstage, Bob Holloway assembled his core musicians and introduced his new percussionist, James Heath, to the sets.

'This'll be the second time I play for the King,' Nelson laughed, strutting around the practise piano as, in dribs and drabs, the rest of the Orchestra arrived. 'The Royal Dansant at the Albert Hall last summer – now, *that* was something.'

Nelson had won that coveted spot courtesy of his uncle. It was the very performance that had led to his offer from the Imperial Hotel.

'Of course, back then, I was just the guest pianist. A few little numbers, to get them *jiving*! By God, I'll bet he remembers. Even the old folks get their feet tapping when I play. Even the King of England himself!'

The doors of the dressing rooms opened, and in stepped none other than Mr Gove's personal valet. 'Gentlemen, your presence is required in the ballroom.'

'Now we get to it!' laughed Nelson.

He was the first to burst into the ballroom. There, in the space above the dance floor – the space where, tonight, the royal party would gather to watch them play – was a banqueting table, fit for thirty-six people. Scarlet red candles flickered above silver platters adorned with twists of holly and fir. Golden goblets shimmered.

Mr Gove was waiting at the table's head. His smile reached from ear to ear, bending his perfectly coiffured whiskers out of shape, as he bade the Orchestra to sit.

In procession came the staff from the Continental Kitchen. First the head chef, and then a succession of underlings approached, each of them wheeling a silver service trolley heaped high with platters of food. Here were golden roast potatoes, curls of Cumberland sausage, vegetables glistening in butter, a fleet of gravy boats brimming with thick, luxurious sauces. And there, in the midst of it all, four enormous serving trays bedecked in slices of rich, bloody lamb; and, pride of place, a Christmas goose, already carved, and steaming with wild garlic and thyme.

'Gentlemen,' Mr Gove began. 'I have presided over nine such Christmases. Nine times have I stood here to announce that the day of our ball is beginning. But this one, oh *this* one, is special. This year, we have outdone ourselves. From this night on, everyone will know: it is the Imperial Hotel – not the Savoy, not the Dorchester or Ritz, and certainly not the Buckingham – where society gathers.' He beamed. 'And so, to stand you in good stead for the triumph of tonight, I present you with your banquet. Before you lies the grandest fare the Continental Kitchen has to offer. Raise your glasses, gentlemen! A toast!'

Nelson leapt to his feet, brandishing his golden goblet high. 'To tonight!' he laughed.

On another occasion, Mr Gove might have thought very dimly of this impertinence – but, right now, he just smiled.

'To tonight!' he repeated.

'Tonight!' the Orchestra and dancers chimed in.

'Ladies and gentlemen, let dinner commence!' Mr Gove called out. 'Enjoy yourselves. Make merry! And then . . . make *music*. My friends, the clock is ticking.'

In the hallway of the house at No 19 Blomfield Road, the carriage clock starting chiming.

It was already two o'clock.

In the sitting room, Raymond clapped his hands together and lifted the needle from the gramophone.

'Gentlemen, I'm afraid it's time.'

It had been a good morning's dancing – though, by the look of them, it seemed to have left the Americans a little ragged. 'The trick,' Raymond had told them, halfway through the morning, 'is to keep it simple. Let Miss Marchmont, or Miss Kainz – whomever you dance with – give it some flair. As long as you listen to the music and don't overthink things, you'll find it starts to flow.'

He only wished the conversation would flow more naturally. He'd tried to draw them into speaking about the war, asking

Ellsworth again about Pearl Harbour, Jonah about his work securing the embassy and McCord what the next year might bring. There was much to discuss, but the Americans trod lightly, as if they didn't want to give anything away.

'There's only one thing certain, Mr de Guise,' said McCord, when they broke for a light lunchtime repast: bread and butter, honey and cheese. 'There'll be war again in Europe before we reach a peace. Mr Hitler won't roll over. At some point soon, we'll have to roll up our sleeves and invade.'

This thought seemed to cast a pall over proceedings, especially when Jonah added, 'It feels golden now, doesn't it? All the killing's so far away. But Henry's right: the battle's going to come back to the Continent before it's over.' He paused. 'All the boys we've brought over here – they're high on the season right now. They're spending Christmas "home away from home". Hell, some of them are even going to be dancing in the Grand Ballroom tonight! But a good number of them are going to be dead by the time this thing is done.'

Raymond seized his chance: 'If only there was something we could do, some weapon we could deploy, to end it all at once.'

McCord's face twisted, but it was Jonah who spoke:

'Enough of this,' he announced. 'It just makes me want to go back out there and take up a gun. Cast off embassy life and get back in the thick of it with our boys. Sometimes I feel useless, sitting on the sidelines.'

Raymond noticed that both Frank and Henry McCord looked shamefaced at this. Of course, they were the only two in the room not to have been soldiers on the frontline.

'Maybe one more song, Mr de Guise, to break the bad feelings?' ventured Ellsworth.

Raymond had been only too happy to oblige – but now the carriage clock was chiming, and his taxicab was idling on the snowy thoroughfare outside. Frank scurried to ready himself, while Raymond followed Vivienne to the kitchen, where Stan and Arthur were sitting at the table, poking at their own lunch-time spread.

The music had started again in the sitting room. Evidently, the Americans were going to keep up their practise until the moment when they too would head for the hotel.

At least it meant Raymond didn't have to whisper.

With one eye on the hallway he said, 'I couldn't find a thing, but I didn't have enough time. Maybe you'll have more luck. You'll have all night, Vivienne. Take the room apart. Leave no stone unturned.'

Vivienne bent over the sink, trembling. 'I know my job, Raymond.' Then she turned to face him. 'But if I find nothing? If there's nothing *to* find? If this secret he's carrying is just up here?' She tapped the side of her head. 'What then? We keep them until Christmas? Raymond, Nancy *knows* something is wrong.'

'I'm going to handle it.'

'How? How, without telling her the truth?'

Raymond had no answer for that.

'Just promise me, Vivienne. Promise me you won't tell her.'

In the sitting room, the music cut out.

'The taxicab's waiting, Raymond,' said Vivienne.

'Vivienne, I need you to trust me.'

The silence grew stranger, more stilted and strained, the longer it went on.

Then, at last, Vivienne crumbled.

'I'll do everything I can, Raymond. Let's just pray that I find something. Then this can all be over, once and for all.'

That was enough for Raymond. He bent low to kiss Vivienne on the cheek – the moment was not lost on Ellsworth, lingering out in the hall – then went to lift Arthur from his seat at the table. 'Wish your father good luck, young man. The Winter Ball awaits.'

Moments later, he was out in the hall, donning his overcoat and gloves, shaking hands with each of the Americans in turn.

'I'll see you on the dance floor, gentlemen.'

Then, with Frank in tow, he hurried into the snow.

By half past two, when Raymond de Guise and Frank Nettleton walked into the Grand and felt the pure anticipation of the coming night, the lunchtime service in the Queen Mary had come to an end. As the pot washers busied themselves scrubbing down surfaces, scouring the remaining roasting pans and stacking crockery, Henri Laurent bent over his countertop, one fat finger moving through the evening menu. He was still debating dessert, furious that the figs he'd used last night were not up to standard, when he heard footsteps behind him. A mute cough announced the appearance of a figure he hadn't thought to see again.

Laurent could hardly look him in the eye.

But Victor stood there regardless, a bulging knapsack over his shoulder.

'Didn't last long, did you, boy?' Laurent muttered darkly.

'No, Chef,' said Victor.

'So it's back where you belong, is that right?'

'Yes, Chef.'

Henri Laurent wheeled round to face him. 'If it was up to me, boy, you wouldn't darken this doorway again.' His face had grown livid. 'Walk out on us in our hour of need, then just walk back in like nothing ever happened? If it was down to me, you could stay in the gutter.' Laurent closed the gap between them with a stride, then prodded Victor in the breast. 'But you must have a guardian angel, boy. I don't know what game Mr Hastings is playing with those dogs at the Imperial, but it turns out it's your lucky day.'

'I know, Chef,' Victor answered, 'and I'll make it right. I promise I will.

'Aye, and you can start right now.'

'Prep for this evening, Chef?'

Laurent's laughter was like the braying of a wounded seal. 'You might have come back to the fold, boy, but don't expect the same station. No, you're in the pot wash tonight – and every night thereafter, until I say otherwise. Do you hear? Go and get yourself ready. We start preparing for the dinner service in an hour. I need you on station by then.'

Victor was grateful the barracking had not been more severe. He'd been filled with a daunted feeling as he approached the Buckingham Hotel, and might have turned tail and fled, if it hadn't been for thoughts of Annie and what his return might mean to her.

Now that his scolding was over, he could go and find her. Sloping out of the kitchens, he circumvented reception and scurried down to the Housekeeping Lounge. Victor didn't suppose there was any way he'd be able to come to the evening shindig; M. Laurent was sure to keep him in the kitchens until long after midnight, but perhaps there'd be time, after that, to raise a glass with Annie. If he was right about how the next few moments would turn out, they were going to deserve it.

There was Annie, halfway up the stepladder, pinning paper stars to the wall. Mrs de Guise was on the other side of the Housekeeping Lounge so Victor didn't feel he could cry out. Instead he just waited until some of the other girls noticed his presence. One of them poked Annie in the ribs to get her attention. She very nearly tumbled from the stepladder in response; then she saw Victor and scrambled to his side.

'You're here!' Annie gasped.

'I'll tell you everything later,' Victor whispered. 'Right now, I need you to come with me.'

Annie couldn't abscond, not without first begging permission from Mrs de Guise – but apparently Nancy was too consumed in other things to worry too much about tinsels and paper stars, so that permission was very quickly granted. Soon, Annie was holding tight to Victor's hand, skipping after him as he marched through the back halls of the Buckingham Hotel.

'What happened, Victor? I thought you were gone – gone for good!'

'So did I,' Victor replied, 'but it was the strangest thing. Me and Mr Hastings, we came to an *understanding*.'

None of this made sense, but Annie didn't care – not if it meant Victor was back at the Buckingham.

Then she realised where they were going.

Up ahead, at the end of the hall, lay the hotel post room.

Victor didn't knock. One moment, he was standing outside the post-room door, avoiding Annie's questioning eyes; the next, he was kicking his way through, to find Billy half asleep at his desk.

'Too many late nights, Bill?' said Victor, closing the door behind him and fastening the latch. 'Or too many early mornings, making deliveries across town?'

'You're back,' he gasped.

'Back for good, as a matter of fact,' said Victor.

Billy didn't understand the look on Victor's face – he thought, at first, it was the look of a man getting ready for a fight, but a moment later he changed his mind: this, he decided, was actually the look of a man about to land a killing blow.

'I'm back to work for the Buckingham Hotel,' Victor announced, 'but I'm finished working for you. And so is Annie.'

Billy rolled his eyes. 'Now, wait one second. You don't get to march in here and start barking out orders. This is *my* outfit, Victor.'

'I offered you a deal, Billy.'

There was much Billy wanted to say, but Victor didn't let him. He reached into the knapsack hanging over his shoulder, pulled out of it a fat bundle wrapped in brown paper and deposited it on Billy's table.

Billy prodded it with a finger.

The paper unfurled.

There, sitting proudly in the middle of the package, was a plump Christmas goose.

'She's a small one,' Victor said, 'but the deal still stands. You get to keep both of your promises – first, the one you made to your mother. And, second, the one you're about to make me.'

'Where did you get this?' Billy marvelled. Down on his knees, he started inspecting it from every angle – just like some archaeologist might, upon unearthing an ancient treasure.

'Does it matter where I got it?' Victor snapped. 'I offered you a trade: one Christmas goose, in return for those ledgers you keep. One Christmas goose, to let me and Annie go.'

'Is it from the larders?'

Victor just stared.

'Did you steal it from the Imperial Hotel?'

Victor snorted, 'We're finished here, Billy.' Then he took Annie by the hand and led her out of the post room.

Annie was breathless. She was quite certain that what she'd just seen was a miracle – but now new fears started to play on her. 'Is that what you did, Victor? Did you steal it from the Imperial? And... aren't they going to find out? Aren't they going to *know*? You didn't have to do it. You didn't have to do it for—'

Victor silenced her with a kiss.

He'd hoped it might calm Annie, but the truth was it left her even more shell-shocked.

'I – I don't understand.'

'I didn't steal it, Annie. I just took a leaf out of Billy's book. I made a deal of my own.'

'But what deal?' Annie gasped. 'Who with?'

For the first time since he'd returned to the Buckingham Hotel, Victor's face broke into a smile. 'Well, with Mr Hastings, of all people,' he laughed. 'Mr Hastings offered me a deal I couldn't refuse. He says – he says it might even save the Buckingham Hotel. He says it might be the making of the Winter Ball.' Victor put his arms around her. He had liked that kiss, as sudden as it was. In a few short moments, he was going to kiss her again.

But first he pressed his lips to her ear and whispered the whole truth.

There wouldn't ever be lies, not between Victor and Annie.

Chapter Twenty-Three

Time, which had flown by so quickly this morning, had slowed to a terrible tread. Vivienne busied herself with the children, prepared the Americans a simple dinner to give them some ballast before the dance, but all the time her eye was on the clock. When Jonah coaxed her into the sitting room to waltz, she watched the clock sitting on the hearth. As Ellsworth took Stan out into the snowbound garden, to make fortresses and wage battle with snowballs and sticks, she counted the minutes. As she brought yet more tea to McCord, every second seemed interminable.

Three o'clock.

Four o'clock.

Five ...

Then, when at last the Americans retreated to the bedroom to put on their evening wear, time seemed to speed up. One moment, she was gathering herself in the kitchen. The next, Ellsworth was standing in front of her, asking for help fixing his collar and tie.

She had to admit: he looked handsome, in a suit of jet black. He'd run pomade through his hair, shaved in the bathroom mirror, applied a scent like coal tar to his stubble.

Surely he didn't need help fixing his bow tie.

Surely it was just an excuse.

So it was. The moment Vivienne stepped close and started straightening his collar, he caressed her arm and said, 'Have you thought about what I said?'

Vivienne knew not what to say. Beyond Ellsworth, she heard footsteps on the stairs.

'Your son would be safe in New York. Vivienne, I know your loyalties are torn. But there's nobody else you have to please in this world. Nobody else you owe a thing to – only that little boy, sitting over there.'

Jonah and McCord appeared in the kitchen doorway.

Vivienne drew back.

'I'm still thinking,' she told him. 'But let's just say: you've got me dreaming.'

The words seemed to melt Ellsworth's heart – and she realised, then, that, in this alone, she wasn't lying. Here she stood, planning on rifling through their belongings as soon as they left his house, hoping above all other things that she could expose one of them as the traitor he was, but right now she was telling the truth. Ellsworth had planted the seed of New York in her mind, and the idea had started to grow.

Stan, growing up in one of the grand townhouses on Washington Square.

A little place in Greenwich Village, and all the places she used to play.

'Time to go, Ellsworth,' Jonah laughed, from out in the hall. 'Your carriage awaits.'

Vivienne swept up Stan and followed the Americans down the hall, her heart beginning to race.

McCord opened the front door. He looked the most debonair of them all, a young man stepping out on his first date with society. Out he went, Ellsworth in his wake.

'I promise we'll be on our best behaviour tonight, ma'am,' laughed Jonah, as he joined them out in the snow.

'I'm not your mother,' Vivienne laughed (heart racing, fingers fidgeting, every breath catching in her throat). 'Have fun, boys. The Grand Ballroom is like no other place in London town.'

The moment she closed the door, Vivienne fell against the wall, still clinging to Stan, and steeled herself with a breath.

Why, when she was separated from the Americans for the first time, did she suddenly feel so scared?

It was, she decided, the thought of what she might find above.

Stan still in her arms, Vivienne rushed upstairs and, venturing into Arthur's nursery, peeled back the blackout blinds. There was no mistaking the taxicab that turned round in Blomfield Road and began its journey to the city.

She watched until it was out of sight, enveloped by darkness.

'Stan, my beautiful boy, we've got a job to do,' she whispered.

Then she fixed the blackout blind back in place and went out into the hall.

Two miracles had happened to Annie Brogan today: the first when she'd been helping decorate the Housekeeping Lounge and looked up to see Victor, and the second during that afternoon's shift, when she hadn't made a single mistake (not torn a single pillowcase, nor spilt a single bucket) working the fourth-storey suites. It was difficult to believe that the sheer elation she'd felt at Victor kissing her in the Housekeeping hall hadn't somehow flowed out of her and manifested the second miracle of the day.

The voices coming from the kitchenette were raucous this evening. The music was loud, the tea had long since been passed over for what was left of the sherry, and Annie was quite certain there was already some dancing. Mrs de Guise had given strict instruction that the girls not arrive in the Housekeeping Lounge until the Orchestra was already playing in the Grand – but Rosa, Mary-Louise and the rest had obviously decided that this did not preclude a little private party beforehand.

Annie fixed one of her mother's embroidered roses in her hair, took one last look in the mirror and smiled.

There were so many reasons to be joyful tonight – but at the centre of every one of them was Victor.

No more thieving for Billy.

No more lying and cheating, and not being able to look Mrs de Guise in the eye.

The new year wasn't even here, but it felt like a new beginning.

She couldn't wait to see Victor again. With any luck, there'd still be time to have a little dance with him in the Housekeeping Lounge after he came off shift.

With a spring in her step, Annie left her bedroom and skipped down the hall to join the other girls in the kitchenette.

'Raucous' hardly described the scene in the kitchenette. 'Chaos' was more appropriate. The girls had cleared the sofas, coffee table and general clutter to make a dance floor – but only one person stood in the heart of it. There, in a gown of sky-blue silk, stood Rosa.

Annie had to admit: she really looked beautiful.

The other girls thought so too. They were clucking around her like she was a princess, Mary-Louise fixing the back of the gown with pins. One of the other girls had put curlers in Rosa's hair.

Annie had never smelt *perfume* in the chambermaids' kitchenette before, but the air was thick with a sweet, floral scent.

The sky blue brought out the shimmer in Rosa's eyes. And the way she was smiling made Annie start dreaming too. That gown wouldn't have looked half as good on Annie – but one day, maybe *one day*, she'd get to wear something half as beautiful, and that would be enough.

'Where'd you get it from, Rosa?' Annie marvelled. The gown seemed to have some gravity of its own. It was drawing her in. She bent down, to touch its flowing hem. 'You'll have to be awful careful dancing in this, Rosa! I'd fall over it every step.'

Rosa laughed, 'You'd fall over your own feet, Annie Brogan.'

'Well, you look beautiful,' Annie said, more mutely now.

Perhaps she oughtn't have come in the kitchenette at all.

There was so much to be happy about tonight. So much to be grateful for. She didn't want to lose this feeling; she wanted to luxuriate in it, until the night was old.

She had almost slipped back out of the kitchenette when, quite without thinking about it, she turned back and said, 'You'll be kind to Frankie tonight, won't you? He'll think you look awful beautiful in that gown as well. But you *will* be kind, won't you?'

Rosa's face, which seemed to reflect the beauty of that gown when she laughed, turned suddenly to a groan. 'If you can't be happy for me, Annie Brogan, don't say anything at all. Frank gets to dance in that ballroom just about every week. This might be the only chance I get in the whole of my life.'

'I was just saying—'

'I know what you're saying, Annie, but it's time to be quiet. You Brogans never do know when to keep your traps shut. This is *my* night, and I'm sorry for Frank – I really am – but I'm allowed to enjoy myself, aren't I? I'm allowed to – to be in *love!*'

Flushing scarlet, Annie hurried along the corridor, down the rickety stairs and rode the service elevator to the hotel's ground floor. The Queen Mary was thronged with diners dressed in their finest attire. Guests in evening wear and beautiful flowing gowns were crossing the starlit reception hall, bound for the cocktail lounges and Candlelight Club. Mr Hastings himself was standing in the glittering light of the Christmas fir, to greet his guests as they came.

Annie allowed her eyes to drift to the marble arch leading down to the Grand.

Perhaps, one day...

If Rosa could do it, why not Annie?

Frank had only been a hotel page, until he learnt how to dance.

Tonight was a night for dreaming. Annie found herself skipping, and hardly stumbling at all, as she made her way down the Housekeeping hall.

Mrs de Guise was just finishing up for the day. It seemed to Annie that some extra decorations had gone up since the girls had left.

'It's a little early yet, Annie.'

'Oh,' Annie stammered, 'I don't mind. I just wanted to see it.'

Nancy brushed past Annie, squeezing her shoulder warmly as she left. 'Have the most wonderful night, Annie. The Buckingham Hotel's been lucky to have you this year.'

Annie was so flabbergasted she could hardly speak.

'Lucky?' she whispered. 'To have *me*?'

Mrs de Guise had marched on, but perhaps Annie didn't need to hear the answer.

She didn't really need to go into the Grand to feel special after all.

As soon as she left the Housekeeping Lounge, Nancy skirted the reception hall by the service corridor and approached the Grand from the dressing-room side.

The first thing she saw, after she knocked and ventured through, was Hélène Marchmont, standing resplendent in a gown of ivory chiffon and lace. Silver thread sparkled at its every seam; under the lights of the ballroom chandeliers, she would look almost angelic. It was, Nancy understood, only the first gown of the evening – for, when the intermission came, Hélène would step into the golden gown hanging behind her.

Hélène squeezed Nancy's hand, as Nancy picked her way through.

On one side of the dressing rooms, the musicians were gathered. Their faces were set in sombre lines, as Max worked through how to accommodate James Heath's betrayal, but at least Alix Monet was keeping spirits high. Nancy could hear her playing on the practise piano through the open doors that led to the studio. The night's guest singers – what were left of them – gathered round her, voices raised in chorus.

Through the bustling dancers, Frank caught Nancy's eye. She winked to him, trying to encourage a smile – and, to his credit, he summoned one from deep within. Mathilde was at his side, fixing his collar.

'Dance like the King really is here tonight,' Nancy told him. 'Frank, don't look Rosa in the eye. I've cautioned her to act with decorum when she's in the ballroom tonight. You...'

Frank sensed some gentle reproach – the kind Nancy had always given him when he was up to some mischief as a little boy. Nancy never had cross words, not for her brother, but that didn't mean she hadn't chased him with a wooden spoon when he was caught with his fingers in the jam jar.

'I know, Nancy. I'll act with decorum too.'

Nancy rolled her eyes. 'I was going to say: just enjoy yourself, Frank. When you dance like you're in love with it, why, the whole ballroom loves you.'

It was as she said the final two words that she saw the shadow in the corner of her eye, and turned to see Raymond. He looked so elegant, a titan in midnight blue, his black hair sailing up from his brow in extravagant curls. If it wasn't for the brooding feeling of discontent Nancy had been carrying all day, she might even have thought it was like the last years hadn't happened, like she was witnessing the Raymond of old. He'd looked so unlike himself with his hair shorn short in a military fuzz. Now there he stood, her husband renewed.

Well, didn't he?

Nancy inclined her head, asking Raymond to follow. Then she picked her way across the dressing rooms, finding a quiet corner in the maelstrom where they could talk.

'I couldn't leave the hotel tonight, not without wishing you good luck.'

Raymond's eyes flashed at the clock on the wall above Nancy's head.

'You're going back home?' he asked. 'You're not staying for the shindig in the Lounge?'

'You should have told me, Raymond. Vivienne ought to have told me too. I don't want secrets under my own roof.' She paused, willing Raymond to enter the conversation – but he only looked at her. 'I've worked hard, Raymond – worked hard to make Blomfield Road feel like a home. Somewhere we can all be safe. Somewhere we can put down our worries. Put down the war. But it feels as if – it feels as if the war's in our house now.'

'They won't be there forever,' Raymond said, stroking her arm. 'It will all be ordinary again.'

'I'm not talking about the Americans, Raymond,' Nancy sighed. 'I'm talking about *you*.'

'I didn't want to worry you, Nancy. You're my wife. I'm meant to protect you.'

Nancy smiled, sadly. 'I don't need protecting. I didn't need protecting before you, and I don't need protecting now.' She reached up, kissed him on the cheek and said, 'I need to know you're right here, at my side.'

Raymond watched as she pulled away.

Before she left the dressing rooms, she looked back and smiled.

Every piece of him wanted to tell her it all, to make her understand.

But...

Just one more night, and it would be over.

If it wasn't, he would blow it open himself.

Out in the reception hall, beneath the boughs of the great fir tree, Mr Hastings waited.

The guests had started arriving an hour ago, but now they were coming in droves. Every time he blinked, the bronze doors revolved, and another one of the ball's elegant invitees appeared. Here came Lord Trevelyan of Kingsclere; here, the Chalfonts of East Sussex. Lord Manningham's party were already in the private dining room behind the Queen Mary. News had come that the Norwegian royal party were due to arrive within the hour.

Hastings greeted Viscount Emlyn, the most notable of a coterie of guests who had travelled from the Welsh Marches specifically for the occasion, personally. He was deep in conversation with the Viscount's wife, whose forest-green gown was augmented by a silver stole, when one of the hotel aides approached from the check-in desks and stood to one side, meaning to catch his attention.

'Sir, there's a telephone call at the front desk.'

Hastings didn't turn round until the aide added, 'It's Mr Gove, sir, from the Imperial Hotel. He says it's urgent.'

Hastings was not a man given to much emotion, but he felt a tingle of something at the mention of Gove's name. Whether it was dread or whether he was pleased, he couldn't quite say.

'Tell Mr Gove that we are hosting our Winter Ball, and that I am currently unavailable.'

The aide nodded, then turned on his heel and marched away.

Ten minutes passed, then twenty. Mr Hastings had greeted a good number of other guests, including the first of the Dutch ministers – attending in advance of their sovereign, Queen Wilhelmina and her exiled family – when the aide approached again.

'The telephone, Mr Hastings. I'm afraid Mr Gove says that it's most urgent.'

Hastings tried not to betray a smile, though inwardly he felt his satisfaction mounting.

There is no adversary more formidable than a reasonable man.

'Tell Mr Gove that my ball is urgent too. I shall return his call as soon as possible.'

As seven o'clock approached, the doors of the Grand were opened to guests.

John Hastings watched them flocking towards the marble arch.

His own Home Away From Home guests appeared and marvelled at the stream of dignitaries bustling through.

'I trust you'll enjoy your evening, Corporal Kaplan,' Mr Hastings smiled, inclining his head in greeting.

'Truth is, we're nervous, sir,' Kaplan replied. 'A night like this – we don't have anything like it back home.'

Hastings drew them closer and smiled. 'I know *precisely* how you feel. But might I suggest a little aperitif, up in the Candlelight Club, before the evening begins? It will steady the nerves. Tell Ramon that it comes courtesy of the Buckingham Hotel.'

The Americans enjoyed the sound of this very much. As they headed for the golden elevator, Hastings heard the corporal say, 'One drink for courage, and I'll go and collect Rosa!'

He was watching them go, thinking what a wonderful memory this would be when the day came for them to face the bullets, when the check-in attendant appeared at his side again.

'I'm sorry, sir. The telephone—'

This time, Mr Hastings just laughed. 'Tell Hubert Gove that, should he call this hotel again, I'll present him an invoice for time spent.'

But the aide just shook his head. 'It isn't Mr Gove this time, sir. Sir, I think you'd better come.'

Some moments later, Mr Hastings was bursting through the doors of the Benefactors Study and waiting for the hotel exchange to transfer the call to the telephone sitting on the desk. All his ordinary reserve was gone.

The telephone trilled.

Hastings whipped up the receiver.

Then, as coolly as he could muster – which wasn't very coolly at all – he intoned, 'John Hastings, director of the Buckingham Hotel.'

'Mr Hastings,' came the rich, plummy baritone on the other end of the line, 'this is Daubney, from the Palace. I need you to listen and listen carefully. There has been a most unusual occurrence.'

'There you go, darling. It's cold tonight. You'll need your blanket.'

Vivienne was still counting the passing seconds as she tucked Arthur in his crib, settled Stan in her own bedroom with his toy trains and milk and readied herself. By now, enough time ought to have passed. She crept along the landing, reached for the door handle, turned it in her fist and slipped into the Americans' bedroom.

It was dark in here. The air smelt of the scent that Ellsworth had been wearing as he made his goodbyes.

She turned on the lamp.

The blackout blinds were in place, so there wasn't any chance she'd be seen from outside.

Where to begin ...

Raymond had taught her well. When Vivienne pulled Jonah's suitcase out from underneath his bed and opened it, she made a mental note of how it was ordered before she pulled it apart. Nothing of note was hidden here, just clothes and a cloth bag comprising razor blades, shaving soap and ointment. Ellsworth's packs were much the same: just the ordinary day-to-day articles a man might need for a trip away from home.

She had left McCord's suitcase to last.

She felt a terrible foreboding as she opened it.

From inside she lifted out shirts, folded neatly and with pride. Slippers.

Balled-up socks.

A cloth bag, closed with a drawstring, where his dirty laundry lay.

Vivienne set that bag aside to continue her search – but, when she found nothing else, she quickly found herself drawn back.

She'd done less pleasant things in her life than sifting through some stranger's dirty laundry, so she wasted no time in opening it.

But nothing was hidden within. No secret lay among Henry McCord's crumpled clothing.

Vivienne closed the suitcase and flung it – with mounting despair – back underneath the bed.

It was then that she heard a clatter on the other side.

Something else had been slipped into the darkness underneath the bed. She'd dislodged it when she thrust the suitcase back. Now, skittering round to the bed's opposite side, she saw it lying on the floorboards, its corner just poking out: the black briefcase, the one McCord carried everywhere he went; the one he'd taken out on those mysterious nocturnal forays.

Vivienne's heart was beating wild percussion as she lifted it up and laid it on the bed.

Of course, he hadn't been able to take it to the Winter Ball. He'd had to hide it away instead.

A combination lock stopped her from opening it: a wheel demanding four digits, a code to make the clasp pop open. Vivienne fumbled with it three times before she understood it was a hopeless task – but there was fire in her belly now, and she didn't mean to give up.

No doubt Raymond would have cautioned against what she did next.

But Raymond wasn't here – so Vivienne hoisted up the briefcase, carted it down the stairs and laid it on the kitchen table.

Then she reached for a knife.

It wasn't easy to pop the lock. Evidently this was a briefcase meant for carrying secrets – or at least the sensitive documents an embassy staffer might need – and consequently the lock held fast. It took a good amount of wrangling, jiggling the knife around to spring the mechanism, before it popped open, revealing all that was inside.

There, on top of a sheaf of papers, was the dog-eared notebook she'd seen McCord trying to hide.

Sitting down at the head of the table, she buried her head in its contents.

This was like no language Vivienne knew. Not English, not French, not German – just a series of squiggles and swirls, dots and lines. It wasn't journalistic shorthand, she felt certain of that, but it was certainly shorthand of a sort – a shorthand for spies. Page after page was inscribed in some strange cypher, a code book that could be proof for only one thing: that Henry McCord wasn't really a staffer at the US Embassy at all. Or, at least, that wasn't *all* he was. He was a spy, just like Raymond de Guise. He was the one Raymond was looking for.

'Mama, look!'

Vivienne had been so lost in the notebook, trying to work out if there was any meaning in this spidery scrawl, that she hadn't heard Stan enter the kitchen. Now, when she looked up, he was on his tiptoes, his hands buried in the briefcase.

Up came his pudgy wrists, his hands wrapped around a black object he'd found buried in the papers.

Vivienne's heart stopped dead.

'Give that to me, Stan. Stan, give it to your mother.'

There, trembling in Stan's hands, was a revolver.

Vivienne recognised it at once. It was a standard-issue Smith & Wesson, the kind many responsible, upstanding householders kept in New York. Stan looked as if he'd unearthed some priceless treasure – his eyes were flashing with delight – but Vivienne could see that he could hardly hold it. Any moment now, it was going to drop to the cold hard stone of the kitchen floor.

Vivienne panicked: if it was loaded, there was no telling what it might do.

'Stan, this is not a game. I'm *ordering* you to give it to your mother.'

She could tell, by the flicker of his eyes, that Stan knew this was wrong. But she could tell, by that same flickering, that his father lived on in him – his father, who could never stand to be told what to do. Stan tottered forward, as if he was about to hand the revolver to Vivienne, then stalled, as if he couldn't quite bear to let go.

'Stan, *now*,' Vivienne commanded.

Suddenly, Stan panicked. He hadn't expected his mother to sound so ferocious. In the same moment that he reached out to give it to her, he staggered backwards – and let the gun fall.

Time seemed to slow down.

Vivienne braced herself.

The revolver hit the cold stone – and spun there, hopelessly, without going off.

Vivienne rushed to seize it, laid it carefully on the table and swept up Stan. 'You silly boy,' she whispered. 'You silly, silly boy.'

What was the best course of action here? Her first instinct was to put everything back precisely as it had been before she unearthed it. That way the secret could be preserved – at least until Raymond broke the news to his superiors. With this in mind, and having first set Stan down to play with pencils and old newspapers, she slipped the revolver back into the briefcase. The notebook should go in too, so that McCord wouldn't know he was discovered – yet, when she tried to close the case again, the lock wouldn't catch. It was broken, and all the evidence of her intrusion was plain to see.

Vivienne clenched her fists in frustration.

Perhaps she wasn't made for spycraft after all.

At once, her mind started whirling. This changed everything. It occurred to her suddenly that the Americans would most likely return from the ball before Raymond did. That meant there was every chance McCord would discover the ruin she'd made of his briefcase before Vivienne could tell Raymond what she knew. What she needed to do was hide the evidence.

She turned on the spot, searching out some space he wouldn't find.

Then she thought: the air raid shelter.

Still cradling Stan, Vivienne fumbled with the back door, finally throwing it open to the whirling white of the night. Some time after the Americans had left, the clouds had closed again over the London skyline. Now the back garden was a miasma of snow and ice, a silvery strobing stage with the Anderson shelter buried at its bottom.

Stan cringed against the cold.

'It's only for a few moments, little one.'

She was about to step out, when suddenly she heard the sound of the front door opening.

Vivienne's heart stilled.

If this was McCord, if he'd found another reason to slip away on another nocturnal foray, there would be no hiding what she'd done.

She heard footsteps.

They were coming down the hall.

'Little one,' she whispered, 'I need you to be brave.'

She set him down, braced him by the shoulders, fixed her eyes upon his own.

'To the shelter, my brave little man, and quickly now.'

'But why, Mama? *Why?*'

'Go,' Vivienne commanded. 'Go now, and don't look back.'

Her heart burst with the twin feelings of terror and pride as Stan took off, his legs flailing wildly through the ever-deepening snow.

He'd be safe out there.

At least for a moment, he'd be safe.

Vivienne didn't know how much she was trembling until, dropping the broken briefcase back on the kitchen table, she reached inside and drew out the Smith & Wesson. She didn't know if it was loaded, barely knew enough to check – but there was no time for that now. Time, which had been cascading past so quickly these last few days, had finally run out.

A shadow appeared in the kitchen doorway.

'Stop right there!' Vivienne shrieked, her voice a mangled tirade. 'One more step and I'll—'

The electric light flared.

Henry McCord didn't stand in the doorway.

It was Nancy de Guise.

Her face was a frightened mask. Her eyes were wide and darting.

She opened her mouth to speak, but no words came out.

Vivienne didn't know why, but she was still pointing the revolver. It trembled violently in her hands, but the rest of her body had turned rigid, every muscle locked in place.

Seconds passed.

Neither Nancy nor Vivienne could move.

Then, by some enormous act of willpower, Vivienne wrenched her body to one side, crashed the revolver back onto the kitchen table and wept, 'Stan! Stan, come back here!'

Stan came rampaging back out of the wild, whirling whiteness, his little face already covered in snow. Still sobbing, Vivienne dropped down to cuddle him. 'It's your Aunt Nancy,' she wept, directly into his ear. 'Go to Aunt Nancy now.'

Nancy was still silent, too shell-shocked to speak. As Vivienne approached, to press Stan into her arms, she only stared – until, with Stan pressed up against her, she breathed, 'What in God's name is happening here, Vivienne? What's happening in my house?'

But Vivienne's throat constricted every time she tried to speak.

'Nancy, I can't. I can't tell. But you've – you've got to look after them now.'

Nancy's eyes burnt with fresh fire. They lacerated Vivienne with a look as, still sobbing, Vivienne pushed past, took up the stairs and hurtled to her bedroom door. Inside, the lamp by which Stan had been playing still flickered. She flung open her wardrobe doors, rifled through all the drab, dreary day clothes she'd been wearing the last year and spied a splash of colour at the very back.

There hung a bright red Grecian gown with gold embellishments, and sequins that shone like stars.

A reminder of days gone by, and not ones Vivienne thought to ever revisit again.

She lifted it out, held it up against herself in the mirror.

In the reflection, she saw Nancy appear.

'Vivienne Cohen, you'll speak to me right now. This is *my* house. *My* home. What in God's name is happening in my home that I'm not allowed to know about it?'

Heedless of propriety, Vivienne started tearing off her day dress and scrabbling into the gown.

'I'm sorry, Nancy,' she said, drying her eyes. 'I've wanted to tell you. I really have. And ... and I need you to trust me. I made an oath. I promised.'

'You promised to be my friend as well,' said Nancy. 'You promised to be my sister.'

Vivienne stifled a sob. It was, perhaps, the first and only time she understood – completely and totally understood – the situation that Raymond de Guise had been in ever since his return from the war.

The gown was on. She drew herself up.

'I'm sorry, Nancy,' she declared. 'I've got to go to the ball.'

Chapter Twenty-Four

On the other side of the dance-floor doors, the ballroom was bustling.

Inside the dressing room, a reverential hush had descended.

Raymond de Guise's mind was still racing with thoughts of Vivienne, still echoing with the disappointment dripping out in Nancy's words, but he took a breath and rallied himself just as the dancers and musicians rallied before him.

Once the first waltz began, he would surely sink into the music. When he and Hélène sailed out to meet the crowd, he would close his mind to the outside world and exist only in the ballroom.

But until that moment, if pretending to be something he wasn't was now his trade, he would have to embrace it.

Here he stood: Raymond de Guise, the King of the Grand.

'My friends,' he ventured, 'this has not been easy. We have, all of us, been sorely tested this winter. But let us forget, for a moment, the manipulations of the Imperial Hotel. Let us set aside every trial and tribulation that has dogged us this December, and for a moment just ... *dream*.'

Raymond turned round, to face the dance-floor doors.

'In a few short minutes, those doors will be open. The band will strike up. The night will begin. And when it does, it is our

duty to make something magical happen out there. No, *wait*.'
He checked himself. 'Perhaps it's wrong to think of it as a duty.
The world is full, right now, of men and woman living up to
their duties. My friends, the war has changed everything. But
tonight it is our *honour* to dance in the Grand. The Grand is
not some place to be battled over. The magic of the ballroom is
not the spoils of some war that must have a victor. This is what
the poor souls at the Imperial Hotel have forgotten. We don't
need to grind some other hotel down to stir up magic tonight.
Magic isn't rationed. It cannot be stolen or squabbled over. It is
lodged inside every one of us. I intend to spin it tonight. I hope
you all feel the same.'

In the dressing rooms, the dancers lifted themselves.

Frank clutched Mathilde's hand.

Max Allgood raised his voice, 'Quite right, sir!', and lifted
Lucille aloft for his musicians to see. 'And the magic, boys – oh,
and you, Miss Monet – the magic starts with *us*. Line up! It's
time to put on a—'

He'd been about to say 'show' – and, indeed, his musicians
were about to cheer in response – when the dressing-room door
opened and an ashen figure, with bags under his bloodshot eyes
and the faint smell of the grave about him, staggered in. It took
Max a few moments to recognise him – but here came James
Heath, drumsticks clutched in a trembling hand.

'Mr Allgood,' Heath slurred, staggering forth, 'I'm glad I
caught you. I'm glad as hell I got here in time.'

Heath looked pale, blue veins prominent at his temples, and
had to steady himself on one of the dressers to catch his breath.

'Mr Heath, what the devil is this?' Max snapped.

The romance Raymond had conjured was in danger of disappearing. He moved to Max's side and put a hand on his

shoulder. 'Mr Heath, it was our understanding that you'd given in to the temptation of the Imperial Hotel?'

'Aye, and what a poisoned apple!' Heath spat. 'I'm sorry, Max.' He cast his eyes around the rest of the Orchestra, eyes wide and grovelling. 'I know it. I'm dirt. Ten years with this Orchestra, and I skipped out. They said I could play for the King. I'm an old musician. It's an old musician's dream. But look at me – just look!'

He lifted his hands, to show how they were shaking.

Max Allgood's eyes flashed at the dance-floor doors.

'We've got to go,' he ventured. 'There's a full house waiting.'

James Heath lurched towards him. 'Let me come?'

'Mr Heath, even if you hadn't walked out on us, I can't let a drunk man play in front of this crowd.' Max was not without sympathy; the fact was, he'd played drunk plenty of times – there'd been a time when he swore Lucille preferred it – but this wasn't the Cotton Club or the Creole House in Chicago. 'This is the Grand!'

'I'm not drunk, Mr Allgood. I swear on my daughter's life I'm not drunk. It's whatever they fed us at the luncheon. The whole Imperial Orchestra, laid to waste! Oh lord, they put on such a spread. You've never eaten finer, Mr Allgood. You'd think we were lords and ladies ourselves. But the meal was hardly over when Mr Holloway came down with it. The old man couldn't keep down his figgy pudding. We laughed it off – one too many glasses of Champagne. But then it started coming for us all and…'

As Mr Heath's story spread around the dressing room, the fevered whispers began.

'Mr Heath,' Raymond intervened, 'do you mean to say the *whole* of the Imperial Orchestra is sick?'

'More than half, Mr de Guise – much more than half. Nelson reckons he'll still play, but at this rate it'll be him and his piano.' Somebody had found a glass of water; Heath took it greedily and started slurping away. 'Half of the dancers too. They're just laid out with it. It's like … like a curse, sir. Like a curse on them, for what they did to us.'

What sympathy Heath had been garnering quickly vanished. 'It wasn't just *them*,' somebody muttered. 'It takes two to tango,' added another.

'And I'm sorry,' Heath spluttered. 'Just – just let me play?'

Max Allgood cradled Lucille. All the eyes of the Orchestra and the dance troupe were upon him.

'And Nelson's at the Imperial, playing alone?' he asked.

James Heath just murmured, 'The curse just didn't touch him like it did the rest of us.'

'I reckon that's because the boy *is* the curse.'

'It's a disaster,' Frank whispered to Mathilde. 'They're in the middle of a disaster.'

Max looked James Heath up and down. 'Somebody get the man some sweet tea. Maybe he can make it by the second act.' Around Max, the Orchestra started groaning. Voices of complaint flurried up from one end of the dressing room to the other. 'Stop!' Max snapped – and the remarkable force in his voice summoned silence to the room. 'We're not like those scoundrels at the Imperial. We won't be like those dogs. Mr Heath can play, if he gets his constitution in order. I don't care about what's happened. I care about what's *going* to happen when we walk through those doors.' Max's eyes bugged out. 'Which is what we oughta be doing right now. Boys, line up!' Max checked himself, once again. 'You too, Miss Monet.'

'Dancers, to me!' Raymond called out.

The dancers rushed to form a line behind Raymond, holding formation as Max strode up to the dance-floor doors and threw them apart. For the first time, the dressing room caught sight of the Grand in all its glory. Max had barely set foot over the threshold when silence swept over the assembly, then turned to tumultuous waves of applause. Out the musicians flocked, streaming up onto stage.

The light of the chandeliers cascaded through the doorway. Raymond waited for the music to begin. 'This is the moment, my friends,' he said. 'Make it count. Make it *magical.*' He squeezed Hélène's hand. 'Once more, for the Grand!'

Out they sailed, to devastating applause. Round and round they turned, alone in the heart of the dance floor, before presenting themselves to the lords and ladies stationed above.

One after another, the couples soared out to fill the dance floor – until, at last, only Frank and Mathilde remained.

On the precipice, they waited for their cue.

Frank's eyes scoured the crowd.

There, by the balustrade, half hidden behind the ranks of the great and the good, was Corporal Joel Kaplan. His hands were raised in applause.

And at his side, unthinkable in sky blue, was Rosa.

She barely looked like the girl Frank used to know, the girl he'd danced with in the Midnight Rooms, the girl he'd held in his arms and whispered of love.

Mathilde knew where he was looking. 'You didn't tell her, did you?' she whispered.

Their cue was almost here.

'Not yet – but I have to do it,' said Frank. 'I thought I had to do it for *me* – but no, I have to do it for *her.* Just look at them. She was in his suite last night, Mathilde. I went to find her but I couldn't catch her in time. She's going to make a terrible mistake.'

Alix Monet hit a cavalcade of chords, and both Frank and Mathilde knew it was their cue.

Together they skipped into the heart of the dance floor.

Frank took Mathilde in hold, turned her around, presented her to the ball.

Up on stage, Mr Allgood was counting down.

Three . . .

The dancers took formation.

Two . . .

Frank fixed his eyes on Mathilde alone.

One . . .

Raymond made a silent vow: the next three hours were for the dance; only after that would he deal with what was happening at Blomfield Road.

The Winter Ball had officially begun.

'Vivienne!' Nancy bawled. 'Vivienne, stop!'

Vivienne burst out of the front door at Blomfield Road, skidding wildly in the snow as she careened along the path. Clutch bag in one hand, McCord's book of code in the other, she clattered through the gate. Nancy was still hollering as she took to the road, but Vivienne tried desperately to push it out of her thoughts. Lies could never be undone, but they could yet be forgiven. There was always tomorrow, she told herself. Tomorrow, she would look Nancy in the eye and beg.

Running through the snowbound city was like gliding through a dream, this otherworldly landscape of snow and scaffolds, bombsites and hoardings, shopfronts and wreckage, churchyards and forests of steel girders. It seemed, somehow, that Vivienne was the only splash of colour in this monochrome world – for, every time she looked down, the scarlet of her ball gown seemed to leap out from the black and white.

The cold had not touched her yet; fear and desperation kept it at bay.

This late at night no taxicab happened by. She was halfway down Edgware Road, Marylebone on the horizon, when she saw one. 'The Buckingham Hotel,' she said, breathless, as she collapsed on the back seat.

The driver took one look at her and baulked, 'You'll catch your death out here!'

'Please sir!' Vivienne gasped.

The driver said no more. Soon, he was rounding Berkeley Square and coming to a halt in front of the marble colonnade.

Begging him to wait, Vivienne burst back into the chill of night.

Up above her, the face of the Buckingham Hotel looked so dark and unknowable that it was difficult to believe the Winter Ball went on inside its blackouts. She strained to hear the music – but all she could hear was the beating of her own heart.

At the top of the steps, the doorman had come to attention. Perhaps there was something a little too wild about her tonight. Perhaps she lacked elegance or poise. Or perhaps he remembered her from those long-ago days when she'd disgraced herself here every Saturday night. Whichever it was, she knew that there would be no entering the hotel through its fêted revolving doors.

It was lucky, then, that she had once known this place like the back of her hand.

Vivienne pivoted on her heel, as elegant as any dancer, and set her sights on the tradesman's entrance on Michaelmas Mews.

In the Grand Ballroom, the music swelled.

From the balustrade, John Hastings watched as the troupe's second piece came to its end and Raymond de Guise welcomed his guests to the dance floor. Holding a regal poise, Raymond himself took the Princess Juliana on his arm. Hélène Marchmont had been promised to one of the Welsh lords, Frank Nettleton to the daughter of one of the ministers working for de Gaulle. Hastings watched with satisfaction as the Orchestra struck up the next song. Alix Monet had caught the eye of the ballroom. People whispered. People pointed. People's eyes lit up when she leant into the piano and turned a song from stately to sublime with the mere flick of her wrists.

Mr Hastings turned.

The members of the Hotel Board would soon fan out among the ball's guests, just like the dancers, but right now they stood in a clot, faceless wives on their arms, working fervently not to catch his eye.

'Gentlemen, is this not a *spectacle*?'

There was no other word for it. There was such an explosion of joy on the dance floor that it was rippling over the balustrade, lighting up even the darkest corners of the Grand. But Bell and Merriweather still glowered. 'You can dress it up all you like, sir. The Grand is never anything but spectacular – but this year we could have had it *all*.'

Hastings risked a glance at the ballroom doors, the ornate marble arch leading out into the hotel. 'We must be patient, gentlemen. The night is yet young.'

The doors trembled.

Somebody was coming through.

'Gentlemen,' Hastings declared. 'I received a telephone call earlier. It seems that fate has one last twist in store this evening. I'm afraid that, earlier today, there was quite a disaster at the Imperial Hotel. I could not begin to say how it happened,' and here John Hastings smiled, for he would never again speak of the pact he'd made with the young man named Victor. 'Perhaps an errant kitchen boy made a terrible mistake. But the most terrible bout of sickness ran through the Imperial Orchestra and dance troupe, only hours before they were due to perform. As a result…'

Hastings was about to tell them of the call from the Palace, when the doors opened.

His heart sank.

Perhaps he'd got it wrong after all.

'Gentlemen, forgive me,' he said. 'We must be patient just a little while more.'

Because it wasn't the King and his royal party who were coming through those doors.

It was a half-bedraggled young lady with striking red hair, and an even more striking scarlet gown.

'I know that face,' growled Uriah Bell.

'It's like seeing a ghost,' snorted Merriweather.

'Lord Edgerton's stepdaughter, back in the Grand Ballroom?'

Merriweather slapped Hastings on the back, propelling him forward. 'You mightn't be able to summon the King, Mr Hastings – but you've definitely summoned something here. That girl's a liability. She's a walking scandal.' He paused. 'You wanted the Buckingham Hotel splashed all over the Society Pages? Well, if that girl's got an ounce of her old passion in her, you're about to get your wish.'

Memories crashed over her. She'd thought it might feel different, walking into the Buckingham Hotel – but in fact the last five years of her life just evaporated. It was the smells that did it. The scent of the Buckingham Hotel at Christmas, of beeswax polish and pine needles, sweet Champagne and luxurious cigars, was so potent that, as she burst into the Grand, it was like she'd never been away.

She was aware that eyes were upon her. That felt familiar too. She tried to ignore them as she picked her way through the tables to reach the balustrade. Before she was halfway there, she could see Raymond dancing below. The lady in his arms was stately and silver-haired, twenty years older than Raymond – and seemed to be dancing in a different world, her eyes taking in Raymond alone. This, Vivienne remembered, was the magic of the Grand. Fleetingly, she wished she'd been more sober in her Buckingham days, so that *this* was what she remembered. For everyone upon this dance floor, as the music arced across them, nothing else existed.

Vivienne felt McCord's code book tucked inside her gown and could only dream of feeling the same thing.

Down on the dance floor, Raymond pivoted past.

It was then that he caught her eye.

He'd been in that other world, that world where only song and dance mattered, but Vivienne watched as reality rushed back in. His eyes darkened. He *knew*. There could be only one reason Vivienne had appeared in the Grand tonight, and that was because her mission had been a success.

But there was Raymond, his silver-haired guest in hold. The song was only just beginning. For a few minutes more, he was a prisoner of the dance floor.

'Vivienne?' came a voice.

Vivienne's heart wrenched.

She knew that voice.

The Max Allgood Orchestra had only just reached the first chorus of the song. That meant it would last another two minutes. Too long to ignore the voice. Too long to pretend she hadn't heard.

She turned round, summoning a smile. 'Ellsworth,' she grinned.

Ellsworth was wearing an expression suspended somewhere between wonder and disbelief. But it wasn't wonder at the ball-room, thought Vivienne – no matter how spectacular it was. The wonder was meant for her alone – for Ellsworth clearly believed she'd had second thoughts, that she'd accepted his invitation, that she'd come here for *him*.

'I didn't think for a second that you'd come.'

Vivienne reached for his arm. Perhaps it felt right, now, to admit that she liked the way he looked at her. Oh, there was a feeling of treachery in this as well – didn't all young widows feel the same, when their hearts were just starting to heal? – but at least she didn't have the niggling feeling that it might have been he, Ellsworth March, in the enemy's employ.

'I catch myself quite unawares sometimes,' Vivienne laughed. Then she gazed up at the chandeliers, if only to avoid looking in his eye. 'Isn't it wonderful in here? I'd quite forgotten how beautiful it can be.'

'Dance with me,' Ellsworth declared.

The song had reached the second chorus. Vivienne could sense it building to its climax. The music in the Grand had never been as lively as this in the old days. Archie Adams' Orchestra had been stately and poised, beautiful and sublime, but it hadn't been as fast as Max Allgood's. It hadn't been as urgent.

If she danced with Ellsworth now, she'd miss Raymond. He'd be in the arms of some old dowager, spinning magic for her, and time would keep cascading by.

Over Ellsworth's shoulder, she saw Henry McCord. He was standing at one of the tables, with Jonah Linden at his side. By the looks of it, they'd found some other Americans – perhaps, Vivienne wondered, the infantrymen who were spending Christmas right here at the Buckingham Hotel?

'A drink, perhaps?' Vivienne said, stroking the back of his hand – if only to encourage him on his way. 'I think I might need a drink, before I dance.'

'Champagne, for the lady?'

Vivienne glanced around the Grand with a smile of her own. 'When in Rome,' she grinned.

The moment Ellsworth left, Vivienne's face changed. Quite how Raymond had kept his act up all year long, she didn't know.

But at least the song was ending. She listened to the piano erupting; to the proud blasts of the trumpeters, to Max's joyful swoon. Then, as the dancers came apart and smatterings of applause broke out across the Grand, she slipped through the balustrade, crashed onto the dance floor – and hurtled towards Raymond.

Another guest was approaching, but before she reached him, Vivienne grabbed him by the hand and compelled him to take her in hold. 'It's a tango,' Raymond whispered. 'You do know how to tango?'

Vivienne snorted. 'We need to get off this dance floor.' But the song had already begun, and soon Raymond was whisking her around. 'It's McCord,' she gasped. 'It was that briefcase he carries – that's why you didn't find it. Raymond, he brought a revolver into our house. I have his notebook. It's all written in codes.'

Raymond's eyes flared. 'You have it with you?'

'Nancy caught me. The gun in my hand and the briefcase torn open.'

'But the book?' Raymond repeated. 'You have it with you? You have it *here*?'

In the same moment that Vivienne nodded, her eyes caught sight of Ellsworth reappearing at the balustrade. There he stood, in the very same spot where he'd left her, two glasses of

Champagne in his hands. Vivienne wrenched as she saw his face turn from confusion to disappointment.

She couldn't hold his gaze.

Lies beget more lies.

They turned everything to heartache.

'It's right here,' she hissed at Raymond. 'Right here in my gown.'

When Vivienne looked again, Ellsworth was not alone. Jonah had appeared alongside him. So too had Henry McCord. At least they were distracting him, thought Vivienne. Except McCord seemed to have one eye on Vivienne as she danced. She couldn't escape the sense that he was *watching*.

'Show me,' said Raymond. Quite without Vivienne realising it, he had danced them to the edge of the dance floor, then skirted around its circumference until he reached the steps leading above. 'Go,' he commanded, driving her up. 'Find a corner. Show me *now*. I need to see.'

Out in the frigid cold of Berkeley Square, stationed on the Buckingham's sweeping marble steps, the hotel doorman heard the crunch of footsteps – and turned round to see the chambermaid Annie Brogan approaching with a mug of hot, sweet tea in her hands.

'Here you are,' she said, breath fogging in the cold. 'Just like Mrs de Guise promised.' Then she lowered her voice. 'It's got just a drop of rum in it. For Christmas cheer.'

'You're a good girl, Annie,' the doorman replied. Even the smell of the tea was enough to revive his senses on this long, bitter night. 'It sounds like things are ticking along in the Grand. How's it going in that Housekeeping Lounge of yours?'

Annie beamed. 'Oh, there's music and there's dancing and …'

'That sweetheart of yours turned up yet?'

Annie flushed red. 'He's still on shift.'

'Aye, well, the night's young yet,' laughed the doorman. 'Go on, Annie. Be off with you. Get out of this cold while you can.'

Annie wrapped her arms around herself. 'I'll bring another mug out for you, shall I? In an hour?'

The doorman grinned, 'You're a good girl, Annie. That kitchen lad's lucky to have . . .'

Then the doorman's face fell.

He gazed out across the whirling white of Berkeley Square.

'Looks like you've got another guest coming,' said Annie. 'But they've missed half the fun!'

The doorman looked momentarily panicked.

He slurped his scalding tea, then found a place to hide the mug in the snow behind one of the marble pillars.

It wasn't a taxicab that was approaching.

Or at least, it wasn't *just* a car that was coming.

It was a convoy: two sleek black Rolls-Royces, driving abreast of one another, and behind them, four noble horses drawing a carriage.

'You're going to want to see this, Annie,' the doorman announced, clapping his hands. 'Go on, girl. You just duck out of sight, but for Heaven's sake keep your eyes peeled. When you get back to that shindig of yours – why, they're not going to believe a word you tell them!'

As Raymond led Vivienne through the crowd, music still filling the cavernous vaults of the Grand, she was distinctly aware of the Americans. The truth was, she wasn't sure which affected her more: McCord's eyes boring into her, as if somehow he *knew*; or Ellsworth, blanched with disappointment. *Don't look back*, she told herself.

Yet, quite without meaning to, she did look over her shoulder – and it was only the fact that some other commotion was going on in the ballroom, that meant she couldn't find Jonah, Ellsworth and McCord in the throng.

In the corner of the Grand, pushed up against the black-out curtains in the windows that ordinarily looked out across Berkeley Square, Vivienne pulled the dog-eared notebook from her gown and pressed it into Raymond's hands.

In a fever, he flicked through it. She watched as the certainty hardened on his face.

He looked up, eyes scouring the ballroom. 'You did well, Vivienne.'

'But he'll know we know, the second he gets back. I didn't mean to, Raymond, but I broke his briefcase when I popped open the lock.'

'Then he'll have to be in a cell before then.' He dragged his hand through his hair, furiously trying to work out how this would work. 'I need to get this to the Deacon Club. It isn't far. I can be there and back in but a few songs. By intermission he could be in custody.'

Vivienne blurted out, 'Nancy *knows*. She's there right now, with his revolver and the children. I couldn't stop it, Raymond. I pointed that gun at her. I thought it was *him*.'

Raymond's eyes twitched rapidly. 'So much for the secret,' he said, through gritted teeth.

'It's better this way, isn't it? No more lies?'

Raymond thrust the notebook into his evening jacket. 'One problem at a time,' Raymond said. 'I've got to get out of this ballroom.'

Up on stage, the song had reached its end. A cascade of piano and drums brought it to a rousing finale. Across the ballroom, applause erupted.

Raymond waited for the next number to begin. He ought to be on the dance floor taking his next partner in hold, but his mind was working furiously to order what he must do: leave the Grand unseen, hurtle for the Deacon Club to make his report, slide back into the ball without breaking stride. His absence would surely go noted, but – like Nancy, alone in the dark of their house – that was a problem for later. Right now, he had a duty to fulfil.

'Why isn't the band playing?' Vivienne whispered.

It was true. The silence had gone on too long. Raymond drew himself to his full height, gazing over the heads of the other guests to catch a glimpse of the dance floor beyond. On stage, Max Allgood was bent down, apparently receiving some message from a hotel page. From this distance, it was impossible to know what was being said – but Max's big, expressive face looked more startled than ever. The second the page scuttled away, Max rallied his musicians. Heads were bowed. Some special communion was taking place.

'Now's my chance,' Raymond told Vivienne.

'What about me?' Vivienne asked.

'Dance,' Raymond said, striding past, meaning to lose himself in the throng and be out of the ballroom before the next waltz began. 'Dance with Ellsworth. Dance with Jonah. By God, dance with McCord if you can. Keep them in the ballroom. By the time the interval comes...'

The band struck up.

Raymond uttered an oath. This was happening too quickly.

He couldn't afford to be dragged back into the dance.

Then he stalled. This was not one of the standards on the set list, nor one of Max's more adventurous creations. This was just the brass section, trumpeting out a fanfare.

Through the sea of heads, Raymond could see the Orchestra. Those that weren't playing were standing to attention, like soldiers on parade. The trumpeters and horn players had formed a phalanx at the front of the stage, with Max Allgood and Lucille at their head.

The fanfare flared.

On the other side of the ballroom, the doors were opening.

In walked Mr Hastings, flanked by the rest of the Hotel Board.

As they peeled apart, to stand on either side of the door, six men in scarlet red regalia marched in and formed a corridor down which more figures marched.

'Good Lord,' breathed Raymond.

Out of the shadows they came, through the marble arch, down into the half-moon of black marble tiles at the opening of the Grand. King George, his wife on his arm; the two princesses in gowns of the finest silk. Yet more courtiers, Palace officials and Metropolitan security officers filled the corridor behind.

The trumpeters' fanfare came to an end, revealing – just for a moment – the Grand full of whispers and gasps.

Then the piano began.

The Orchestra rushed back to their positions.

Up flew Max Allgood's rendition of 'God Save the King', tinged with just the slightest hint of jazz from Alix Monet's rolling wrists and fingers.

The whole ballroom had started to sing.

Raymond seized Vivienne's hand.

'I can't go,' he whispered, shock carving deep lines into his features. 'Vivienne, I can't leave the ballroom.'

He drew her near, their voices almost drowned out by a ballroom in full song.

'God save our gracious King…'

He grabbed her shoulders, bowing down to look her in the eye. 'You're going to have to do it.'

'Long live our noble King…'

'Me?'

While Vivienne was still reeling, Raymond took the notebook from his jacket and pushed it into her hands. Swiftly, she slipped it into the folds of her gown.

'Listen to me. You've done brilliantly tonight. You've done more than I could have hoped. You're the reason he'll be in a cell tonight, and all the world safer for it. But I need you to run this last mile. I can't go. Not now.' Raymond's eyes flashed into the crowd. Yes, he was quite certain now – John Hastings had detached himself from the royal party and was weaving through the crowd in his direction.

'I'll do it,' Vivienne gasped. 'Just tell me where.'

'There's a place off Piccadilly. They call it the Deacon Club. No, you haven't heard of it – and no, not just because it's a gentleman's affair. Look for the unmarked black door between the Erstwhile Tannery and Saville's the tailors. They won't let you in, not at first. But tell them who you are. Tell them where you've come from. Tell them you need to see Vernon Fox. Do you hear me?'

'Vernon Fox,' Vivienne said, determinedly. 'I don't need telling twice, Raymond.'

John Hastings was almost upon them.

'Then go,' Raymond told her. 'Vivienne, fly!'

Vivienne streaked off, as if to leave the Grand by the main exit. Then she stalled. That way lay the King, his princesses, all the might of the Palace officials. No, there was no way out of the ballroom by that route – not now.

She turned on her heel, streaked past John Hastings and made for the dance floor itself. Down there, the dancers were only just recovering their wits.

Ellsworth March was hanging above. Somehow, he seemed to know she was there. The other Americans were turning, marvelling at the spectacle of the King and his courtiers, but Ellsworth seemed to have eyes only for Vivienne as she ploughed through the dancers, crashed through the backstage doors and was gone.

In the corner of the ballroom, Raymond watched.

His heart was in tumult.

One problem at a time, he'd told her – but in truth they were all exploding inside him, right now. Not just Henry McCord, not just Vernon Fox, not just the King freshly arrived at the Grand – but Nancy, all the lies, the lies he would yet have to tell to make it right.

'Raymond,' John Hastings called out, reaching him at last, 'I need you on the dance floor.'

'What happened tonight, sir?'

'I believe,' smiled John Hastings, 'they call it "victory from the jaws of defeat".' He grasped Raymond's hand, shook it and beamed. 'Mr de Guise, the night has only just begun!'

Chapter Twenty-Five

The moment the royal party appeared, Rosa fell against Joel's shoulder, grasped his hand and squeezed it tight in disbelief. She'd seen the King once, out on parade in the city, but the idea that she might share a ballroom with him was too much to comprehend. This night was proving itself to be more and more of a fairytale with every passing moment.

The music was yet to strike up, but the Orchestra were almost ready. At the head of the ballroom, the princesses were being greeted by the most esteemed among the guests, the King was receiving ladies and lords, the Palace officials marching out to take up positions of security and authority in the hall. 'Joel,' she breathed, 'could it be more *perfect*? I hope – I hope it never ends. We'll remember this forever.'

On the dance floor, Frank could hardly believe his eyes. He was quite certain that that had been Vivienne, tumbling across the dance floor in a dress of scarlet red. He'd watched her careening past, seen her burst through the dressing-room doors – but it had all happened in such a flash, and so many other unlikely occurrences were exploding across the ballroom, that he wasn't entirely sure it was real.

Then he looked up.

Raymond was making his way back onto the dance floor – quite where he'd been, Frank didn't know. 'Dancers!' he declared, his voice slicing through the hubbub.

Frank swept round to join the rest of the troupe – but, as he did so, he saw Rosa melting into Joel at the balustrade above.

Suddenly, every shred of wonder he'd felt at the appearance of the royal party fizzled away.

'Not now, Frankie,' Mathilde whispered, scurrying to join the assembled troupe.

But Frank thought: *no*. It might be the only opportunity he got.

The ballroom was still reorienting itself to the new reality, that this was now a Royal Ball, when Frank rushed to balustrade, slipped through the rails and approached Rosa and Joel from behind.

'R-Rosa?' he ventured.

He had to say it twice before it pierced Rosa's wonder. She was still whispering in Joel's ear when she finally heard. To her credit, she looked flushed with uncertainty the moment she turned to face him. 'Frankie,' she said. She smiled wanly, as if to acknowledge the absurdity of the situation, and stuttered, 'C-can you believe it? King George, right here in the Grand?'

It seemed more believable to Frank that King George should be here than Rosa, but he was wise enough not to say it. 'Rosa, can we talk?'

Until that moment, Joel had been fixed upon the royal party, his fellow infantrymen rushing in to share the moment, but now he turned and looked Frank up and down. The two had met before, of course, out in the clubs – but that had been before the betrayal.

Joel had little of Rosa's willingness to be civil. 'Now look here, son – this is a once-in-a-lifetime situation. Let's not spoil it now, shall we?'

Frank bristled. It wasn't often that he felt any emotion that bordered on anger, but now it was rising in him, hot and fast.

'I know this is your world, son, but Rosa's here as my guest this evening. You'll be down there, dancing with your princesses, no doubt – well, I got a princess of my own to be dancing with.'

It was the way he said 'son' that rankled Frank the most. Frank Nettleton was nobody's son, and hadn't been for some years.

But perhaps the best thing to do was not acknowledge him at all.

'Rosa, I wondered if you might want to dance with me – one more time, for old time's sake?'

Rosa's eyes flashed between Frank and Joel. 'Er – Frankie, I'm not sure that...'

Joel looked fit to bustle Frank bodily out of the way, but at that moment Mathilde's voice chimed out, 'I'd like to dance with the corporal myself, actually.' She sailed past Frank, detached Joel's arm from Rosa's shoulder and inveigled her way into it herself. 'I was watching you from the dance floor, sir. This next one's a quickstep. Do you think you can keep up?'

Joel didn't seem to know what had happened to him as he was swept down to the dance floor by Mathilde. Caught unawares, he was being dragged onto the dance floor, just in time for the band to strike up.

'It's better that we don't pretend the other one doesn't exist,' said Frank. 'It's better we just dance and then – then you spend the evening with Joel, and I'll get back to my work. Rosa, please?'

Rosa looked torn. It was only when she directed her gaze at the dance floor, to see Joel taking the first steps of his dance with Mathilde, that she shrugged and said, 'One dance, Frank – to show... to show there's no hard feelings.'

Frank smiled and, offering her his arm, took her to the dance floor.

No hard feelings, she'd said.

Well, not yet, anyway...

Vivienne flew through the dressing rooms, out through the rehearsal studio – where the percussionist James Heath was desperately trying to reconstitute himself with tea and hot toast – and through the warren of passageways that led to the reception hall.

The cold of Berkeley Square hit her with the full force of a gale. Palace officials were stationed around the colonnade, the square itself lined with security cars and Metropolitan police. Vivienne paused for just one moment, steeling herself against the burning cold, then hoisted up her gown and picked her way down the steps. Twice she slipped and pitched to the ground as she crossed the white expanse of the square. Twice she drew the eye of curious policemen as she picked herself up and battled onward, heading south towards Piccadilly.

It hadn't been the first time she stumbled and fallen outside the Buckingham Hotel.

She only wished she had enough Champagne coursing through her veins to guard against this bitter chill.

She was on the southern side of the square, about to disappear between the townhouses, when she heard someone calling her name. If she'd known it was Ellsworth March, coming running through the white to catch her, she might have kept going.

'Vivienne, Vivienne stop!'

Ellsworth didn't seem to feel the cold like Vivienne did. Then again, Ellsworth wasn't wearing nothing but a ball gown and dancing shoes.

'I don't understand,' Ellsworth said, with an unexpectedly plaintive edge. 'I'd given up hope of you coming to the ball, but there you were. Dancing with *him*, I know – but I thought… I thought there might be room for me as well. I thought we might waltz, and then you'd *see*.' He stopped. 'King George, Vivienne! The whole ballroom is enraptured with King George – but me? I was only thinking of you.'

Vivienne floundered for something to say. Every piece of her knew she needed to keep running.

'Why come and then just go, Vivienne? Is it something *he* did? Something *he* said?'

'It isn't Raymond,' Vivienne blurted out. 'I've told you. I tried to explain. I didn't come here for Raymond de Guise.'

'I can still take you away from all this. I could be drinking a martini with you in Times Square on New Year's night. Damn it, I could have you there by Christmas if the will is there. By all that's holy, Vivienne, I could have you on a plane this very night. All you'd have to do is say you want it, instead of being beholden to—'

Vivienne had heard enough.

'I'm not in love with Raymond de Guise,' she raged. 'I'm *working* for him!'

Ellsworth looked so deflated that he shrank into himself. 'I've never known a gentleman task his housekeeper with going to a ball.'

'I'm not working for him as a housekeeper. Ellsworth, you're not a stupid man – but you've been blind! How could you not know? Henry McCord isn't just an intelligence analyst. He isn't a patriot, slaving hard in the embassy day and night. He's a damn traitor. He's about to betray us all – he's been plotting it all along, and he's been doing it in plain sight!'

Vivienne reached into her ball gown and drew out the note-book.

'It's all here, every last thing,' she said.

There was silence out on Berkeley Square.

The silence of winter.

The silence of snow.

A world away from the glamour and light of the Grand Ballroom, Vivienne watched as Ellsworth absorbed the horror in front of him. She watched, as realisation contorted his face – and, at last, he understood what he ought to have seen all along.

'I've got to take it to Raymond's colleagues,' she said, more softly now. 'I haven't got a second to lose.'

Ellsworth straightened.

Handing the notebook back to Vivienne, he clasped hold of her hand.

'Then neither have I,' he told her.

Together, they started to run.

This dance was like no other.

Raymond's eyes darted. He was quite sure Vivienne had got out of the ballroom – that, by now, she would be halfway across Mayfair. But how long might it take until this was over? How long to convince them she was genuine, and for officers to descend en masse upon the Buckingham Hotel? One song, two songs, three songs, four?

McCord was watching from the balustrade.

Did he know?

The royal party had gathered, with the Hotel Board, up above. Security officers and Palace staff watched them from every single corner of the Grand.

How could he keep it from them?

With his partner in his arms, Raymond pivoted past Mathilde. She appeared to be dancing with Corporal Kaplan.

And there was Frank, his dark blue suit a stark contrast to the girl in sky blue in his arms.

Rosa, thought Raymond.

It couldn't be.

What was even stranger: they seemed to be talking as they danced. Frank seemed to be blathering – and, in turn, Rosa's face was darkening, her smile turning to a scowl, the dark red flush of fury moving its way up her cheeks.

The song reached its height.

Surely Vivienne had reached the Deacon Club by now?

Crashing cymbals and trumpets marked the climax of the song. Lucille's voice soared out over the Grand.

And one more drumbeat punctuated the music:

In the middle of the dance floor, Rosa stepped out of hold, planted her feet squarely on the ground – and slapped Frank hard, with the flat of her palm, across the cheek.

Raymond didn't break the flow of his own dance – but he scoured the balustrade above. The slap had certainly been seen – but only by a scant few, for the royal party still drew the eye of the ballroom. Of all the things he had to worry about in this moment, perhaps this was the least important.

But what was least important to him could still devastate Frank...

Moments after she struck Frank, Rosa stifled a sob and started running. Joel Kaplan, realising what had happened, might have marched directly over to Frank, if Raymond and his partner hadn't pivoted into his path, obscuring his view. Instead, he gathered himself and took flight after Rosa.

Frank was beached on the dance floor, upright and trembling, for only a second. Without a partner of her own, Mathilde skipped gracefully to his side – and, within instants, she slipped into his arms.

The dance continued, sweeping Frank and Mathilde back into its rhythms as if nothing had ever happened.

'You had to do it, Frank,' Mathilde whispered, voice drowned out by trumpets and drums.

Frank nodded.

'It isn't nice breaking a heart.'

'No,' said Mathilde, 'but there's every chance you just saved one.'

In the Housekeeping Lounge, where the chambermaids and concierges, porters and pages – and those few kitchen hands who'd been spared a night's toil in the Queen Mary – gathered to dance, the music was so loud that not a soul heard the telephone ringing in the office.

In the reception hall, where the music sailing out of the Grand was at once faint and yet bombastic, the attendants were so consumed with thoughts of King George that the telephone ringing on the check-in desk went forever unanswered.

In the Candlelight Club – though few patrons populated its corners and booths on this, the most prestigious night in the hotel's history – too many waiters had been seconded to the ballroom, and consequently, when the telephone behind the bar started trilling, nobody was there to pick it up.

And in Blomfield Road, where shock had given way to confusion and fear, Nancy slammed down the telephone for the seventh time – and, hearing Arthur crying in his nursery above, hurried upstairs to console him.

She'd tried to settle Stan in Vivienne's room, but the moment he heard her in the nursery, he started shouting out. Soon, with Arthur in arms, she went to see him. The strangeness of the evening had unsettled him – but, whereas Nancy had paced and prowled, gone into each room in turn, called the Buckingham Hotel time and again, Stan had torn off his bedclothes, upended the bedroom, opened and emptied every drawer.

Nancy knew she ought to have admonished him, but instead she just held him tight.

'What happened here tonight?' she whispered.

But Stan had no words for her. He just clung to her as she levered back downstairs.

The briefcase still lay on the kitchen table.

Nancy had hidden the Smith & Wesson inside it, but somehow it seemed to draw her eye.

'Not in here, boys,' she trembled. 'Let's settle by the fire.'

In the sitting room, the embers were still glowing. Nancy wrapped Stan in a blanket on the armchair and told him to cuddle Arthur while she brought biscuits from the jar on the kitchen shelf. It was Vivienne's own shortbread, dusted in brown sugar from the Buckingham Hotel. She made them every Sunday, the boys' favourite treat – made with love and care and…

What had she been doing?

What had happened, here in Nancy's own home?

The urgency took hold of her again. Having first delivered the boys their biscuits, then put on a record to soothe their nerves, Nancy went to the telephone in the hall and dialled again for the Buckingham Hotel.

The telephone buzzed.

It clicked.

It started to ring.

On and on it went, on and on again. In the living room, the sounds of Duke Ellington rose up. There was music all across London tonight – music in the Grand Ballroom, music at the Imperial Hotel, music in the Housekeeping Lounge where all

Nancy's girls were dancing away – but all that Nancy heard was this interminable ringing.

Finally, somebody picked up.

'Buckingham Hotel?'

It was Billy, Nancy realised. Billy Brogan. The telephone exchange had clicked through and sent her call to the hotel post room.

'Billy,' she gasped, 'it's me. It's Nancy. Billy, thank God. I need your help. I need you to do something for me.'

'Anything, Mrs de Guise!' Billy's tinny voice chirped back.

'I need you to go to the Grand Ballroom. I need you to fetch Raymond to the phone. I know he ought to be dancing. I know he's with the guests – but Billy, you have to promise me.'

There was wonder going on in the Buckingham Hotel tonight, but no number of Kings and Queens could change the feeling in Billy's heart – that the real wonder was here, sitting right in front of him: the goose he'd promised his family for Christmas dinner, wrapped in brown paper, ready to be cooked.

'I don't know if I can do that, Nancy.'

'You have to,' Nancy swore.

'You don't understand. Everything's changed. The royal party arrived! They're in the ballroom right now. I reckon Raymond's dancing with one of the princesses this very minute.'

Nancy's knuckles whitened around the telephone receiver.

'I don't care, Billy,' she said, at last. 'This is more important. You get to the Grand Ballroom straight away and get him a message. He has to call home, right now. Billy, King George or not, this simply cannot wait.'

Chapter Twenty-Six

In the Grand Ballroom, the song reached its height, exploding in a climax of piano and trombone. Max Allgood lifted Lucille from his lips and thrust her triumphantly into the air. With his other hand, he reached for Alix Monet. Together, they stood like returning heroes at the edge of the stage. When they bowed, the whole ballroom cheered.

Max looked at Alix. 'Did you ever think you'd make a debut like this, Miss Monet?'

Alix was breathless. 'I want to sing,' she said.

Max's eyes goggled.

'Let me sing, Mr Allgood?'

Max shrugged. Tonight, it seemed anything was possible – and they were, after all, missing one guest singer.

'It's the 'Christmas Cantana' up next, boys!' Max exclaimed, sliding back into place with Lucille in his hands. 'And we've got a surprise for these good folks. Rally up!'

In the same moment that Alix struck the first notes of Max's own 'Christmas Cantana', Rosa was reeling along the Housekeeping hall, tears drawing black lines of make-up down each cheek.

'Rosa!' Joel's voice chased her down the hall. 'Rosa, stop. Rosa, what did he say to you?' Then, when Rosa – desperate to reach

the doors of the Housekeeping Lounge, to be among her girls –
refused to obey, he added, 'I'll knock his head off his shoulders.
King George or not, I'll finish his dancing right now!'

Rosa froze.

Then she turned over her shoulder and said, 'It isn't Frank
who deserves his head off his shoulders, Joel – it's *you*. Frank
only told me the truth. It's all he's ever done.'

'You're the one who slapped him, Rosa.'

It silenced Rosa for only a second. She was well aware that
she could be a walking contradiction – but the one thing she
wasn't was a fool.

'Who is she?' Rosa demanded.

Joel took a step towards her, but Rosa only lifted her hand,
as if she might strike him too.

'Who's who?'

'Your *wife*,' Rosa snarled.

At that moment, the door to the Housekeeping Lounge
opened. Out burst music, laughter – and one particularly green-
around-the-gills concierge, who gripped his stomach and made
for the nearest washroom.

'I'm going to see the girls,' Rosa snapped, when Joel's silence
told her everything she needed to know. 'Don't even look at me
again. I thought – I thought you were the one I'd grow old with.'

Joel took hold of her and whirled her round.

'Are you going to let me speak?' he demanded. 'Are you going
to let me explain?'

'You don't deny it,' snapped Rosa, her eyes tear-stained and
black.

Joel took a breath before he whispered, 'No.'

'Then what is there to talk about?'

Rosa tried to wrench herself free, but Joel was too strong. 'Not
in there,' he told her, his voice as domineering as it was when he

spoke to his boys at the barracks. 'Damn it Rosa, give me five minutes. Five minutes and I'll explain it all. You owe me that.'

'I don't owe you a damn thing!'

She brought back her hand to slap him then, but Joel caught it and held it there.

Then, holding her eye, he pressed the hand that meant to strike him close against his face.

He nuzzled it.

He said, 'Not in there. Five minutes, Rosa. Walk with me now.'

The tradesman's entrance was not far. Joel, taking off his jacket, draped it around her shoulders, and for now Rosa did not complain.

In silence they tramped through the snowdrifts, until they stood together on the edge of Berkeley Square. Some of the Palace security officials watched them curiously, but nobody moved to intervene.

'She's called Michelle,' Joel said at last – and, when Rosa turned away from him, trembling further, he said, 'and she means nothing to me. Not one thing.'

Rosa refused to hold his eye. 'I bet that's what you say to all the girls. I trusted you,' she bleated. 'I did a dirty thing to Frank because I fell for you. And now . . . now, I suppose, I deserve everything I'm about to get. What goes around comes around, isn't that right?'

He lifted his hand to gently touch Rosa's chin and compel her to look him in the eye. At first she resisted – yet Joel was persistent and, eventually, she gave in. He studied every contour of her face, with eyes that seemed to see straight to her soul.

'People get what they deserve,' he told her, 'and you got *me*.'

Something in Rosa thawed. She tried to cling on to the bitterness and rage which had fuelled her, but it was like ice melting in her fist.

'Michelle was my childhood sweetheart. I don't know what it's like where you come from, but back in Madison it's just how it was. She lived down the street. My father did business with her father. She came to parties and our moms drank coffee and smoked while us kids were out in the yard. I was nineteen when I got married. Our folks built us a little house six streets over.' He stopped. 'And that's where it went wrong.'

When Rosa heard the words, it was like a gap opening in the storm clouds.

Hope was resurgent inside her.

'I was away from home so much. The 32nd Infantry. I'd wanted to be a soldier since I was a boy, but it meant long months away from home – even in peacetime, we had to be ready.' He stopped. 'The first time I realised that we weren't *really* married was the summer of '38. They'd sent us all down to Fort Knox for command exercises. Kentucky, Rosa – it's as far away from Madison as London from Berlin. I must have been gone three months. And when I got back – well, Michelle had stopped making a secret of it by then. There was a kid we'd grown up with – he worked as a mechanic, somewhere out in Dane County, and when he wasn't servicing cars, he was servicing…'

'Michelle,' Rosa whispered.

'I found out, in the end, that he wasn't the only one,' Joel shrugged, 'but the strangest thing was, I didn't mind. Now, I'm not saying I didn't get hot-headed – and I'm not saying I didn't march down to his garage and give him a piece of my mind. But I stopped short of giving that guy a hiding, because it hit me: he could have her.' He paused. 'Of course, once I told her she was free to do as she pleased, she started thinking of everything she'd lose. But I was past caring. I wanted to leave Madison, live my own life, see something of the world. And then…'

'Pearl Harbour.'

'I was summoned to the war, like I'd always hoped I would be.'

Rosa was still trying to make sense of everything Joel had said. 'You *wanted* a war?'

'I wanted to change my life,' smiled Joel, 'and here I am!' For the first time, he let go of Rosa, turned round and surveyed the black-and-white expanse of Berkeley Square. 'I'm going to end my marriage as soon as the war's over. But that's just paper. That's just courts and laws. In here,' and he thumped his heart, 'it's been over for years. Michelle can pretend if she wants to, but I'm not. I've got *you*.'

Rosa gazed out over the square too. The tears she'd been crying had turned to trails of frost down her cheeks.

'But what happens *then*?' she asked, faintly. 'When the war's over and you get a divorce ... and you're in America and I'm right here, changing bedsheets at the Buckingham Hotel?'

Joel put an arm around her, so that they could gaze out over the wintry splendour together.

'Isn't it incredible,' he said, 'that we're here, talking about *when* the war's over? Last Christmas, it wasn't like this. Back then it was: what happens when there are Nazis goosestepping on the Strand? Listen to yourself, Rosa – you're thinking, *dreaming*, about the future again!'

'I am,' she admitted – and it was as if all the passion of the ballroom had turned back to peace.

'I don't know what happens in the future,' Joel said. 'All I want to do is think about *now*, right here and now – me, standing here with you, on the most prestigious night of our lives.' He bent to kiss her – and Rosa did not resist. 'Some day soon, we're going to saddle up and invade France. The word's going to go round: it's time to march on Berlin.'

'Don't say that,' Rosa whispered.

'Oh, but I have to. It's what I'm for. And, who knows, maybe it'll be the making of me. Maybe I'll rise up. Or maybe I'll die.' He stopped. 'But all that's for the future. Right now, you and me, we're missing out on the most magical thing that ever happened to us. It's like destiny's flung us together, and given us this chance – but, instead of dancing in the Grand Ballroom, we're standing out here in the cold. What do you say, Rosa? Back to the dance, and live for the moment?'

Rosa hesitated. Dancing in the Grand had seemed the dream of a lifetime

'Let's dance, Corporal Kaplan,' she said.

'But perhaps not *straight* away,' she added, and heaved him into a kiss.

On the dance floor, Alix Monet's voice rose to a crescendo.

The Orchestra had reached its climax. As the dancers stepped out of hold, wild applause broke out across the Grand.

In the heart of the dance floor, Raymond bowed graciously at his guest. Not a soul in the ballroom would have known it – for outwardly he seemed perfectly composed – but inside, his heart was racing three beats ahead of the music, his eyes scouring the balustrade at every opportunity to keep sight of McCord.

There he was now.

Mathilde, who'd just broken from the dance with Frank, was inviting him to the dance floor.

At least, Raymond thought, it would keep him occupied. Vivienne was surely at the Deacon Club by now, so it wouldn't be long. By the end of this dance, perhaps, it might be over.

Raymond was about to open his arms to the crowd, inviting some other guest into his arms, when he saw the royal party watching from the head of the dance floor. The King and his officers stood imperious, while his daughter, the Princess Elizabeth, held Raymond's eye.

At her father's acknowledgement, the Princess approached.

With one eye still on McCord, Raymond welcomed her to the floor.

'We meet again, Mr de Guise.'

Raymond bowed. He had had the honour of dancing with the princesses this summer – it had been the pinnacle of the Royal Dansant at the Albert Hall – but he hadn't dreamt of seeing them right here in the Grand.

Was this the worst night of his life, or was it one of the best?

Fate plays cruel tricks.

'Shall we?' Raymond asked, offering his hand.

The music struck up: Max Allgood's 'Express Train', a fast, flowing foxtrot – and, Raymond remembered now, the finale to the evening's first half.

With the Princess in his arms, Raymond crossed the dance floor, pivoted, then crossed it again. She was light and nimble – such a pleasure to dance with that, for fleeting moments, Raymond almost forgot his worry. Onward they glided, on and on – and Raymond thought that, if only his mind hadn't been broken into a dozen pieces and each of them given their own separate task, this might have been the crowning moment in his career.

Up above, John Hastings certainly thought it: Raymond caught sight of him, standing as nobly as the King himself, the rest of the Hotel Board looking on in astonishment.

Keep it out of the ballroom, Raymond told himself.

If McCord was seized on the dance floor, it would sully the evening.

If officers had to drag him away, it would ruin the Buckingham Hotel.

Every other soul here ought to remember the splendour of the night.

The mounting tension was for Raymond alone.

Halfway through the song, Alix Monet lent her voice to the Orchestra again. Sublimely, it rose up, to dovetail with the swooning trombone, the driving trumpet blasts. Raymond hadn't even known there were lyrics to this piece; he wondered, perhaps, if Miss Monet was improvising with her voice, just as the best musicians could improvise with their instruments.

What a talent she was, to welcome to the Grand. The moment her voice rose up, the dance changed *feeling*. Raymond's heart was still pounding, but he gave himself to the moment. The dancers seemed to part for him and the Princess. Into the heart of the dance floor they sailed – and, as the song came to its end, in rippling piano, Alix's long graceful call and Lucille's gentle lament, they danced more and more slowly, until together they came to a stop.

Raymond and the Princess stood upon the dance floor, still holding one another. He was about to step back and bow, the applause ringing out on every side, when he realised Max Allgood had marched up to the front of the stage, thrust Lucille into the air and beamed.

'Ladies and Gentlemen,' he cried out, 'we'll be back in a quarter of an hour. Enough time to rest those dancing feet! Take a breath, folks. Take a drink. The night's not over yet!'

The dance floor became a blitz around Raymond, as the dancers parted ways and followed the Orchestra back into the dressing rooms – but Raymond and the Princess remained, an oasis of calm in the tumult of the Grand.

Slowly, steadily, Raymond bowed.

'Save a dance for me later this evening?' the Princess smiled.

'You may count on it, Your Highness,' Raymond returned.

The moment she left him, reality rushed back in.

Raymond turned on his heel.

He could quite clearly see that John Hastings was approaching, as if to congratulate him on a spectacular opening to the evening – but he could quite clearly see McCord vanishing into the crowd as well.

His eyes flashed to the marble arch, willing the doors to open, willing Vivienne to appear with Vernon Fox and his fellows in tow.

But, no matter how much he willed it, nothing happened.

Fifteen minutes, Max had said.

In Raymond's experience, the intermission of a Buckingham Ball often lasted longer – but perhaps fifteen minutes would do.

Perhaps Vivienne was still at the Deacon Club.

Perhaps a messenger simply wouldn't do.

The moment he stepped backstage, the dancers fell upon him in a rhapsody of disbelief, wonder and cheer. Mathilde started gabbling about the Princess, Hélène gave him a wry look from across the room – as if to say that, whatever it was that made Raymond so special, he still had it, after all these years – but Raymond had no time for them.

He rushed out of the dressing rooms, skirted the reception hall and made for the tradesman's entrance on Michaelmas Mews.

Two figures were locked in a passionate embrace at exactly the point where Michaelmas Mews opened onto Berkeley Square. It wasn't until Raymond came abreast of them that they drew apart – and Raymond recognised Rosa and her corporal.

'I'm sorry, Mr de Guise,' she stammered. 'I was just...'

Raymond didn't care, but his instinctive duty to the hotel made him blurt out, 'Decorum, Rosa. You might be a guest in the Grand, but you're still a representative of this hotel.'

'I – I know,' she stammered. 'Please don't tell Nance... I mean, Mrs de Guise?'

Nancy. In the chaos of the last moments, Raymond had hardly thought about his wife – alone, the evidence of his lies all around her, not knowing what was happening, nor perhaps even *who* he was.

He had no words.

He just glared at Rosa.

Then he ran, and kept on running.

The snow wreathed around him as he burst from the grand thoroughfares of Mayfair, the palatial townhouses all crowned in white, and hit Piccadilly. An army truck was wheeling by in the blackness. A WAAF station was set up on a corner, underneath a shop awning groaning under the weight of the falling snow. Raymond ploughed past them all, and bowed into one of the lesser back streets, where the door to the Deacon Club lay.

He knocked.

He knocked again.

When the doorman appeared, he looked taken aback at seeing Raymond bedecked in his midnight-blue dinner jacket, his black hair crested in white – but Raymond wasted no time, sliding directly inside.

The warmth of the Deacon Club prickled up and down his arms and legs.

'Is she still here?' Raymond asked.

The doorman, a leonine fellow dressed in black, furrowed his eyes and said, '*She*, sir?'

'Vivienne Cohen,' Raymond returned. 'I sent her with a message for Mr Fox. It's quite urgent. They're in Mr Fox's office, I presume?'

The doorman just arched an eyebrow. 'I think there must be some mistake, sir. Mr Fox is dining with the director right now. He's had no guest.'

Raymond peered up the darkness of the stairwell.

An uneasy feeling opened in his gut.

'Are you sure?'

This time, the doorman gave him a withering look.

'I might remember if a *woman* had come into the Club, sir.'

'But I sent her,' Raymond began.

'And yet...'

The doorman had given such an insouciant shrug that Raymond felt his blood boiling. 'Bring me Mr Fox, sir.'

'As I said, he is dining with the director.'

Raymond had no time for this. It still amazed him that His Majesty's intelligence service operated as if they were the Academy des Artistes.

'Then I'll fetch him myself,' he roared – and, ignoring the doorman's protests, started loping up the stairs.

The Deacon Club's restaurant dominated the first storey of the narrow building – the food it served was indulgent and rich, but the restaurant itself was only a collection of tables and threadbare chairs, arranged around a sweeping bar. Raymond crashed through its doors to find the room a miasma of grey cigar smoke. He located Vernon Fox sitting in one of the corner booths. Under the low lamplight, up against the blackout blinds, he was whispering intently with a rotund man dressed in brown tweeds, his shirtsleeves rolled up to his elbows, golden braces criss-crossing his back.

Raymond waited for no man's permission.

He wasted no time.

In a split second he was standing directly in front of Vernon Fox.

Mr Fox looked up, startled.

But he looked more startled still when Raymond opened his mouth.

'I've no time to explain, sir. I'm due on the dance floor in minutes – and King George himself is attending the Grand. I sent a messenger to reach you, but she hasn't got through.' He paused. 'The man you're looking for is named Henry McCord. He's the intelligence analyst Mr Charles sent to stay with my family – and it's him, sir. He's the one planning the trade with the enemy – and he's dancing in my ballroom right now.' Raymond turned on his heel, marched halfway back across the restaurant, then turned to glare at Vernon Fox through the swirling restaurant smoke. 'Sir, the clock's been ticking all week – but, right now, it's ticking more urgently than ever, and we're running out of time. We have to go!'

Chapter Twenty-Seven

Life could be very complicated.

If you let yourself get carried away with things, there was so much to agonise over: there was love and war, poverty and wealth, honour and duty – and this was without even thinking about 'right' and 'wrong', two nebulous concepts that Billy Brogan was quite certain ought to be redefined for the modern age.

But the one thing that was completely and totally *uncomplicated* was joy – and Billy had rarely felt the simple, unadulterated joy he felt as he packaged up his Christmas goose, locked up the hotel post room and limped along the hall, whistling to himself as he came.

On another Christmas night, he might have gone down to the Housekeeping Lounge to have a drink or two, catch up on the gossip of the day, perhaps even try his hand at romancing one of the girls – well, stranger things had happened! – but tonight Billy felt as if nothing could surpass the magic he was already feeling. Consequently, he decided to head directly home. Once he got there, and presented his trophy to his ma and pa, there would be no better feeling in the world.

There was just one stop he had to make first.

The intermission had come in the Grand Ballroom, so when Billy approached the dressing-room doors he could hear quite a hubbub bubbling behind. He knocked once, knocked twice – it wasn't until the third knock that the door opened. There stood Hélène Marchmont, resplendent in a gown of shimmering gold.

'Billy Brogan,' she smiled, 'as I live and breathe.'

'Good Lord, Miss Marchmont – it's like I've been yanked back in time.' Billy stuck his head into the dressing room. 'Is Raymond there, Miss Marchmont? I've got a—'

Billy had been about to say 'message', but a sudden bustling behind him cut him off. Wheeling round, he saw Rosa marching purposefully to the doors. Somewhere behind her, Corporal Kaplan was waiting with a vaguely exasperated air.

'I want to see Frank,' Rosa declared, and cut a course directly across the room.

Hélène looked at Billy, faintly concerned. 'The course of true love,' she smiled, sadly. Then, remembering Billy's request, she added, 'Raymond isn't here. We don't know where he went. Hotel business, I think.' She glanced back into the dressing room, nervously searching for a clock. 'He'll be back soon. I'm sure he'll be back soon.'

Billy didn't like the idea of waiting, not when he had his prize goose to show off. 'Nancy called the hotel. She wants to speak with him. Now, I told her – Nancy, I said, there's the *King* here. Raymond's dancing for the *King!*' He shrugged. 'Anyway, she made me promise, so here I am. You'll tell him, won't you?'

That was enough for Billy. As soon as he'd said the words, his promise fulfilled, he grinned, and turned to leave.

He was still whistling jauntily as he left the hotel and limped along the frozen mews.

A little while later, while chaos reigned at the Buckingham Hotel, Billy Brogan sauntered through the doors at No 62 Albert Yard, unfurled his bundle of wax paper on the dining-room table, flung open his arms and cried, 'I told you, Ma! I told you,

Pa. It isn't rabbit stew for dinner this Christmas. We're going to celebrate like we should. We're Brogans, and we deserve the *best!*'

It was (though some might find it strange) the happiest day of Billy Brogan's life.

In the dressing room behind the Grand, as the clock ticked down to the moment the music would resume, Max Allgood rallied his musicians, Hélène Marchmont paced nervously – and Rosa, her cheeks still bearing the marks of the tears she'd been crying, carved her way between the dancers, bustled Mathilde aside and seized Frank by the hand.

'We can do this in front of everyone if you like, Frank Nettleton, or you can come with me.'

Frank looked about as shell-shocked as he'd been when Rosa slapped him, so it was Mathilde who cried out, 'Who do you think you are, just bursting in here?'

Rosa scolded her with her eyes. 'Are you going to let her talk to me like that, Frank?'

Frank wrenched his hand free. 'She's right, Rosa,' he said, simply. 'This is the dressing room of the Grand Ballroom. It's no place for . . .' It was on the tip of his tongue to say 'chambermaids', but Frank had never said anything as waspish in his life – so, in the end, he just said 'guests'. Then he lifted his shoulders, puffed out his chest – and, seizing the moment, grabbed Rosa by the wrist instead. 'I'll be back in a moment, Mathilde.'

'Make sure you are, Frank – and without another bruise from that woman. We haven't got much time!'

Rosa had never known Frank so domineering – so, in spite of the vitriol coursing through her, she let him lead her out of the dressing rooms, into the practise studio where James Heath was still trembling over his tea. The moment he saw Frank and

Rosa, he picked himself up. 'Are we almost ready?' he stammered. Then, clutching his stomach, he lurched towards the dressing room – as if there was still some hope Max might let him up on stage.

'Well, say what you have to say,' said Frank, releasing Rosa by the piano and stepping back. 'Be as angry with me as you like – but I couldn't not tell you. I still *care* about you. I couldn't let him take you for a fool.'

'It's you who's taking me for a fool,' Rosa burst in.

Frank just stared.

'It's only paper,' she sobbed. 'He's only married on paper. It isn't his heart. And when the war's over, he's going to…

Frank could hardly believe what he was hearing. 'Did you already know?' he whispered.

'He told me everything, just now.'

Frank didn't know what she expected. Was it an apology she wanted? Or was he just to be the man that she slapped, while in truth it was Joel who deserved every blow?

What was his duty? His responsibility?

Then he said the one thing he'd been working hard not to say all year long, ever since that terrible summer's day when he'd first seen Rosa and Joel together.

'It isn't nice to be lied to, is it, Rosa?'

Rosa dried her tears. 'I see how it is. I see it now. You want me ruined, because of what I did to you. Well, I'm sorry, Frank. How many times do you want me to say sorry? I thought we were friends.'

Frank had to stop himself rushing to her. 'We *are* friends,' he said. 'That's *why* I told you. That's *why* you had to know.'

'He loves me,' Rosa said.

Frank had no answer.

They stood in silence – until the studio door opened, and Mathilde beckoned Frank with her eyes. The dance, it seemed, was ready to resume.

'I hope you're right,' Frank whispered – and Rosa did not resist when he crossed the studio to kiss her on the cheek. 'For your own sake, Rosa, I hope you're right.'

Three cars burst onto Berkeley Square in an explosion of snow and ice, drawing the eyes of the Palace officials arrayed around the townhouses, the security officers positioned beyond the hotel colonnade.

Raymond de Guise was the first to emerge. Soon after him, Vernon Fox appeared; soon after that, every other officer who'd been dining at the Deacon Club this evening was spilling out into the night.

Raymond cocked his head, but all he could hear was the soft susurration of falling snow. That could only mean he had made it in time: the Orchestra had not yet marched out to enrapture the crowd for their second act. If things went smoothly from this moment on, he might even make it back to the dance floor by the time the dancers fanned out for their showpiece.

'Mr de Guise?'

It was the voice of the doorman, spying him from the top of the marble steps.

Raymond looked up. 'These men are with me,' he said, and turned to Vernon Fox. 'The tradesman's entrance. I'll lead.'

Fox turned to issue orders to his men. At his command, they took up stations around the hotel doors, as well as the entrance to the mews; McCord had no military training, but there was no telling what a man might do when he was cornered – at least, this way, his avenues of escape would be cut off.

Raymond marched in quickstep along Michaelmas Mews, forcing open the tradesman's entrance and escorting Vernon Fox through. From here he could hear the duck and dive of frenetic music – but it was only the raucous sounds of the shindig in the Housekeeping Lounge.

Together, they reached the hotel reception.

'Is he a fighting man, de Guise?'

Raymond said, 'Aren't all men, when they're cornered?'

Vernon Fox nodded. 'If we're to keep this civilised, you'll have to lead. Approach him as a friend. Ask him to take a drink. Bring him to the bar, and I'll do the rest.' His eyes flashed back and forth. 'Is there a place we can detain him, while I bring out my men?'

'There's a rehearsal studio, behind the Grand.'

'What are the chances of getting him there, without drawing the eyes of the ballroom? Without exposing to management what you really are?'

Raymond brooded on this. 'Perhaps that's a problem for tomorrow, sir?'

Vernon Fox grumbled, 'Like all the very worst problems. So be it. Let's march, de Guise.'

Both Palace and hotel officials stood on sentry by the ornate mahogany doors – but no man questioned Raymond de Guise's right to be in the ballroom. They stepped aside – and, moments later, Raymond and Fox were entering the bustle of the Grand.

Nor were they the only ones.

Max Allgood's Orchestra were marching out.

'They must be panicked backstage. They must be wondering where I am.' Raymond's eyes scoured the crowd – but the guests were packed too closely; he saw Rosa leaning into Corporal Kaplan, but of McCord he could see nothing. 'The Orchestra will play one number to announce themselves – after that, Mr Fox, I'm due to dance.'

'Find him,' said Vernon Fox, inclining his head to the long, sweeping bar. 'I'll be waiting.'

Raymond ploughed into the ranks of guests flocking to the balustrade. He skirted the royal party, weaved past the members of the Hotel Board (praying that John Hastings didn't see him so out of place), then picked his way past Princess Juliana and Queen Wilhelmina's party. A cadre of officials from de Gaulle's Free French were at the very head of the balustrade – and there, beyond them, the infantrymen who were staying at the hotel.

The music had started. Alix Monet rolled her wrists, summoning a storm of minor chords which eventually resolved into a brooding melody.

Then the atmosphere changed.

The trumpets launched in.

The drums rattled and rolled.

Max lifted Lucille.

Now it was a party...

Raymond looked directly across the dance floor. In less than two minutes, the doors would open again, revealing the dancers to the crowd – but there, raising his glass with Jonah Linden, was Henry McCord.

It wasn't easy to reach him. Raymond had to tread on toes, dazzle with smiles, promise half a dozen dances – but, eventually, he came upon McCord from behind.

'Mr McCord, how about a glass of something, something to whet the whistle for the dance ahead?'

'Oughtn't you be dancing?' grinned McCord turning round.

He was right. In the corner of his eye, Raymond saw the dance-floor doors fluttering as the dancers lined up behind. Even now, he was letting the troupe down. The only saving grace was that, for this dance, he and Hélène would be the final couple through the doors. There was yet time.

'Some Champagne for our guests,' Raymond smiled. 'Step right this way.'

It wasn't easy to charm McCord – the young man evidently wanted to stay at the balustrade and watch the dancers come out – but Raymond had the sort of smile that, properly deployed, wouldn't take no for an answer. He continued chatting amiably as McCord followed him back through the press of guests crowding the dance floor, out into the emptier environs of the ballroom, until they were finally approaching the bar.

Vernon Fox was waiting some distance along the bar. The moment Raymond drew near, he lifted himself, marched to McCord's side and took his arm. 'Mr McCord,' he whispered, 'I'm glad we can meet at last. There are some questions I need to ask you, and I'm afraid they're quite urgent.'

Henry McCord's face soured in a second. He made to step away from Fox, but Fox was holding him fast.

'Mr de Guise, do you know this fellow?'

'I'm afraid so, Henry.'

A fresh wave of applause broke out.

The dance-floor doors had opened, and out pirouetted the first of the second act's couples, Frank and Mathilde, to whirl around the dance floor.

'Henry,' Raymond ventured, 'perhaps we can go somewhere quieter?'

Vernon Fox's eyes flashed around. By now, several of the Palace guard had started watching them keenly.

'Do I have any choice?' McCord seethed.

'Henry,' Raymond whispered, 'this ballroom is swarmed with security officers. All I have to do is click my fingers.' Raymond smiled. 'Let us be gentlemen.'

There was nothing gentlemanly about marching McCord to the ballroom doors, Vernon Fox with his arm hooked around one side and Raymond the other – but, to McCord's credit, he didn't seek to tussle. Perhaps there was honour among traitors after all. Together, as another wave of applause broke out in the Grand – and another couple spirited through the dance-floor doors to present themselves to the guests – they marched out of the ballroom, skirting the barren reception to approach the dressing rooms from the rear and enter the rehearsal studio.

James Heath had taken sanctuary here again – apparently he was still deemed unfit to play – but, wasting no time, Raymond ordered him to find some other corner to nurse his troubled soul.

Then they were alone.

'What's the meaning of this?' McCord demanded, shaking off both men. 'I was under the impression I was a guest here tonight.'

'You may drop the act now, Henry,' snapped Fox, kicking at the piano stool. 'And you may sit down.'

There was a moment in which Raymond thought McCord was about to resist – but only a moment. Still putting up a front – as if this had all been some terrible mistake – he sat down and declared, 'Now tell me what this is all about.'

It was only when Fox produced a pair of handcuffs – and, taking advantage of Henry's momentary disbelief, cuffed him to the stool – that his face darkened.

'I demand an explanation! I demand to call the embassy!'

The rehearsal studio door flew open. Raymond turned, expecting to have to barrack James Heath – but there stood Hélène Marchmont. She must have been alerted to Raymond's presence by Heath, staggering into the dressing room in search of some other corner to haunt.

'Raymond, where on earth have you been? It's us up next! We have thirty seconds!'

Her final exclamation petered out as she saw the unusual scene in front of her – but, the moment Raymond realised that she'd *seen*, he swept towards her and ushered her back through the door. 'I'll be there, Hélène. Just one moment!' He turned to Fox and said, 'I'll have to dance.'

'Go!' Fox seethed. 'This man's going nowhere.'

Raymond heard McCord put up another protest, but he wasted no time. In one fluid motion, he opened the door, spun directly across the dressing room and seized Hélène's hand.

'Raymond, what the devil…'

'I'll tell you *everything* later,' he said (one more lie couldn't hurt – not on a night like this), 'but first, Hélène? First, to dance!'

The Grand Ballroom, already alive with music and applause, exploded yet further when Raymond led Hélène onto the dance floor. At first, he could tell that she was tense, but within moments, she melted into the dance. Together they sailed into a clearing among the other couples. Raymond presented Hélène; Hélène presented Raymond. Then, body to body, in the tightest of holds, they turned together, inviting the other couples into a constantly shifting spiral of dance.

The song reached its zenith.

One by one, the instruments fell away.

Couple by couple, the dancers came to a stop.

Finally, it was only Raymond and Hélène turning in the ballroom.

He saw the whole host wheeling past. He saw the Hotel Board, the infantrymen, the King and the royal party. All of them, the great and the good, the lowborn and high, of the Buckingham Hotel.

And, for perhaps the first time in days, he breathed a sigh of relief.

It was done.

McCord was in handcuffs, waiting to be broken by Vernon Fox and his men.

'Ladies and Gentlemen,' Max Allgood cried out from the stage, 'get ready to dance!'

Raymond released Hélène from hold. Her beautiful, glacial eyes were still appraising him strangely but Raymond just winked and whispered, 'Dance on!' Around them, the troupe were already fanning out to accept new partners to the dance floor. The band was about to strike up its next big number. He turned, knowing that Mr Hastings would expect him to fill this second half with drama and romance – but first he *needed* to know.

Avoiding the tantalising eyes of the guests desperate to dance with him, he turned and sailed back through the dressing-room doors and into the studio beyond.

Still shackled to the piano stool, McCord bucked upwards at Raymond's appearance.

'Let's give him credit for this,' said Fox the moment Raymond appeared, 'he's got some acting talents. He's still acting the innocent. If you won't take it from me, McCord, take it from the man who exposed you.'

'I'm sorry, Henry,' said Raymond. 'The game's over. It's time to come clean.'

Fox gestured to one of his men, who marched off through the rehearsal-room door. 'If you don't want to play nicely, we'll just do it a different way. Bring round the cars. Let's move this on. We can interrogate him better at the Office.'

McCord pleaded with Raymond with his eyes. 'Interrogate? Oh, you damn fools. You've got this all wrong. You don't know who I am!'

'I know exactly who you are, and I know exactly what you've been planning. You were sent to my house to be unmasked, McCord. I didn't want it. I didn't want my family exposed to it – but here we are.'

McCord's face turned ashen white. 'Now listen to me—'

'I don't need to listen to you,' Raymond snapped. 'I've seen it with my own eyes. Your book of codes, Mr McCord. Page after page of cyphers, showing exactly what you are.'

Stunned into silence, McCord could do nothing but stare. 'You went through my case.'

'It's why you're in my house this Christmas. You know, I've had my run-ins with traitors before, McCord, but none like—'

'Traitor?' laughed McCord. 'You call *me* a traitor?'

'I've held the evidence in my hands. You're planning to deliver to the enemy the secret that could win this war.'

McCord's eyes flared. 'You goddamn fools,' he snorted, and Raymond thought he had never seen a man sound as righteous as he did right then. 'My name,' he declared, 'is Henry James McCord. My number is 774631. I am an agent of the Office of Strategic Services, straight out of Washington DC. I'm no traitor, you bumbling English fools – I'm the man dispatched by my government to hunt traitors down. I'm the one tasked with bringing them in!'

Chapter Twenty-Eight

Raymond flashed a look back towards the ballroom. Music and applause ricocheted throughout the Buckingham Hotel.

But it all seemed so distant now.

All he could hear was Henry McCord.

'What I'm about to tell you is highly classified information,' McCord spat. 'By rights, I ought to kill you for even hearing the words I'm about to spill – but it sounds as if we might be working towards the same ends, and if you've already broken cover and searched my packs, that means you've set the clock ticking…' McCord took a breath. He didn't strain at his cuffs, just presented them to Fox as if he might scuttle over and remove them. For the moment, Fox demurred, just barked at McCord to carry on. 'A short time ago, scientists in the employ of my government made a strategic breakthrough – a breakthrough that, if weaponised correctly, might end this war in one decisive stroke. Indeed, this breakthrough is of such staggering significance that there's a chance it might end all wars – that it might usher in an era of world peace, under the guidance of American might. I won't pretend to understand the particulars. Suffice to say, the technology could develop a bomb so powerful as to level cities. A bomb so potent that every enemy ranged up against us would be compelled to come to terms.'

Raymond hadn't heard the secret described quite as luridly as this – it curdled his stomach to imagine such preposterous power – but at this point he interjected, 'My colleagues know this. A young man in the Pink Sink brought it to the attention of my superiors.'

'Several weeks ago, a technician on the Project reported a disturbance in the records. It was established that a copy had been made of a certain file pertinent to the project. We traced the leak to a man named Erlick, who worked in the laboratories – but Erlick was no longer in possession of the copy he made, and he refused to give up his contacts. Naturally, we assumed he was in the enemy's employ. It wasn't until the day after we found him hanged in his cell that we were able to ascertain the facts. Erlick hadn't sent the information to the enemy. He'd sent it to a dead letter drop right here in London. He'd sent it to an American friend.

'At first we didn't understand. But Erlick was a man of conscience. He'd confided in his wife that what the Manhattan Project are developing is too powerful for any one country to wield. To control that power would be to hold the world to ransom. It wouldn't usher in peace. It would usher in an epoch of darkness and domination.'

'Where is that file now?' breathed Vernon Fox.

'That's the problem,' McCord replied. 'We can't be sure. The address it was sent to is a safehouse my government keeps in the city. Its comings and goings are not recorded, for obvious reasons. But we know that only members of our intelligence community are aware of it – and that one of us picked it up. Where they've stashed it is a secret only they could say. But it has been my job, for the last weeks, to vet our staff and certify their loyalty. It has been my job to watch them, to draw profiles of them, and somehow put the traitor in our sights. The notebook you robbed from me, Mr de Guise, is nothing more than a record of the observations I've made on Jonah Linden and Ellsworth March. Notes about Linden's obsession for detail – and Ellsworth's sudden infatuation with your housekeeper!'

Vernon Fox's hands turned to fists. He kicked, wildly, at the piano. A discordant sound burst up as the strings rattled inside. 'Unlock him,' he snapped, tossing the keys to Raymond.

Raymond snatched the keys from the air, then bowed nervously to unshackle McCord.

'Are you close to finding the man?' Raymond asked.

McCord shook himself as he stood, rubbing the red rings around his wrists. 'Well, I haven't made any false arrests yet – so I'm one step ahead of you.'

'We know he's in the embassy,' Vernon Fox snapped. 'That much we knew from the start. Once he had the file, he spilled his guts to some poor sot, who spilled *his* guts to one of our boys working the Pink Sink. One of the new appointees at the embassy – that was our intelligence. You know, McCord – it would have been a damn sight easier if your government kept to its promises and actually *shared* its intelligence with ours.'

McCord scowled, 'I'm sure MI5 has reams of intelligence it deems unfit for American ears as well.'

'Jonah Linden? Ellsworth March? Are they clean?' Raymond cut in.

McCord just snapped, 'I'll show you exactly how banal those two are if you hand me back my notebook. Well? Where is it?'

'It's with Vivienne,' Raymond replied.

'And where is *she*?'

Raymond said, 'She was taking it to the club when…'

Then he stalled.

He looked at Vernon Fox.

'What is it, de Guise?' he asked.

A look like revelation was ghosting across Raymond's face. In silence, without a word of explanation, he turned and cantered out of the studio, back across the dressing room and into the Grand. Across the dance floor, couples wheeled and soared. Frank, Mathilde, Karina and the rest – they were doing exactly what Raymond ought to have been doing. They were spellbinding guests.

Guests…

He scoured the crowd for the Americans. First, he saw Corporal Kaplan; then, the infantrymen Eugene Tuck and Buxton May. Then, at last, he found Jonah Linden – now romancing Lord Manningtree's daughter with a magnum of Champagne.

He turned and ran, bursting back into the studio to find McCord readying to leave.

'Vivienne didn't make it to the Deacon Club,' he said. 'I sent her with a message – but she didn't arrive. I thought she was lost. Just spiralling through the streets, looking for the entrance. But Ellsworth March isn't in the ballroom.'

McCord stopped dead.

'What of it?' Vernon Fox demanded.

'Ellsworth became enamoured of her. He asked her to the ball. He told her he could take her away from London – spirit her back to New York, to sit out the war. I saw the look on his face when she came to the ballroom. It was like she'd agreed to all of his terms. Except she wasn't here for him. She was here for me.' Raymond gathered his breath. 'What if Ellsworth was watching her as she fled from the ballroom? And what if…'

'What if he followed her out of the ballroom?' McCord interjected.

'He might have gone to convince her,' said Fox.

'And instead discovered what she was really about,' said McCord.

'And if it isn't you, Mr McCord, who's planning to deal with the enemy, then...' Raymond took a breath. 'What if Ellsworth March is the reason Vivienne didn't reach the Deacon Club?'

There would be no sleep tonight. The fury, the confusion, the urgency must have been leaching out of Nancy, unsettling both of the boys. Every time she tried to take them upstairs, the tears started flowing – so, in the end, all she could think to do was put on more records in the sitting room while, out in the hall, she hung by the phone.

Billy Brogan must have delivered his message by now.

Any moment now, Raymond would call her – and then she'd know what was going on.

Nancy lingered in the sitting-room doorway, trying to let the music weave its magic on her, as it was spellbinding the boys. But it was no use. When the telephone had sat silent for too long, Nancy marched back to it.

Again, she called for the Buckingham Hotel.

Again, it rang and rang.

Until finally a tinny voice, drowned out by the music of the Housekeeping Lounge, piped up: 'Buckingham Hotel, Housekeeping department!'

Nancy knew that voice. *Annie Brogan.* At least she knew she could count on her. 'Annie, it's Mrs de Guise.'

'Oh, Mrs de Guise!' Annie's distant voice trilled. 'It's quite civilised in here. I promise it is! The girls absolutely aren't dancing on the tables, Mrs de Guise. Mary-Lousie absolutely *isn't* asleep in the chair at your desk. There definitely isn't any punch soaked into the...'

'Annie!'

Annie Brogan's shocked voice said, 'Yes, Mrs de Guise?'

'I need you to go the Grand this moment. I need you to find Raymond. Get him here. Drag him to the phone if you must.'

Annie whispered, 'I'm not sure I could really *drag* him, Mrs de Guise.'

'Just go!' Nancy snapped. Then, because she hated the flinty sound of her voice, she took a breath and said, 'I'm sorry, Annie. I just need the help tonight.'

'I'm on my way, Mrs de Guise.'

'Don't hang up,' she blurted. 'Just set down the telephone and run. Annie, I'll make it worth your while.'

Nancy braced herself against the wall, the receiver dangling in her hand, and tried to gather her composure. For a moment all she could hear was the pounding of her own heart. Not even the sounds of Duke Ellington swirling out of the sitting room reached her ears.

Then, as her breathing slowed and her heartbeat gentled, the world came back into focus.

The music was filling the boys' hearts.

But it wasn't the only sound that she heard.

Outside, somewhere on Blomfield Road, was the sound of a car engine idling.

And closer, much closer: the crunch of footsteps upon snow.

A voice, rising out of the darkness in the garden:

'You don't need much. An overnight bag and your boy. The rest I'll figure out on the way.'

It was the voice of Ellsworth March – and he was coming this way.

Raymond emerged from the studio, McCord and Fox following. 'I'm going to have to put in a call to the embassy,' McCord began. 'Where can I get to a telephone?'

'The Benefactors Study,' Raymond declared. 'This way.'

He was leading them across reception, past the towering fir tree, when Annie Brogan appeared from the Housekeeping hall and started cantering their way.

'If March knows he's rumbled, he'll go to ground,' said McCord.

'Or try and leave the country,' Raymond remarked. 'It's what he's been trying to convince Vivienne of all along.' He stopped. By now, he was quite sure that Annie Brogan was calling his name. 'Could he really do that? Just skip out on a diplomatic flight?'

'It's entirely possible,' McCord returned as they reached the check-in desks. 'March was in Washington only last month. He'd need to call in favours, and it wouldn't be easy, but the diplomatic airfield at Northolt would...' He paused. 'We need to call them too.'

'Mr de Guise, STOP!'

Raymond turned.

'I'm sorry,' Annie fretted. 'I didn't mean to shout. Only – nobody ever listens to a Brogan. They think I'm just yapping but I'm not yapping, yapping's what little dogs do, and I'm not a little dog – I've got a message for you and I need to pass it on and...'

'Miss Brogan,' Raymond exclaimed, 'perhaps just take a breath and spit it out?'

Annie did as she was told.

'Mrs de Guise wants you. She's been trying all night. She's on the phone in the Housekeeping Lounge and...'

Raymond's heart sank. He could deny the image no longer: Nancy, alone with the children, a revolver and a mystery; Nancy, pulling at the threads of the lies, her whole world upended.

How much longer could he tell himself it was a problem for tomorrow?

'Annie,' he said, 'show these men to the Benefactors Study and leave them there. Do you understand?'

Annie looked slightly crestfallen to have been given another errand, instead of being able to go back to the dance, but Raymond had no time to waste consoling her. 'I'll meet you in the study,' he called to Henry McCord and Vernon Fox.

Raymond had never experienced the full chaotic majesty of a shindig in the Housekeeping Lounge – but the way Nancy spoke about them did not prepare him for the pandemonium that greeted him. The dance floor – if dance floor it still was – was a press of bodies. Concierges danced with chambermaids. Pages danced with porters. One particularly inebriated member of the kitchen staff appeared to be dancing with a broom handle, while countless others lounged in the chairs spread around the circumference. That the Buckingham Hotel could host both the exquisite elegance of the Grand and the bawdy bedlam of this shindig on the same night was a miracle.

Nancy's office had not escaped the party – but at least it was quieter in here. One of the Housekeeping girls was asleep in Nancy's chair, a teapot had been turned over – Nancy's collection of barley sugars had all been unwrapped and scattered around the desk – but Raymond was able to ignore all of that as he reached for the telephone receiver, lying on the table where Annie had left it.

'Nancy?' he ventured, steeling himself for what she had to say as he picked it up.

But in reply, there was only distant, crackling silence.

No, Raymond realised at last, *not quite silence after all...*

*

Nancy heard the footsteps approach, Ellsworth's voice growing louder and louder – until it was joined by a second voice, equally as ragged.

'You don't have to do this. There must be some other way.'

Vivienne.

In the sitting room, the sounds of Duke Ellington faded away as one song came to an end.

A thousand thoughts exploded inside Nancy.

Something was terribly wrong. On the other side of the front door, Vivienne's voice was trembling ... Raymond had been lying to her ... The last time Vivienne had looked at her was down the barrel of a gun ...

Nobody was telling the truth.

And now Ellsworth March seemed to be compelling Vivienne up the steps to her house.

There was still time to hide. The blackout blinds sealed what was happening within from what was happening without, and there was yet hope that they hadn't heard music rippling through the walls. Vivienne must surely have known Nancy was here, but if the house was in darkness she could introduce some element of doubt, perhaps suggest that she and the boys were already tucked up safely in bed.

Turning out the electric light, she tumbled across the living room, lifted the needle from the record player and crouched in front of the boys.

Stan was half-dozing in the armchair, Arthur fast asleep in his lap.

His eyes opened at seeing the ghost of Nancy crouching in front of him.

Nancy lifted a finger to her lips and whispered, 'It's a game.'

Stan grumbled.

'Shhh!' Nancy grinned. 'They'll *hear*...'

Out in the hall, the front door opened. Footsteps clattered through. Nancy didn't have a plain view of the hallway, but she was quite certain it had been Vivienne. She heard the door slam behind her. Then Ellsworth's voice rang out, 'Fetch the boy – and don't wake the house. We don't have long.'

The hallway light flared.

'The car's waiting, Vivienne. We need to *move*.' Then, more tenderly, Ellsworth said, 'It's going to be OK. You do believe me, don't you? It will just,' and he paused, as if to let her take breath, 'take some finessing. Some careful thought. But Vivienne, this is your chance: you *have* to believe me.'

Something about his voice made Nancy tremble. It made Stan tremble too – but it wasn't until he heard his mother's voice ring out that he stirred fully from sleep:

'I do believe you,' Vivienne said. 'I really do.'

Nancy started. There was a quality to Vivienne's voice that she had never heard before, something meek and gentle, almost *coquettish* and helpless. There could only be one explanation for it: this was another lie. She realised that Vivienne was not here of her own free will, that she was walking along the hallway under duress – assuming, no doubt, that the house was sleeping and Stan to be found in their bedroom – because Ellsworth was driving her along.

'Mama?'

Stan was still waking, so at least his voice didn't carry. Though she hated herself for it, Nancy pressed her hand against his lips. He wrestled back, but Nancy wrestled further. 'It's a game,' she whispered.

But even Stan knew this was no game.

'Go!' Ellsworth snapped, out in the hall. 'We can't get stranded here, Vivienne. We don't have time.'

Vivienne's voice broke: 'I don't know if it's right. I don't know if it's what I want.'

'It's for your own good,' Ellsworth snarled. 'You don't know what they're planning. They'll win this war any way that they can – and, if millions die, then so be it. Do you want to be among them? Do you want your boy to live? Do as I say, Vivienne. Get the boy and bring him downstairs. I'll get my packs.'

Nancy lifted herself upwards, only a fraction of an inch – and, spying over the top of the armchair, saw the silhouette of Ellsworth march past the sitting-room door. Moments later, she heard his heavy boots following Vivienne onto the stairs.

In moments, Vivienne would find the bedrooms empty.

In moments, the cry would go out.

'Stay here,' Nancy whispered.

Then, daring to steal out into the hall, she reached for the telephone receiver, on the table where she'd left it.

The line was dead.

Somewhere along the way, the call had been killed.

And from the bedroom above, Vivienne's voice cried out, 'Stan! Stan, where are you?'

Henry McCord was still on the line to the embassy, instructing them to send direct word to Northolt and every other US airfield, when the door of the Benefactors Study flew open – and in strode Raymond de Guise.

'I know where they are,' he declared. 'McCord, we've got to go.'

Raymond wasted not another breath. He was already back in the Housekeeping hall by the time Vernon Fox and Henry McCord caught up, striding through the cluttered store room just inside the tradesman's entrance by the time he started to explain.

'It was just voices, just fleeting voices – but it was definitely them.' The moment he stepped into the bitter chill of Michaelmas Mews, he rounded on McCord and snapped, 'My wife's in the house. My nephew and son.'

Vernon Fox's men were still standing sentry at the end of the alley. They looked to him for instruction – and, moments later, one of the cars burst to life.

'If we're right, Ellsworth March isn't a dangerous man,' said Fox, sliding into the car alongside Raymond and McCord. 'A man of dangerous morals. A man of corrupted conscience. But not a violent man. Not a danger to women and children.'

The car burst forward, kicking up waves of snow on its way out of Berkeley Square.

'You still don't understand this secret he's carrying,' roared McCord. 'The man's a danger to every woman and child on God's green Earth. Now – *drive!*'

Nancy heard Vivienne call Stan's name, and time seemed to slow down. She dropped the telephone receiver, staggered into the sitting room – but she was never going to be quick enough to stop Stan from shouting back. 'Mama!' his voice chimed, and all Nancy could do was lift Arthur, grab Stan by the hand and heave him into the hall.

Vivienne was calling out again. Nancy could hear the clatter of footsteps on the landing above.

'Stay with me,' Nancy instructed the boys, tightening her grasp on Stan as she led him into the hall. She reached out and killed the light that Vivienne and Ellsworth had put on. Darkness would help, but she needed more than the night to protect her. Stan was straining, as if – sensing the unusual panic in the house – he might bolt straight for his mother. Nancy hustled him down the hall, past the bottom of the stairs and into the kitchen.

'It's all right, little ones. Just pretend it's an air raid. An air raid without any sirens.'

It was impossible to open the back door, with Arthur pressed against one shoulder and Stan holding the other hand. Momentarily, she let Stan go, urging him to stay where he was – but Vivienne's voice was growing louder now, her footsteps pounding as she came down the stairs. Nancy had only just opened the door, when Vivienne appeared in the kitchen doorway. Stan rushed towards her.

'Nancy, there you are,' Vivienne said. 'Listen to me and listen good – we've got to ...'

Nancy backed towards the open door, arms wrapping around Arthur as she hovered on the threshold. 'This is the second time I've asked you, Vivienne. What in God's name is happening in my house?'

There was a moment in which Vivienne might have chosen silence once again.

But then she burst out:

'They were sent here to be spied on.'

More footsteps clattered on the stairs, just outside the kitchen door.

Ellsworth's voice rang out.

'Raymond works for military intelligence,' Vivienne continued, her words as rapid as anti-aircraft guns. 'It's why they sent him home from Africa. They deployed him as a spy, straight into the Buckingham. He didn't ask for it, he didn't *want* it, but his department arranged for the Americans to come here this Christmas. Raymond had to ...'

'Expose me,' stated Ellsworth, appearing behind Vivienne, then shouldering her out of the way as he stepped into the kitchen. 'Mrs de Guise, I'm afraid it's all become a terrible mess. I didn't want to bring madness to your home. Believe it or not, I was looking forward to Christmas Day. But this is a house of too many secrets. Sooner or later, it was all going to burst.' He took Vivienne's arm. 'Tell her, Vivienne.'

'He thinks I'm Raymond's mistress. He thinks to save me from it.'

'Not that!' Ellsworth snarled. 'Tell her what I told you.'

Vivienne hadn't understood, until they reached Piccadilly, that Ellsworth March wasn't really accompanying her to the Deacon Club at all. It wasn't until he whistled for a taxicab, shovelled her inside and commanded the driver to head towards Maida Vale that reality dawned on her. 'I'm sorry, Vivienne,' Ellsworth had said. 'I couldn't possibly let you get to that club.' Then he'd plucked McCord's notebook out of her hands, slipped it inside his dinner jacket and hung his head. 'I should have known,' he murmured. 'But there's still a hope, Vivienne. I can still see it through. You don't see it now – all you see is a madman – but, by God, I'm trying to save the world.'

In the darkness of the kitchen, snow now clawing inside, Vivienne said, 'The Americans are building something. A weapon to end the war. It sounds incredible, Nancy. It doesn't sound real.'

'Oh, but it is,' said Ellsworth, heavily, 'and if they achieve it, it won't just be the war that's over. It will be the world.' He paused. 'I'm a patriot, Mrs de Guise – but, before that, I'm a brother and a son, a cousin and a friend – a man with a future, and perhaps a family of his own.' He looked askance at Vivienne. 'I need the world to survive. We all need the world to survive.'

'He means to trade with the enemy,' Vivienne interjected.

Ellsworth hauled her near. 'I mean to save lives,' he snapped. 'I mean to keep the world in balance. You've no idea the devastation this might cause. You lived through the raids over London, but it's as nothing compared to this. How many bombs fell on your houses? How many tens of thousands? Well, ladies, it would take just *one* to level this city. One bomb to render it inhabitable for generations to come.' He snorted. 'You look at me as if I'm a fantasist, Mrs de Guise. Well, the world's about to find out. And if I can keep a single soul safe from it, that's what I'm going to do.'

Ellsworth reached into Vivienne's arms, trying to pry Stan away. The boy clung to his mother desperately, his arms locked around her neck, refusing to let go.

'Mrs de Guise,' Ellsworth said, as he struggled to keep the boy from kicking out, 'I thank you for your hospitality this Christmas – but Vivienne and I, we've got to go.'

There came the distinctive sound of a click.

Still battling Stan's ceaseless scrabbling, Ellsworth looked up.

While the tussle had been going on, Nancy – still cradling Arthur to her shoulder with one arm – had reached down into the briefcase on the kitchen table.

Now McCord's Smith & Wesson trembled in her hand, its eye pointing directly at Ellsworth's breast.

'Now, Nancy...'

It was on the tip of her tongue to tell him to go, to scream out that he should leave the house this moment – that she didn't care what he did, where he went, what he sold to who, as long as he left Vivienne and Stan behind.

But a deeper thought had opened inside her.

And perhaps it was the very same thought that had been driving Raymond – her lying, faithless, *honourable* contradiction of a husband – all year long.

That if somebody didn't stand up, if somebody didn't look the devil in the eye and face him down, if somebody didn't make the sacrifices and fight the good fight on whatever front they could find, then all that was good about the world would be lost.

'You're not going anywhere, Mr March,' she declared.

At once, Ellsworth released Stan – and Vivienne staggered backwards, clinging on to her beautiful, feral, petrified boy.

Then Ellsworth started striding forward, directly into the path of the gun.

'Mrs de Guise, I don't believe you want to do this.' He stopped advancing, held his ground in the middle of the kitchen. 'Give me the gun.'

'I won't,' she trembled. 'Sit down, Mr March. Sit down while we call for help.'

Ellsworth brooded on it, for only a second. 'I'm afraid I won't be doing that, Nancy.'

He closed the gap between them in a single stride.

He extended his hand, clicked his fingers.

'The gun, Mrs de Guise. I may yet have need of it tonight.'

Nancy stood, resolute, and shook her head.

'Mrs de Guise, you have your son in your arms. And here I stand, an unarmed man. You're not going to shoot me – so why don't you make a rational decision, and *give – me – the – gun.*'

'Rational decision?' Nancy snorted. 'To take a secret like that and trade it to the enemy?' She waved the gun. 'No, Mr March, I don't think you're a man to lecture me on rational decisions. This is *my* house. This is *my* country. There's precious little I can do for the war, Mr March, but there is *this*. You're going to sit down and put your hands flat on the table, or so help me, I'll—'

'I always did admire the pluck of the British,' said Ellsworth. 'I'm sorry, Mrs de Guise.'

There was a moment in which Nancy thought she'd got through to him, that the twin threats of reason and the gun in his face were about to make him see sense. But it was only a feint. The moment Ellsworth said 'I'm sorry', he threw himself forward.

In the darkness of the kitchen, his hands grappled for the gun.

The first sounds to fill the air were the panicked cries of Arthur and Stan.

The second: a gunshot, rending a hole in the night.

The Rolls-Royce flew along Blomfield Road, the driver wrestling with the wheel to keep it from slewing sideways into the frozen canal. Before it came to a stop, Raymond kicked open the door and reeled out into the snow. Right there, right outside his house, a taxicab sat with its engine idling. Fox and McCord were still picking themselves out of the car when Raymond threw open the taxi door and heaved the driver out.

'You brought them here? To that house?'

He pointed at his own house, just an outline of black set against snow.

'The Americans,' the driver stammered. 'A man decked out for the night, and his lady in a gown.'

'They're still in there?' Raymond demanded.

'I was told to wait. That's all I know, sir.'

'Get out of here,' Raymond told him. 'There's no more fare tonight.'

Raymond turned to the house.

And a single gunshot obliterated the silence.

Ellsworth was on top of her. One moment he was lunging; the next, he was a dead weight, crashing down.

Nancy staggered backwards. Only now, with Arthur bawling at her shoulder, did she see the blood coursing down her front.

The gun, scorching hot, had bucked and tumbled from her grasp.

For a second, Nancy wasn't sure whose the blood was.

She wondered: is this how it ends? Is this the fundamental truth at the end of all the lies?

Nancy had been eight years old when she lost her own mother.

But at least she remembered her.

At least she had fragments to cling on to.

She lifted her hand, drenched in scarlet gore.

What memories would Arthur have?

Then Ellsworth March dropped at her feet.

The world, in all its madness, rushed back in. The ringing in Nancy's ears faded to the screaming of her child, the unearthly howl coming from Vivienne.

Ellsworth rolled on the floor.

Blood was pumping out of a place between his shoulder and breast, his collar bone decimated in the blast.

'You did it,' he gasped. 'You fool. You goddamn fool. You don't know what you've done.'

His good arm reached upward, like a dying man clawing for the light.

'Help me,' he said. 'You have to help...'

She cradled her sobbing boy, stepped over Ellsworth's recumbent form and handed the baby to Vivienne. Then she turned, seeking out whatever tea towels, aprons and tablecloths she could find.

Moments later, she was on hands and knees, trying to stem the blood that pumped like a geyser from Ellsworth's wound.

'I didn't mean that kind of help,' Ellsworth gasped. 'You have to finish it. You have to *see*. The file – I left the file – a deposit box – Paddington Station. You have to retrieve it. Do what I couldn't.' His good hand shot up, as if to drag Nancy down. 'Take me there. I have to—'

The front door flew open.

A storm of footsteps raged up the hall.

Nancy was still bent over Ellsworth March, thrusting all her weight into the injury – anything, absolutely anything, to stop his life's blood leaching out onto her kitchen floor when, suddenly, McCord was on his knees alongside her, sliding his hands into the place where hers were pressed.

'Henry, see sense,' Ellsworth gasped, as the strength left his body. Out in the hall, Vernon Fox's distant voice could be heard rattling into the telephone receiver as he summoned an ambulance to the house. 'You don't know what they've done. It's too great a cost. The scales must be balanced. I want peace, Henry. Peace, not the end of all things.'

Nancy didn't hear the rest. Up on her feet, she felt Raymond's arms close around her. It was on her mind to push him away, to let loose with fire and tell him that he was a liar, that he should have told her, that he had no right to bring such wickedness into her house and keep it from her, that she didn't know who he was – but the terror of the moment had seized her, and for a moment she needed his arms.

'I'm not a traitor,' Ellsworth's faint voice flurried up. 'All those people. All those beautiful people. They don't deserve to die. *I – I don't deserve to …*'

Nancy leant into Raymond, until all she could hear was the beating of his heart.

There would be so much to discuss.

But that was for tomorrow.

Right now, in spite of all the lies, she needed but one truth: He was here.

For the moment, that was enough.

Day Five:

Sunday, 20 December 1942
And Beyond...

Chapter Twenty-Nine

There was always a strange feeling in the air the day after a ball at the Buckingham Hotel. It would be wrong to say it was an empty feeling, because the daily rhythms of the hotel had begun anew – there were still suites to be changed, still meals to be prepared, still drinks to be poured and errands to run – but, this morning, John Hastings approached his work with a certain fresh élan. Triumphs were good for a man's soul.

They were good for the soul of the hotel as well.

In the hotel director's office, the telephone rang. Hastings let it chime several times, savouring the moment, before he picked it up.

'It's Mr Gove again, sir,' said the girl from the telephone exchange.

Hastings had been ignoring Gove's entreaties since dawn, but this time he relented. 'I'll take it.'

He waited while the connection was made, then smiled into the receiver, 'Mr Gove, it's tremendously magnanimous of you to call and congratulate us on our Winter Ball.'

Gove's voice was even more brimming with vitriol than Hastings had expected. Indeed, he had to hold the receiver away from his ear for fear of incurring an injury. Then, when Gove seemed to have expended himself – perhaps the terrible sickness had claimed him too? – Mr Hastings allowed all the joviality to drain out of his voice, and sternly said, 'You instigated a dirty war, Mr Gove. You and your staff waged an ungentlemanly campaign against this hotel. I don't claim credit for last night's unfortunate occurrence in your ballroom, but nor will I stand by and let you go unchallenged. Bullies must be told *no*.'

'You're smug now, Mr Hastings, but your night wasn't an unalloyed success. I know about the cracks that appeared in your ballroom. I know your very own King of the Grand vanished – no, *absconded* – for your second act. Walked out on King George and his daughters, no less. There'll be whispers about him, sir. The disloyalty he showed. The effrontery in the face of his King.'

Of all the venomous things Mr Gove had poured down the telephone line, this was the only one that soured Mr Hastings' sense of elation and triumph. He was yet to discover where Raymond de Guise had vanished to – indeed, his prize asset had seemed distracted all week – and, some day soon, he would have to make an account of it. De Guise was the Buckingham Hotel's shining star. They were lucky to have him. And yet, at the moment he was needed the most, he had vanished into thin air.

He would need to summon de Guise back to the hotel and ask him, face to face.

But, right now, he didn't mean to give Mr Gove a single inch.

'There's no mystery in it, Mr Gove. My star dancer has sustained an injury – one he will recover from, in time for our new year preparations to begin. I do, however, thank you for your concern.'

Gove's voice was searing as it came down the line, 'This is not the end, sir. My Board is meeting this evening. It is their intention to hold you accountable for a gross act of vandalism upon this hotel.'

'Now, Mr Gove!' Hastings rejoined. 'Christmas is coming. The New Year promises all sorts of splendours – for London, as well as the war. Who knows, we might be at peace by next Christmas night. So perhaps our hotels should enter a period of truce?'

At first the reply was just stony silence.

Then, incandescent, Mr Gove seethed, 'You should know something about we British, Mr Hastings: we don't make treaties with the enemy. I'll fight you for every last guest in London. I'll fight you for every last farthing. I'll fight you in the suites, Mr Hastings. I'll fight you in the cocktail lounge …'

Hastings didn't hear the rest. He had already lain the telephone receiver down on the desk, so that Mr Gove was unleashing his unrivalled venom to nobody at all.

A knock came at the door.

Mr Hastings went to open it.

There stood one of the attendants from the reception desks.

'It arrived just now, sir,' he said, handing over a small ivory envelope, sealed in red wax. 'Hand delivered by the Palace equerry.'

Gove's voice was still buzzing down the line as Mr Hastings sat back at his desk, felt every contour of the envelope, then opened it.

'HIS ROYAL HIGHNESS, KING GEORGE VI AND HIS FAMILY WOULD LIKE TO THANK THE MANAGEMENT AND STAFF OF THE BUCKINGHAM HOTEL FOR A WONDERFUL WINTER BALL, AND GRACIOUSLY ACCEPTING OUR PARTY'S ATTENDANCE AT SUCH SHORT NOTICE.'

Mr Hastings smiled. The Board of the Imperial Hotel might have been meeting tonight to discuss the devilry of the Buckingham – but, when his own Board next convened, this ought to be enough to keep all his naysayers at bay.

'Happy Christmas, Mr Gove,' he declared, and finally hung up.

*

It had been a long night at Blomfield Road.

The last Raymond, Nancy and Vivienne had seen of Ellsworth March, he'd been strapped to a stretcher, being ferried into a waiting ambulance by the physicians Vernon Fox had summoned to the house. Soon after that, another taxicab arrived to deposit Jonah Linden back home, and he and McCord left for the embassy to brief the ambassador. Vernon Fox was the last to leave. 'I'll need you at the Deacon Club tomorrow,' he told Raymond, before he vanished into the night. 'In fact, it's possible I'll require all three of you.' His eyes took in Nancy, hands scrubbed clean, but still stained by blood, and Vivienne, cradling the children. 'Until that moment, not a word of what happens here gets breathed. I recommend you don't even speak about it amongst yourselves.'

The moment he left, it was clear that would not be the case. As the shock and horror faded in Nancy's eyes, leaving behind only a bereft, bewildered soul, Raymond said, 'I'll tell you everything.'

And that was what he did.

Long after the midnight hour, after the children were settled with Vivienne standing sentry by their bedside, he looked Nancy in the eye and said, 'I didn't plan any of this. I thought I'd be serving my country out there until the war was won. But then, one day, I was in barracks in Cairo and there was a telephone call...'

He started from the beginning: the summons from Maynard Charles; the port in Liverpool; the requisitioned manor house where he'd been taken to learn his new trade. 'At first, I imagined they'd let me tell you.' But the rules were hard and the rules were fast, and the story they concocted had to be so watertight that not a soul, not even the closest soul to him in all of the world, was permitted to know.

'I always knew you could spin a good story, Ray Cohen,' said Nancy, trying hard to mask her bitterness. 'But I never thought you'd spin one to me.'

'I've sometimes thought it's what my whole life's been preparing me for. I lived a lie for years at the Grand Ballroom. At the beginning, they truly thought me an aristocrat – one of their own. If a street boy from Whitechapel could play that role, well, why not this?' He paused. 'Nancy, you have to see – it's for…'

'For King and Country,' she said, sadly. Then her voice broke: 'Did I kill a man tonight, for King and Country?'

Raymond went to put his arms around her, but Nancy demurred.

'If he does die,' Raymond said, 'then he died by his own hand. You bear no blame.'

But Nancy could still see Ellsworth's blood in the lines of her hand and she said, 'I'm tired, Raymond. Let's talk tomorrow.'

And when Raymond turned towards bed, she stopped him and added, 'I think, perhaps, I need to sleep alone tonight.'

Of all the things Raymond had experienced in the last few days, this was the bitterest blow.

He was still wearing it in the morning, when he awoke in front of the fire – Frank having been asked to stay in quarters at the Buckingham Hotel – to discover Vivienne already in the kitchen, working by rote through the duties of the day. 'I'm sorry, Vivienne,' he said.

When Vivienne said, 'We stopped it. That's the important thing,' he was more grateful than he'd known he could possibly be.

Nancy was still upstairs, tending to Arthur, when the telephone rang in the hall, one of the secretaries from the Office instructing Raymond that they were sending a car. When Raymond went upstairs to tell Nancy, she looked up at him from the side of Arthur's crib and said, 'My heart bled for you, when you came back home. I was so worried – my husband, wounded at war. Would you still love music? Could you still dance? Would you even *hear* it anymore, when I said that I loved you?' She barely looked him in the eye. 'I know why you did what you did, Raymond. I know you had no choice. But I feel like a damn fool.'

'You're no fool, Nancy.'

'This damn war,' she said, her voice cracking apart. 'It was bad enough when it was out there, Raymond. Bad enough when the bombs were falling down. But now it's … here, right here in my house.' She looked at her palms. 'And right here in my hands. I just cleaned up Arthur – cleaned him with the same hands that killed a man last night.'

Raymond whispered, 'He isn't dead.'

Nancy shot him a look.

'They told me just now. He's under lock and guard in a hospital bed – and, God knows, they'd hang him for what he was trying to do – but he isn't dead. You haven't killed a soul.' He wanted to go to her, but dared not. 'You'll never have to know what that's like, Nancy.'

He nearly added, 'not like I do', but instead he just looked at her longingly, willing the tears in her eyes to run dry. What it truly felt like to take a life – perhaps that would be the only secret Raymond had to keep from her from this moment on.

'They're sending a car,' he said. 'You've got to come too.'

'And the children?'

It looked like they might need the help of Mrs Fitzwilliam again, but Raymond added, 'And after that, it's just you, me, Vivienne and Frank. The quietest of Christmases – and not a lie that needs telling, neither for King nor Country, ever again.'

Raymond had expected the car to deliver them directly to the Deacon Club, but another surprise was waiting. The driver's name was Cartwright. He was, Raymond understood, one of the Office's regular drivers, a grizzled veteran of the Great War – and the very man who had been there with Maynard Charles on that fateful winter night.

'That's where I'm taking you, sir,' said Cartwright, as Blomfield Road turned to a blur around them. 'St Thomas's Hospital. It's Mr Charles. We thought we'd lost him – but he's finally awake.'

Raymond's heart surged at the news. He tried to take Nancy's hand, but she remained brittle. 'I haven't thought about Mr Charles in years,' she said, eyes on the window glass.

'He's one of the good ones,' said Cartwright. 'One of the best. And we almost lost him.'

St Thomas's Hospital sat, grey and austere, on the banks of the snow-wreathed river. To Vivienne, who had been here only days before, there was a sense of dizzying déjà vu about being shepherded into the hospital halls. The last time she'd come here, it had been as an intruder. Now, she was given a military guard as she followed Raymond and Nancy onto the King James ward, past the watchful eyes of the ward sister and up to the private room where Maynard Charles lay.

Vernon Fox was waiting at the door.

'Raymond, Mr Charles will see you first.' He inclined his head at Nancy and Vivienne. 'Excuse us, ladies.'

Nancy tried not to be resentful as Raymond was led into the room. There was much she was going to have to get used to, much she was going to have to do – and the first was to forgive. She felt certain she'd find the strength for it, but right now it still rankled.

In the back of her mind, she could still hear Arthur screaming.

The erstwhile director of the Buckingham Hotel was propped up in bed, looking ashen; a line fed into the cannula on the back of his hand. Raymond had seen corpses look healthier. He stood by the bedside and was readying to salute when Maynard rasped, 'You don't stand on parade for me, de Guise. Take a chair.'

So Raymond did.

'I understand you've accomplished all that I could ask of you, while I've been lounging in bed.'

Hope, like embers flurrying back into flames, sprang in Raymond's breast. If Maynard Charles could summon his usual sardonic wit at a time like this, then perhaps there was a chance he'd be back on his feet and ready to rejoin the war before winter was out.

'I'd hardly call it lounging, sir.'

'From what I'm told, you acquitted yourself perfectly, de Guise.'

'I'm afraid not, sir. I'm afraid the fact that March is behind bars is down to Nancy, and Vivienne.'

'Vivienne Edgerton,' Maynard rasped.

'She's a Cohen now, sir. You won't recognise her as the girl you used to know.' Raymond paused. 'Mr Charles, the man who shot you – was it Ellsworth March?'

'The Office tells me not. It turns out that, in our trade, any number of different men might want you dead, for any number of different reasons. The war is changing, Raymond. London swarms with spies. The Americans brought infantry and airmen and a tidal wave of wealth to the war, but where armies go, so do espionage artistes. It's the Wild West again. It's hard enough keeping track of your enemies, without keeping track of your allies as well.'

'It seems as if we ought to pool our resources with the Americans, sir. If I'd only known McCord was more than just an analyst...'

Maynard reached for his hand. 'This is a complicated world. Your cover story has been compromised, has it not?'

Raymond looked over his shoulder. Through the glass in the door, he could just about make out Nancy and Vivienne standing in the hall.

'Mr Charles doesn't mean them,' intoned Vernon Fox, prowling the edges of the room. 'He means the hotel. You absconded in the middle of the Winter Ball. Walked out on King George himself. Questions are going to be asked.'

Raymond stammered, 'I'll find a way to make it work again.'

Maynard Charles took a ragged breath. 'We'll get to that. Right now, it's time to invite your family in. They need to hear this too.'

Nancy said nothing as Raymond invited her into the room, but at least she let him take her by the hand; that had to mean *something*. Maynard gathered himself and said, 'Strange times call for strange fellowships. I'm glad to see you again, Nancy. I'm glad to see you too, Vivienne.' He tried to lift himself, but just guttered for breath instead. 'I imagine I look like death, so you must forgive me. They tell me I'm getting better. And they also tell me that, thanks to the pair of you, this government has avoided a damning situation. Ladies, I have already said it to Raymond, but I must say it to you, openly and without hesitation: *thank you.*' He had to gather his strength again before going on, 'Thanks to your swift actions, your astuteness and unimpeachable instincts, Ellsworth March is behind bars. That you did all this without fully understanding the gravity of the situation, without an ounce of training, and without the possibility of back-up from my Office, is worthy of royal commendation. Alas, there are no medals in our world. There will be no parade. No letter from the King, and no stories to tell. What you have done may yet affect the course of this war – but I have asked you here, today, because I need to make it clear: you may never speak of it again.'

Maynard Charles had grown pale again – the effort of speaking at such length sapped him of strength – so at this point Vernon Fox intervened. 'My office is preparing the paperwork, ladies, but you are being invited to sign the Official Secrets Act. I'm afraid we must insist.'

Nancy and Vivienne hardly knew what to say.

'Raymond,' Vernon Fox went on, 'I've requested that a file be created with the Metropolitan Police. According to the paperwork we'll introduce, last night there was an attempted break-in at your house on Blomfield Road. Nancy called you at the Buckingham Hotel and you rushed home to make sure she was safe. For official purposes, that's why you missed the second half of the ball. You'll write personally, of course, to the Palace to apologise for any presumed slight.'

'It isn't a perfect story, sir, but perhaps it will work.'

'This is an imperfect world,' rasped Maynard Charles. 'We do the best we can. And you three in front of me, you have gone further than I could have hoped.'

'Sir,' Vivienne ventured, 'is it *real*? What Ellsworth March said – about a bomb to end wars. Can it really exist?'

Maynard said, 'Some things are beyond even my understanding.'

'And Ellsworth March?' Vivienne whispered. 'What will become of him?'

Maynard sensed some hesitation in Vivienne's voice. 'You liked the man?'

'I think most people can be redeemed, sir.'

Maynard looked her up and down. 'Yes, I can see that you would. You've come a long way, Vivienne. You've come further than I thought you might – which is to credit you, girl, and to diminish me.' He paused. 'Ellsworth March's fate is for his countrymen now. We five in this room must look to our own nation, and our own endeavours. I couldn't tell you what the next twelve months will bring. But I can tell you that this isn't the end of the dangers we face. Mrs de Guise,' he breathed. 'Nancy. When I asked Raymond to come home and work for me, it was expressly forbidden that he share the nature of his new life with another soul – and this included you.'

Nancy's eyes darted at Raymond. He could tell that she was torn, stranded somewhere between duty and obligation, and the pain he'd brought into their life.

'To disobey would be to betray,' said Maynard, 'but hear me now: *I was wrong*.'

'Sir?' Nancy ventured.

'Raymond's activities in the Buckingham Hotel are of paramount importance. Secrecy is hard currency in this world. But the moment I dictated that he become a spy in his own house – that, Nancy, was the moment I should have inducted you into our fellowship. I hope you can forgive me.'

'It's a family home, sir,' said Nancy. 'It's a sanctuary. Right now, it feels broken. Like the walls have come down.'

'I see that,' said Maynard, 'and I give you a solemn oath that, come what may, I won't ask it of you again. You must rebuild those walls, Nancy – and you must know that the sacrifice you made has been worth it.' He paused again; what little colour there had been in his cheeks was rapidly fading. 'And now, I believe,

I have earned some rest. As have you all. Nancy, Raymond – I wish you the happiest of Christmases with your little boy.'

Raymond squeezed Maynard's hand gently, then turned to leave. As they reached the door, it filled his heart that Nancy was walking alongside him, her shoulder grazing his.

Behind them, Vernon Fox reached out and tapped Vivienne on the shoulder. 'Perhaps you might stay behind, one moment, ma'am.'

Nancy and Raymond were already out in the hall, so – although they looked back in bewilderment – there wasn't time to ask what was happening before the door closed again, Vivienne on the other side.

In the hallway, Nancy held Raymond's hands. 'Where do we go from here?' she asked.

'Back to the Buckingham Hotel,' he said.

'I didn't mean it like that.'

But of course, Raymond knew that. 'Back to normal life,' he said softly. 'But it will be different now. I won't have to bring the lie home from the hotel. I won't have to pretend.' He stopped. 'We'll be in it together. Will it be enough?'

'The war corrupts everything it touches. I know you couldn't tell me. I understand it. I just – I want it to be over, and for Arthur to grow up in a world without shadow. I want him to have brothers and sisters, and for Blomfield Road to be the beating heart of the world.' She paused. 'Will you promise me something?'

Raymond nodded.

'When the war's over, when peace has come, will you leave it behind? Will you go back to the ballroom and just dance? Dance until you're too old and tired to keep a partner in hold? Dance, so that our children can grow up seeing their father doing what he *loves*? There'll always be another challenge, Raymond. There'll always be something more we can do for the world. But one day, when the battle's won, can our world be *smaller* again?'

A future that was only music, family and dance.

Yes, Raymond could imagine that.

He was about to fold his arms around Nancy again when the door opened, and Vivienne emerged, looking almost as pale as Maynard Charles.

Nancy rushed to her side. 'Vivienne, what happened? Vivienne, what did he say?'

Vivienne faltered before she found the words to explain. 'Well, he said he's on a long, winding road back to full health – but he's going to start working the very moment he can. Only – he might need some *help*, back at the Office. He's always needed help. There aren't enough hands. And he wondered if a woman like me, someone who's resourceful and hard-working and knows a little bit about the seamier side of life, might be just the sort of person he needs.'

'He offered you a job?' Nancy asked.

Vivienne smiled.

'Well, yes. I suppose that he did.'

Christmas was coming.

The goose was getting fat.

In the days that followed, the aftermath of the Winter Ball could be felt all across the Buckingham Hotel. It wasn't just in the smell of vinegar and carbolic where the Housekeeping girls had scrubbed and scrubbed to make sure Mrs de Guise saw none of the after-effects of the shindig in the lounge. It wasn't only that the Hotel Board were suddenly (and quite unexpectedly) appreciative of their director; it wasn't just how Max Allgood looked to the year ahead with fresh belief filling his sails; it wasn't just the glittering feeling that Annie and Victor got when, keeping up his end of the bargain, Billy gathered them in the hotel post room so that they could watch him feeding his ledgerbooks, and all the evidence of their misdeeds, into the fire. No, the feeling was even deeper, even richer than that. It seemed to lift the very soul of the hotel, promising good things for the future – an oath that, when the thaw finally came, the snow and ice would retreat to leave the Buckingham Hotel, Berkeley Square, the whole of London, looking forward with fresh hope and expectation.

Christmas was coming.

So, they had started daring to whisper, was the end of the war...

And if, right now, this was only hope speaking – if, in their hearts, the chambermaids and concierges, musicians and dancers, porters, pages and department managers, all knew that there was still a continent to be conquered, blood to be spilt and lives to be lost before the moment of victory was assured – that didn't change the feeling of it.

Nor had any of that good feeling worn away by the time Christmas Day came along. As Annie worked the suites in the morning, dreaming of Christmas dinner at home (Billy's goose would taste even better now that she was free), as Victor toiled through the lunchtime service in the Grand, as Frank left the observation post for home, the Buckingham Hotel seemed to exist in a perfect pocket of peace. Touched by the hand of victory, graced by the footsteps of the King, the magic of the Winter Ball stretched on and on, reaching out as if to bless the New Year, and all that was yet to come.

And in Blomfield Road, a family gathered...

Christmas morning had passed in a whirlwind of gifts, music and celebration – but Nancy, Raymond and Vivienne had waited for Frank to be finished his duties at the Buckingham Hotel before lighting the candles for Christmas dinner. Only when he crashed through the door, shaking the snow off his coat and boots, were they ready to begin. In the kitchen, a table that ought to have been set for nine was now laid out for six. For the first time in an age, this meant that the rations were piled high. Fat sausages had been baked with a Cornish hen unexpectedly donated by Billy Brogan. Potatoes glistened in butter. The lamb shank melted from the bone as Raymond took it to task, the carving knife in his hand.

At the head of the table, he stood and marvelled: this was his first Christmas at home since the darkest days of the Blitz.

The first Christmas he got to spend with his son.

A rush of emotion coursed through him: not only did he get to spend Christmas with his family; he got to spend it free of all the falsehoods as well.

'Happy Christmas,' he said to Nancy, to Vivienne, to Frank and Arthur and Stan – and was surprised to discover that he truly felt it as well.

Christmas bells did not toll this year, as they had not tolled in any of the years since war was declared. But in Blomfield Road, as at the Buckingham Hotel, the clouds of suspicion, doubt and fear had parted, leaving only a crystalline winter light.

Around the table, glasses were raised.

'To the New Year,' Raymond declared, 'and new beginnings for us all.'

'New beginnings!' they all chimed.

The clock had been counting down to disaster for far too long.

Now, thought Raymond, as he brought the glass to his lips, it could start counting *up*.

Acknowledgements

Thank you to the team who worked with me on *The Winter Ball*.

Thank you to the team behind me – my manager Melissa Chappell, my literary agent Kerr MacRae, my brilliant assistant Yvonne, and Lou & Grace and the team at Plank PR.

Huge and heartfelt thanks to my editor at Orion, Sam Eades.

And to booksellers and readers all over the world – thank you for being such wonderful supporters of my books. I am so grateful for your support.

And, lastly but most importantly, a special thank you to my wife Hannah and my children George and Henrietta for your endless support and love.

Credits

Orion Fiction would like to thank everyone at Orion who worked on the publication of *The Winter Ball*.

Editor
Charlotte Mursell

Copy-editor
Francine Brody

Proofreader
Alex Davis

Editorial Management
Anshuman Yadav
Jane Hughes
Charlie Panayiotou
Lucy Bilton
Patrice Nelson

Photo Shoots & Image Research
Natalie Dawkins

Audio
Paul Stark
Louise Richardson
Georgina Cutler-Ross

Contracts
Rachel Monte
Ellie Bowker
Tabitha Gresty

Design
Charlotte Abrams-Simpson
Nick Shah
Deborah Francois
Helen Ewing

Inventory
Jo Jacobs
Dan Stevens

Finance
Nick Gibson
Jasdip Nandra
Sue Baker
Tom Costello

Publicity
Sarah Lundy

Sales
Dave Murphy
Victoria Laws
Esther Waters
Group Sales teams across
Digital, Field, International
and Non-Trade

Production
Ruth Sharvell
Katie Horrocks

Operations
Group Sales Operations team

Rights
Rebecca Folland
Tara Hiatt
Ben Fowler
Maddie Stephens
Ruth Blakemore
Marie Henckel